Seminole Bend

Seminole Bend

A NOVEL

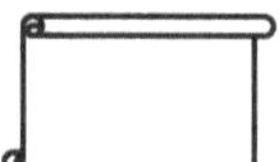

Tom Hansen

Seminole Bend is a work of fiction. All incidents, dialogue, and all characters except some well-known historical figures are products of the author's imagination and are not to be construed as real. Some locations, businesses, and organizations are real but are used only to support the fictitious nature of this novel. In all other respects, any resemblance to actual persons, living or dead, events, or locales is entirely coincidental.

Cultural Unity Publishing
4106 N. St. Elias
Mesa, AZ 85215

Cultural Unity Publishing is a division of Educational Video Training Concepts, LLC.

First Printing: December 2016
Second Printing: November 2018
Third Printing: December 2019

ISBN: 978-1-7328182-3-1

Printed in the United States of America

Cover by Luke Hansen

DEDICATION

For my wife, Meg,
my children, Marc, Luke, and Shea,
and my daughter-in-law Jeanne:
You are why I enjoy life!

For your reading pleasure, a character reference chart is located in the appendix.

PROLOGUE
Seminole Bend, Florida

History is inflexible, unchangeable, and impossible to destroy. However, in March of 1982, the president of the United States rewrote the rules of history.

My name is William "Billy" Gorman, and I was born on a dairy ranch in southern Florida on January 22, 1971. Yep, you heard me right, a dairy ranch in Florida. Sorry to ruin your image of palm trees, orange juice, and Coppertoned beach bums sipping pina coladas out of coconut shells, but just a mere forty miles west of the Atlantic coast is some of the finest milk this side of Wisconsin!

Let me start by asking you to pardon my English, which wasn't the best back in the good old days of elementary school. Hate to say it, but it still ain't. Then again, most of the folks I grew up with around here didn't really care much about vocabulary and phonics as long as they got their point across.

My fifth-grade teacher, Miss Norma Foss, cared, and she insisted that all of her students learn a new word each day—one that had at least three syllables. Okay, you probably won't guess it, so I'll just come right out and say it. I was in love with Miss Foss, so just to impress my gorgeous teacher, I took her up on that three-syllable challenge, and in front of the whole class, I spitted it out like she did when she taught us new words.

"Sumptuous. Miss Foss is sumptuous. Sumptuous." My first three-syllable word was pretty darn good; wouldn't you say? Well, Miss Foss turned all red in the face, and I had to stay in at recess and scrape gum from underneath the desks.

I was born to Marvin and Maxine Gorman during the folly of the Vietnam War and the struggle for civil rights. I entered this world on the night *Rowan and Martin's Laugh-In* debuted on TV, but I never made it to Gregorson General Hospital where most babies in Seminole Bend were born. Instead, I took my first breath of our earthly atmosphere on the passenger seat of Daddy's Ford pickup truck. Mama said she was having contractions, but thought it was from giggling and snorting while watching *Laugh-In*. Then, I kicked her a good one from inside her belly, and she screamed at Daddy to get her to the hospital. We never even made it to the end of the gravel driveway. Now, this is where it gets a bit fuzzy, depending on who's telling the story. Let's just say Daddy was Mama's midwife and leave it at that!

Mama said I survived Kiddy Kare Preschool because of my good looks. Unfortunately, when I got to fifth grade, Mr. Rambert, the principal of Seminole Bend Elementary, couldn't see the beauty I possessed. On the ride home from my suspension for putting a king snake down Mickey Patton's britches, Mama offered maternal comfort by telling me that I was a normal, active eleven-year-old boy. But at the dinner table that night, my older brother, Kenny, called me a "rambunctious meddling brat." When I went back to my room, I sounded out those words the best I could and wrote them on a piece of paper, but I had to wait out my suspension torture on the ranch before I could return to school and ask Miss Foss what they meant. Meanwhile, Daddy told Kenny that I had a bundle of youthful energy wrapped around my heart, and he needed him to be a positive role model for me. I didn't know exactly what that meant either, but I always looked up to my big brother and wanted to be just like him.

Principal Rambert said he was doing me a favor by keeping my home prison term to just two days. Had the king snake been a coral snake, I'd be telling you this story up on

Death Row at Raiford prison. But, getting up at four in the morning to do chores with Daddy was purely rancorous, which was another three-syllable word I learned from Miss Foss. Then, having to do homework with Mama until sundown was just plain cruel. My sentence was way beyond the limits of reasonableness and worse than a felony conviction! No recess, gym class, or chocolate milk breaks! I was sure thrilled for dinner to start even if I had to put up with Kenny messing with my head.

Bobby Joe Plank and me were best buddies, and we were looking forward to being proud graduates of Seminole Bend Elementary School. One night I dreamt that Principal Rambert praised me on the gymnasium's loudspeaker: "And now, walking on the stage to accept the award for *Most Rambunctious Graduate*, the one, the only, Billy Gorman!"

Just in case you were wondering, squeezing cow udders in blistering hot Florida was not a pleasurable way to grow up. Especially in the summer months when afternoon downpours and burning sunshine found a way to keep my shirts soaking wet and me downright stinky. But Daddy insisted that good Southern boys like me and Kenny had to make an honest living and always remember to put things in proper order: God, family, school, and chores. But shoot if it didn't seem like even God answered to chores around the Gorman house!

One night back in January of 1982, Daddy was mad at our neighbor, Roy Jackson, who had tons of money and paid people to do his chores for him. Well, Daddy used some choice words, and Mama told me later he had let his spirituality slip for a moment. Daddy's motor mouth brother, Uncle Johnny, had joined us for another one of Mama's magnificent meals. Kenny and me could see that a little bit of anxiety had been escaping from Daddy's normally calm and collective manner when he told us he couldn't imagine how Mr. Jackson got out of another open and shut case of unlawful ignorance.

"Doing at least 107 in a fifty-five zone, he was! Caused Clem Riker to slam on his tractor's brakes, sending a load of hay bales all over Highway 441! I mean, how could Deputy Willy Banks not give him a ticket for speeding or reckless driving or for just being a high falootin cocky son of a bitch?!"

Mama told Daddy to watch his mouth.

Willy was a good cop, big and tough like the ones you see in the movies, with biceps bigger than my two legs put together, and he could run faster than a thoroughbred galloping around the track at Hialeah. My friend Jesse Dagos said he once saw Willy wrestling an alligator that had decided to sun himself five feet from the dog pen that housed Willy's pit bull, Clyde. Old Clyde wasn't afraid of no gator, and he dang near dug himself through a hole under the fence just to let the web-footed monster know that his dog pen wasn't no beach for ugly reptiles! Willy got there just as the old gator woke up and started licking his chops and moving in on the canine lunch. Willy dove headfirst at the eight-foot reptile's elongated face and clamped its jaws shut with his bionic arms. He literally dragged the tail-slapping gator about a hundred yards to the pond behind his house and tossed him in with very little effort. The stunned ruler of the swamp quickly submerged into the black water and swam away, no doubt embarrassed to be seen by those he ruled over, especially the laughing egrets.

Anyway, Willy had hidden the sheriff's squad car perfectly in the sunken ditch behind two fat palmetto bushes and fingered the trigger of his fancy new radar gun. He had already nailed a Mustang and a Cutlass and even a beat-up Plymouth Duster. Suddenly, Roy zoomed by blowing dust and gravel onto Willy's windshield. Roy had zipped past the dawdle-driving farmers and the gray-haired, slow-moving Yankee snowbirds who were bumper to bumper on the two-lane highway, and forced oncoming traffic to take evasive action. By the way, Uncle Johnny said them damn snowbirds would be the end of him because they drive half the speed of their age and can't see five feet beyond their front fender! Course, Mama told Johnny that swearing ain't allowed in the Gorman home. But Daddy's little brother never did listen to her, especially when it came to cussing at those old fools from Pennsylvania who swap their snow shovels for fishing poles every winter.

Okay, I got off track there a little bit. So, after school was out, my buddy Bobby Joe Plank was selling strawberry Kool-Aid alongside the road when Willy finally caught up with Roy's Corvette about ten miles down from the ditch he'd been hiding in. Willy stopped Mr. Jackson right smack dab in front of Bobby Joe's orange crate table. Bobby Joe pretended not to listen to all the squabbling, but being only eleven-years-old with a whole bunch of curiosity dancing around in his head, well, not listening was no easy task. I asked him if Willy clamped the handcuffs around Roy's wrists and hauled him off to the county jail, but Bobby Joe said nothing happened! At least nothing juicy to gossip about around Seminole Bend County. No ticket, no warning, nothing!

Daddy was pissed off about Roy breaking the sound barrier with his Vette and Willy letting him off scot-free. Yep, a bit of jealousy no doubt came into play here. You see, Daddy got up before the sun every morning to milk our herd of dairy cows and wasn't finished with farm business until well after dinnertime. Meanwhile, Roy Jackson had twenty-something hired hands to work his enormous ranch while he flaunted his money and power all around the county. Roy had a deep voice that portrayed a strong man, but he ate enough southern fried chicken and cornbread to keep a well-rounded gut and one wide old ass to boot. He was a pompous, self-centered, Southern son-of-a-bitch, and everyone knew it!

My bro' Kenny is living proof. He was a helluva basketball player for the Seminole Bend High School Warriors. He was one of two token white kids on a team that consisted of seven African-Americans and a Seminole Indian, who, by the way, was affectionately known as Leaping Chief. Kenny was a lights-out shooter, which is why Coach Berry kept him.

But Kenny wasn't a starter. Kenny's only other white-skinned counterpart was Jimmy Jackson, the oldest son of the infamous pompous ass, Roy Jackson. Kenny had cleaned Jimmy's clock in every game of one-on-one they ever played in practice. Coach Berry knew Kenny was better but refused to start him in place of Jimmy.

Roy once poked Coach Berry in the chest with his finger and told him, "By God, that white flunky Gormon kid ain't playing before Jimmy, ya hear me?!" Then, Roy told Coach that there would be hell to pay if Jimmy didn't get a basketball scholarship to the University of Florida. Roy made sure none of the colored boys played more minutes than Jimmy, either. Coach Berry was rewarded with a new color TV and a Lazy Boy recliner for his efforts, but no paper trail could ever prove it. Strangely, after threatening the coach, Roy bought all the black kids and Leaping Chief new leather Nikes. More hush money, I guess. But I never could understand why Jimmy Jackson needed a basketball scholarship because heck, Roy could buy the Florida Gator team and every house in Gainesville if they was for sale!

Then there was Jimmy Jackson's younger sister, Jenny. She was drop-dead gorgeous. Her sandy blond hair was drawn slightly back from her perfect dimples, and her blue eyes matched that of the Florida skies. Jenny was a sophomore cheerleader for the basketball and football teams. However, she was the first and only sophomore to cheer on the varsity squad. Back when Jenny was selected by unscrupulous judges who would gladly accept cold hard cash under the table, my daddy just shook his head in jealous disgust. Plain and simple, it was another example of Roy's fat old money belt getting in the way of fairness and integrity. Mama told Daddy that just maybe Jenny Jackson was good enough to cheer varsity, and he shouldn't make no snap judgments. Daddy said that was bunk, so Mama got mad and walked away.

Deputy Willy Banks' nephew, Tyrone, was the sophomore center on the Warriors basketball team. Tyrone was known in these parts for dunking the ball so hard that many a glass backboard was shattered. In fact, one night, nobody in Clewiston dared guard him, so he thunder-smashed two backboards into millions of minuscule glass fragments. Took two hours just to replace both glass boards with the tin ones that hung from the side walls of the gym. They finished the game with only one referee because the other whistleblower got glass in his eye and had to be sent over to the local hospital.

Roy Jackson didn't much like Tyrone Banks, even though he knew Tyrone's court skills could help the Warriors team win a championship. He was riled because Tyrone had the hots for Jenny. Seemed Jenny would come home after games and talk and talk and talk about Tyrone and his basketball dominance. Then one night, Jenny didn't get back to the Jackson ranch until about one-thirty in the morning, and instead of catching a ride with a cheerleader friend like she told her daddy she was going to do, Roy saw Tyrone's rusty Volkswagen Beetle hustle backward down the long driveway. Roy didn't get outside in time to shoot poor old Tyrone, but he did grab Jenny by the arm and placed her rather ungracefully down on the couch in the living room. Jenny had been hoping that her daddy was sleeping when she got home. Not a chance. Jenny told her daddy that she only caught a ride with Tyrone because he just so happened to be heading this way. Jenny said Tyrone told her he was driving down to Nubbin Slough for some night fishing, practicing up on catching the biggest crappie so he could win the $500 award during the Speckled Perch Festival in nearby Okeechobee. Her usual ride, Connie Lou, a senior cheerleader, left the party at the north side beach of Lake Okeechobee early, and Tyrone just wanted to be a nice fella and offer Jenny a ride home. Roy Jackson didn't buy it, and Jenny was grounded for life, or maybe longer.

So, going back to that Saturday morning in January of 1982 over by the Kool-Aid stand, Bobby Joe heard Roy Jackson tell Deputy Willy Banks to make sure his nephew, Tyrone, stayed away from his daughter or he'd have his badge. Because he had orders from Sheriff Al Bonty to back off of Roy Jackson at all costs, there was not much Willy could say or do. Give him a ticket for excessive speed or reckless driving? Haul him in for threatening a police officer? Willy wanted to extract Roy's head from his shoulders and toss it in the pond in back of his house as a little dessert for the gator, but he knew better. It wasn't just Willy's career on the line—it was his life.

CHAPTER 1
The Jackson Brothers
1940s and 1950s

Ray Jackson was two years older than his brother, Roy, but they were best friends. Mammy and Pappy Jackson owned a used car lot in Pahokee, Florida, a small town of about 4,000 hard-working, but low-income folks on the eastern banks of Lake Okeechobee. All four of the Jacksons lived in a one-bedroom trailer that doubled as the sales office. To makes ends meet, Mammy and Pappy opened the store seven days a week and told little Ray and Roy to play elsewhere during business hours.

The boys began their life of crime at an early age, five and seven to be exact, when to pass time they stole bubble gum from Kuppa's Convenience Store so they could read the cartoons wrapped inside. They enjoyed cartoons so much that they elevated their plunder to *Dell* comic books. A few years later, as Ray and Roy were moving into the age of adolescence, *Playboy* hit the newsstands, and the boys would steal several copies and sell them to their wide-eyed pubescent pals. The crime spree continued until Ray was caught his junior year in high school by Pappy as he tried to steal a Pontiac sedan right off his father's own car lot. Ray planned to sell it to Betty Wills over in Clewiston, a young lady he happened to run into while they both were burglarizing Jake's Standard Oil gas station in Belle Glade one night. Pappy kicked Ray out of the trailer and told him never to come back. Roy packed a bag and left home with his older brother.

Ray and Roy hitchhiked to Cocoa Beach and enrolled in Causeway High School by forging their parents' names on the registration documents. They built a hut made from palm fronds on Cape Canaveral and went to school using a stolen Harley Davidson motorcycle. Instead of completing homework assignments, their nights were spent robbing stores and burglarizing homes.

Ray's first of many murders began after Principal Loughten, an ex-congressman from Florida and a single man in his late forties, told Ray after school one day that his grades were not sufficient for him to graduate with his class. By that time, Ray and Roy had raided every pawn shop in central Florida and had a collection of guns and weapons that would rival most police stations. Later on, the same night that Ray was told of his academic fate, Principal Loughten was snoring soundly in his bed. Moments later, his face was smothered by a foam pillow and blasted into eternity from a sawed-off double-barrel shotgun.

When teachers and staff heard the news of their principal's murder the next morning and were grieving together with bereaved students in the gym, Ray Jackson was forging out a new permanent record in Loughten's office. His F's had miraculously transformed into A's, and he added his name to the list of honor students who would be wearing gold tassels the night of graduation.

But Ray struck gold when he found an old piece of stationery from Principal Loughten's days in Congress next to the paper he used as a Cocoa Beach Causeway school administrator. Using the stationery with *United States Congress* emblazed on top, Ray typed out a letter of recommendation to the Naval Academy in Annapolis, Maryland. After falsifying Principal Loughten's signature once more, he left the office and joined his mourning classmates. One week after graduation, Ray purchased a mailbox in the local post office, then mailed a letter of application to the Naval Academy with a copy of his falsified transcript and Principal Loughten's recommendation enclosed in the envelope. Three weeks later, Ray was accepted into the Naval Academy's Officer Training Program. It was there where he met Oliver Harfield.

The day Ray graduated with honors from Causeway High, his little brother Roy officially dropped out of school. During the last two months of his sophomore year, Roy was able to lift more than $500 from the purses of every female teacher at the high school. After methodically plotting the times for after-school faculty and grade level team meetings from the bulletins posted next to the office door, Roy would sneak into the teachers' classrooms, pull out their billfolds from their purses and take only a couple of ones or fives. Not one teacher reported a theft because no one realized the money was missing.

In June of 1955, Roy Jackson bought a Greyhound ticket to Milwaukee. He wanted to work in a brewery surrounded by hops and yeast and alcohol. Roy got off Bus 149 in Cincinnati at midnight to change to Bus 167 that would take him to the city of suds, but instead, he accidentally boarded Bus 197 to Pittsburgh. The driver wasn't paying much attention, and Roy was fatigued from the long ride north from Florida, so he found the first open seat and collapsed into a snore-laced stupor. He awoke outside of Wheeling, West Virginia, but didn't have enough geographical sense to know he was traveling in the wrong direction. US Geography was taught in eleventh grade at Causeway High.

"The next bus to Milwaukee isn't until ten tomorrow morning," said the attractive brunette Greyhound ticket agent in Pittsburgh. "You're kinda cute, kid, so I won't charge you anything for the mess up." The ticket agent smiled and winked at Roy.

"So what's there to do in this city?" asked Roy as he looked at his watch, not noticing that the googly-eyed ticket agent was making passes at him. It was mid-morning, and he had the day to kill. "You know any cheap place I can bunk down for the night.

"It's such a nice day, you should walk downtown and stroll along the three rivers that come together here. There's the Monongahela, the Allegheny, and the Ohio. Very pretty, I must say."

The gal was so sweet that Roy didn't want to offend her by letting her know he wasn't much for strolling. "Okay, that sounds like fun. So do you have any cheap hotels around here?"

The agent thought a moment and pondered her next response carefully. "Well, there's no need for you to waste money at some dirty hotel. Why not stay at my apartment? My husband sells insurance, so he's out in Harrisburg today, and we have plenty of room for guests." That was a stretch. The young lady actually lived in a one-bedroom apartment about the size of a large treehouse.

Roy finally got the hint and was anxious to confirm spending the evening with this beautiful gal who looked to be just a couple of years older. He wrote down her address and directions. She got off work at five.

Roy left the Greyhound station, checked the city map the cute ticket agent had given him, then walked a few blocks southwest down Grant Street. He noticed a green section on the map that indicated Mellon Park Square was located just a block away up Sixth Avenue, and he decided to hunker down there to kill some time before checking out the Allegheny River.

"Wow, what a place!" whispered Roy to himself. He was looking at greenery and fountains that had just been erected on top of a parking garage. Then, he sat down on a park bench and gazed across the street at a skyscraper. It too looked new. Fifteen minutes later, Roy decided to check it out. There was a sign next to the entrance of the building that said: *Pennsylvania, Ohio, and West Virginia Aluminum Company World Headquarters (Built 1953).*

The revolving doors were a novelty that Roy had never experienced. He started toward the open wedge of the door, but then stopped. The door was revolving quickly, and he wasn't sure his timing was just right. But then he got a nudge on his shoulder.

"Come on, buddy. I don't have all day." A man in a dark gray pinstripe suit, white shirt, and a narrow silver and black-striped tie gripping a black leather briefcase stood waiting impatiently for Roy to make his move. Roy jumped into the next opening and tiptoed quickly until the door opened on the other side, and he emerged into a grand lobby. He stopped and looked up and down and all around, stunned by the beauty of this towering superstructure.

Roy wondered if working here would be better than scrubbing and polishing copper fermentation vessels at Pabst Blue Ribbon. He had nothing to lose, so he strutted up to the receptionist.

Roy was wearing faded blue jeans, a red t-shirt, and worn down tennis shoes. The receptionist gave him a once over and decided whoever this young man was, he needed to go. But Roy had a different plan.

"Howdy, young lady," Roy said with sheer confidence. "My name is Roy Jackson, and I am the head of marketing for Clyde Hayes Western Wear, and I have an appointment with your personnel department manager."

The receptionist looked back at him incredulously. "You have an appointment with Marvin Adams? Is that the way you always dress for an interview?"

"Yes, ma'am! This is how Clyde Hayes wants us to present ourselves, just like we want our customers to look."

"You've got to be kidding, right?" sputtered the receptionist. "Oh well, okay, but I need to give Mr. Adams a few minutes to get up to his desk. He was the man right behind you when you came through the revolving door."

Roy's face turned bright red. "Oh sure, yes, I thought that was him," he lied. "I'll just take a seat over here." Roy sat down on a fabric chair by the window and picked up a copy of *Life Magazine*. He wanted to appear literate.

Ten minutes later, the receptionist motioned for Roy to approach her desk. "Mr. Adams says he has no appointment scheduled with you, Mr. Jackson."

"You're right, I lied. But I know my experience working with Clyde Hayes is something that could be very beneficial to POWVAC."

"Is that right," replied the receptionist with skepticism. "You said you work at Clyde Hayes' headquarters, Mr. Jackson. Where exactly is that?"

Roy had to think quickly. He wasn't prepared for that question. "Well, it's in Milwaukee, of course."

"Is that so? Sorry to tell you this, but Clyde Hayes Western Wear is headquartered in San Francisco. I just got off the phone with their personnel department. They have no record of a Roy Jackson being employed there." After a moment of dead silence, the receptionist added, "Is there something you want to say? If not, I suggest you leave."

"Yes, ma'am, I am very sorry that I wasted your time. But I am motivated by this company and would really like to work here someday. By any chance, could you get me Mr. Adam's business card?"

The receptionist looked around and saw that no one was waiting for her assistance. Roy had already checked that out, too. She reluctantly decided to go to the personnel department and grab Marvin Adam's business card from his secretary. Customer service is what her company was all about, and she aimed to please, regardless of how much she loathed the customer.

"Alright, Mr. Jackson. Please have a seat again, and I'll be back soon." The receptionist locked her desk and headed for the elevators.

Roy looked around again. Still, no one was in the lobby. He reached in his pocket and took out his multifaceted Swiss Army knife. Nary a teacher's desk at Causeway High School had survived this trusty tool. Roy picked the receptionist's desk in less than a minute and had ducked down where no one could see him. Her purse was in the bottom right file drawer. As luck would have it, she had two crisp hundred dollar bills tucked into a hidden compartment that only petty thieves like Roy Jackson would know where to look. He closed the purse, shut the drawer, and waited as patiently as possible for the receptionist to return. Three minutes later, she returned and handed Roy the business card while bidding him farewell. The revolving door bumped his ankle, and he stumbled to the ground face-first onto the Sixth Avenue concrete sidewalk. People covered their mouths to hide their laughter.

Roy strolled aimlessly, trying to find a clothing store. On the other side of Mellon Square, he found the Union Trust Building. In an old railroad ticket office on the corner of Oliver and William Penn, Roy saw a luxury clothier with the name Larrimor's posted above the entrance. He looked in the huge picture window and saw a black suit fitting superbly on an equally superb manikin. A placard hanging from the ceiling just above the dummy said: *Made from 100% washable Dacron.*

Roy walked in the store and fifteen minutes later walked out wearing a dark blue Dacron suit, white shirt, red tie, a pair of Frank Brothers shoes, and a dollar bill he received in change from one of the stolen hundred dollar bills. He tossed his t-shirt, blue jeans, and tennis shoes into the garbage can by the door and walked out, proudly raising his chin in the air due to his new-found opulence.

Having no destination in mind, Roy walked northwest on Oliver Street for a block until he came to Smithfield Street. Looking to his right, he saw another skyscraper with many offices. He crossed the street and entered the Henry W. Oliver Building with a strut as dapper as his dress. To his left were the offices of *Marks, Taylor, and Smith, Attorneys at*

Law. "Why not?" Roy thought with a grin of confidence smeared all over his face.

Roy walked over to the men's room in the lobby and pulled out his Swiss Army knife once more. One of the gadgets that was tucked into it was a small metal file. He pulled out the POWVAC business card, unfolded the filing instrument, and scratched off *Director of Personnel* underneath Marvin Adam's name. Then Roy dipped his forefinger in water and lightly rubbed the flakes off the card. He used the electric hand dryer to remove the moisture, then held the card up to the light. "Not bad, if I do say so myself," whispered Roy.

After exiting the bathroom, Roy walked purposefully through the doors of Marks, Taylor, and Smith and straight to Doris Doth's reception desk. Doris was an attractive, middle-aged lady with curly blond hair and wearing a smart, yet elegant navy blue dress. Roy wished he had a briefcase. It would have looked much more professional. He smiled and handed the business card to Doris.

"Hello, gorgeous," cajoled Roy. "My name is Marvin Adams, lead attorney for POWVAC." He added a wink to his smile.

"My, my," replied Doris, totally flattered. "You look awfully young to be a lawyer."

"Yes, I've heard that before. Personally, I don't see it, but I sure appreciate the compliments."

Doris handed the business card back to Roy. "So how may I help you today, Mr. Adams?"

"Please call me Marvin, thanks. Yes, is Mr. Marks or Mr. Taylor available this morning? If not, perhaps I could speak with Mr. Smith?"

"I'm sorry, Marvin. All three partners are in Minneapolis this week."

"Ah, the Minny Apple, are they? What are they doing there?"

"Northwest Orient Airlines is our biggest client, and they are still involved in a lawsuit over the crash that happened back in 1950. The family of the house that was destroyed is suing them."

"Interesting," proclaimed Roy thoughtfully. "What is your defense strategy?" He wasn't sure that was the right lawyer talk, but it sure sounded good.

"We believe there was some sort of malfunction in the control tower's radar system. I only hear this second hand, you know, in the lounge at lunch, but the talk is that some unknown radio wave accidentally interfered with the tower's communication to and from the airplane. So the plane had to land on its own in a snowstorm with very little visibility."

"Well, that's just plain awful!" exclaimed Roy as he was pondering his next move. "So getting back to my visit, is there someone I can talk to for a few minutes about a lawsuit we are involved in? We might like some assistance from your firm on this one."

"Certainly, Marvin. I think Hank Daughtry would be available. Hank's our new associate. Fresh out of Yale, but you'll have to listen closely when he speaks because he still talks with a southern accent. He's from somewhere way down in Florida. Anyway, Hank is doing scientific research for the Northwest case."

"Well, that would be splendid, Doris. Thank you very much."

Doris picked up the phone and dialed Hank's office. Roy sat down in the visitor's chair and stared at a picture of the three partners that were framed on the wall. He was in deep thought. Perhaps this Daughtry fella could be duped. He had nothing to lose by trying. If Marks, Taylor, and Smith didn't work out, there were plenty of other law firms nearby.

Hank Daughtry appeared a few minutes later, introduced himself to Roy, and led him up two floors on the elevator to his office. Roy looked around at the messy room. Boxes of files were scattered everywhere, and Roy saw only two personal items, both hanging on the wall behind Hank's desk. Roy walked up and looked at the diploma from Yale, then glanced over to the picture next to it. It was a photo of Hank wearing Yale shorts and t-shirt uniform holding a soccer ball in his left hand while his right arm was draped around the neck of a dark-skinned teammate with curly black hair.

"Who is this?" asked Roy as he pointed to the teammate.

"That's my college roommate and best friend," replied Hank. "We were the captains of the Yale soccer team. His name is Yussef Jasur, the son of a prince from Jasurbia."

"Jasurbia? Isn't that the place where there's supposed to be a bunch of oil?" As soon as Roy said it, he wished he hadn't. He didn't think a lawyer would use the word bunch, but it just slipped. He needed to step up his game, and he wished now that he had studied those twenty vocabulary words he was supposed to learn in grade school each week.

"More than just a bunch, Mister, uh, oh, I'm sorry. I forgot your name."

This was Roy's chance for the switch. If he were to be employed in a law firm, it would be much easier using his real name.

"Jackson. Roy Jackson is my name, and there is absolutely no reason to apologize. It happens all the time."

"Yes, thank you, Roy. As I was saying, SoCal discovered an abundance of petroleum in Jasurbia back in the thirties, and a few years later, King Mustafa ibn Jasur and his family became very rich. The king's son, Adil Al Jasur, sent his son, Yussef, to America to learn about petroleum engineering at MIT, but Yussef excelled at soccer and wanted to play for an Ivy League team. He ended up at Yale and received a BS in electrical engineering, then transferred to MIT and got a master's in physics. Smart man, if I do say so myself!"

"Sounds like it. So you're new to Marks, Taylor, and Smith? Are you enjoying it here?"

"Well, I just started a few weeks ago. Down the road, I'd like to get into politics, but for now, this will help me pay off my student loan."

“I see,” said Roy. Hank was very amiable, but Roy noticed he was giving him the once over. Roy suspected that Hank was curious about his age. “Yes, I just graduated from Penn. I, too, have a large amount of debt.” Roy hoped that Penn had a law school.

“Well, I must say, Roy, you certainly look awfully young to have a law degree.”

“Yes, actually, I’m much younger than most. You see, I was accelerated through junior and senior high school and graduated when I was fifteen. Got a BS degree from Florida in two years and finished law school in three.”

“That’s quite impressive! So, are you from Florida? I’m from Haines City.”

“Well, what a coincidence. I’m from a small town on Lake Okeechobee called Pahokee. Ever heard of it?”

“Can’t say that I have, but I’ve fished the Big O many times. Best bass fishing around, right?”

“Sure is, Hank.” Roy guessed that Hank had bought his string of lies.

“So, how can I help you today, Roy?”

“Well, I understand you are conducting some research into the crash of that Northwest flight a few years back, right?” asked Roy, and Hank affirmed with a nod. Hank had no idea that Roy received that information from Doris. “I just started as an attorney over at POWVAC, but the aluminum industry doesn’t exactly excite me. My bachelor’s is in aeronautical engineering, and I would like to assist you in your research if you happen to have an opening.” Now Roy hoped that the University of Florida had an aeronautical engineering program.

“It’s your lucky day, Roy. This case is huge, and Mr. Marks called me this morning saying I should hire an assistant to help me out. He wanted me to work with someone who has a science background. You must be my gift from God!”

“I can start today, Hank. I just need to run back to POWVAC and give them my resignation.”

"That fast? You don't need to give them a two-week notice?"

"I'm sure I can work that out," replied Roy. "So, where do I fill out my employment paperwork?"

"Doris can take care of that," said Hank. "Well, welcome aboard Roy. I sure look forward to working with you!"

"I'll be back first thing in the morning, Hank. Thank you so very much!" Roy left Hank's office and went back to Doris' desk. Hank had called down to her, and she had the paperwork in hand. He needed to list a home address, so he wrote the address of the Greyhound ticket agent's apartment. Roy would open a post office box as soon as he left Marks, Taylor, and Smith, and then would change the address tomorrow. But tonight he would celebrate his good fortune.

With the few dollars he had left, Roy bought a bottle of fine champagne and searched for the Greyhound agent's apartment. She lived in a worn-down building on Mittenberger Street, just east of Duquesne University. The young lady was very impressed with Roy's new threads and the bottle of Veuve Clicquot, but she wondered where he found the money to pay for it. He told her he met up with his rich Aunt Mamey, who inherited a fortune from her late hubby, Uncle Mel. Roy claimed that he was always Aunty Mamey's and Unc Mel's favorite nephew. The naïve young Greyhound ticket agent bought it: lock, stock, and barrel. Tomorrow her husband would return from Harrisburg, but tonight she would enjoy being wined and dined in style.

They ate at Tuscan's, an expensive Italian restaurant on the riverfront overlooking the Monongahela. The bill arrived in a leather binder from a waiter wearing a black tux. Roy put a dollar bill inside and closed the binder without his date noticing. The gorgeous gal and Roy left the restaurant and thanked the waiter on the way out. As soon as the door closed behind him, Roy suggested that they walk briskly back to her apartment. He claimed to be overstuffed from pasta and needed a bit of exercise. In reality, he wanted to be as far from the restaurant as possible when the waiter realized he had been stiffed.

With the one night stand successfully completed, the young lady kissed Roy and said she would see him at the Greyhound station a little before ten so he could catch the bus to Milwaukee. Roy nodded, but then got dressed and walked quickly to Marks, Taylor, and Smith for his first day of work. At ten o'clock, the bus pulled out from the station and headed west to Wisconsin. The ticket agent was bewildered that Roy hadn't shown up, then became disconsolate with the thought that she may never see him again. But the memories of last night would never fade, especially nine months later when her only son would be born.

CHAPTER 2
House of Jasur
1940s and 1950s

Landlocked and surrounded by Iraq, Jordan, and Saudi Arabia is Jasurbia, a wasteland country of windswept sand dunes and a smattering of date palm oases containing a few patches of fertile soil. Once oil was discovered in the 1940s, no one cared much about the dates.

Prince Adil Al Jasur was given his name because it meant fair, honest, and just in Arabic. He was anything but. His father, King Mustafa ibn Jasur, relishing the newfound oil riches, proceeded to provide a lavish lifestyle for the Jasur family, building extravagant palaces in each of the five Jasurbian provinces. The king's oldest son, Hakim, flaunting his wealth around Europe, built a mountain chalet in the Swiss Alps and a gambling hall in Monte Carlo. Prince Adil craved the same lifestyle as his brother Hakim but was jealous that the crown prince had received all the family attention. When Adil turned fifteen, he was sent to govern the Al Qadir region of Jasurbia while Hakim became the Minister of Defense. Prince Adil was fascinated with the new attack planes built by the United States and was hoping his father would have named him to oversee the defense of his country instead of his brother. He had always been envious of Hakim, and he vowed to someday embarrass his brother in hopes that his father would reassign him to the defense position. Adil made this his life mission, and he didn't care how long it took to accomplish. Meanwhile, he was a powerful prince in an adolescent boy's body, and it was time to build his harem.

By the time he was sixteen, Adil had twenty wives and a countless number of concubines. He was never lonely!

Yussef, born in 1933, was the oldest son of seventy-six children fathered by Adil and was the prince's pride and joy. Yussef was a soccer star by the age of six and wanted to be just like his Italian idol, Giuseppe Meazza, when he grew up. But Yussef was intellectually gifted in the sciences, and Adil saw an opportunity to use his son's brainpower to finally unseat Hakim as Minister of Defense. The House of Jasur was wealthy beyond imagination with petroleum reserves in abundance under the arid desert just waiting to be tapped.

Prince Adil sent Yussef to America at the age of fourteen to learn engineering skills from American professors in the hopes that his son could find a way to prevent enemies from attacking Al Qadir Province by air. Well, at least that's what he told Yussef. Actually, the prince's motive was to collapse the novice Jasurbian military aviation industry that his brother had implemented as a means of national defense. If successful, his father, King Mustafa, would surely replace Hakim's ministerial position with himself. Yussef passed Yale's entrance exams with perfect scores while his daddy sent a donation for one million dollars to the Yale Scholarship Fund, which prompted Yale administrators to welcome the youngest Ivy League student ever with open arms. Yussef played soccer at Yale and left three years later with a bachelor's degree in electrical engineering, then transferred to the Massachusetts Institute of Technology to specialize in physics. One summer, he was employed as a consultant for Marks, Taylor, and Smith, a law firm in Pittsburgh.

Upon graduation, Yussef returned to Jasurbia and was appointed Al Qadir Province Chief Science and Technology Officer by his father. Prince Adil wasted no time asking him to design some sort of device that could disrupt air traffic control communications with airplanes. Yussef thought his father wanted him to create a new defense system for Uncle

Hakim in Fayez, the capital of Jasurbia. He had no idea that his father was trying to depose the crown prince from his ministry position by finding a way to bring down Jasurbian military planes.

CHAPTER 3
April 15, 1960

When Ray Jackson learned that his baby brother had been working at a law firm in Pittsburgh as an attorney for the past four years without a law degree or even passing the Pennsylvania state bar exam, he laughed uncontrollably. "That little con artist," Ray said, shaking his head. He was sitting at the Officer's Club in Annapolis drinking with Oliver Harfield.

"How did he get that job anyway?" asked Oliver in between sips of Miller draft beer. He and Ray had been living the Hi-Life themselves for some time, as well. Both had graduated with honors from the Naval Academy: Oliver because he was smart and Ray because he was a master at cheating. Now officially ranked as ensigns, the two friends were awaiting orders for their first command position.

"Some lawyer name Daughtry hired him to help research an airplane crash investigation. Their biggest client is Northwest Orient, and there was some sort of radar malfunction in Minneapolis back in 1950. They finally settled out of court last week. Roy said a Jasurbian prince's kid was hired as a consultant to help out with all the technical stuff."

"Should have hired us," joked Oliver. "I'm sure we know more about radar malfunctions than a spoiled rich kid from Jasurbia. Shoot, they don't even have airplanes over there. I don't think they even have electricity!"

"Our training with naval radar functions is top secret, Ollie. I don't think we should be talking too loud here with all these officers hanging out."

"Yep, you're right, Ray. But you know, I bet there's a lot of money that changes hands when an airplane crashes. Lawsuits galore!" Ray looked up from what was left of the foam head in his glass and met eyes with Oliver.

"I hope you're not thinking what I think you're thinking, Ensign Harfield?"

"Well, I might just be, Ensign Jackson. Any chance your little con artist brother, Counselor Roy, would like to take a nice vacation to Maryland someday soon? Sure would like to chat with him." Oliver and Roy toasted each other and ordered up another round.

* * * * *

On May 1, 1960, the USSR shot down an American military U-2 reconnaissance jet that was searching for nuclear weapons over Soviet territory. Suddenly, the Central Intelligence Agency shifted from a fledgling spy service to the fundamental organization used to protect America from foreign adversaries.

Those cadets and midshipmen who had graduated with honors from West Point and the Naval Academy were swiftly recruited into covert duty and assigned to an international location by President Eisenhower himself. Ensigns Oliver Harfield and Ray Jackson were given orders to report to a secret CIA research laboratory stationed underneath the Al Raha Bayt Hotel in Jeddah, then locate and convince a Jasurbian radio electronics expert named Yussef Jasur to come work for the CIA in the Saudi Arabian facility. Their mission was to oversee and assist the Yale and MIT grad in finding a way to prevent the Soviet Union's military from shooting down American reconnaissance planes. But on the flight to the Middle East, Harfield and Jackson had a better idea, one their bosses must never know about. After all, treason was still punishable by death in the United States.

*****

Oliver and Ray received no resistance signing a deal with the devil. Prince Adil gladly offered up his oldest son, Yussef, and all the cash necessary to successfully carry out Harfield and Jackson's newly created master plan.

"How dastardly!" thought Prince Adil as visions of himself ruling the world danced in his head. "Why didn't I think of that myself?"

All the prince wanted in return for loaning out Yussef was a piece of the action and a chance to bring down one of the world's two superpowers—the mighty US of A. Then he would prove to his father, King Mustafa, that he, not his brother Hakim, should have been appointed Crown Prince and the next ruler of Jasurbia.

Yussef was sent to Jeddah and set up shop in an unused rat hole of a cellar built underneath the Al Raha Bayt Hotel that the CIA called a laboratory. Working around the clock, in a few short weeks, Yussef was close to inventing a radar jamming device that could scramble and falsify air traffic signals. All he needed was a little more time to test it and tweak it.

Oliver lied to President Eisenhower and told him that the special assignment was sadly going absolutely nowhere, but he would continue to monitor Yussef's progress and report back to Washington every week. The president was disappointed and considered ending the project. Oliver was running out of time.

To successfully complete the task and tie up loose ends quickly, Yussef asked to have an MIT buddy who majored in electromagnetism, Abdul Samad, join him on this project. Abdul had returned to Jasurbia and started up the first Radio Shack franchise in the country. Oliver and Ray agreed that Yussef could use some help, and Abdul was happy to partner up again with his old friend.

Laboring relentlessly nonstop through twelve-hour days, five weeks later, Yussef and Abdul finalized the creation of a small, electrical instrument they believed would jam radar functions if the correct frequency were located. But it would need to be installed in a flight control tower's computer mainframe to work.

Pretending to hold written orders from President Eisenhower, Harfield and Jackson commanded a low-ranking rookie CIA agent to break into a Soviet military aircraft center and position the jammer into the mainframe. A daunting task, but it could be done. Bringing down a MiG jet would be the ultimate test.

CHAPTER 4
July 3, 1960

Yussef and Abdul knew an important piece of Oliver and Ray's plot was missing. Simply put, jamming the radar and providing false data signals between the control tower and airplane would not necessarily cause an accident. A well-trained MiG pilot would be able to see that the radar data feed was inaccurate and attempt to land visually. If the weather and visibility were terrible, the jamming device would most likely work just fine, but at other times—it was just a crapshoot.

Years earlier, while working on an end of semester project at MIT, Abdul had invented a remote control instrument that could infiltrate automobile steering functionality using radio band technology, thus controlling cars from a long-distance away. The automobiles required the newfangled power steering option to be installed in the vehicle for the remote control to work. Abdul had used a 1951 Chrysler Imperial in his experimental tests at MIT. He believed that the same type of apparatus could be used to guide aircraft from a remote location. It was time to sell the idea to Oliver and Ray.

"Mr. Oliver, please, sir, Abdul and I have something to discuss with you," Yussef uttered politely as he bowed his head and did not look Oliver or Ray directly in their eyes. He knew the CIA traitors would not be happy about another delay necessary to efficaciously complete their grand scheme.

"What is it, Yussef?"

"You are planning to secretly install our new jammer into a Soviet military base control tower next week, correct?"

asked Yussef with a bit of trepidation. “What makes you think that will bring down a MiG-21 jet?”

“What are you getting at, Yussef?” Oliver was puzzled. “You know damn well what our plans are!”

“Well, sir, if successfully placed into the Soviet’s computer guidance system, I’m sure the jam will scramble signals effectively. However, the MiG pilot can still land the aircraft using his own visual acuity.”

“Go on,” said Oliver, now listening carefully. He and Ray had thought about that possibility but guessed that jamming would occur only on a foggy or stormy night when visibility was deeply hampered.

Abdul explained in great detail his remote control experiment at MIT and how, in theory, it could be used to pilot aircraft from a long distance away. It would require some sort of video guidance system so that the operators on the ground could have eyes in the air. Used together with the radar jamming device, Oliver’s master plan would be fail-safe.

Oliver and Ray talked about it, then Oliver went to the phone and called the CIA operative who was awaiting orders at Baranovichi Air Force Base in the Belarus Republic. He ordered him to stand down and wait for further instructions.

Two days later, Oliver and Ray were sitting cross-legged on huge, silk pillows and sipping tea served from a brass pot as honored guests of Prince Adil of Al Qadir Province. The prince had just written a check to each man in the amount of one million United States dollars drawn from a Swiss bank account. The House of Jasur now had a finger in the pot of American espionage, albeit with rogue agents hell-bent on personal gain.

CHAPTER 5
November 7, 1960

On November 7, 1960, Oliver Harfield phoned CIA Director Alex Dulles to tell him that he and agent Ray Jackson were forced to execute Yussef Jasur after they caught him red-handed selling secrets to the USSR. It was a lie. Harfield claimed that Yussef was providing Soviet KGB agents with technical information that would be used to crash Air Force One during President Eisenhower's trip to New York to celebrate Richard Nixon's anticipated presidential win over John F. Kennedy. They telegraphed a completely fabricated official report detailing the KGB's use of implausible technical advancements that were going to be used to bring down the world's most famous airplane.

Coincidently, the report also appeared to demonstrate Harfield and Jackson's extraordinary heroics in the face of immense danger to protect the president. Director Dulles and President Eisenhower discussed the shocking details of the apocryphal report and immediately promoted Oliver Harfield and Ray Jackson to CIA Supervisors.

Harfield's first assignment was to head up intelligence operations in the Bahamas and Caribbean Islands, but use Florida as his home base due to the covert activity passing between Cuba and the Sunshine State. Meanwhile, Ray Jackson was assigned to oversee operations in the northern countries of South America. Harfield and Jackson needed to solidify their credentials, and for the next two years, they were exemplary employees of the nation's clandestine spy agency.

*****

MacDill Air Force Base in Tampa had morphed into a Tactical Air Command facility in the 1960s when the fear of a nuclear attack by Russia raised the blood pressure of many Americans, military personnel, and citizens alike. But with the possibility that the Cold War would soon become hot and espionage out of control, it was time to ramp up America's surreptitious warmongering efforts.

Nike missile bases had been constructed throughout the United States to protect our homeland from mass destruction. On October 29, 1962, the day after the Cuban Missile Crisis ended, President Kennedy ordered the covert development of an underground nuclear weapons control facility in Gainesville, Florida. From that secret command center, atomic weapons located in Nike bases around the country could be aimed and launched at enemies of the US. The current command center located at the Pentagon would be decommissioned and used only as a decoy.

Kennedy dispatched fifty-five high-ranking Corps of Engineers officers, architects, construction supervisors, electricians, and communication experts to create and assemble a subterranean structure in Gainesville. They would be required to handle the manual labor involved in excavating the dig and shelling up the concrete and triple-reinforced steel structure. Due to the top-secret nature of the project, Kennedy wanted only trusted officers deployed to complete the mission. The men began by erecting a thirty-five-foot opaque canvas fence around the perimeter of the site. Two digging cranes and a bulldozer were transported in by Army flatbed semis, as were steel beams and construction materials. The president ordered two recently promoted top CIA staff members to oversee the mission. Chief Supervisor Oliver Harfield and Senior Supervisor Raymond Jackson were assigned by the new CIA Director, John McCone, for this duty.

The project location was selected because it was a vacant area within the environs of the University of Florida. Director McCone explained to President Kennedy that by constructing on the college campus, residents of Gainesville would assume the university was merely building another dormitory or classroom building and would suspect nothing out of the ordinary. College administrators were told that the Corps of Engineers needed to construct an underground sewage pumping station to enhance drainage during times of flooding. Kennedy himself had issued the letter and assured the university that the federal government would pick up the tab, and the project would be completed in less than a month. College officials were perplexed that the president would write the letter personally, but seeing they didn't need to provide any funding, and the construction zone was in a vacant area of campus, they were satisfied and did not question any further.

Construction of the subterranean facility was completed in twenty-five days, but the trench wasn't finished for another month. The Corps of Engineers was building dedicated railroad tracks for military use only that linked all Nike bases throughout America for the transport of missiles and nuclear warheads. The tracks had already been completed from Site TU-79 in Albany, Georgia, to Site HM-97 in Homestead, Florida. Those tracks ran directly through the city of Gainesville and less than a quarter-mile from the new underground command center. Electrical engineers carefully ran one-inch-thick cable wire from the facility to a connection box next to the military tracks. From there, cable ran along the rails to every Nike site in the United States.

On December 25, 1962, ignition switches were ready to go that could fire an electrical impulse from the new secret command center to each Nike base, and within minutes there could be the total destruction of Moscow, Havana, and any other city we didn't like. Merry Christmas!

Early in the evening on the 25th, CIA supervisors' Oliver Harfield and Raymond Jackson thanked the fifty-five men for their service and provided Army transportation to MacDill AFB so they could be home with their families for what remained of the holidays. The Lockheed military transport plane crashed into the Gulf of Mexico shortly after takeoff, killing all on board. Harfield and Jackson watched the news report on the black and white television from a barstool in Gainesville's Oldfield Saloon. They raised their glasses of spiked eggnog and lightly tapped each other's until a small clang could be heard.

"Cheers, Oliver."

"Yes, cheers to you, too, Raymond."

CHAPTER 6

December 26, 1962

After the military transport plane crashed off the Gulf Coast killing all fifty-five Corps of Engineers soldiers on Christmas Day in 1962, President Kennedy was devastated. On December 26th, the day after the tragedy, Kennedy met with CIA Director John McCone. McCone recommended CIA supervisors Oliver Harfield and Raymond Jackson be assigned to oversee operations at the new underground nuclear launch command center.

Because of its ultra, top-secret nature, McCone ordered Harfield and Jackson to keep silent, both within the intelligence agency and outside of it. Only McCone, Harfield, Jackson, and President Kennedy were now aware of the existence of the subterranean facility that could control the fate of the world.

As a diversion, Kennedy purposely leaked to the *Washington Post* that the nuclear command center lay several floors beneath the Pentagon and was untouchable by enemy missiles. Russian President Nikita Khrushchev ordered his US-based spies to devise a plan that would destroy America's nuclear launching capabilities, and because of the *Post's* article, the espionage focus was centered around the Pentagon. The diversion was successful. Oliver Harfield, if authorized to do so by President Kennedy, would push the button that could start World War Three. But Oliver Harfield had a better idea. Power. The world had controlled him for too long, so now it was time for him to control the world. He and his colleague Ray Jackson had been ordered around by McCone long enough. This was their chance.

CHAPTER 7

January 1, 1963

On New Year's Day, 1963, Oliver Harfield invited Ray Jackson's brother, Roy, and his colleague Hank Daughtry to a housewarming party at Oliver's new mansion built amidst palm trees and green pastureland near Seminole Bend in south-central Florida. Oliver paid for a chartered Lockheed JetStar flight from Pittsburgh to Orlando for his guests and provided ground transportation in a limousine from Orlando to Seminole Bend. Needless to say, Hank and Roy were impressed! But they were astonished to see another limousine pull up right behind them, and a dark-skinned man with two-armed bodyguards exit the vehicle. The obviously Arab man was wearing a white, gold-embroidered thobe that hung like a bedsheet from his neck down to the leather sandals on his feet. Wrapped around his pate was a red and white checkered kufiyah that was tucked neatly under a black agal. It was pressed snuggly against the wealthy Arab man's forehead. Oliver invited everyone into his home and cordially introduced his highness, Prince Adil, to Roy and Hank.

* * * * *

Oliver and Ray had been planning and patiently waiting for this day since leaving Adil's Jasurbian palace two years earlier. Now that the prince's son Yussef's radar jamming device and Abdul's video remote controller were successful in bringing down the military transport plane on Christmas that disposed of fifty-five potential witnesses to Oliver and Ray's scheme, the two CIA chiefs ramped up their efforts and initiated the masterplan. Once the second chocolate raspberry martini had been consumed by all guests, Ray brought out a wooden easel with a thirty-by-twenty-five-inch lined paper attached. Using a red marker for emphasis to strongly suggest plenty of blood be spilled, the plan was outlined on six sheets of the oversized paper and in great detail.

Hank Daughtry had never been involved in any criminal activity, and he was hesitant to start now. He had been fooled into believing this trip to Florida was simply a party to ring in the New Year and welcome Roy's brother's friend into his new house. But once Oliver handed him a briefcase with 10,000 crisp one hundred dollar bills, Hank decided it was time to change his career path! In truth, he had no choice. If he had turned down Oliver's caseload of Benjamins, Hank would have been the first meal of the new year for a family of alligators sunning themselves in the backyard. The scheme was actually doubly enticing for Hank, who had a lifelong desire to get into politics. The first step in Oliver's plan would be to get Hank elected as governor of Florida. Prince Adil's Swiss bank account would fund his campaign. It would be a slam dunk.

If all went as planned, Hank Daughtry would assume the office of governor of the great state of Florida on January 7, 1975, twelve years and six days from today. Once he became governor, Daughtry would appoint Sam Dulie as the new South Florida DNR supervisor in Homestead. Thanks to the CIA's covert operative skills, no one would know that Sam Dulie was really Abdul Samad, a graduate of the Massachusetts Institute of Technology who actually knew nothing about protecting natural resources. Sam would use his office as a decoy for a communications facility.

Daughtry would then secretly transfer government-owned swamp and grazing land to Ray Jackson's little brother, Roy.

Roy's new massive ranch would serve as the distribution center for the radar jamming equipment being assembled in Columbia and the remote control devices air freighted from Jasurbia. Meanwhile, Ray would construct an electronics factory in the mountains between Bogota and Medellin, disguised as a secret underground surveillance building used to track the new drug cartels that were springing up throughout the country.

Ray assured CIA Director McCone he could successfully lead two significant projects at the same time. He would fly back and forth from Columbia to Gainesville and oversee both the South American intelligence operations and Florida's nuclear missile command center at the same time.

Al Qadir oil revenue would flow freely from Prince Adil's Swiss bank account directly into Rancher Roy's bank account in Seminole Bend. The mission would be complete once the United States of America was held hostage firmly in the grips of Oliver Harfield and the Jackson brothers, and then a ransom of one billion dollars was paid in cash or gold. Prince Adil had plenty of money, so for his part in the operation, he only wanted power. He dreamed he would become the first King of the Monarchy of America.

Recruiting the players would be difficult and complex. They would be ruthless in finding and engaging erudite men and women who, under the intimidation of a deadly weapon, would leave their families to protect the ones they loved. The timeline for the master plan to be successful would be twenty years. By the summer of 1982, the pieces would be in place. The radar jamming and remote control equipment would be plentiful, tested for accuracy, and distributed to targeted locations. The federal government would have closed the Nike missile bases. However, Ray Jackson would ensure they were fully armed and operable and undetected by the Soviet spies or even US intelligence agencies.

Once the takeover of America was complete with the ransom paid, Ray, Roy, and Oliver would change their names, move to an uncharted Bahama island, and retire in blissful obscurity.

As the strategy meeting came to a close, Prince Adil began to daydream. In his delusional reverie, he envisioned himself accompanied by a barrage of Jasurbian military personnel who would tear down the White House and build the first White Palace on the Mall across Pennsylvania Avenue. It would completely surround the Washington Monument, and the obelisk's observatory would be replaced with the world's grandest throne.

The Prince smiled at the thought, but no one caught it. Sometimes dreams do come true.

CHAPTER 8

Fall of 1964 to Fall of 1970

Bo Yardly was the most famous resident of the Seminole Bend subdivision known as "Slum City" by the white folks who resided outside the northeast section of town. The area was identified by cheap concrete block homes, hourly cacophonic freight train noises, and young black children playing stickball on the dusty gravel streets. Well heck, Bo Yardley was actually the only famous resident of that subdivision, a symbolic cliché of Deep South African-American living conditions that Martin Luther King so despised. Bo was the first three-time high school All-American from the state of Florida in any sport, and following his sensational senior football season in 1964, consummate Alabama college coach Paul "Bear" Bryant visited Seminole Bend and recruited Bo to become the next Crimson Tide featured running back. Had Bo any hair on his back, I'm sure the follicles would have been standing straight up at attention! Anyway, Bo led the Tide to the very top of the AP National Poll by rushing for 1,523 yards his freshman year, and things just kept improving from that point on.

On January 28, 1969, with four stellar college seasons under his belt, Bo was drafted second overall into the National Football League by the Atlanta Falcons. Second was good enough for all his friends and followers back in Seminole Bend, considering USC's Heisman winner, O.J. Simpson, went first to the Buffalo Bills. Then, amid a spectacular rookie season for the Falcons, on the third day of December in 1969, Bo was redrafted. And this time he was selected first—by none other than good old Uncle Sam. Yep, that's right, Bo's birthdate was September 14th, and as soon as the NFL season ended, he headed up to Fort Sill, Oklahoma, for eight weeks of basic training with the US Army. From there, he was sent to Fort Carson in Colorado for eight weeks of Advanced Infantry Training with the Signal Corps. Bo was always fascinated with radios, and he would take apart and put back together his dad's transistor every chance he could get.

On June 27, 1970, Bo was shipped via a Lockheed C-141 Starlifter to Saigon with ninety-four men from his company, supposedly the elite soldiers of the Fourth Infantry. On September 12th, two days shy of his twenty-third birthday, Bo was shot in the back of his skull and killed instantly by friendly fire in southeastern Laos. He was the only American to die during Operation Tailwind, a covert incursion that was merely supposed to be a diversion for the Royal Lao Army. His mama didn't want him buried in obscurity with all the other grunts in Arlington, so he was laid to rest peacefully in Seminole Bend's Calvary Baptist Cemetery with his little sister, Bea, who died during childbirth.

Because Bo's unrecognizable head had been shattered into several thousand bone fragments and gray matter, his funeral was closed-casket. The memorial service was attended by every single neighbor, including three-week-old Elva Simmers and 104-year-old Herman Cobert. Even most of the white folks who cheered for Bo found their way to Calvary Baptist that day. Standing dolefully in line, forty-eight friends and relatives stood ready to eulogize Bo. When it was Rupert Dockins' turn to speak, instead of words of respect and remembrance, he offered up a rather strange proposal, considering it was right in the middle of the memorial service. He suggested that the neighborhood adopts an official name, perhaps one the whites could use instead of Slum City, and that name would be "Yardlyville." After several minutes of joyous hoots and hollers, Rupert asked for a vote by a show of hands. No need for a count – it was unanimous, and Seminole Bend now had an official de facto "suburb" called Yardlyville.

* * * * *

Willy Banks and Bo Yardly had been neighbors, school buddies, teammates, and best friends. Together, at age seven, they began lifting weights in Willy's front yard. Willy found the weights while he and Bo were exploring down at the dump looking for old transistor radios. Someone must have given up on bulking up and thrown the barbell and 300 pounds worth of sand-filled plastic cylinders into the trash. Ironically, for all the comic book fans of the world, the steel barbell was rusting out right next to an empty can of spinach. Whoever tossed the weight set must have decided to try Popeye's muscle-building green leaf program instead. Willy and Bo soon began weightlifting contests with each other, and before they reached the ripe old age of eight, both were bench pressing 140 pounds. In high school, Willy was the fullback on the Warriors football team, and his main task was to block for Bo. Bo went on to break every rushing record ever created at Seminole Bend High School and received a full-ride scholarship to Alabama, while Willy broke the record for the most "good job" pats on the back.

In the early sixties, just as the boys were starting high school, they took it upon themselves to be the neighborhood protectors. On occasion, drug dealers would enter the neighborhood looking for youngsters to peddle their goods. Few left without broken jaws and other bodily encumbrances straight from the fists of Willy and Bo. But along with keeping out the riffraff, Willy and Bo would volunteer to carry groceries for the women and mow lawns for the elderly, never expecting anything in return. When Bo headed off to Alabama, Willy joined the army. After surviving three tours to ‘Nam and four bullets to the torso, Willy came home and signed on with the Seminole Bend Sheriff's Department.

CHAPTER 9

September 26, 1965

While Willy was patrolling the jungles west of Saigon in the fall of 1965, his older brother, Tyrus, met up one night with Abelina Charles, the prettiest girl on the planet (according to Tyrus). Abby never wanted to get serious with any boy unless she could land Tyrus—the most gorgeous man in the universe (according to Abby).

Tyrus had his eyes set on Abby since they sat across the play table from each other in kindergarten, but he was way too shy to cozy up with her until the moment finally hit him during the annual Set de flo' dance competition at the church. Calvary Baptist continued the Nineteenth Century tradition out back in the picnic area under the shade of the old banyan trees. Folks just sat on top of the picnic tables waiting for their turns to be called to enter the dance ring, which was simply a circle drawn in the dirt with sticks. Fiddler Freddy Jones was supposed to call out the numbers randomly to see whose turn it was to compete, but it sure looked fishy when Tyrus and Abby's numbers were "randomly" called first. Anyway, Abby placed her hands on her hips and winked at Tyrus, and Tyrus complied with the tradition by rolling his eyes amidst claps, cheers, and laughter from the crowd. Freddy called out the Cakewalk for the first required dance steps, then laid aside his fiddle, picked up his banjo, and started strumming away.

It wasn't but a few seconds into the dance that Abby fell down and tumbled outside the circle. She grimaced, grabbed her ankle, and rubbed it soothingly with both hands. Even though Tyrus was declared the winner of the first dance, he ran over to Abby, lifted her off the ground with both arms, and carried her to a banyan tree about a hundred yards away. He gently leaned her up against the uncomfortable braided trunk and lifted her injured leg so it could rest on his lap. But when he rolled down her sock to examine the wound, she reached over and grabbed his neck with both of her hands and pulled his face next to hers. The kiss was their first. Tyrus had waited fifteen years for this moment, ever since the two of them created stick figure dolls with Play Dough back in kindergarten. Abby's ankle was just fine, thanks to that medical miracle called smooching.

Tyrus went back and excused himself from the dance competition, claiming he needed to get Abby to a doctor. Several concerned friends offered to help, but Tyrus said he could manage alone. He carried Abby out of sight of the revelry behind the church, then, smiling and chuckling, they both started running down the muddy path to the creek. On the grassy bank came the second kiss. Nine months later, on June 6, 1966, Tyrone Banks was born.

* * * * *

The day Tyrone was born, Tyrus left Abby at Gregorson General Hospital for a few minutes and jogged down to Mattie's Toy Store. He returned with a small ball made from cloth and stuffed with cotton. The fabric was painted orange with black stripes to look like a miniature basketball. Tyrone was officially twelve hours old, lying very comfortably in his mama's arms, when his daddy Tyrus wiggled the ball in front of his son's eyes, then tucked it under the newborn baby's armpit. Abby, who was sitting up in the hospital bed, raised her eyebrows and grinned at her proud boyfriend. Seconds later, the ball rolled off Tyrone and onto the floor.

"So, Abby, can we get hitched now? I want to be Tyrone's official daddy!"

"You are his official daddy, Ty," Abby replied with a smile that showed off her delightful dimples. "And yes, I think it's time I officially become Abby Banks."

Tyrus leaned over and hugged and kissed his new fiancé, careful not to squish his future NBA star. He wanted to call his little brother Willy to tell him the great news that not only was he a new uncle, but he was also going to be a new brother-in-law. Unfortunately, Willy signed on for a second tour and was again serving his country somewhere in the jungles of Vietnam. Airmailed letters were the only way to keep in touch.

After two hours admiring his new son and trying to teach him to palm a cloth basketball, a nurse shooed Tyrus out of the hospital room. Visiting hours were over, and Abby and Tyrone needed some rest. If everything checked out satisfactorily, they would be coming home tomorrow. Reluctantly, Tyrus kissed his family goodnight and headed for the exit. It would take him about twenty minutes to get back.

After Abby found out that she was pregnant, she and Tyrus had moved into a one-bedroom rusty trailer that had been used as a fish camp south of town on Taylor Creek, just a stone's throw, if you could get it over the dike, from Lake Okeechobee. Every now and then, a speckled perch scale would flake up from the faded orange shag carpet, but for the most part, the fishy smell had been removed with the help of gallons of Lysol and open windows.

As soon as Tyrus left the hospital parking lot, he realized that he hadn't told his little brother, Otis, about the baby yet. It was almost time for supper, so Tyrus decided to detour to his old neighborhood and fry up some catfish for Otis and himself as a way to celebrate the good news. He would write his letter to Willy while at the house so that way he could drop it in a mailbox before going home.

Otis had been living with Willy together in the family house ever since Mama Banks passed the night of Willy's high school graduation. Mama Banks wasn't the best manager of her own blood glucose, and skipping an insulin shot in the tummy was a frequent occurrence. Before President Johnson signed into law the act that created Medicaid a year earlier, Mama had no way to pay for the expensive drug. But once she began receiving it for free, the daily painful shots were easy for her to ignore. She made it to the graduation ceremony and cheered as Willy crossed the stage to receive his diploma. When the students tossed their caps into the air, and hugs and kisses were rampant, Mama Banks' blood vessels gave out. She died before even reaching the ambulance.

Of the three brothers, only Tyrus remembered his daddy. He was five years old when Papa Banks ran away with Clover Bane, a waitress at Marvin's Southern Barbecue where Papa Banks worked as a dish washer. Rumor had it that Papa and Clover were both doing twenty-five years to life for armed robbery up in Virginia somewhere.

Tyrus smothered the catfish in an egg and cornmeal coating, then fried it in used bacon grease that was left on the stove since yesterday's breakfast. Otis didn't have any Mazola lying around, but he figured that grease and oil were basically the same things when it came to gourmet cooking. And who could eat catfish without sipping on a few Budweiser's, right? Otis raised a toast to his big brother, ate a couple pounds of catfish, then moved on over to the couch to digest his dinner and watch *Gunsmoke* on his thirteen-inch black and white TV with twenty-inch rabbit ears. Someday he would marry Miss Kitty, he dreamed. Otis burped a few times and was snoring by the time Chester met up with Matt Dillon over at the Long Branch Saloon.

By the telephone, Tyrus found a notepad and a pencil that had been sharpened down to a length of about a half-inch. There was a pocket knife next to the pad, and Tyrus figured that Otis whittled away on the pencil to get to the lead. The eraser was worn down and leveled equally with the top of its tin holder. Otis was well-known for making mistakes, and here was irrefutable evidence!

Just like his younger brothers, Tyrus wasn't much for letter writing, so the lack of pencil lead served as a good excuse for keeping his communications short and sweet. One long sentence should be good enough for a baby announcement, he thought: "bro, yur an uncle and baby name is Tyrone and now yur uncle willy and abby is good and they come home tomoro." Tyrus passed his English courses in high school because he got extra credit for clapping the chalk dust out of the black felt erasers.

Airmail from the US was sent only once a week by military transport from the nearest Army Post Office in Miami. However, after leaving Miami, it stopped to pick up mail in San Francisco and Seattle before flying on to Vietnam. The flight plan included a holding and refueling stop in Tokyo, where the plane would wait for clearance to proceed into Indochina airspace. Ho Chi Minh would like nothing better than to gun down a US aircraft full of good tidings and cheerful family pictures for the enemy soldiers on the ground. Once the plane landed in Vietnam, the mail was held in Saigon until the soldiers could be located, and a dangerous delivery through Viet Cong guerilla positions could be made. Tyrus knew that Willy probably wouldn't find out about his new nephew for a couple of months.

Tyrus had taken an instant color photograph of baby Tyrone using a Polaroid Land camera that Gregorson Hospital purchased for those happy occasions in the maternity ward. He put the picture in an envelope along with his note and sealed it. Tyrus couldn't find a stamp anywhere in the house, so he thought he would run over to Yardly's house and see if Bo's mama had one that he could borrow. It was eight o'clock, and the sun was setting, so most likely the Yardly's were done eating, and Tyrus wouldn't be interrupting their dinner. Otis was sound asleep on the couch, so Tyrus didn't bother to tell him where he was going.

* * * * *

"Cute kid. Pretty girl."

Tyrus flinched on his way over to Yardly's house. Did he hear something? He looked around but couldn't see anyone. The sun had set just a few minutes earlier, and only a handful of streetlights were working. The others had been used as rock-throwing targets, and fragments of glass that had fallen to the street were sparkling in the moonlight. Tyrus paused a moment, then shook his head and walked on.

"I be talking to you, boy."

Tyrus recoiled, then quickly turned around. From behind two palmetto trees that served as Al Franklin's only front yard landscaping, appeared a crew cut, vast-stomached white dude. "Did he call me boy?" thought Tyrus.

Tyrus had a good mind to march right up to the unknown man and smack him for using a derogatory racial slur right to his face. White folks should know better than to call a black man boy, especially on his own turf. But Tyrus held back. The white dude had a gun aimed at Tyrus' head.

"Please don't shoot, man. I got fourteen dollars and some change. It's all yours, you can have it!" Tyrus was afraid. The Civil Rights movement was supposed to be creating equal rights for all people, but instead, it was creating more hatred in the Deep South. A white man in this neighborhood at night could only mean one thing—another lesson to be delivered to those blamed for ending the Confederacy. When would it stop? Would it ever?

The man walked right up to Tyrus and placed the barrel of the pistol on his nose. He cocked the hammer back and began to squeeze the trigger. Tyrus froze. Would he be a daddy for less than a day?

"I don't need your money, boy. I have a job for you to do. It involves leaving this here country, and you will never return," the man said bluntly as he pushed the weapon harder into the cartilage of Tyrus' nose.

"Please, man, I got a newborn son and soon a new wife." Tyrus was pleading with not only his lips but with his eyes. A teardrop fell onto the man's gun.

"Yes, I know that. I already told you they were cute." The man smiled and winked. "And if you want them to live a long life, you'll come with me."

"What you saying, man?" Tyrus' fear turned to sheer panic. How did this guy know about Abby and Tyrone? He called them cute. Had he been to the hospital? Had he actually seen them?

"Listen boy, you're coming with me. If you decide otherwise, there will be three dead bodies in Seminole Bend. Two of them in the maternity ward at Gregorson Hospital."

"Okay, man. I come with you, but can I sees them one more time? Only a minute or two at the hospital, please, man!"

"You don't seem to get it, do you, boy?" The man pushed Tyrus back a few feet with the barrel of his pistol. "It's over, you're done being a family man. You come with me, everyone lives. You give me any problems, three die. Simple, understand? Now lie down on the ground, face first, and put your hands behind your back!"

Tyrus did as he was told. The man kneeled on Tyrus' back. He was a big guy, 250 pounds, at least, Tyrus thought. With his left hand, the man took out a pair of handcuffs and slapped them on Tyrus' wrists. He then stood up and yanked Tyrus back on his feet. A car started up a block away, turned on its lights, and drove up to the man and Tyrus. It was a black Chrysler New Yorker, brand new. The driver got out and opened the back door. The man shoved Tyrus face-first into the luxurious white leather seat, then shut the door.

"Get him out of here fast," the man shouted at the driver.

The driver promptly returned to the front seat and slammed the pedal. A cloud of dust rose up as the New Yorker sped away. Tyrus moved his handcuffed hands towards the back pocket of his blue jeans. With the tips of his fingers, he felt the envelope that contained a note for his brother, but more importantly, a picture of his newborn son. He may never see Abelina Charles again, but he was determined never to let the picture of Tyrone Banks and his mama become separated from his body.

Meanwhile, just a few feet from the two palmetto trees, Roy Jackson slipped his pistol back into a small holster attached to his belt and walked away into the darkness.

Tyrus Banks was never seen or heard from again.

CHAPTER 10
July 2, 1966

Abby and baby Tyrone stayed in the hospital for a week. When Tyrus didn't come back the next morning to pick them up and take them home, Abby was bewildered and distressed. Doc Stanley, who delivered Tyrone, decided Abby should stay in the hospital until she could physically and mentally take care of Tyrone by herself. Abby's mother was not willing to take her daughter and grandson in with her family, a stubborn result of Abby getting pregnant during what her mama called a "one-night stand." But she was willing to call the sheriff's office to report Tyrus as missing.

Four sheriff's deputies checked his trailer and talked to neighbors and determined that no foul play was detected. Otis confirmed that Tyrus stopped by for catfish and a few beers after leaving Gregorson, but he fell asleep and figured that Tyrus went home. Abby was crushed. She presumed that Tyrus got cold feet after leaving the hospital thinking about his new parental responsibilities and decided to bolt.

The following week Abby wrote a letter to Willy letting him know about the birth of his first nephew and the perplexing vanishing act of his older brother. Willy finally received Abby's letter in September of 1966 while recuperating at the Eighth Field Hospital in Nha Trang. Willy had been completing his third tour of duty in Vietnam, the last two voluntary, and it would be his grand finale. At the end of his previous mission, Willy was one of eight tired soldiers that remained from his platoon, and they had trudged through the rain-soaked bush on their way back to Ninh Hoa from Xa

Ninh Sim where helicopters would transport them back to Saigon. They knew Viet Cong guerillas were lurking all around, but they couldn't see them. While crossing a rice field during a torrential downfall, the platoon was ambushed from their northern flank. Being outnumbered by twenty-five men, the American soldiers tried to run south into the cover of the wilderness. All were gunned down, leaving a crimson tint in the flooded paddy field.

Willy took two 7.62 millimeter bullets from a Soviet-made AK47 to his muscular torso, one lodging in his right shoulder and the other in his left shoulder, both finding bone and tissues between the scapula and clavicle of each arm. His face splashed directly in the groundwater, and he laid there dazed for a moment. Upon hearing screams of pain behind him, he noticed two fellow soldiers wounded and lying face up in the rice paddy. Willy ignored the searing pain in his upper body and crawled the twenty feet back to his buddies as the Viet Cong began to move in his direction. With enormous adrenaline pumping through his system, Willy took a squat position in front of the wounded men and power-lifted both soldiers onto his broad, severely injured shoulders. But could he get all three of them safely to the rainforest about a hundred yards away? He had no choice. Willy lumbered the best anyone could with nearly 400 pounds on his bullet-shredded back.

The soldiers were only five yards from the edge of the bush when shots rang out, and Willy was hit by two more bullets, both hitting flesh and tissue on the right side of his body, but missing the internal organs of his abdominal cavity. Although bleeding profusely, Willy managed to dive headfirst into the thick forest with his human cargo in tow. However, Lieutenant Connelly was already dead. His skull was shattered from a projectile that hit him directly on top of the cranium during his transport on Willy's back.

Willy's other passenger, Private Buck Scott, was unconscious from loss of blood. Although it was too late to help Lieutenant Connelly, Willy was determined to get Buck to safety. With his strength beginning to wither from his own blood loss, Willy managed to drag Buck into a hole, and then covered both of them in decaying leaves fallen from the jungle canopy. He remembered seeing a Burmese python in a similar hole a few days earlier, and he hoped that if he and Buck were lodgers in some Pythonid's home, the reptile would be a gracious host!

Buck had been hit in the lower back, and Willy couldn't tell if he had ruptured any internal organs. Willy untied the private's boot and took off a sock, then squeezed the water out, hoping to remove any loose dirt. He ignored his own pain and blood loss and held the sock firmly on Buck's wound, trying to stop the bleeding. At this point, he had no idea how they were going to escape. It was then that Willy heard the chopping sound of several Bell UH-1 Iroquois helicopters advancing towards the rice paddy, and a few moments later, the sweet music of ammunition peppering the field from the M60D door guns attached to the Huey.

With difficulty, Willy crawled out of his hiding space in time to see the last of the Viet Cong guerrillas gunned down next to the fallen men of his own platoon. He limped out into the open, waving his arms, praying that his fellow comrades in the air recognized his American uniform. They did, and both Willy Banks and Buck Scott were evacuated to the Eighth Field Hospital. Willy miraculously endured the ordeal with no permanent disability other than bullet hole scars in four locations on his back. Buck lived to tell his story but did so in a wheelchair as he became a paraplegic survivor that war protesters back home would use for propaganda, then soon forget.

While recuperating in the hospital, Willy opened an officially sealed congratulatory letter from General William Westmoreland that indicated he would be receiving the Purple Heart from President Johnson after returning to the States. The letter also noted he was being considered for the

Medal of Honor for his acts of valor that resulted in saving the life of Private Buck Scott. Heroics really didn't excite Willy. He was just thankful that he could lengthen Private Scott's existence here on earth, but terribly saddened he couldn't have done the same for Lieutenant Connelly. Willy put the letter down on the bedside table and picked up another one. He noticed it had been postmarked July 9th, a little over two months earlier. The return address read: Abby Charles, Seminole Bend, Florida, USA.

CHAPTER 11
October 27, 1966

Near the end of October 1966, the medical staff at Walter Reed Army Medical Center in Washington D.C. wrote a letter to Army Chief of Staff, General Harold Johnson, recommending that Corporal Willy Banks be assigned light duty activities for the remainder of his enlistment period. By then, Willy had been promoted to the rank of corporal and presented with both a Purple Heart and Medal of Honor, and was well known and respected among officers and enlisted men throughout all branches of the armed forces. However, he refused to speak to television, radio, or newspaper reporters who wanted to let the world know about his bravery. In his own mind, he was merely a random GI doing his part to protect freedom and democracy for the country he loved.

On November 2, 1966, Willy was honorably discharged from active service and would finish the terms of his enlistment in the Army reserves at the base in Orlando. As a corporal, he would train new recruits and ensure that orders from high ranking officers were implemented.

Orlando was only a couple of hours from Seminole Bend, and soon he would take over the responsibilities of raising Tyrone Banks—the same duties that his older brother had mysteriously absconded.

CHAPTER 12

Fifteen Years and Nine Months Later
Monday, February 8, 1982
10:30 p.m.

Willy Banks had suspected for some time that Roy Jackson's mammoth income wasn't entirely made by peddling milk, butter, and cheese curds. A couple of months ago, while patrolling the north end of the county, Willy and his partner on the night shift, Sam McCormick, witnessed several Piper Cubs flying suspiciously low over the vast Jackson estate. It looked as though they were going to land somewhere in a field on the other side of the mounds of hay bales piled high near the distant swamp. Or maybe they were actually putting down right on the swamp itself with some sort of seaplane. The airplanes were too far in the distance to see if floats were attached to the frames. They would sink below the horizon, then rise again like hawks hunting for field mice.

Willy believed that the swamp served as a moat filled with gators and poisonous snakes to keep intruders away from the Jackson property. The ominous, shallow blackwater prevented anyone from entering the wealthy man's home from the rear, at least with all his limbs attached.

Phil Bennett owned *Bennett's Airboat Palace*, which was about as much like a palace as nearby Belle Glade was like Beverly Hills. Old Phil must've been dreaming he was a king or emperor or something when he called it a palace, and those dreams were mighty far-fetched! Anyway, the airboats, new and used, were kept in a run-down shack on Bennett's lot that ran adjacent to Lake Okeechobee's rim canal, about six miles southeast of Taylor Creek. The driveway leading into his property was plain old white sand with cracked miniature seashells, not exactly the kind of entryway that would lead up to a monarch's castle. Fortunately, his prices were fit more for a peasant than an emperor, and Sam and Willy decided to rent one with cash out of their own pockets so they could cruise down and check out Roy Jackson's enigmatic backyard.

The deputies didn't use police allocated taxpayer money to rent the airboat because Sheriff Al Bonty told them to stay away from Roy's place. In fact, Bonty advised all his deputies to simply "ignore" Roy Jackson's transgressions, or face dismissal from the sheriff's department. When asked why, Sheriff Bonty claimed that he had orders from the FBI. However, as far as Willy was concerned, Roy's world of total disregard for the law ended last Saturday when Willy clocked him doing 107 in a 55 zone. Willy was met by threats and intimidation as he approached Roy's car, but because of Bonty's orders, Willy didn't give Roy a ticket. Nonetheless, as Roy hammered down the pedal and fishtailed back on the road, kicking up gravel and chipping the windshield on the squad car, Willy swore that someday he would ensure that Roy Jackson faced justice, the legal kind—or otherwise.

The day after witnessing the Piper Cubs hovering around the Jackson estate back in December, Sam and Willy told the sheriff that they were concerned that some kind of unlawful activity was taking place. Sheriff Bonty smiled and said, "Never mind them little airplanes, boys. They are just being flown by harmless folks who like to pretend that they are birds, that's all." What kind of grown man pretends he's a bird?

Since that night in December, Sam and Willy noticed that on Mondays after sunset, for some unknown reason, the Piper Cubs would rendezvous over the Jackson estate. Finally, curiosity, or maybe nosiness is a better word, got the best of them. So on Monday, February 8th, the boys set sail for what would prove to be a fatal mistake.

Sam figured the route over water would be long, but the airboat could cover the territory in no time flat. The plan was to put in on the rim canal behind Bennett's, swing around to the Taylor Creek locks on the north end of the lake, cross eight miles over Lake Okeechobee to the mouth of the Kissimmee River, and head northwest for another twenty-two miles. There, with the flowage tucked under a forest of mangroves, they would enter a small tributary creek that ran straight east for five miles and merge into the widespread, murky swamp, better known as Jackson's Moat. Finding the tributary creek would be the most challenging task, especially in the bitter blackness of the cool and moonless February evening. Would it be better to wait a few days until there was a full moon to shine some of nature's light, or would that make the risk of being seen on Jackson's land even more likely? Sam and Willy decided that no moon on the eighth was the safest bet.

Crossing the big, shallow lake in the airboat was no problem, although the strong winds from the west almost flipped the boat into the gloomy water. Sam and Willy didn't worry about drowning, seeing the depth of the lake was barely over their heads; however, the more predominant fear came from Betsy, the sixteen-foot gator who was Florida's version of the Lochness Monster. Betsy's last victim was an unlucky water skier from Scranton who was visiting his retired parents back in November. The thirty-year-old man couldn't wait to ski in the Florida sunshine, seeing just the week before he was actually snowboarding the frozen Pocono's mountains of the northeast Pennsylvania Appalachians. Who would have guessed that Lake Okeechobee could produce a four-foot wave? The young man could have easily handled the surf, but his dad eased down on the throttle to keep the boat from flipping, which caused his son to wipe out. Hungry Ol' Betsy left only the plastic skis floating in the red-stained wake.

Willy and Sam found the mouth of the Kissimmee River with little effort thanks to the lights encompassing the Angler's Delight marina and restaurant. Most of the bass boats were moored for the evening; just a few night fishermen remained on the lake to shine for crappies. Actually, with two cases of Bud Lite tucked away into their built-in deck coolers, most of the so-called "sportsmen" hoped the fish wouldn't bother them!

About a mile upstream and away from the sleeping residents of Mill's Trailer Court, Willy gassed the throttle for the twenty-two-mile trip northward. The huge fan attached to the strident, six-cylinder Banks-Maxwell engine pushed back the crisp nighttime air, and the boat raced swiftly upriver. A short time later, Willy eased up, and then completely shut down the engine as the two audacious men approached the hidden inlet that led to the Jackson estate. They paddled with beat-up wooden oars the last mile on the Kissimmee to keep the noise from startling any of Roy Jackson's lookouts that might be watching from the moat. Rowing the five-mile trip against the flow of the stream on the small tributary creek took a couple of hours. Sam and Willy were upset that they didn't think to take along a small, quiet electric motor for the final leg of the journey.

The men had departed Bennett's at 10:30 p.m. on the eighth and had finally arrived on the outskirts of the swamp just before 2:30 a.m. on the ninth. Willy sculled close to shore, dropped a small anchor, and the airboat bobbed gently in the mild current. The two police officers hid behind a large mangrove tree with arched branches that reached out about three feet over the water's edge. The past five Monday nights, while working the graveyard shift patrolling State Road 98, they had witnessed the Piper Cubs approaching Jackson's property between three and four in the morning. Sam wanted Willy to row closer to the estate, seeing there was no moon to illuminate the box-shaped airboat, but Willy refused to budge from the safe haven of the river bank.

After fruitlessly waiting, watching, and listening for almost two hours, Sam and Willy were about to start paddling back to the Kissimmee River, when both heard a diminutive buzz in the distance, seemingly coming from the south. They put the oars back into the boat's side slots and lifted the binoculars to their eyes. The buzz became louder with each passing second, and soon Sam saw the single-engine Piper on the horizon heading straight for them. About two or three miles out, the plane's navigational lights were shut down, but Sam could still make out the faint silhouette of the aircraft as it approached Jackson's property. The pilot immediately made a steep descent and came close enough to the swamp to cause ripples in the water.

Sam and Willy were anticipating that the plane would make an easterly turn to approach Jackson's cracked asphalt airstrip and land into the slight breeze moving from the west. But as the aircraft flew nearer, the deputies noticed two oblong pontoons budding from the fuselage and realized the Piper had been converted into a seaplane. Moments later, five barrel-shaped containers dropped from the belly of the plane onto the swamp where they sunk, then emerged and bobbed on the water's surface. The pilot pushed full throttle, and the aircraft rose quickly into the dark night sky. The navigational lights reappeared as the plane circled to the east then turned south, heading toward Florida's Gold Coast.

Sam and Willy glanced at the wooden containers floating and bobbing quietly on the tranquil swamp. Through the binoculars, they could see the barrels were aided in floatation by Styrofoam supports. Each container was approximately a foot in diameter, and now sat portentously perched above the hungry heads of the many nocturnal marsh creatures. Sam grabbed an oar and quickly snapped it into the holder, but Willy reached over and clutched his arms.

“Where the hell do you think you’re going?” Willy whispered forcefully as he peered angrily into Sam’s energetic eyes.

“We got to get them barrels before Jackson does!” steamed Sam, on the verge of breaking the whispering soft talk with a roar of thunder.

“So you think Jackson doesn’t already have eyes locked in on them targets?”

“So, what’s your plan, Willy? Just sit here like we watching the damn fishing channel on TV!” The sarcasm carelessly flowed from Sam’s tongue as his eyes danced with excitement and impatience.

“We’re police officers, Sam. Let’s see who snatches them barrels and where they take them. If they head to Jackson’s, we get ourselves a search warrant and arrest them bastards.”

“And Chief Bonty would have our asses! He told us to leave Jackson alone,” Sam murmured as spit was spraying off his tongue, trying to keep the conversation to a whisper.

“But if we bust Roy legally with a shitload of drugs, we’ll be heroes. Bonty will give us a promotion, and all else will be forgotten.”

“Jackson owns this damn town. Bonty would be too dang chicken to get a warrant from Judge Boone cuz the judge and Jackson are fishing buddies. Our only chance is to snag one of them barrels and get the hell out of here on this swamp jet, so let’s get cracking Willy.”

Suddenly, two flat-topped bass boats appeared out of the darkness and hovered near the barrel that was floating the farthest distance from Sam and Willy. Within seconds, the barrel was snared out of the water by a supersized, silhouetted figure in the first boat, while the second boat headed to the next container. Before Willy could stop him, Sam slid over the side of the airboat into the dark water. He submerged quickly to quiet his strokes as he swam to the closest barrel that lay about twenty yards away. Willy stood recklessly balanced in the rocking boat as he peered through the binoculars, but he couldn't see Sam or any trace of a human wake. The first boat was now heading right towards Willy, but it stopped to pick up the third barrel that was floating gently in the middle of the low, grassy swamp. Finally, Willy saw the back of Sam's head surface alongside the last container.

The simultaneous blasts echoed through the mangrove trees and rang for several seconds in Willy's ears. A double-barrel, twelve-gauge shotgun peppered the surface of the water with copper BBs, while nearby herons screamed and scattered through the thick brush. Willy looked up to see both bass boats racing to the last container, and he quickly scoped the surrounding water with binoculars to find Sam. He muttered his best Baptist prayer, trying to convince the Lord to bring his buddy back to the airboat, but the Lord had a different destination for Sam.

A mallard that had just arrived for the winter from his Minnesota home took to flight at the thunderous sound of the gun, but his left wing had been grazed by several stray pellets from the shotgun cartridge shell. He flew for several seconds, then belly-flopped back to the swamp directly behind Willy's airboat. Both bass boat lookouts heard the splash and looked over at the direction of Willy's hiding place. The men pointed and gunned their boats toward the mangrove tree hideout. Willy rammed the ignition button that fired up the engine and then yanked up the anchor from its muddy basin. He quickly pushed off the shore with his oar, reversing the airboat 180 degrees. When he slammed the throttle down, Willy left the bass boat riders sucking both wind and wake from the huge fan.

Branches of mangrove trees scratched Willy's face and arms as he soared westward towards the Kissimmee River. The darkness had become his enemy, making the "s" turns in the small tributary creek a perilous venture. Willy remembered paddling by a partially submerged log stump during the trip inland but forgot its exact location—until now.

The menacing wood chunk appeared too late for Willy to avoid, and the boat's front float caught it dead on, jilting the rear of the vessel upward and sending the colossal-sized police officer airborne. Willy flew twenty feet before his body slammed into the shore, and his skull hit a turtle-sized oval rock protruding from the mud and tropical undergrowth. His body lay still and silent, while his face and nose were jammed into the soft ground. Willy had no air inlet through the mouth, and what little pocket existed through his nasal passages was filling quickly with blood.

CHAPTER 13

Tuesday, February 9, 1982

7:00 a.m.

Willy coughed and moaned, then opened one eye. He wanted to rub it, but for some reason, he couldn't move his arms. Willy rolled his body over so that he was lying flat on his back, and then realized his arms were bound with thick rope, the kind used to lasso cattle. He blinked several times to clear his vision and noticed Roy Jackson and a group of five or six gun-toting thugs standing ostentatiously over him. A putrid smell was rising from the wooden floorboards on which he lay, and it dawned on him that his uncomfortable bed was actually a foul mixture of hay and cow manure. The walls of the structure that surrounded him were made of concrete blocks that were stained brown with feces, probably from the artistic wagging tail of Ol' Bessy. It was obvious no one took much pride in keeping the milking bins clean, but then again, the dairy industry was just a mask for Roy's real business.

Willy wasn't sure how he got there, nor how long he'd been there. His Seiko watch was shattered, which most likely happened during the catapult into the rocky shore of the riverbed. But the sky was becoming light, and that meant sunrise was commencing, and a new day was about to begin.

"Sit your fat ass up and listen to me, Willy Banks," Roy bellowed as he stooped on his haunches, then grabbed Willy's chin and pulled him into a sitting position. Willy flinched and winced in pain, but his eyes made contact with Roy's, and an evil look of hatred radiated from them, sending the message that Willy was fearless, regardless of the current predicament.

"Sam? How is Sam? Where the hell is Sam?!" Willy hollered, even though the slightest sound from his mouth left a throbbing pain in his temples.

"Shut up, you mutt! I'm doing the talking, and you're doing the listening. It's too bad, but your buddy became a midnight snack for a couple of gators last night. Trespassing is against the law, but I bet you know that, seeing you're a smartass lawman, Willy Banks."

Willy glared at Roy but decided to say nothing. He wasn't convinced that Sam died in the jaws of an alligator, but getting himself dead wouldn't save his friend and colleague. If Sam had met his death in the swamp, he wanted to check the body and see for himself if shotgun pellets or reptile teeth were responsible for Sam's final demise.

"I'm sure Sheriff Bonty would like to know why Seminole Bend's finest was violating state law. Think a felony conviction would help your career much, Willy? You'd be cleaning fish guts off the floor at Mucker's Produce Market for the rest of your life, just like your damn brother!"

* * * * *

Willy had two brothers, Tyrus and Otis. Tyrus, the oldest of the Bank's family, had the looks, Willy had the brawn, and the youngest, Otis, well, he was still searching for his talent. Otis struggled in school: he never could make much sense out of learning A's, B's, and C's or how knowing that stuff might help him be a better fisherman.

Otis found his dream job working for Slim's Guide Service, a fly-by-night group of three brothers who overcharged tourists to find and catch bass. Otis rode along on the boat to bait hooks for the affluent customers and then filleted the fish upon returning to shore. One night, Otis finished slicing and deboning his ninth largemouth for some folks from Indiana, and then went down to the beach and dumped the heads, guts, and scaly skin into the muddy water for the catfish to feed on. He glanced to his left and noticed a small, wooden rowboat rocking and rolling in the weeds about ten yards away. Now, Otis was not exactly the sharpest knife in the drawer, but he figured something wasn't right because the boat was moving all over, and there wasn't a puff of wind anywhere to be found. Otis snuck up quietly, just in case a hungry gator was resting close by, or worse yet, was in the dinghy. He tiptoed into the knee-deep water, lifted up the loose canvas cover, and peeked nervously inside of the boat. Suddenly, a large, dark-skinned creature with long hair braided into a ponytail jumped up and was face to face with Otis. Startled, Otis slipped and fell backward into the water. He looked up to see the human beast grabbing an object from the floorboards, and then noticed a young lady behind the man covering her body with the other end of the canvas. Otis pushed up with his arms and scrambled backward, splashing wildly in the shallow water. He managed to duck beneath the swinging oar aimed directly at his forehead. He rolled and wallowed, then sprang to his feet and made a mad dash back to Slim's.

Otis was out of breath and sweating profusely, trying to explain to Slim and his brothers what he saw.

"It was Jenny Jackson doing a little hanky-panky with some damn big Injun, it was!"

"No way, Otis! You gotta be shittin' us! Roy Jackson's daughter?"

"I knows it was her cuz my nephew Tyrone's been tugging at her skirt, ya know! I sees him eyeing her while he be warming up before basketball games. Tyrone be out on the warpath iffin he knew she was rolling in that boat with a Seminole!"

Trying to be proactive to save her hide, Jenny Jackson returned home and told her papa that Otis Banks had been putting the moves on her. The next morning Otis was looking for another job, and Slim got a brand new, twenty-four foot Bayliner Cabin Cruiser as his reward for firing Otis. Otis looked at Slim with tears welling up in his eyes and asked, "Why did ya sack me, Slim? I works real hard for ya."

Slim didn't have the heart to look at Otis when he replied, "Tourism has dropped round here, you know, and I can't afford you anymore, Otis."

"I ain't had much schooling, Slim, but if this here business of yours is so bad, why am I's always up all night cleaning fish? And why is there a sparkling new mini-yacht tied up over yonder on your docks?" Otis had no idea that Roy Jackson's powerfully intimidating pocketbook was hard at work again.

Otis moved in with Willy, and after three months living and dining off his brother's trifling paycheck, Otis finally got a janitor job at Mucker's Produce. But Deputy Willy had to surreptitiously take care of Matt Mucker's citation from the county health department so he could stay in business. That was the only way to keep his little brother duly employed.

* * * * *

"Otis is living an honest life, Jackson. More than can be said for you," Willy proclaimed proudly while staring up at Roy. Roy stood up and placed his boot directly on the center of Willy's face and pushed his head back to the ground. He then twisted the rubber soul back and forth into Willy's nostrils and mouth. Brahman cattle dung jammed into both nasal cavities causing Willy to choke and spit. Roy's thugs took turns kicking Willy in the ribs, and when one pointed, steel-toed cowboy boot landed square on his temple, Willy was out cold again.

CHAPTER 14
Tuesday, February 9, 1982
9:00 a.m.

The powerful jaws of an American alligator can easily crush the shell of a turtle or the bones of any animal. Willy's skull was the target of the hungry monster of the swamp, and it was time for the beast to do a little grocery shopping. The huge, muscular sheriff's deputy had been dragged and abandoned at the edge of the moat by Roy's thugs, left there for a reptilian breakfast. If not for a pesky mosquito buzzing in Willy's ear, he may have drowned before being eaten. As he lifted his head to the annoying sound of the hovering insect, he began to snort the water that had seeped into his nasal passage. The inundating sensation burned from his chest all the way up his throat as Willy choked and coughed out the slimy mixture of cow feces and swamp water. The rope tied to his wrists behind his back had loosened a bit, most likely due to Willy being dragged to the water, but it still firmly held his hands in place. Suddenly, goosebumps covered his limbs, and fear triggered an arrhythmia Willy had never experienced in his superiorly fit body. Glancing to his left, Willy noticed two green eyes and large, coarse nostrils floating on the surface of the water, terrifyingly motionless, only four feet away.

A sales representative from the Gaston Glock Company had been very pushy working off straight commission while trying to sell several of the company's newly designed, waterproof pistols to Sheriff Al Bonty. The Glock has a synthetic polymer frame and a ferritic nitrocarburizing surface that is corrosion-proof. Al never received a grade higher than C- in any science class. However, he nodded affirmatively at the salesman just the same. Wanting the rep to take a hike, but knowing that an elected sheriff needs to use tact when dealing with the public, Bonty said he would be happy to try out one of the small guns for a month to see if it had any value. When the rep left, he tossed the weapon on Willy's desk and told the deputy to "shoot up" a few garfish for dinner. The Glock came with a holster that could be strapped to the calf of a leg, and Willy had been wearing it dutifully for the past two weeks, thinking that he might just have a chance to hunt some water moccasins for sport. The thought never occurred that the pistol might save his life.

With awkward agility in the muddy water, Willy was able to slowly reposition himself to his knees. But the moment of truth came next. Willy purposely fell forward, face down into the swamp so that his legs would bend upward behind his back. With nothing to breathe but slime, his time was expiring. The elongated fingers that could palm a basketball and enable the athletic deputy to slam dunk were a Godsend at this critical moment. His fingers barely touched the holster snap; however, Willy was able to undo the strap after several attempts. But time was running out. He could only hold his breath for a few more seconds.

Water pressure provided slight levity on the Glock, and it slid scarcely into Willy's fingers. With all ten fingers working as a single unit, he turned the gun in his hand, placing the cylinder on the rope. The top of his middle finger touched the trigger, but he would have to engage the finger in a backward motion to fire. Did he have the strength in his fingers as he did the rest of his body? Would the pistol actually work underwater? No time to rethink his decision, for as he turned his head beneath the surface, he could see the scaly, pointed toes of the carnivorous reptile moving toward him. The gator was on the move.

The muffled explosion rippled the water, and Willy felt a sharp pain in his upper back. The bullet had torn through the rope thread and lodged in his scapula. Willy's hands were free, but could he get on his feet? The nine-millimeter cartridge was causing a searing sensation throughout his body. Sheer adrenaline kicked in, and Willy rose uneasily in the shallow water as a thunderous sound racked his eardrums. The gator's huge muscular tail slapped the surface, and the creature sprang at Willy with his jaws wide open. Willy tried to backpedal out of the water, but the gator was too fast and locked Willy's massive thigh into his gigantic mouth, then whipped him vigorously left and right, trying to break the deputy into two pieces. The swamp ruler pulled Willy into deeper water and rolled several times trying to drown his victim, but the gator could see his human fodder wasn't going to be an easy lunch. With all the torso flexibility and bicep power he could muster, Willy grabbed the gator's jaws in his bare hands and pried the reptile's mouth just enough to escape for the moment.

Along with the open wound under his shoulder, blood was squirting madly out of Willy's leg as the alligator had severed the femoral artery with his sharp molars, and puncture wounds deeply penetrated the thick skin of his hands. Then, without hesitating, but in extreme pain, Willy circled behind the gator and jumped onto the leathery back of his attacker and clamped the reptile's mouth shut with his left bicep. He took the forefinger of his right hand and jammed it deep into the gator's right eye, then extracted quickly and did the same with the left eye. The creature snorted in pain and submerged into the dark water, then promptly surfaced and floated awkwardly to the shore. He no longer could see what his nose could smell.

Willy scrambled back onshore and smothered his leg wound with his injured hands. In scorching pain from the bullet gore, he then lifted his top hand, reached up to his neck, and ripped his t-shirt vertically off his body. Letting go of the pressure to the artery momentarily, blood once again gushed out, and Willy began to feel light-headed and dizzy. He knew soon the loss of blood would cause him to faint and lead to certain death. With his last bit of strength, Willy wrapped the dirty makeshift bandage around his leg and tied tightly. He laid his head back on the mud and couldn't fight off the overwhelming feeling of tiredness. Bright white lights, then sudden darkness. Willy had passed out.

* * * * *

Pancho Sanchez didn't much care for his job picking grapefruit and oranges for the Gold Coast Fruit Company with a hundred other migrant workers from Mexico, some imported legally and some not so legal. In fact, he didn't like picking cotton in north Texas last month, either. But Pancho sure liked catching catfish, whether it be the big mama Mississippi River variety, or the small, tasty Taylor Creek scavengers from the good old Sunshine State. Problem was, Pancho liked fishing when he should've liked working.

Each morning, he would squish into a rusty, one-ton Chevy cargo van with fifteen other migrants and be transported to the groves near Fort Pierce. As a daily ritual, the caravan of workers would stop for a few moments at Quick Stuff on the east side of Seminole Bend so the driver could get coffee and Little Debbies for the forty-five-minute ride down Highway 74.

On days when Pancho felt like fishing instead of picking, which was most days, he would purposely position himself last in line at the convenience store's restroom door out back. As soon as his buddy in front of him entered the biffy, Pancho would make a mad dash to the rear of the dumpster located across the alley and hide until the van pulled away.

A supervisor checked off the migrant workers in the morning when they were picked up from their rundown shacks west of town, and then again in the evening after taking them home. But, no one thought to do a headcount following the daily pit stop at Quick Stuff. On those days that he felt he could get away with it, Pancho would be off to the river. Later that evening, he would sneak back in with the gang of migrant workers when they made their customary dinner stop at McDonald's, a daily company perk following a hard day's labor in the groves. Pancho would slip into the van while the rest ate in the restaurant. He didn't need to eat because he was by no means hungry. By late afternoon, he usually had his fill of cypress wood-smoked catfish fresh off the river bottom. That was much more tasty and healthy than American junk food anyway.

So today, after the van pulled away, Pancho came out from behind the dumpster and hustled down to the creek. He picked up his cane pole and a milk carton full of black dirt stuffed with squirming nightcrawlers that were hidden under several shrubs near the riverbank. Then he scrambled down a worn path to his fishing hole, a route he could maneuver in his sleep.

Every time he skipped work and went fishing, he walked past a small Alumicraft boat with a twenty-five horsepower Johnson outboard tied to a dock jutting out into Taylor Creek. He had trekked this path many times, each time becoming more envious of the boat's owner. The owner's house was located about a hundred feet from the dock, but Pancho noticed that several large grapefruit trees covered the picture window, thus blocking the view of the vessel. Hmmm. Who would know if today he borrowed the watercraft and dumped it later somewhere along the riverbank?

Pancho figured he had fished the muddy banks of Taylor Creek long enough, so this morning he decided to upgrade his angling adventure and take a little joy ride in the boat. He would cruise over Lake Okeechobee and test out those cane-bending catfish critters that dwelt in the mighty Kissimmee River. Well, the Kissimmee wasn't anything like the Mississippi, but nobody told the catfish that!

The mooring rope was loosely wrapped around the dock anchor, making it an easy task of undoing the boat. Pancho softly tossed in his cane pole and bait. He glanced nervously left and right, then pushed the boat off the dock and quickly jumped in. The Alumicraft shimmied outward, and Pancho fell backward, landing clumsily on the floorboard. He regained composure, grabbed the oars, and rowed quietly down the shoreline. He didn't want the engine noise to startle the owner or his neighbors, so he waited until he reached a bend in the creek to fire up the Johnson. One pull on the starter rope and the engine sprang into action. Pancho twisted the throttle that doubled as a steering handle, and off he headed towards the Taylor Creek locks.

Ernie Hyle, the bald-headed, obese lock operator, gave Pancho a puzzled look when he entered the water elevator. It was as if Ernie recognized the boat, but not the owner. Three other small craft came into the lock at the same time, and all the captains and passengers reached out to grab the side safety ropes that dangled from above. Ernie picked up his binoculars and glared downward, searching for Pancho's license number. The Florida marine sticker attached to the bow of the stolen boat was the right color for the current year, so the actual number should be listed with the Department of Natural Resources. Ernie picked up the phone to dial the DNR, but the phone's cord knocked his jelly donut off the counter. As he reached out to catch the donut, his elbow struck the open thermos bottle of coffee, and it spilled onto his khaki work pants. The boats in the chamber had almost risen the six feet needed to equalize the water in the lock with Lake Okeechobee when Ernie put the phone down to wipe the hot liquid that was beginning to penetrate through his pants and onto the skin of his leg. After dabbing up the Folgers, it was time to open the lock's spill gates. The boats revved up their outboards and headed out into the vast expanse of the lake. Ernie was too busy rinsing off his jelly donut stains, and he plain forgot about checking out the name and nationality of the Alumicraft's owner.

Pancho clipped briskly across the lake and soon reached the mouth of the Kissimmee River near the Angler's Delight marina. He was afraid fishermen might recognize the stolen boat, so as Pancho cruised up the Kissimmee, he kept it at full throttle until he was many miles north and out of sight of the locals. When he noticed a partially hidden, small creek running eastward, Pancho thought it looked like a mighty catfish-biting tributary, so he headed directly into the mangrove-lined stream. Five miles upriver, he came to a large opening that appeared to be a swampy grand finale to his anxious voyage. Across the bayou, Pancho could see a substantial grassy pasture that led to a luxurious, three-story ranch mansion. Pancho decided it was best to veer away from the ranch so he wouldn't be seen on what looked like private property. Soon, he found what he was searching for: a shaded narrow section of the swamp with lily pads floating close to the banks. Pancho killed the engine, dropped the anchor that hung over the bow, baited his hook with a worm, and then flung the hook, line, and red bobber over the side.

Almost immediately, the bobber submerged, and the end of the cane pole arched wildly, looking like it could snap in half at any minute. Pancho knew to let the fish take the line slightly, and then he jerked the pole straight upward. Bingo! The barbed copper hook caught the fat lips of the catfish, and the rest was history. Pancho grabbed the fishnet that the boat's owner had left on the floorboard and then reached over the boat with the net while slowly guiding his pole toward it. Soon he could see the whiskers of the catfish as he pulled the tail-flapping little rascal to the surface. Pancho scooped the net underneath the fish, and the capture was complete. One minute, one catfish. Dinner today was going to be a feast!

By noon, Pancho had fourteen catfish, two speckled perch, and a small bass, now all strung through the gills with a thin rope that he tied onto the oar post and hung over into the water. With the midday sun beating down on him, Pancho was getting a bit sleepy, and he didn't much care if another fish bothered him for a while. So he baited the small hook and tossed it softly into the water by the lily pads. Then he laid his head down on some greasy towels, propped his feet up onto the bench seat, and took a snooze. An hour later, he awoke to find the pole slipping out of his relaxed hands and the bobber nowhere in sight. Pancho quickly arose, and his adrenalin was pumping—it must be a ten-pound bass! Strange though, it wasn't putting up much of a fight.

Pancho could barely see the fish through the murky water as he slowly pulled it toward the net. When he finally did see it, he didn't recognize the shape. Could it be a garfish? Pancho slipped the net under the fish and lifted up. By God, it wasn't a fish! The shiny hook had snared a human finger that was attached to a human hand that was attached to a human forearm! The arm was ripped to shreds just below where it connects to the elbow, and the blood had completely drained out, leaving a puffy, cloud-white human extremity in a net that should be holding fish!

Pancho damn near fell out of the boat! He dropped the cane pole and net over the side and scrambled over the bench seats to the motor. The engine fired on the first pull, and Pancho twisted the handle to full throttle. The stern began to lift, and the bow tilted toward the swamp before Pancho realized the anchor was still stuck on the river bottom. He reached overboard and under the surface of the water to grab the anchor rope, and then yanked. As he pulled, Pancho fell backward onto the boat floor, but his hands held on tightly to the line. But it wasn't rope, it was hair—with a head attached! The skull's eyes were wide open and staring directly into Pancho's terror-stricken pupils!

Lying on his back, holding tight to the hair, Pancho yelped, "Oh, mierda!" He tried desperately to toss the bloated head overboard, but it hit the edge of the boat and rolled backward, finally settling at Pancho's bare feet, and once again, the glassy, lifeless eyes peered directly into the Mexican's panicky pupils!

Pancho grabbed the skull again by the hair, closed his eyes, and with all his might, tossed it onto the shore. This time he took his pocketknife out of his pants pocket and slashed the actual anchor rope to shreds. He then noticed that the string of fish was still dangling over the port side of the boat. He quickly untied the line from the oar post and was beginning to haul the barely alive-and-kicking fish in, when an enraged, psychotic gator opened its jaws and snapped the string in two just six inches from Pancho's hands.

Pancho was overcome by fright, and the denim surrounding his buttoned fly became soaked with urine. The alligator's throat expanded, and in one large gulp, devoured his southern sushi appetizer. The black beast was now ready for the main course and was moving back toward the boat as Pancho scrambled to the motor and gunned the throttle. The Alumicraft jerked forward momentarily, and then the engine sputtered to a halt in a puff of smoke.

The gator scurried, heading directly for the stern where Pancho was pulling madly on the ignition rope. The reptile submerged, and Pancho knew what was going to happen next. He stopped pulling and grabbed the wooden oar tightly with his hands. Sure enough, the gator whipped his powerful tail, and his head splashed out of the water, the pink of its throat lunging at Pancho's belly. Pancho never played baseball, but his stance and swing could have rivaled Babe Ruth's! The oar connected into the basin of the gator's throat, and Pancho pushed with every bit of strength he could muster. The jaw slammed shut, breaking the oar like it was a toothpick, but the gator slipped back down into the murky water readying itself for round two. Pancho again yanked hard and fast on the engine rope, and it coughed and choked to a start. Slowly, so as not to kill the motor, Pancho opened the throttle, and the boat began to move. The gator sprang at the outboard's propeller and just missed as Pancho made a beeline for the creek that connected the swamp with the Kissimmee River.

"What the hell is going on?" Pancho muttered under his breath. Alligators are definitely flesh-eating creatures, but they usually avoid any type of engine noise. And whose body was lying in pieces on the bottom of the swamp? Pancho needed this nightmare to end. Never again would he sneak away from his citrus-picking partners to go fishing! He would savor the life of an orange picker, hopefully for many, many more years to come. But as the stolen boat cruised forward, Pancho noticed something lying on the shore to his right.

"Leave it, damn it, just leave it alone," Pancho thought. But Pancho could see it was a body covered with blood, and if it was alive, it was surely suffering. He turned the boat toward the sand and then noticed a strange sight. About twenty feet away from the body was another gator just sitting on the beach. Could the gator have no appetite? Why wasn't he lunching on the bloody body?

Pancho decided it was best for his own health to first check out the status of the gator on the shore. He idled down the motor to a purr. Moving slowly and very carefully, he came closer to the cold-blooded reptile, hoping it wasn't hungry for a Mexican lunch. Pancho edged the boat towards the embankment and then began a parallel turn northward. If the gator attacked, he could open the throttle quickly. But what Pancho saw startled him: the alligator appeared to have no eyes!

No wonder the large swamp creature didn't prey on his wounded victim—he couldn't see him. But surely he could smell him. Pancho decided not to hypothesize, and he turned the boat toward the shore to check out the bloody body. When he could hear sand rubbing on the underside of the Alumicraft, he jumped out of the bow and yanked the boat on land with what was left of the anchor line. Pancho glanced at the ghastly, injured body—and damn if he didn't see the big man's chest rise!

As he stood directly over Willy, Pancho dang near passed out. The deputy's leg was limp where the bloody shirt was wrapped around the enormous, muscular thigh. Pancho put his ear to Willy's nose to see if he was breathing. Then, with lightning-fast quickness, Willy opened his eyes and grabbed Pancho's neck firmly with his two robust hands. Pancho's heart was beating way beyond the speed limit as he gasped for breath. Willy whispered to Pancho as he held him at bay with his outstretched arms, "Help me. Help me." Pancho's face was beginning to turn blue as he tried to undo the grip Willy had on his neck.

Seconds later, Willy's eyes rolled upward into his skull, and then his burly grip loosened, dropping Pancho right on top of the deputy's belly. Pancho scrambled up and was going to run, but stopped himself. He glanced down at Willy and noticed there was no more rising and lowering of his chest. Pancho placed his left hand over Willy's nose and couldn't feel any air. Then he turned his head and put his ear right up to Willy's nose, but couldn't hear anything. Pancho panicked, but he remembered watching a lifeguard out at Sand's Beach save the life of his buddy, Jose, after Jose tried to swim for the first time in the Atlantic Ocean. Pancho gambled that his memory of that life-saving lesson he had witnessed might also help save this massive man.

Willy's mouth was dribbling mud and muck, which was quite different than the clear saltwater that had erupted from Jose's mouth shortly after the lifeguard pressed his chest downward. Pancho wasn't sure his stomach was up to this task. But then he shook his head to get a grip on what was happening and muttered to himself, "What the hell, if it were me, I would hope this hombre would do the same."

Pancho kneeled by Willy's side and tilted the deputy's head back. Nope, Pancho could tell that was only choking the man even more. He needed to clear out some of the mud in Willy's mouth, which he did with his eyes closed! Pancho then pinched Willy's nose, clamped his lips around Willy's, and breathed air until he saw Willy's chest rise. As he released, Willy's chest fell to its original position. Pancho then crossed and overlapped his hands, just like the lifeguard did, and placed them firmly on Willy's heart. He pushed six times. Nothing. He tried again, pushing with all his might against the muscular chest. Nothing. Time to get out of here!

Pancho rose and was turning to hi-tail it out of the swamp when he heard a cough and sputter. The big man was still alive. Pancho mustered enough strength to roll him over on his side, and a blast of black slime ejected from Willy's mouth.

"Mierda!" Pancho knelt back down and pounded his fist on Willy's back until he once again regained consciousness. Willy then rolled over, facing upward.

Pancho sprinkled a few drops of water from his canteen onto Willy's face and mouth. Willy coughed again and looked at Pancho helplessly. Pancho shook his finger at Willy and said, "Now, you keep them fat black fingers offin my neck, and I'll try to get you some help!"

Pancho reached under Willy's shoulders and with all his might, began to drag the wounded deputy to the boat. As he approached the side of the tiny vessel, his arms were weakening quickly.

"How the hell am I going to get you in this damn thing?" Pancho gasped.

Seeing a chance at revival and rescue before him, Willy sat up. He placed his arms on the boat's rim and pushed himself up, fighting off the searing pain of the bullet lodged in his scapula. To keep from further bleeding, Willy tried to put a minimal amount of weight on his gashed leg. He then turned and flopped himself into the boat, head first, and his nose smashed into a dead nightcrawler that was lying stiffly on the floorboard. Rigor mortis had shriveled the earthworm to half its original size, and the dryness of the open air sucked the fatty tissue away, making it look like a string of beef jerky from an emaciated cow. Willy rolled onto his back, and

Pancho lifted his legs, placing them oh so gently on the bench seat.

Pancho then jumped out of the boat and tried to push the front end back into the water. He heard an inauspicious snapping sound. Turning around, he saw the blind alligator at his feet trying desperately to seek revenge for his loss of sight. Pancho dashed into the swamp and grabbed the boat's stern handle that was just to the side of the motor. He yanked with a newfound strength that was generated from pure adrenaline. The Alumicraft slid off the sandy shore into the water as Pancho struggled to climb back in. But his weight and the weight of Willy lying in the boat caused the vessel to tip to one side, and it looked as if it were about to roll.

The colossal alligator slipped into the water and dove underneath where it couldn't be seen from the surface. Willy knew that within seconds, Pancho would be a tasty meal for the hungry reptile. He reached over and grabbed Pancho's wrist, lifted him out of the water, and placed him on the thin ridge of the boat's side panel. Pancho was now bent backward at his midsection, balancing his torso in the vessel while his legs dangled just over the water. Willy let go of Pancho's wrist and clutched the crotch of his pants, yanking the petrified Mexican into the boat as the gator plunged wildly at the sound of Pancho's flapping legs. With sight, the gator wouldn't have missed.

Pancho scrambled to the stern. The motor started this time with the first pull of the rope. Pancho headed directly for the channel that linked the backwater with the Kissimmee River. As they came in sight of the Jackson ranch, Willy whispered to Pancho to go slowly and make no wake. The engine barely hummed as it crept along the far banks of the swamp. Across the way, Pancho noticed several men talking by some docks that moored three bass boats. He felt his heart pulse rapidly, hoping they wouldn't look in his direction.

Pancho turned into the channel and gunned the engine. Too early—the noise echoed across the swamp, and the men at Jackson's ranch caught a glimpse of the stolen boat as it sped into the narrow waterway. They quickly hopped into their flat bottom bass boat cruisers and began to chase Pancho and Willy. The 200-horsepower engines steamrolled the bass boats across the swamp in no time, but they had to slow down to maneuver the winding channel. Jackson's bad boys were only ten yards behind the stolen Alumicraft when Pancho and Willy cut into the wide Kissimmee, almost broadsiding a pontoon cabin cruiser that was returning to Seminole Bend from the Chain of Lakes.

The bass boats throttled down, not wanting to raise suspicion from pleasure boaters who may be on the river. However, although they couldn't make out the man driving the boat, one of Jackson's men did get the DNR license number before it veered left and became hidden out of sight behind the cabin cruiser. The bass boats turned around, and Pancho could hear their loud engines fade as they headed back to the ranch.

An hour passed before Pancho reached the Angler's Delight marina. Willy was slowly losing blood and slipping in and out of consciousness. Pancho tied the boat up at the end of the dock so the gas tender wouldn't offer his services. He sprinted to the restaurant and headed to the payphone just outside the front door. He dialed "O" and connected with the operator, thus avoiding the twenty-five cent charge. The operator answered, "May I help you?"

Pancho shrieked, "Emergency! Doctor needed now! Black man dying in a boat at the end of the dock at Angler's Delight!" Before the operator could reply, Pancho hung up and ran toward the highway. He couldn't miss his rendezvous with the migrant van at McDonald's, especially not today!

CHAPTER 15

Wednesday, February 10, 1982
8:00 a.m.

The Department of Natural Resources confirmed to Roy Jackson that the small boat with plate number *JL 4106 FL* belonged to Calvin Potts, a retired appliance salesman from Ann Arbor, Michigan. Calvin's double-wide manufactured home on Taylor Creek was his annual winter home. He left his snow shovel back in Michigan every October, hoping he would have no need for it upon his return in April. Roy had no trouble extracting the boat's identification from Sam Dulie, the South Florida DNR Supervisor, because Sam was appointed to his administrative position by Governor Hank Daughtry, a key player in Roy's secret business. Sam's job description: oversee the DNR operations in the state from Tampa to Melbourne to Key West, and most importantly, take good care of Roy Jackson.

Sam's office was in Homestead, just miles from the entrance to the Everglades National Park. On a desk near the window in Sam's office was an unusual looking electronic contraption that was wired through the wall to an even more unusual looking contraption located in a secure, fenced-in area outdoors behind the building. It was a six-foot diameter saucer with a four-foot antenna in the middle. The contraption was actually a satellite receiving system that Sam explained to the visiting commonfolk as being a short-band radio wave gadget used for rapid communication with his DNR officers out in the field. Sam was a liar.

Sam was also known as Abdul Samad, an honor graduate with an earned doctorate from the Massachusetts Institute of Technology in the area of electromagnetism. However, it appeared his background relative to his expertise in the field of his current job, Natural Resources Supervisor, was limited to a college all-night beer party at the Glen Charlie Pond up New England way in Wareham. It started as a simple fishing trip—Abdul's first and last. A buddy, Jimmy Granger, who attended nearby Dartmouth, got together with Abdul one night and offered to teach Abdul the fine art of angling. Now Abdul had no problem measuring oscillation wavelengths of the electromagnetic spectrum, but handling a fishing pole with grace was beyond his comprehension. After the first attempted lob of a Spinnerbait lure went awry, Jimmy had to rip two hooks from Abdul's sweatshirt when the cast snagged him by the collar. While Jimmy was extracting the barbed copper hooks, Abdul noticed a fire pit on the shore with a bunch of rowdy kids hooting and hollering. The Rolling Stones blasted from a car radio parked behind them. Jimmy and Abdul rowed over to the party and joined in the fun. So much for the fishing lesson.

Abdul officially changed his name to Sam Dulie in late January of 1979, two weeks after Ayatollah Khomeini forced Shah Pahlavi into exile. During the Islamic Revolution, a Middle Eastern immigrant could find it a daunting task securing employment in the United States. No one's sure if Sam wrote that he was an "elite one-night fisherman" on either his resume or DNR application, but for some unknown reason, Governor Daughtry appointed him as the first electromagnetism graduate of MIT to head up a department that protects flora and fauna of southern Florida!

Shortly after arriving in Homestead, Sam conceived a way to jam aircraft radar functions at Miami International Airport based upon research data he had compiled working covertly with rogue CIA agents a few years earlier. Roy Jackson was delighted with Inventor Sam Dulie! His partners' business plan was ready for action, and his suppliers could fly undetected by the Federal Aviation Administration and the FBI.

* * * * *

"You're sure the plate number was *JL 4106 FL*?" asked Roy to the head of security at his ranch.

"No doubt about it, boss. Two of my boys had binoculars, and each saw the number clearly."

Roy couldn't understand why an old man like Calvin Potts would be fishing so far away from his home when the bass were biting like crazy just off the weeds on the other side of the Taylor Creek locks. But Roy really didn't care: all he knew was that Calvin may have found something he shouldn't have. Jackson's lookouts said the seventy-two-year-old snowbird was undoubtedly in a hurry to get out of the vast swamp. The strange thing was that Roy's men didn't think the man in the fishing boat looked very old, and he seemed to have darker skin like a Mexican. However, they couldn't tell for sure because their view from behind was restricted, and they were in the midst of a mad water chase.

Meanwhile, Calvin's decision to play golf with his poker buddies Monday and Tuesday proved to be unfortunate, for he did not happen to notice that his boat was missing until early Wednesday morning when he traipsed out the back door of his Florida room and headed for the dock.

"What . . . the . . . hell?" Calvin muttered to himself when he found he had no boat in which to toss his casting rod and net. He glanced downriver and across the creek, just in case the mooring line had come undone and the boat floated away. No such luck.

"Stolen, damn it, couldn't be anything but stolen. Dang high school kids, no doubt!"

Calvin stomped back to his house and called the sheriff's office. Deputy Johnny Murphree answered the phone. Calvin described his situation to Johnny and wanted to file a police report right away.

"Can't come over right now, Mr. Potts. Most of the sheriff's department is down at Angler's Delight investigating an accident one of our boys had with a gator yesterday. But if you don't mind coming down to the station, I'll file you a report right here," Johnny explained to Calvin. Calvin said he'd be right there.

Calvin's wife, Agnes, never got up before 9:00 am, and Calvin figured he'd be back home before she even knew he was missing. He quietly opened and closed the screen door leading to the carport, and then hopped into his unlocked car. Calvin backed out of his crescent-shaped, crushed seashell and sand driveway at 8:15 am. With the stolen Alumicraft boat on his mind, he didn't see the dark blue Ford LTD parked across the street, or the big man wearing black Levi's, cowboy boots, and a muscle t-shirt climb out the passenger-side door of the car and dash to the back porch of Calvin's manufactured home.

Max Miller worked as a driver for Roy Jackson for several years, but no one in Seminole Bend had ever seen him. He was always shielded behind a virtually opaque tinted windshield that didn't draw too much suspicion in the bright Florida sun. Calvin didn't happen to notice Max in the rearview mirror following his Chevy Nova during the two-mile drive to the sheriff's office.

Why would Calvin be going to the sheriff's office, Max wondered? He assumed Calvin was about to file a report and provide details of his terrifying escape from Jackson's swamp yesterday. When he saw Calvin heading into the sheriff's station, Max diverted quickly into the Dixie Food and Drug parking lot across the street and then floored it to a phone booth perched on top of a cracked and warped blacktop parking space on the far end.

Lance Billips called that phone booth "home" ever since he lost his last job at the sugar cane factory. The foreman laid him off for being tardy to work each and every day of the two weeks he was employed there. Of course, it wasn't Lance's fault that the convenience store next to his apartment had a broken backdoor lock, and he could accidentally sneak in and steal a bottle of liquor each night. How was he expected to get any sleep and get up on time for work with all that temptation? Wasn't long after losing his job that Lance was looking for a new home, one where the rent was free.

Anyway, he was curled up inside the small booth, snoring like a buzz saw while clutching a half-empty bottle of Mad Dog like it was the Crown Jewels or something. You couldn't find Mad Dog around Seminole Bend, but Lance's cousin, Lenny from Stuart, would bring a bottle for him almost every week when he was passing through on his delivery job. However, a bottle of Mad Dog was hard to keep around an entire week for a wine connoisseur like Lance. He indeed wasn't planning on sharing it with anyone, except maybe his lady friend, Ev.

Lance was the self-appointed emperor of the local homeless clan. He had deep, dark-shadowed eye sockets and a long, crooked nose that had hair hanging out a good half inch below the nostrils. Yes, Lance was disgusting, even for those who pitied his predicament. His particular financial mode of operation was mobile panhandling. He was such a repulsive, sorry sight that every snowbird or retired Seminole Bend resident would gladly part with a quarter to keep Lance from following them. He was six foot, six inches tall with a long beard, scraggly mustache, and narrow lips that were too thin to filter out his nasty liquor breath. Lance's shadow, extending over your shoulder onto the sidewalk in front of you, would induce you to strut down the pavement at a record pace.

Max Miller, the driver of the Ford LTD, had little time to mess around. After slamming his brakes and causing a high-pitched squeal clearly noticeable by all the grocery shoppers, he jumped out of the car and ran to the booth. Max had no time to spare and no patience for a human grub snoring the morning away in the only phone booth for blocks, perhaps miles. He grabbed Lance by his flowing reddish-blond beard and yanked his head up. Pulling groggily out of a whopping good dream, Lance sat up in shock and looked into the driver's glaring eyes. He wanted to take his bottle of MD 20 and crack the phone booth perpetrator in the skull, but hey, it was Mad Dog, and the fruit of the vine should never be wasted! Lance scrambled to his feet, and Max shoved him out the door. Lance stumbled a few feet, and then fell off the curb, shattering his beloved bottle into pieces. He squinted up at his home, now occupied by an alien, and Lance swore he would remember that face.

The driver dialed seven digits and was curtly greeted after two rings, "Speak."

"Danny's at the house. I followed the old man to the sheriff's office. He was in a big hurry. Knows something, I'm sure of it! Bet he found that dead Buckwheat cop in your swamp yesterday, Roy."

"Eliminate him. Make it an accident."

Max bolted out of the phone booth, jumped back into the front seat of the LTD, and jammed the key into the ignition. He fired the eight cylinders and raced northward through the parking lot at light speed, sending gravel and broken glass flying clear over Lance's lanky body! Yep, Lance would definitely remember that face.

At the end of the parking lot was a traffic light where the lot intersected with Main Street. With no thought to who might be noticing from the sheriff's office across the street, the blue Ford ran the red light and turned sharply left onto Main forcing an oncoming Pinto station wagon to veer right and fly uncontrollably into the ditch. The momentum caused the station wagon to bounce back out the other side of the trench into the Dixie Food and Drug parking lot. There, the car's front bumper struck Ev Pritchard's shopping cart, sending egg yolks and milk to omelet heaven. Fortunately, Ev had seen the out-of-control car aimed, loaded, and torpedoing right at her, and in sheer panic, she dove headfirst to the asphalt.

Ev's two muscular legs were her only mode of transportation, and she walked three miles each week to Dixie Food from the northeast ghetto to cash in her food stamps. She pounded her fists on the ground in frustration, knowing she certainly couldn't afford to pay for a second round of goodies back in the grocery store.

Several yards back, still lying on the asphalt where the Ford LTD's driver had shoved him, Lance Billips witnessed the whole accident. He clambered to his feet and came running to check out Ev's condition. Ev Pritchard was his Friday night fling, and the couple probably would get hitched except for two big problems: neither had any money, and Ev had a husband. A gigantic, ornery, and jealous husband.

Ev was okay, a little stunned by the whole ordeal, but more upset about losing this week's food rations. After checking on her, Lance started trotting towards Main Street to see if he could figure out where the LTD was heading. Most weeks, his fitness program consisted of short shoplifting hikes to the nearby grocery store and Friday night heavy breathing exercises with Ev. But today, with adrenaline-induced energy, Lance decided to cross Main Street and jog to the sheriff's office to report the incident at the phone booth. He was hoping he'd get lucky, and perhaps the phone booth assaulter dude was a wanted felon who had a reward on his head. But regardless, Lance wasn't about to let the son-of-a-bitch get away scot-free. First, the dang bastard shattered Lance's Mad Dog, then he almost shattered Lance's lover. Lance vowed revenge.

* * * * *

Calvin Potts backed his Chevy Nova out from the sheriff's office parking lot onto the service road that ran parallel to

Main Street, and then shifted the car from reverse to forward. A block down the service road was an entryway onto Main Street. Calvin stopped at the intersection and noticed a big blue car veering onto the shoulder and heading right at him at warp speed. Calvin froze. He couldn't think fast enough to decide whether to reverse backward with his automatic transmission or jolt forward to avoid a collision, so he did neither. Instead, his mouth gaped wide open as he stared out the driver's side window at the blue box of steel bolting directly at his door, only a few feet away. A split second later came a thunderous sound of metal on metal and an explosion that could be heard all the way to the lake!

Lance's jogging came to a sudden halt, and he glanced west toward the direction of the blast. He could see black smoke rising into the clear blue sky like Hiroshima revisited. Lance could barely make out the tail end of what looked like the infamous blue LTD he was chasing, and sure enough, one of the cars on fire was none other than the one owned by Mr. Bully. Lance's lips curled, and he started a slow laugh. The son-of-a-bitch blew the hell out of himself, he thought. Lance wasn't sure who the unlucky sucker was that the LTD struck, and he really didn't care. The big jerk in the blue Ford wasn't going to be smashing anyone's Mad Dog again!

The Seminole Bend volunteer fire department workers were several blocks away, over by Taylor Creek. They were putting out a grass and weed fire in the backyard of a resident whose cigarette smoking habit not only was burning his lungs but now it was burning his property. They didn't have to wait for a call from dispatch; they, too, heard the collision and saw the smoke rising about a mile away. The backyard fire was almost out, so they unraveled the garden hose from the man's house and told him to keep watering until they returned. The four volunteer firemen, who also cooked at Jake's BBQ at night, hopped into the red fire truck and raced to the scene of the accident. By the time they arrived, both cars were charred black as coal. Approaching the bigger vehicle first, they could find no trace of life or even see anything that resembled a body in the LTD.

The firemen then shifted their attention quickly toward the Nova and made a hurried dash to the driver side door, but stopped dead in their tracks when they noticed a horror flick unfolding before their eyes. The firefighters could see the skin on the face of Calvin Potts sizzle and melt like wax while the old man's empty eyes gazed at the interior roof of his car. All four of the heroes by day and cooks by night became nauseous and staggered away to get their hose from the truck. By the time they returned to the Chevy, the old man's bones were turning to ash. They sprayed massive gallons of water on the two cars, but to no avail as both vehicles smoldered in the street in full view of hundreds of permanent Seminole Bend citizens and snowbirds alike. Traffic on Main Street came to a complete stop as the gawkers couldn't believe their eyes! Everywhere around, people covered their mouths and stared in awe at the incredible sight. But while the Seminole Bend attraction of the century stunned the onlookers as they observed in horror and disbelief, Lance happened to notice a large, muscular man enter the back door to Elmer's Hardware Store. Lance recognized his face, even from a distance.

* * * * *

Danny Martin, the brawny cowboy who was Max Miller's partner, had no trouble getting into the Potts' home. Calvin, in his haste to visit the sheriff, forgot to lock both the outside entrance to the Florida room and the sliding glass door that led into the house's master bedroom. Danny yanked the banana plant, roots and all, from the large ceramic pot in the corner of the bedroom and tossed the tree behind him onto the porch. As he focused his eyes on the lightly snoring body under the covers, Danny picked up the plant-holder, slowly raised it over his head, and walked delicately over to the bed where Agnes Potts was sleeping soundly. She felt no conscious pain when Danny slammed the hundred-pound pot into her face, jamming bones from her nasal cavity into the frontal lobe area of her brain and causing immediate head hemorrhaging. Underneath the black dirt mounded on her face from the moist earth inside the pot, trickles of blood streamed out from Agnes' ears and eye sockets. Her left eyeball hung down by muscle and nerve tissue to where her nose once was located. The ghastly sight even caused Danny to weaken, and he turned his ashen face to the door. But before he left, he ripped open the jewelry case on the dresser and took two gold watches and a diamond solitaire necklace so authorities would suspect the old lady's death was from a burglary.

* * * * *

Lance Billips grabbed a plumbing wrench from the shelf in Elmer's Hardware store and followed the drops of blood that led to the small bathroom tucked away in the back. There was no way the big ox in the blue LTD could have escaped from that collision! Lance guessed that the man must have jammed the accelerator with a heavy oblong object, then jumped out of the car a few seconds before impact. The blood droplets in Elmer's store most likely indicated he was injured doing so.

The bathroom door handle was locked, so with the wrench weapon in hand, Lance backed up and waited precariously behind the shelf of paint just outside of the restroom. Several minutes passed, then finally, the handle turned, and the door began to open. As Max limped out, Lance raised the wrench above his head, looked the stunned car-crashing murderer in the eyes, and said, "This is for hurting my Evie, you bastard!" He swung hard in a swooping hook motion and landed the steel instrument solidly on the big man's temple, causing him to quiver first to the side and then fall backward. Max tried to stand up, but his knees wobbled, and he stumbled dizzily into the bathroom. Then his legs gave out, and he slipped and fell hard. The base of Max's head crashed on the porcelain sink, and Lance heard the ominous crack of his opponent's skull. Lance didn't wait to see the outcome of his blow; he wheeled around, turned left into the storeroom, and sprinted out the back door of the hardware store. But as it turned out, he really didn't need to rush because no one was inside the hardware store, or as a matter of fact, anywhere near the outside of the shop either. Curiosity had gotten the best of the locals, and everyone was down the street watching the aftermath of the worst car accident in Seminole Bend history.

CHAPTER 16

Wednesday, February 10, 1982

11:00 a.m.

Willy Banks awoke to the screaming sound of ambulance sirens all around him. He slowly opened his eyes and tried desperately to focus his vision while a tremendous headache pounded his temples. Facing the ceiling, Willy stared directly at the dim fluorescent lights above the elevated bed on which he lay. As he looked around and saw the transparent plastic tube that ran from a bottle of blood into his left arm, he knew he must be passing time at Gregorson General Hospital. He dared not look at his injured leg in the event that it wasn't attached to his body.

Willy could barely recall the last twenty-four hours, and he was desperate to find out what happened to his partner, Sam McCormick. He knew it was very likely that Sam had died from shotgun pellet wounds or drowned in the Jackson moat, and he laid the blame squarely with Roy's thugs. Willy was convinced that it was high time for someone to put an end to Roy Jackson's Seminole Bend dictatorship. It wouldn't be easy.

Gloria Peters, the forty-something, curly brown-haired-this-week-but-most-likely-redhead-next-week, lead nurse, opened the door to the deputy's private room and said smiling, "What you doing up, Willy Banks? We gave you enough knock-out juice to put a horse to sleep for several years!"

"I'm fraid to look, Gloria. Do I have one or two legs underneath that big black butt of mine?"

"Well, Willy, we ain't seen such a muscular, beautiful specimen of human flesh in years as your leg, so we stuffed it and hung it on the wall in the lobby. But we attached a huge catfish in its place at your hip, so now you will be known as 'Willy the Merman'."

"Well, ain't you the hilarious and sympathetic nurse lady? So what's up with all the sirens?"

"You ain't the only casualty, Willy. This morning we had a huge accident right out front of the sheriff's office. A big old Ford LTD rammed into Calvin Potts' Chevy Nova and blew Calvin to pieces. What was left of him fried and melted like a candle! When the sheriff went over to tell Agnes, they found the back door of the Florida room, you know, the one that leads to the master bedroom, open, and they went in. I overheard the call come in just a few minutes ago: they found Agnes lying in her bed with her face crushed to pieces by what I thought they said was a big ceramic planting pot. Her jewelry was missing. Dang, what a coincidence; some damn thief killing her at the very same time her hubby gets into a fatal accident!"

"I got to go, Gloria!" said Willy authoritatively as his eyes scrambled around the hospital room. "Unhook me from this miserable tube."

"You ain't going nowhere, Willy Banks. We just finished giving you four quarts of blood and sewed up your leg. Not even one of them aliens on *Star Trek* could heal that fast, you fool!"

"Gloria, I have a good suspicion that Calvin Potts' accident and Agnes Potts' killing were not just a coincidence. I got to get to the scene of the murder before—well, it ain't none of your business. Now unhook that damn thing!"

"Willy, I can't let you out of here. You'll pop them stitches just climbing out of bed, then we got to find you some more dang blood!"

"Damn it, Gloria, I'll just do it myself!" Willy ripped the IV out of his arm, then sat up and reached for the bottle of alcohol and a cotton swab that was sitting on a cart near his bed. The blood trickled down to his fingers, but he swabbed the tiny hole in his arm and found a circular bandage to put over it. Gloria stood back with her hands on her hips and just shook her head.

As Willy slid his good leg off the bed, sharp pain in his injured leg caused him to wince. He carefully placed the leg on the floor, but it buckled at the knee, and Willy collapsed, planting his backside firmly on the linoleum.

"That's what you get for being a pain in the ass, Willy Banks," Gloria stammered. But Gloria knew her friend was bound and determined to check out the Potts' house, and she could tell something important was eating at Willy. "Alright, I'll help ya kill yourself, seeing that's what you seem to want. But if anyone asks, I don't know nothing!"

Gloria put her arms under Willy's armpits and yanked with all her strength. "Not even a hydraulic hoist could lift you, ya big ox."

Willy raised his hands and placed them on the side of the bed. Again Gloria heaved, and this time with Willy's help, he stood erect.

Willy's clothes were on hangers in the closet by the bathroom. Gloria helped him to the closet, but then Willy gave her an insistent look. "Don't you be looking while I get outa this dang bed sheet miniskirt, Gloria Peters!"

"Ain't nothing to see that I ain't seen every day that I work here, you dang fool."

Willy grabbed his bloodstained, khaki police shorts and a navy blue t-shirt. He couldn't remember what happened to his socks and tennis shoes, but he didn't have time to look. Willy limped down the hospital hallway with Gloria helping him to keep his balance and then headed straight to the employee parking lot out back. Gloria had offered to let Willy use her ten-year-old Mercury Bobcat, but she began to think twice about the offer as she watched Willy wince in pain trying to get into the driver's side bucket seat. He would have difficulty engaging the clutch and maneuvering the stick shift, but fortunately, the Potts' house was only four miles away. Willy winked at Gloria as he backed out, then sped through the parking lot to the main road. She could see he was trying to hide the severe pain written all over his face.

* * * * *

"And just what in hell's name do you think you're doing here, Willy?" Sheriff Bonty glared at Willy, but had that look in his eyes like a mom or dad has when they find their missing child: first relief, then anger for running off. "You're supposed to be recuperating at Gregorson General. From what I hear, your leg was about ripped off."

"I'm okay, Al. What happened here?"

Two men from the coroner's office lingered by the bedroom door with a black body bag waiting for Sheriff Bonty and his officers to finish their initial investigation. Agnes Potts' corpse was lying on the bed exactly where she was found. Willy gazed down and saw her brutally damaged and unrecognizable face staring upward. He turned his head to the side, covered his mouth and gagged. Although he was nauseous, Willy regained his composure and looked back at Bonty.

"Looks like some damn thief broke into Potts' home, and Agnes unfortunately caught the bastard stealing, so he bashed her with that ceramic pot right in the face," answered Sheriff Bonty, rather sure of himself.

"If she caught him stealing, why was she lying on the bed like she was still sleeping?" Willy asked with a suspicious glance over at the sheriff.

"Don't know for sure she was sleeping. I think the thief pushed her back on the bed and then smashed the pot down over her face."

"But when he pushed her, how did he have enough time to lift a heavy pot and get back over to the bed before she ran?"

"Come on, Willy. Agnes was no spring chicken. She probably was stunned when he pushed her to the bed, and she froze there frightened about what he might do to her."

Willy didn't buy that for a minute, but he could tell Sheriff Bonty was covering something up. "So, Sheriff, don't you think it's a little more than a coincidence that Agnes and Calvin should die on the same morning in two separate, strange accidents?"

"Why are you grilling me, Willy Banks? I oughta fire your ass for disregarding my orders. I told you and Sam McCormick to stay away from Roy Jackson's place, and what do you do? You go right over there! By the way, where is Sam? No one has seen him for a couple of days."

"So, how is it that you knew that Sam and me was at Jackson's place? Did you talk with Roy Jackson, Al?"

"Roy was smoking mad that you were trespassing a couple of nights ago, and he was reporting you. Ya know, Willy, trespassing is a violation of the law in all fifty states. I can't be having my officers violating the law, now can I?"

"You said you knew Sam was with me at Jackson's, Al. That means Roy snitched on both of us, right? So, how come you don't know where Sam is now? Sam was with me, Al, and I think you know dang well Jackson killed him after Sam swam out in the swamp to intercept one of those drug barrels that was dropped from a little Cessna plane! You know, Al, the plane that you said wasn't there so we wouldn't spy on the jerk?"

"I don't know nothing about Roy killing Sam. I'm just asking you because I wanted to make sure he was okay," the sheriff explained, but not too convincingly.

"So when do we start the investigation, Sheriff? One of our finest officers is missing, and you ain't done nothing to try and find him."

"Sam is considered a missing person, and we can't go looking for forty-eight hours, which is coming up real soon. But right now, I'm a little busy, first tending to your gator accident, then Calvin's car blowing up, and now Agnes getting her face smashed in!"

"Gator accident? I'm telling you, Al, it was no damn accident that I was just about an alligator's hors d'oeuvre! Roy's thugs shot at me and Sam when we discovered his boys picking up barrels that were dropped from that airplane. They chased me and my airboat into a rock, and I knocked myself out. Then they beat the living hell out of me in one of Roy's barns, dragged me back to the swamp, and left me to be buried in a gator's belly! And I'm thinking, Sheriff, that Calvin and Agnes' deaths are related to Sam and me somehow, and Roy Jackson is the common denominator. And I'm thinking you know that, too, Al."

The coroner's men and other officers pretended they didn't hear the exchange between Willy and Al, but it was more than evident to the sheriff that they did. Bonty's faced turned a bright red, and he glared at Willy while pointing his finger an inch from Willy's forehead. "Are you accusing me of something, Willy? What the hell evidence do you have that the Potts' deaths are related to your trespassing incident?"

"Just a suspicious bug in the back of my brain. Now, if you don't have time to investigate Sam's disappearance, then I would like to head up a posse to search Jackson's ranch from cover to cover. I just want a search warrant."

"You stay away from Roy's place! Do you hear me, Willy? You're in enough trouble with the law, trespassing and all. I'll take care of finding Sam just as soon as we wrap up the report on Agnes. Detectives Jones and Harper from the Seminole Bend PD will be assigned to the Agnes Potts' case, and then I can shift gears."

"Who's assigned to Calvin's case, Chief?" Willy offered with a hint of sarcasm.

"There is no 'Calvin Case'! It's a traffic investigation, that's all."

"Yeah, right, Al." Willy shook his head and headed back to return the Mercury Bobcat to Gloria. Blood was trickling out from his stitches.

CHAPTER 17

Wednesday, February 10, 1982

12:30 p.m.

On the way back to the hospital, Willy stopped into the sheriff's office. Johnny Murphree was at the front desk, and things were hopping! The sheriff's office and the Seminole Bend Police Department had never been so busy. The worst crime in the past couple of months was when two kids were caught stealing nightcrawlers from Pinky's Bait & Tackle shop. Of course, the worst crime on a nightly basis was never investigated because Roy Jackson's ranch was off-limits to everyone, except maybe God. Willy couldn't figure out how Roy's money could buy so much power. He was beginning to think if anyone was going to stop Roy, it would have to be him, and most likely, going at it alone.

"Hey, Johnny. How's things?" Willy said with a smile.

"Well, I'll be sun-dried and left to wrinkle! What the hell are you doing here, Willy? I heard you beat the crap outa another gator, but he took a chunk outa one of them scrawny little legs of yours!" replied Johnny. "I thought you were supposed to be in the hospital."

"Ain't no chicken shit gator gonna stop me from being the toughest SOB in Seminole Bend County! No make that Florida! No, actually make that the US of A! Oh, let's get it right, the entire planet Earth!"

"Yeah, you must be okay cuz you're still full of it! So why the visit? I think if it was me who was hurting, I'd take a few years of long-term disability, buy a new bass boat, and fish my life away."

"Just wanted to ask you a few questions, Johnny. Were you working this morning when Calvin Potts had his accident?"

"Sure was. Sad thing, he had just left my desk, headed out to his Chevy Nova, backed up, then started down the service road. Then bang, it was over. I ran out, but the whole road looked like nuclear war was raging."

"Are you saying that Calvin stopped into the sheriff's office before the accident? Why was he here?"

"Calvin called me this morning when he was about to go fishing and found out his boat was missing from the dock. I told him to come down, and I'd take the report here because all the boys were down at Angler's Delight trying to find out what happened to you yesterday. Ken Belop checked in for work a couple of minutes later, so I sent him over to Calvin's place on Taylor Creek, hoping he could catch Calvin before he left. He missed him, but it was Ken who found Agnes in bed. Poor lady."

"What kind of boat was Calvin missing?"

"Who the hell cares about the damn boat, Willy!? Both Potts are dead, and you're thinking about the boat? Shoot, man, that's a little sick, wouldn't you say!?"

"Johnny, if you have the report, just tell me what his boat looked like and the plate number."

"It was a silver Alumicraft with a twenty-five horse Johnson motor. You know, they all look alike. Just a tin rowboat that won't scare the fish."

"What was his plate number?"

"Let's see, okay, here it is: *JL 4106 FL.*"

"Thanks, man. I'll talk to you later."

"Not if you die from blood loss, Willy. Look at the floor. You've been dripping hemoglobin all over our shiny linoleum." smirked Johnny.

"Shiny floor? The linoleum was dirty the day they laid it, you damn fool! Got to go." Willy limped out the door and back to the Mercury Bobcat.

*****

Gloria rewrapped Willy's leg with a new cloth. The stitches were holding, but just barely. He thanked her for letting him use her car and then asked for a ride to Bennett's Airboat Palace to pick up his own car that he left there on Monday. She obliged like any southern girl would do for a stranded human being, especially one of the male sex with rock-solid, bulging muscles like Willy's.

Phil Bennett stared in disbelief when Willy confessed he had totaled out the rented airboat on a rock. Willy promised to pay double the cost if Phil could wait a few months to get paid. Phil had been a fan of Willy's when Willy played football and basketball at the high school, and now he was proud to call the one-time star turned sheriff's deputy a friend. Of course, he would take that deal. Anything for a local sports icon.

"Not too pleased about losing a quarter of my income for a few months, Willy, but I'll do it for you and Sam," remarked Phil while thinking how he was going to get by with only three boats left to rent out. He looked Willy up and down, just now noticing his bandages. "Just glad you and Sam weren't hurt real bad or nothing. I mean, you weren't hurt real bad, was ya?" Phil couldn't afford liability insurance, so he was hoping for the right answer to come out of Willy's mouth.

"I'm fine, Phil, but I do need to get a move on." Willy intentionally didn't mention the condition of Sam McCormick. Phil played poker with the guys on Friday nights, and he didn't want Sam's disappearance to create rumors among the locals. The boys were bigger gossipers than the ladies.

Willy started up his car and headed back around the dirt road that ran adjacent to the rim canal. As he approached the Taylor Creek locks, he parked his car and hiked up the flight of spiral concrete stairs to the lock operator's lookout. Inside the tiny room that not only overlooked the locks but provided a great view of Lake Okeechobee, Ernie Hyle was busy brushing the crumbs off his XXXL pants onto the floor from the dozen pieces of Kentucky Fried Chicken he'd just devoured. He caught a glimpse of Willy out of the corner of his eye and smiled embarrassingly, "Someone's got to feed them cockroaches. The bigger they are, the more attractive they are to the largemouth bass. And they wiggle better on the hook!"

Willy thought that Ernie Hyle kind of looked like a different species of largemouth, like a largemouth hippo that just escaped from Africa. "Hello, Ernie. I hope I'm not disturbing your lunch."

"It don't appear anybody's disturbed my lunch in quite some time, wouldn't you agree, Willy?" the big man answered, smiling while he patted his plump belly with his hands. Willy chuckled at Ernie's self-inflicted sarcasm.

"Ernie, I'd like to ask you some questions about yesterday."

"I heard you were injured in a gator fight yesterday, Willy. What's you doing up and about so soon. Are you actually one of them plastic Rock 'Em Sock 'Em robots or something?"

"Yeah, might be. Anyway, this may sound like an impossible question to answer, but do you remember seeing a skinny Mexican guy with a long mustache come through the locks yesterday in a fishing boat."

Ernie paused momentarily to ponder the question, and then slowly began nodding his head as if to say yes. "As a matter of fact, Willy, I do remember a Mexican man come through the locks. I remember because I thought it was strange: the boat he was driving looked just like Calvin Potts' Alumicraft. It had a twenty-five horse Johnson on it. Calvin comes through these here locks almost every day."

"Did you get the plate number?"

"Well, I didn't get a chance to write it down, cuz you see I was doing a bunch of other important stuff. But I think I remember: it started with 'JL.' That I remember because my car license plate starts that way, too. Then the numbers after the 'JL' were 4601, or 4016, or something like that. I can always remember numbers, but I'm a little dyslexic when it comes to remembering which order they come in.

"So what's up, Willy? Do you know this Mexican guy or something?"

"Yep, I think so. You've been a big help, Ernie. Oh, by the way, Calvin Potts won't be coming through your locks anymore. He was killed in a car accident this morning."

"Oh my God! Was that what them sirens and that big cloud of smoke I saw rising in the distance was all about? Man, what a coincidence that we was just talking about him and his boat, eh Willy?"

"Yeah, Ernie. Quite a coincidence."

Willy walked back down the stairs and into his car. The police scanner was beeping, blinking, and crackling with static. Then he heard his name called. "Willy. This is Johnny Murphree. What's your twenty? Can you come down to the station quick?"

"I can be there in ten minutes. What's up, Johnny?"

"Just come down. I'll tell you when you get here. Over."

CHAPTER 18

Wednesday, February 10, 1982
2:00 p.m.

Willy turned left onto US 98 and headed west towards the intersection of US 441 that would take him back through town. After making the right turn onto 441, he noticed in the rearview mirror that a black Lincoln Continental was several cars back. Willy remembered that exact same black Lincoln was parked under a palm tree in the parking lot at Bennett's Airboat Palace. Willy had a sneaking suspicion that the black Lincoln belonged to none other than Roy Jackson.

Traveling at forty miles per hour, Willy made a sharp right turn and squealed tire rubber as he pulled into the BoldMart Shopping Plaza, and sure enough, the Lincoln followed him. Willy stopped his car in a slot that needed its lines repainted. Standing nearby were several people talking about something and shaking their heads while covering their mouths with their hands. No doubt they heard the news about Calvin or Agnes Potts, or both. In a small town, everyone knows everyone, including the snowbirds.

Willy reached under the passenger seat and grabbed a holster with a loaded Beretta pistol. He didn't like guns and just hoped his gargantuan biceps would do the trick and scare potential villains away. He opened his door, stood up, strapped on the holster, and then limped the best he could directly to the Lincoln that had parked about fifty yards behind him. When the Lincoln's driver saw Willy coming, he tried to back out but was blocked in by a string of cars that had just entered the parking lot. Willy didn't figure he had to worry too much about someone shooting at him or trying to mess with him. He could see a whole bunch of curious potential witnesses wondering why a sheriff's car just sailed into the BoldMart lot like it was an Indy pit stop. Willy marched right up to the Lincoln driver's window and pounded on the glass with his massive fist. The driver scanned his rearview and side mirrors looking for options to get away, but he refused to open the window. The dark smoked glass kept Willy from seeing who or how many people were in the big expensive car.

Willy knocked one more time but didn't wait long to see if he was going to get a response. He pulled his t-shirt over his head, wrapped it around his fist, cocked his elbow, and smashed the glass window almost back into the sand from which it came! Shattered glass shards flew all around, but mostly in the lap of the startled driver. Willy noticed a well-dressed, ornery-looking male passenger in the front seat and one in the back who quickly deposited something into a handbag he was carrying. All three men looked shocked.

"Hi, boys. You gents looking for a BoldMart Daily Special or something? I can tell by the looks of your automobile that you ain't got much money, so I suppose you're headed into BoldMart for a great deal on something, right? Though I'm not sure they sell machine gun bullets here. Say, don't I remember you boys from somewhere? Could swear you look like the welcoming committee over at Roy Jackson's ranch."

The driver leaned back to keep a safe distance from Willy's bear-sized biceps, but the man in the back seat moved closer. "You're a dead man, Willy Banks." He then reached into his bag to pull out the pistol he had just placed in it, but Willy was too quick. Through the broken window, he grabbed the driver around the neck with both hands and yanked with awesome force, jerking the man forward and through the jagged glass. Both Willy and the driver tumbled to the ground, but Willy manhandled him over onto his glass-impaled belly and clamped his biceps under the stunned man's chin. He then stood up, using the terrified driver as his shield.

Willy's new cloth bandage around his leg was soaking up blood again, but that was nothing compared to the driver's cuts and scrapes up and down his body. In the car, the armed gunman sitting in the back climbed over the seat to the front and cranked the ignition. He slammed the transmission into reverse and gunned the accelerator, ramming a wide seam between two slow-moving cars that had moments before been bumper to bumper. However, the front end of one car clipped an old man who was pushing his shopping cart loaded with citrus fertilizer and hadn't noticed the commotion. The man tried to steady himself with the shopping cart, but just then, the Lincoln smashed its rear fender into the wire buggy, sending the man reeling to the ground and pinning the cart on top of him. The Lincoln reversed course and sped out of the parking lot in a dust storm.

Willy pushed the Lincoln's driver to the ground to help out the old man, who was now unconscious. The driver quickly got up and ran like the dickens trying to catch up with his buddies, but they weren't about to stop, so he sprinted across the road and disappeared into the palm-forested residential area of southwest Seminole Bend.

Willy lifted the shopping cart off of the old man and brushed away the fertilizer that had spilled through a rip in the bag and onto the man's t-shirt. Willy grabbed the old man's wrist and checked for a pulse. Nothing. He put his ear up to the man's nose to check for breathing. Nothing again! Willy yelled at a couple of startled customers who had witnessed the entire incident and now stood there like statues with their mouths wide open. "Call for an ambulance! Hurry!"

The couple both ran for the entrance to BoldMart while Willy tore the old man's t-shirt to shreds and began administering CPR. Because all the rescue vehicles were on location either at Calvin Potts' car accident scene or Agnes' murder, it took the ambulance twenty-five minutes to arrive. Willy had given it his best shot, but the old man was dead before the EMTs pulled into the parking lot. The coroner would subsequently rule the cause of death as massive heart failure.

In Willy's mind, Roy Jackson was now a mass murderer! Sam, Calvin, Agnes, and now the old man in the Bold Mart parking lot were all killed by Roy's disciples. How many others had suffered or died so Roy's illicit business dealings could thrive? Willy assumed Roy was a drug dealer, but he had no concrete proof. Maybe it was weapons that were being dropped from the small aircraft into his swamp. Willy was bound and determined to find out what exactly Roy was involved in.

Willy got back into his car and headed to the sheriff's office. Had Johnny Murphree not summoned him to come quickly, perhaps the old man would still be alive. Had Willy ignored the Lincoln that he saw in his rearview mirror, surely it would have gone elsewhere when Willy arrived at the station. Had Willy not been so aggressive and approached Roy's bandits in the parking lot, the whole mess would never have happened. Willy wiped away the tears and tried to think of something else, but that was impossible. On the road to the sheriff's office, Willy vowed justice, or if that didn't work, he vowed revenge.

*****

Willy limped into the sheriff's office, blood again seeping from the bandage on his leg. Sweat and dirt covered his face and clothes, and the huge man could easily have been mistaken for the feared Swamp Creature in the next Disney flick. Johnny dashed around his desk and helped Willy to a chair.

"Dang, Willy, I heard the 911 call through the hospital scanner for an ambulance. Some employee dude who was gathering up shopping carts out in the parking lot at BoldMart called it in. He was frantically describing the scene, you know, cars crunched and people injured. I knew it was you out there! The guy said a black giant cop with arms like an elephant's trunk yanked some poor bastard right through his windshield, and while they was rolling on the ground, a Cadillac smashed a couple of cars and run right over some old man and his shopping cart."

"It was a Lincoln, not a Caddy, and it belonged to Roy Jackson. I am an eyewitness to a voluntary manslaughter slaying. Write that fact down now on a piece of paper, and I'll sign it Johnny, and then lock the paper up in a safe. In case I don't see you again, that paper can launch an investigation, as long as you give it to the FBI and not to Sheriff Bonty."

"Whoa, calm down, Willy. I don't know where you're going with the Sheriff Bonty thing, but I don't want to be no part of insubordination."

"Insubordination hell, Johnny! Sheriff and Roy are in cahoots, and nobody in this here town is safe with that combination. Now, what the hell did you want me to come down here for?"

"Just before I called you, Elmer Hudster called from his hardware store. Said some big fella he didn't know must have slipped and fallen in his bathroom and hit his head on the sink. Blood was gurgling from his nose, and he thought the guy was dead. I sent Toby over to investigate, but with all the crap going on today, I thought you might like to know."

"Has Toby called you back?"

"Not yet. But I can't leave cuz nobody's left to mind the station."

"I'll check it out." Willy was out the door so fast he probably forgot his leg was only half attached.

CHAPTER 19
Wednesday, February 10, 1982
3:30 p.m.

Willy pulled into the handicapped parking spot in front of Elmer's Hardware Store. There was no doubt in Willy's mind that he was a wee bit handicapped right now. He opened the door and managed to get his upper body out of the front seat, but his injured leg wasn't exactly cooperating. Willy finally limped into the hardware store.

Elmer was waiting in the back by the restroom with Toby. Toby had a notebook open and was taking notes.

"What happened?" Willy asked as he looked down at the corpse of a huge man lying face up whose head appeared to have been split in half. Barely noticeable, a grayish bulge protruded from the base of the man's skull and was covered in blood. Deciding not to bother with rubber gloves, Willy reached under the man's neck and rolled his head to one side. The bulge was the man's herniated brain. Toby dropped his notebook into the pool of blood and vomited all over the evidence.

Elmer grabbed Toby by the arm and dragged him to a stool just outside the bathroom. Elmer then decided that he may as well join the party, and he too launched his breakfast onto the floor. Willy stepped back out of the bathroom and gave Elmer and Toby an evil glance.

When Elmer regained his composure, he shot a confused look at the dead man, then at Willy. "How could that guy fall so hard that his head gets broken in half? I ain't got much liability insurance, Willy. Dang, is this the end of me and my store?"

"I don't think this fella is gonna be suing anybody, Elmer. Can't say if he's got a family, though. But something's funny: I feel like I've seen him somewhere before, but I just can't place it."

"He ain't never been in my store before. Strange happenings today, Willy. Calvin blowing up in that car, then this."

"Stranger than you even know, Elmer. Stay here, Toby. I'm going back to the station. Don't touch anything. I'll send our detective squad and the coroner over right away."

As Willy limped to the front of the store, he saw something sparkle on the tile floor. He knelt down and picked up a jagged piece of broken glass about the size of a dime. Willy instinctively put the glass to his nose and took a whiff. He thought it smelled like wine, but he couldn't be sure. Willy turned and yelled back to Elmer, who was helping Toby back to the stool after another bout with a sour stomach, "Hey Elmer. You sell liquor in this here hardware store?"

"Now, I ain't no moonshiner if that's what you're asking Willy."

"When was the last time you swept your floors, Elmer?"

"Matter of fact I was sweeping when I heard the car crash outside. Only a couple of customers was in here, and we all ran out to see what happened."

"You remember sweeping up any broken glass?"

"Naw. Wasn't no broken glass in here, Willy. I would have seen it."

Willy took out his hanky and carefully wrapped the glass into it, then stuck it back in his pocket.

* * * * *

Sheriff Bonty's hands were perched on his hips, and if looks could kill, Willy was a dead man. "Get your butt into my office, Banks." The sheriff turned and marched toward his office in the back of the station.

Willy stopped momentarily at the front desk and pulled the hanky from his pocket. He opened the hanky and laid it carefully in front of Johnny Murphree.

"Johnny," whispered Willy, "send this down to the lab and let me know what they find. Don't tell anyone but me, you got it?" As Willy headed down the hall toward the sheriff's office, he looked back at Johnny and said, "And Toby needs the detectives and coroner sent over to Elmer's right away."

After hearing Willy's request for the detectives and coroner, Sheriff Bonty paused outside the door to his office and turned toward Willy. "Hell, Willy! You know dang well half of our detectives are at Agnes' and the other half are investigating that old man at BoldMart. Lord knows where the coroner is!"

"Then call down to Fort Pierce, man. We got to get some guys who can assist us now! This town is a law-breaking mess if you haven't noticed!"

Willy wasn't sure precisely what Sheriff Bonty was pissed about now, it could be any number of things. But he had a sneaking suspicion that he probably deserved the tongue lashing that was about to happen.

"Sit down, Willy." The look in the sheriff's eyes told Willy that arguing with him some more might just start World War Three. "What the hell were you thinking about at BoldMart? Smashing a citizen's car window is one thing, bad enough, you know, but then reaching in and dragging him out of the car by his neck, no less!"

"Thought some proactive self-defense might help me live longer than thirty bullets in my chest, Al," Willy replied sarcastically.

"Yanking a man through the window of his car was self-defense?"

"He was my shield. Jackson's hitman in the back seat was going for his gun."

“And what makes you think it was Jackson’s man?”

“All of them was at his ranch kicking the shit out of me the other night, Sheriff. I think we had this conversation earlier.”

“What had the men in that car done to cause you to approach their vehicle?”

“They’d been following me all morning.”

“Was that a crime, Willy?”

“You tell me, Sheriff. Was a crime about to happen, like them thugs ramming my car into a palm tree or something?”

“Well, the way you handled the situation caused that old man’s death. I’ve contacted the Florida Department of Public Safety, Internal Affairs Division, as I’m required to do, Willy. They’re sending someone over soon. In the meantime, you’re assigned to traffic duty. And if you even think about giving Roy Jackson a ticket for speeding or even spitting on the highway, you’re history.”

“And why is Roy so damned special, Sheriff?”

“He ain’t. But for your own sake, I’m keeping you away from him. That’s an order. Any tickets or harassing Roy Jackson, and I’ll take your badge. Permanently! Got it, Willy? Now get the hell out of here!”

CHAPTER 20
Friday, February 12, 1982
8:00 a.m.

Willy snored Thursday away in la-la land and awoke on Friday morning after a thirty-hour sleep. Not sure how he slept so long considering the vivid dreams that swirled around inside his brain the entire time during his deep slumber. The worst hallucination surrounded a nightmarish vision of an alligator beer party with him being deep-fried in a massive pot of bacon grease while the wild singing reptiles licked their chops and high-fived (or high-foured, depending on how many dang fingers them creatures got!) each other as they danced in circles on their hind legs! Fortunately, the telephone rang and stirred him from the depths of hell. Willy could barely mutter a "hello."

"Mad Dog Twenty," Johnny reported to Willy over the phone.

"Who is this?" Willy stammered, trying to get his thoughts back into reality.

"It's me, Johnny Murphree, and I got your *A-Number One* analysis back for you. But I don't think it's going to be much help, Willy. It's Mad Dog Twenty, you know, MD20, the numero uno pick of winos everywhere!"

"What's MD20, Johnny, I mean, what the hell are you talking about?"

"Your shiny little piece of glass you found over at Elmer's. You got a bit of amnesia, or what, Willy?"

"Are you saying the glass is a broken piece of an MD20 bottle?"

“Yes, sir! Sure you wasn’t boozing it a little with the gators on the Kissimmee, Willy?”

“Hey, after my dream last night, I’m not too sure! Anyway, did you happen to pick up any prints with it?”

“Just yours, Willy. Didn’t think to pick up the evidence with a glove like they teach you in the whiz-bang detective course, did you?”

“No, that wasn’t exactly out of the book, was it, Johnny?”

“No, sir, not exactly. Hey, by the way, there was a tiny speck of fiber that was stuck to the broken glass. It matched the fiber from the shirt worn by the dead man with the bad headache. He didn’t appear to be a cheap wine type of guy, did he, Willy?”

“Have you identified the man yet?”

“No such luck. He was carrying over a thousand dollars on a money clip, but no wallet. No one has called to report a missing person, either.”

“Strange, isn’t it Johnny? You got a dead rich man with no honey to claim the big inheritance. Doubtful a man with that kind of dough would be drinking MD20.”

“So, where did the broken glass come from?”

“That’s what I’m going to try and find out.”

“Now dang it, Willy. First, you need to heal that ugly scar on your behind, and then you got to remember you’re a traffic-only cop for the time being.”

“Yeah, right. Thanks for the info, Johnny.”

CHAPTER 21

Friday, February 12, 1982
7:00 p.m.

The Warriors basketball team was sixteen and one with a shot at revenge for their only loss. Martin Park was in town, and they had destroyed Seminole Bend High the second game of the season at Martin Park. Not much love lost in this one. Martin Park held the Florida high school record for most consecutive wins, had won the state championship two years running, and hadn't lost to the Warriors since the sixties! Good thing for fans down in these parts that Seminole Bend's football team made up for what the basketball team couldn't seem to do on the court. So the arch rivalry was now cooking up some steam, thanks to Seminole Bend's newfound mastery on the hardcourt, and Martin Park was setting their sights on win number seventy-three in a row! Even the *Miami Sentinel's* sport's columnist, Bard Smith, found his way northward to the central Florida swamplands for this one.

Kenny Gormon played only three minutes at the end of the first game in Martin Park back in December and had entered that game when the Warriors were down, ninety-eight to sixty-four. It was merely another game where Martin Park sat their starters the entire fourth quarter. Meanwhile, Jimmy Jackson played the other twenty-nine minutes. Papa Roy Jackson watched that game sitting two rows behind Coach Brett Berry, while the University of Florida hoop scouts took notes and stats from the top row of the bleachers. During a time-out in the third quarter, Berry was going to give Jimmy a breather on the bench and called for Kenny to check in. That was until the coach looked up and detected smoke and flames coming out of Roy's ears and nose. Jimmy sucked it up, and Kenny put his warm-up top back on and sat down again. Jimmy scored fourteen points in the three and a half quarters he played. Kenny scored ten points in his only action on the court, the last three minutes of the game.

Although Coach Brett Berry enjoyed the luxurious fixings for his house that Roy provided, he was an athlete at heart, and he also coveted winning. As the season progressed, it was obvious Kenny was more skilled than Jimmy, and if given the opportunity, Kenny could play major college basketball. Jimmy, on the other hand, would have to have his daddy "purchase" that honor. But tonight, Coach believed his Warriors could be the first team to beat Martin Park in three years, and he needed his shooting sensation, Kenny Gormon, in the game to make that happen.

When the starting five was announced, both Kenny and Jimmy trotted out to center court high-fiving each other. Kenny replaced Willis Mann in the starting lineup at guard, even though Willis was the team leader in assists. Willis asked Coach Berry why he was being benched, and Coach said he needed Kenny's shooting ability to win the game. Willis agreed with that, but he wanted to know, as did most of the Warriors fans, why Jimmy Jackson wasn't the guy picking splinters from his butt. Coach said he had a "gut feeling" about that move.

Roy was ticked off! Not only were the Gators scouting this game, so were the Florida State Seminoles, Miami Hurricanes, and Georgia Bulldogs. Roy could care less about FSU, Miami and Georgia, it was the University of Florida that he wanted his son to attend, and by God, that was going to happen. Roy certainly didn't want Kenny Gormon stealing any thunder from his boy Jimmy.

Roy hopped down to the floor and barked in the coach's face, "What the hell are you doing, Berry? You need Willis and Jimmy in this game if you're going to beat Martin Park."

"Just trying some things, Roy. Jimmy will do fine!"

Roy strutted up and down the sideline before the buzzer sounded to start the game. His daughter, Jenny Jackson, was at the end of the gym by the padded wall mats with the rest of the cheerleaders. She tried to motion with her arms to get her daddy to sit down because he was embarrassing her and Jimmy. Hands staked firmly on his waist, Roy shook his head in disgust and parked himself on the front row of the bleachers, so close to the Warriors team that if he had a uniform and lost several layers of blubber around his waist, he might be mistaken for a player!

Willy's nephew and Warriors center, Tyrone Banks, tipped the opening jump ball over to Marcelus Cleaver, who threw a nifty bounce pass to Jimmy Jackson for a reverse layup and the Warriors were up two to nothing. Seminole Bend immediately set up in a one-two-one-one full-court press, and Jimmy stole the Martin Park in-bounds pass. He could have easily gone in for another layup, but he saw Kenny Gormon open at the top of the key, and he passed it over to him quickly. Kenny's shot was more than pretty as it arched delicately over the top of the rim and barely skimmed the net on the way through. Four zip, Seminole Bend. Roy's eyes caught his son's eyes, and the look of anger was powerful.

"Damn it, Jimmy. What's up with passing? Take the easy layup!" Roy shouted as Jimmy took his position at the frontcourt wing of the zone press. Jimmy ignored his father, and that irked Roy even more.

Midway through the second quarter, Martin Park began to light it up. They finished fourteen for fifteen on short-range jump shots following dynamic picks and sensational passes and then tossed in another five points on free throws. The thirty-three second-quarter points put them up fifty-one to forty-two at the half. But Kenny Gormon one-upped the entire Martin Park team in the first half, hitting fifteen for fifteen on everything from a driving layup to a baby hook and even a left-handed fallaway shot from the baseline. Needless to say, the scouts were impressed. Needless to say, Roy Jackson was fit to be tied!

Kenny's thirty half-time points were a school record. He needed only fifteen more to break the single-game scoring record, and twenty-two in the second half would break the conference record. Roy was going to make sure that didn't happen. As the Warriors broke from the locker room, Coach Berry was bringing up the caboose. Roy met him in the hallway and told the assistant coaches to keep on moving out to the gym.

"Kenny needs a rest, Coach," Roy uttered in a stern tone of voice.

"Dang it, Roy. We can win this game. Kenny is hotter than all get out!"

"Kenny needs a rest, damn it! I'll let you know if you need him anytime soon!"

"I can't Roy. Everyone in the gym, including Martin Park, would know something's up. How the hell can I justify taking out a guy who just scored thirty points in a half without missing? Smith from the *Sentinel* would have a field day with that!"

"You and your pregnant wife came in two separate cars, right Coach? They say a big rainstorm is brewing outside. You wouldn't want her vehicle slipping and sliding going home alone on Highway 441, now would you?" Roy stuck his crooked finger into Coach Berry's chest. "Gormon sits, got it?" Roy turned abruptly and headed back to the gym, leaving the flabbergasted coach standing alone in the hallway.

Coach Berry was numb, perplexed, and unfocused as he shuffled back to the bench with only fifty seconds to go before the start of the second half. Instead of conjuring up one last motivational oration in the huddle, he jotted and folded a Post-It note for his wife and had his manager send it up to her. Sheryl Berry was sitting on the top row of the bleachers, mainly so she could prop her back up against the concrete wall. Her first child was seven months in the making and practicing karate in her stomach. The note was scribbled quickly and said, "Don't go home after the game! Stay in gym!" Sheryl glanced strangely at her husband, who was shouting second half instructions to his team just as they were about to break the huddle. He looked up at her briefly and nodded with a serious look on his face.

"Kenny," said Coach Berry as he grabbed Gormon's jersey and pulled him back. "Willis is going to start the second half."

The entire Warriors team, starters and subs, looked up at the coach, and their mouths dropped open in unison.

"Coach, Kenny's got to play. He ain't missed a shot. I'll sit right here on the bench and cheer for him like I did in the first half," Willis pleaded.

"You don't want to play? What the hell kind of attitude is that, Mann? Now get your butt in the game and make a difference, you hear me?!"

Willis hopped up and joined the other four starters as they made their way onto the floor, all of them shaking their heads in confusion and muttering under their breaths. As soon as the Warriors fans saw that Kenny was on the bench, angry shouts and a few cuss words were bellowed towards the beleaguered coach. Sheryl Berry knew something was wrong. So did Willy Banks, who was standing in the doorway.

The Warriors had no answer for the Martin Park starting five in the third quarter, and Jimmy Jackson shot one for eleven. Sophomore Tyrone Banks knew it was up to him to step it up, or they would be blown right off their own home court. He ripped down rebounds from the few Martin Park missed shots, and added three thunderous dunks. Marcelus hit a few key shots, but at the end of the third quarter, Martin Park's lead had grown to twenty-four points, eighty-three to fifty-nine. All that was left was the fat lady hooking up her karaoke machine.

When Jimmy's first shot of the fourth quarter missed everything except the back wall, Coach Berry called for a timeout. He then pulled Jimmy and put Kenny back into the game. By then, the scouts were long gone, as they departed at the end of the third quarter. Roy got up and took a new seat, directly behind the coach.

"Are your windows up, Coach? I think it's raining outside." Roy's threatening sarcasm rang through Berry's ears, but he didn't flinch.

Kenny Gormon took over right where he left off in the first half. The Martin Park defense couldn't even locate Kenny as he moved with blinding speed around their two-one-two zone, hitting jumper after jumper. Meanwhile, Tyrone Banks had blocked the last three Martin Park shots in the paint, setting up three successful fast breaks for Seminole Bend and causing the defending state champs to start shooting longer shots, something they never had to do before. With two minutes and four seconds left in the game, Martin Park called timeout as their lead had sunk to ten points, eighty-nine to seventy-nine. Albeit still a daunting task against a superior team, this was the last chance opportunity the Warriors needed. During a timeout, Martin Park devised a plan to break the Seminole Bend one-two-one-one full-court press that had caused four turnovers in the quarter.

"Okay, boys," Coach Berry said calmly. "We're now going to switch to a half-court, one-three-one trap. They'll be looking to break the full-court zone by going deep, and maybe we can confuse them."

"But Coach, we're down ten! We need to keep pressure right up front," hollered Marcelus. "There's only two minutes left!"

"We'll go half-court this time down the floor on defense, and then three-quarter court trap the next, then full court man to man. But that will only work if we keep making our shots. We'll keep up that pattern until the end of the game. But you need to concentrate and always be thinking about which defense you're in. Defensive pressure is the only way we can get the ball back. Everyone needs to be on the same page, got it?"

In unison, the entire team responded, "Got it!"

Martin Park was confused! Where was the full-court pressure? As their High School All-American point guard, Clevus Mathune, dribbled across the half-court line, Willis and Marcelus clamped on the trap and forced an errant throw that Tyrone picked off. Kenny had already sprinted down the floor, and Tyrone threw a strike for an easy layup, eighty-nine to eighty-one.

Expecting now to wait for the half-court trap, Martin Park was bewildered to find the trap had moved up to three-quarters court. Johnny Jones slapped the balled away from Martin Park's Matt Russell into the hands of Willis Mann, who flipped it behind his back to Tyrone for another slam dunk! One minute and thirty-five seconds remained; however, Seminole Bend had closed the lead to six.

The full-court man to man pressure startled Martin Park again, and they couldn't get the inbounds pass in within the allotted five seconds. Another turnover! One minute and thirty seconds to go, Jones passed the ball to Kenny, who flipped it over to Willis and then broke for the basket on a give and go. Willis' pass was intercepted by Clevus, but he was immediately tackled by Tyrone. Clevus Mathune hadn't missed a free throw in his last seventeen attempts, three games ago. His first shot was nothing but net. So was his second, but the Martin Park center stepped in the lane too soon, nullifying the basket and making the score ninety to eighty-three.

Jones again inbounded the ball to Willis, who dribbled and streaked elegantly through the Martin Park full-court zone, then cut towards the corner before lobbing a perfect pass to Tyrone for his sixth dunk of the night. Score: ninety to eighty-five.

So why are they falling back, away from the full-court press again, thought Clevus? Those damn Warriors were now back to a half-court trap. Clevus dribbled the ball just short of the half-court line, then stopped his forward motion, but kept dribbling. He was going to wear off the ten backcourt seconds that he was allowed before penetrating into the half-court zone. As the clock showed fifty-five seconds remaining, Clevus put his shoulder down and drove like a madman towards the basket. Tyrone just waited in the lane with his arms up high. Clevus hit Tyrone like a bowling ball hits wooden pins, but Tyrone didn't budge. The ball lofted towards the basket and bounced off, but it didn't matter. Both officials had blown their whistle, placed one hand behind their head, and pointed toward the Warriors basket: charging on Clevus!

Martin Park called a timeout for two reasons, the first to let the men in stripes learn some new choice words from the litany of assistant coaches the Martin Park taxpayers were paying for, the second to set up a tight box and one zone. Four players would form a box in the lane, and Clevus would stick to Kenny Gormon like glue.

Ten seconds later, a confused Warriors team called timeout. They were still down five, but now only forty-one seconds were left in the game. Coach Berry called for a back pick on the zone and a dangerous lob over the top to Johnny Jones. That was the last man Martin Park would have guessed to get the ball, and Johnny's shot from ten feet out on the baseline rolled around the rim twice before swirling through the net. Ninety to eighty-seven, with twenty-seven seconds left to play.

The three-quarter-court trap would have been easily broken by Martin Park; however, Johnny Jones forgot where he was going on defense after making the crucial shot, and he accidentally got in the way of the Martin Park sideline pass! In one airborne athletic move, Johnny intercepted it and then tossed it over to Willis as he was about to fly headfirst into the stands. With only twenty-two seconds left, Willis couldn't wait for Johnny to return to the offensive set, so he dribbled into Martin Park territory, four on five. Marcelus set a perfect back pick on Clevus Mathune, freeing up Kenny for an easy twenty-foot jumper. As usual, nothing but net. Martin Park was up one, ninety to eighty-nine with only fourteen seconds remaining.

Clevus' ball-handling skills were a sight to behold as he weaved through the full-court man-to-man press, avoiding defenders that were trying to foul him. Finally, with five seconds to go, Tyrone grabbed his shirt and hung on. The whistle blew, foul number five, the last one allowed, on Tyrone. Seminole Bend called their final timeout.

"If Clevus misses, we need to set another pick for Kenny. They'll be watching for Marcelus, so Johnny, you screen for him," Coach said. His voice was beginning to fade from all the shouting.

Marcelus looked down at the floor, shook his head, and muttered, "Don't matter. Clevus never misses. Dang, we came close."

"None of that talk on my bench, ya hear me!" barked Tyrone. He reached over and grabbed Marcelus by the jersey and brandished him. "We do the job and don't ever give up!"

Clevus made the first free throw, and then smiled and winked at his opponents. The official tossed him the ball for the shot that, barring a wing and a prayer, would wrap up win number seventy-four in a row. But as soon as he received it from the official, his teammate George Bernd left his spot in the lane to fall back into a prevent defense. The whistle blew for the dead-ball violation—and a last chance for the Warriors. Martin Park called their final time out. George Bernd was ordered to sit on the bench by his coach, who had just grown red horns and a pointy tail!

On his green basketball court clipboard, Coach Berry assumed some sort of full-court pressure would be applied with only five seconds to go, so he designed another back pick play for Kenny to be set by Johnny Jones around mid-court. The officials blew the whistle and handed the ball to Marcelus under the Martin Park basket. But as Marcelus was trying to make the inbounds pass, he saw that Kenny was now guarded closely by two Martin Park defenders. Johnny couldn't pick both of them! He wanted to call timeout but knew the Warriors were all out of them. His pass went to Willis, who was wide open at half court thanks to Kenny's double team. Kenny also realized that a single pick would do no good, so he feigned a dash for the basket, stopped suddenly, and reversed direction. His defenders couldn't stop on a dime with him, but they tried to hustle back to Kenny after both had momentarily slipped on the court. Willis passed Kenny the ball at the top of the key, and as the buzzer sounded, Kenny's shot floated like slow motion in a perfect arc to the hoop. Swish, but his right foot was inside the three-point line—game tied! However, as Kenny had reached the peak of his jump, Clevus tried desperately to block the shot and hit Kenny's wrist when the ball was released. Whistle blew, foul on Clevus Mathune! No time on the clock: score even at ninety-one apiece.

Because the play clock had expired, all the players took a position at half court to watch the free throw attempt. While Kenny walked to the line, Clevus shouted at him, "Come on, honky, hit the wall!"

Kenny dribbled twice at the line, then stopped. He stepped back from the line, turned his head, and glanced over at Clevus. Then he smiled and winked, stepped back to the line, dribbled twice again, and swished the free throw that ended the longest winning streak in Florida high school history.

Kenny's teammates and others in the gym mobbed him, tackled him to the floor, and piled on high! The cheerleaders were waiting for the pile to unfold, ready with hugs and kisses. Classmates who had avoided the mob danced and pranced on the scuffed gym floor. The Martin Park team sat on the bench with their heads in their hands.

Coach Berry looked up at the top row of the bleachers to blow his wife a kiss, but Sheryl was nowhere to be found. Either was Roy Jackson.

CHAPTER 22

Friday, February 12, 1982
9:30 p.m.

Coach Brett Berry took home $928 a month for teaching history and coaching basketball at Seminole Bend High School. And even if the coach's wife happened to be working, which she wasn't, Uncle Sam wasn't bound to get rich from the Berry family tax base. The Berry's rented a two-bedroom, one-bath, 980 square-foot cement block house that resembled a Civil War munitions armory. The fortress on Twenty-Fourth Avenue had no garage but plenty of cockroaches. A few neighbors raised an eyebrow when the Berry's told them that they just purchased a new two-story, four-bedroom, three-bath, wood-frame home north of town. The beautiful dwelling was located behind a few palmetto trees on the seventh hole of the Seminole Bend Golf Course, but even the Berry's close friends had no clue about the exact location. The Berrys hadn't concocted a viable story that would explain how they could afford an expensive house on their minimal salary, so they simply didn't invite guests over.

Just a few new homes scattered the area that ran parallel to the seventh hole, and those abodes became an attractive nuisance to the Titleist and Top Flight dimpled balls that were sent flying into backyards by the slashing slicers of the Seminole Bend golf world. The nine-hole course and country club, situated about twelve miles north of town and right smack dab in the middle of nowhere, attracted many of the prominent and not-so-prominent citizens of the county. It was a great place to play golf, but more importantly, a wonderful hideaway for poker, beer, and Monday Night Football say nothing of a perfect way to escape a nagging wife. The new residences being built were prime topics for the nineteenth hole imbibers.

Arguments replaced good sportsmanship all along the seventh hole as golfers found their balls lying just a few feet on the other side of the red and white out-of-bounds stakes in the lovely landscaped yards of the new homeowners. No one wanted to take a penalty stroke drop when just a few years ago the duffers wouldn't have been out-of-bounds. Before "them damn homes" were built, golfers could merely hack their way back onto the fairway, or do it the Irish way with a few Mulligans, of course.

Set back from the course a bit and mostly hidden by the palmetto trees, Berry's new home may never have been noticed if it wasn't for a large swimming pool being dug in the backyard. The wrap-a-round oak wood deck could easily be seen looking back from the tee box on the eighth hole. Teachers' salaries were public information, and most everyone in town wanted to know where their hard-earned taxes were being spent. So every faculty member, from the principal on down to the school crossing guard, had their annual income printed on a sheet of paper and handed out to every citizen in attendance by the board of education at their first meeting each August. Knowing how much Coach Berry grossed, then considering the new house he was building, caused rumors that either someone in the family died and left the Berrys a good deal of money or Roy Jackson was up to something again. As the basketball season progressed and it was evident that Jimmy Jackson never took a rest regardless of his production on the court, the latter was most likely the truth. But still, it was hard to believe that Coach Berry could be bought. Both he and his wife were solid citizens and dang near patron saints of the local Catholic Church. They both taught Sunday school and organized most of the fundraising efforts for the diocese. Father O'Shea, the fastest talker on this side of Dublin, would even take twenty-seven seconds out of his twenty-nine-minute church service to thank the Berrys every Sunday. That is, of course, unless a hurricane was coming, or the Miami Dolphins were on TV. Then Father made sure all the good Catholic folks were back in their cars headed for home in twelve minutes flat!

US Highway 441 ran straight north out of Seminole Bend with barely a crook in the road until you got just outside of Rabbit Hollow. The road was heavily traveled in the winter when the snowbirds began their migration down the turnpike heading for the land of largemouth bass and crappies, better known to Southerners as speckled perch. Although it was just two lanes wide, it was a safe concrete road with a few cracks here and there. Of course, you needed to be ready to dodge the last second passer, usually someone in a Chevy pickup with a Confederate flag pasted on his rear window who had no patience for old folks that dwelt most of the year north of the Mason Dixon line.

Sheryl Berry had frequently driven the twelve-mile stretch of US 441 in both the daylight hours and at nighttime, in the searing hot sun and the pouring rain. Since she became pregnant, Sheryl kept her vehicle at fifty miles-per-hour in the fifty-five zone, just to make sure her unborn child would never be at risk. And Coach Berry changed his Ford L-Series pickup truck's oil and had the tires rotated and checked every three thousand miles, just to make sure everything was running correctly, and the vehicle was safe. He couldn't wait to play one-on-one with his future son.

* * * * *

Willy Banks had watched the game standing behind two teachers who were supposed to be supervising the school grounds, but got too wrapped up in the biggest basketball game in Warriors history to pay much attention to the hallways. Willy wanted to be in the bleachers cheering on his nephew Tyrone and his alma mater, but he knew Roy Jackson would be there as well. By now, Willy was sure that Roy knew he had escaped the swamp alive and would most likely be back hunting him down. He wasn't afraid of Roy, but he didn't plan on being an easy target.

After the biggest win of his life, Coach Berry was frantic. As players and fans lifted him on their shoulders and began to parade their beloved coach around the gym, Berry was searching the arena for his wife. Willy noticed the coach's eyes had tears starting to form around the swollen sockets, but they weren't filled with liquid drops of joy. Willy was curious why it appeared that there was a look of panic transmitting from the coach's flushed face as he nervously made quick glances back and forth. He was definitely conveying a look of fear, but no one seemed to notice amid the wildest celebration in Warriors history.

As Coach was gently placed back on the floor while sustaining a load of slaps on the back and hugs from the unknown, Willy made his way forward and grabbed the coach's wrist as he was about to start jogging for the exit.

"What's up, Coach?" Willy asked inquisitively.

"What do you mean, 'what's up,' Willy? I just want to get home."

"Why the rush, and by the way, where's Sheryl?"

"I can't talk right now, Willy. I've got to run!"

"She's in trouble, isn't she, Coach?" Willy turned the coach around so the two men's faces were just several inches apart.

"I don't know, Willy!" Coach Berry said aggressively. "I've got to find out."

"Let me help you, damn it! Tell me what you know!" Willy was beginning to see a picture in his mind that he didn't like.

"I can't right now. Listen, I'll stop down to the station in the morning, and we'll chat, okay, Willy?"

Coach Berry's jog became a sprint as he exited the gym and jumped into his 1963 orange Plymouth Fury, the same car he used to drive to his own high school back in the early seventies. The car was originally red, but several winters of salted slush on US Highway 119 in Pennsylvania transformed it into a faded rust bucket, but it was and always would be Brett's pride and joy. No air conditioner, no radio, and a stick shift that slipped into second gear when it dang well felt like it! But it was superbly equipped with an eight-track player, thanks to a small scholarship Coach Berry received after graduating from Uniontown High.

The 225 cubic inch slant six Fury did zero to sixty in about four minutes as long as the mosquitoes didn't get caught in the carburetor. Coach was out of the parking lot in a flash, speeding north onto US 441 in the light rain. Willy pulled out behind him in the squad car and kept a safe distance. No need to startle the already rattled coach.

The flames could be seen from three miles away. Willy radioed headquarters to see if a fire had been reported anywhere in the north county. When the night dispatcher told him "no," Willy put on his flashing red lights and zipped past Coach Berry's Fury. Coach didn't pull over, nor did he even slow down. He was probably thinking the same thing that Willy was.

The Ford pickup truck was almost vertical, lying ten feet down in the culvert that was used to cross Brahman cattle under the highway. It was engulfed in a towering blaze of orange, red, and blue, and the heat seared Willy's face as he rushed to get close to the wholly destroyed vehicle with a small fire extinguisher. Coach Berry ran up behind him, then seeing that it was his own Ford truck, he tried to pass Willy and make his way to the door. Willy clamped his enormous arms around the coach's chest and jerked him back from the inferno.

"Let me go, damn it!" Coach barked.

"You can't get into your truck with those flames, you'll kill yourself," Willy yelled back. "Take my extinguisher while I call the fire department!"

"Hurry, Willy. Damn it, hurry up!"

Willy raced to his squad car and called in the emergency.

As Coach Berry frantically sprayed the wreckage with white foam, he knew the impossible nature of the task-at-hand would not prevent the inevitable death of his wife and unborn child. He ripped off his shirt and sprayed the remaining liquid from the extinguisher on it, thoroughly soaking the cotton garment. He then tossed the extinguisher down into the ditch. Coach wrapped the wet shirt around his left hand and wrist and hurried to the door while shielding his eyes with his right hand. As he fought back the intense heat while trying to rip open the crunched door frame, he could see through the window his wife's head lying helplessly at a slant against the steering wheel. There was no hair or skin to be found, the pupils of the cadaver's eyes staring directly into the coach's. Coach Berry yanked on the door handle with a reserve of strength fed by pure adrenaline. The door was jammed and sealed tight and very difficult to maneuver due to the awkward angle from the truck's vertical position. As the coach made one last futile attempt to disengage the door handle, the pickup began to tip on its front fender and fall sideways toward him. Coach lost his footing on the oily culvert bank, and then slipped and fell on his back. The Ford truck's 1,500-pound frame slammed on top of him, and the flames instantly ignited his hair.

Willy saw what was happening and rushed back to save the town hero, but to no avail. He knelt down on the ridge of the embankment overlooking the debris of mangled steel and burning flesh, both inside the truck and out, and he grabbed the back of his head, sobbing uncontrollably. He heard the sirens in the distance, but the only thing Willy could do now was offer a prayer.

The next few minutes seemed like an eternity for Willy as three red fire engines stormed the scene of the accident. Fire Chief Bobby Williams quickly directed his crew, and within seconds, hundreds of gallons of water were emptying from the belly of the truck onto what was left of the Ford pickup.

Five minutes later, the entire crew of fifteen volunteer firemen hopped down into the culvert and pushed the truck until it rolled off Coach Berry and flipped into an upright position. The ambulance from Gregorson General had just arrived, and two paramedics raced to the coach who was lying motionless on his back, the skin on his face seared down to his skull. No pulse, no movement, no life.

Meanwhile, the fire crew had managed to pry open the door to the pickup. As they saw the ashen remains of the driver, three men pulled back and dropped to their knees, vomiting on the damp ground. Soon they would climb back up to their hoses and complete the soak down of the accident scene. Many of the firemen remembered back a few days earlier and thought about the eerie similarity of Calvin Potts' death by burning flesh with what now lay before them in the culvert.

Too many coincidences lately for Willy Banks to believe, and the common denominator was Roy Jackson. But the game was getting very dangerous, and Willy knew others would get hurt and killed if he pursued Roy without a lot of caution and assistance. The legal system did not appear to be the answer because corruption was the tune singing throughout south-central Florida. As much as it appalled him to do so, Willy knew he had to lay low until he found the solution.

The coroner pronounced Coach Berry and his wife deceased, with the time of death being only seven minutes apart. The basketball celebration in the gym was still going on. An autopsy would follow.

CHAPTER 23

Friday, February 19, 1982

11:00 a.m.

The entire town and then some attended the memorial service for Coach Berry and his wife. Seemed like every high school basketball coach in southern Florida was there, as were several college athletic dignitaries from major Division I schools, including the University of Miami, Florida, and Florida State. In his short time as the head basketball coach at Seminole Bend High School, Coach Berry had turned out top prep performers who were gobbled up at the collegiate level.

The *Miami Sentinel* printed a detailed description of the accident, a quarter-page obituary, and a notice for the ensuing memorial service in their Sunday edition. The report of the crash by a beat writer would have been plenty, but several photos accompanied the write-up that left little to the imagination of the *Sentinel's* readers.

The deaths of Brett and Sheryl Berry were given top billing and plenty of coverage by the state's most widely read newspaper. Interestingly though, there was never any mention of Calvin Potts' fatal accident on the same day his wife was murdered, or the snowbird who was run over in the BoldMart parking lot, or the huge, bloodied cowboy found dead in the hardware store: all casualties that were considered "coincidental happenings" to everyone in Seminole Bend except for Willy Banks.

Brett's mom, Janet Berry, was devastated and extremely depressed. She told her husband, Lew, that she was too heartbroken to make the trip to Florida for the memorial service in the Seminole Bend gymnasium. The burial of what was left of Brett and Sheryl's corpses would take place back in Berry's home state of Pennsylvania. But each time Brett's father would call to make arrangements to transport the ashen remains northward, Seminole Bend coroner Cliff Sutton would delay the shipment.

"Something strange that I need to clear up before I can give the okay for release," was Coroner Sutton's latest response. Both Janet and Lew were miffed, but they were also beginning to form a variety of suspicions in their minds. They had been told by Sheriff Bonty that it was just an awful accident, so why another delay?

"What's going on down there, Doctor Sutton?" Lew Berry asked into the phone.

"Well, Mr. Berry, this is difficult for me to tell you. As you're probably aware, the only anatomical vestiges found at the scene were ashes and charred skeletal residue. Your son's remains seem okay; however, Sheryl's don't seem quite right."

"What the hell do you mean by that?!"

"Well, the length and thickness of the skeletal parts found inside the vehicle seem to fit a person who is in the six-foot range. I believe your daughter-in-law was about five feet, eight inches, isn't that correct?"

"I guess so. So what are you trying to say?" Lew Berry asked with a puzzled look on his face that the good coroner could only imagine from a thousand or so miles away.

"Quite frankly, I'm not sure. At this point, I'm just curious. Experts from Tallahassee are coming down to measure what's left of the bone residue. If they tell me the person in the car was six feet tall, well, you probably know what I'm saying." The doctor hoped Mr. Berry was getting the picture.

"So what you're trying to tell me is the person in Sheryl's car may not be her? Do you know how confusing this is to me? What happened that night, anyway?"

“I suggest you give the sheriff’s department a call to answer that question, Mr. Berry.”

“If what you’re saying is correct and the bones are enlarged, is it still possible it could be Sheryl’s body? I mean, with the intense heat, could the bones expand or something?” Lew Berry was trying his best to make this just a horrible accident and not something out of the occult.

“I’d rather answer that when I know what the experts have to say. They are coming today and may want to interview the emergency responders. However, all of them are at Brett and Sheryl’s memorial right now. With a rush, we should have the results in forty-eight hours or less. I’ll give you a call as soon as I know something.”

“I’m not going anywhere until I hear from you. Please call immediately!”

* * * * *

The final two games of the Warriors basketball regular season would be forfeited to the opposing teams. Greg James, the assistant coach, had reluctantly assumed the head coaching job left vacant by Brett Berry. He had the dubious duty of trying to assemble a group of heartbroken high school athletes and have them ready for playoffs. No doubt, Martin Park would once again be looming on the horizon during the sectional tournaments.

Following the memorial service in the gym, Tyrone Banks sauntered down the sidewalk to his Volkswagen Bug that was parked in the high school lot. Tyrone was still four months away from his sixteenth birthday, but he had his driver’s permit, and because of his size, most of the lawmen around Seminole Bend figured him to be of age to drive alone. His uncle Willy knew better but wasn’t about to spill the beans seeing he helped Tyrone pay for the Bug. Jenny Jackson jogged down the walk, grabbed Tyrone’s elbow from behind, and whirled him about. “Hey, big boy,” she smiled with a provocative look that gleamed from her sparkling blue eyes down to her glossy lips.

"Jenny, not here, not now. I'm sure your old man is watching somewhere."

Jenny locked her left arm into Tyrone's right one and led him down to his car. "Daddy's not here. He wasn't interested in the service," she said, somewhat disappointed and somewhat embarrassed.

"I'm shocked, I mean I knew he didn't give a damn about Coach Berry, but with all the university coaches hanging out, I just thought he'd be sucking up!" Tyrone rolled his eyes and looked away from Jenny.

Trying to get Tyrone's mind off Coach Berry and his wife, Jenny said, "Come on, Ty. Let's go down to the lake. Nobody's using our pontoon. We can catch a few rays and a few crappies to boot."

"Do I really look like a tan is going to do me much good, Jenny?" Tyrone chuckled as he brushed his ebony skin with his fingertips.

Jenny hopped in the front passenger seat of the tiny car, and both doors closed simultaneously. Jimmy Jackson happened to notice his sister and Tyrone getting into the Volkswagen as he walked out the gym door and peered down the sidewalk through the array of black suits and dresses of those folks just leaving the service. He shook his head and walked down to his own car, certainly wondering what Jenny was up to.

CHAPTER 24

Friday, February 19, 1982
8:00 p.m.

Visibility was near zero as the Trans South Airline's jet taxied to Runway 36R at Miami International Airport. In the winter and spring, tropical southern Florida rarely saw a torrential downpour like the one today. Those types of cloudbursts usually saved themselves for the summer months when immense precipitation became an almost daily late afternoon event. Air Traffic Control advised a delay but did not demand it. Thus, the pilots could choose their own course of action. Captain Harry Hutter, best known by his aviator colleagues as "Hurricane Hutter" due to his enjoyment of gliding several tons of metal through dark, cumulous clouds for the sheer purpose of providing a terrifying turbulent landing to high paying customers, was at the controls. Tonight, Harry thought he could stir up some excitement by initiating a thrilling takeoff into the wet and wild southern Florida atmosphere. Harry said many folks pay astronomical prices at amusement parks to ride roller coasters that dip and dive and twist and turn at heart attack speeds, so why not put a little fun into business travel?

*****

Following customer complaints, Harry had been written up for several company violations in the past, but Trans South execs knew damn well he was the best pilot they had. His planes never arrived late to their destination, which made corporate travelers ecstatic, unless ground control forced a delay in the departure city due to mechanical problems. The Federal Aviation Administration could never ground Harry because when air traffic controllers required a particular path or route be followed, he did so without argument. But when the ATCs merely suggested a smoother altitude, he knew he had the option to follow their directions—or mix up a few drinks in the coach cabin with the kind of turbulence that only the Florida prevailing winds could provide. Not many pilots had the self-confidence that Harry had, so Trans South assigned him to primarily short flights in and out of the southeastern United States where the weather could be a challenge in any season.

Three years ago, Harry was deadheading in an exit row seat to West Palm Beach from Atlanta when the jet he was riding in nosed-dived somewhere over the Okefenokee Swamp in southern Georgia. He knew right away that major engine failure had occurred, and amidst the screams of all 108 passengers and dangling oxygen masks, he made his way through the cabin and noticed the pilot lying face down in the galley and the copilot in the cockpit with his head resting on the steering wheel. The airplane was on autopilot at 38,000 feet when the copilot had become ill and passed out from some lousy fish he had eaten a couple of hours earlier in an airport restaurant. Knowing the flight attendants were busy serving up passengers, the pilot left the cabin to grab a bottled water from the galley for his partner when he heard a loud "bang" and the plane began to free fall. An unsecured coffee pot landed on the pilot's head knocking him unconscious, and nasty hot Maxwell House began rolling down the back of his neck. Harry quickly jumped into the captain's seat and noticed engine number one was on fire. Something had triggered an automatic shutdown of all three engines, and Harry couldn't get them restarted. He grabbed the controls, pulled up on the flaps while depressing the right rudder, and the plane began to level off. Harry radioed the

Valdosta Control Tower and mandated them to get the Georgia State Patrol to cordon off a five-mile section of Interstate 75 and to do so pronto! As red lights and sirens were scattering cars down into the ditches, he glided the aircraft to a smooth landing, however, the reverse thrusters were not operable. Remaining calm in the face of horror, Harry veered the jet into a muddy field of cotton on the east side of the freeway. After bouncing belly first from the ditch to the field, the plane's landing gear snapped, but the aircraft slid to a halt, and no one was injured—at least not physically! Members of the Georgia house and senate discussed petitioning Harry for a Congressional Medal of Honor for saving the lives of everyone on board, including seven passengers who were Navy seamen. Unfortunately, the Georgia State Patrol wanted to hang him from the closest tree for endangering the lives of everyone on the road. The *Atlanta Constitution* printed a front-page story that made Harry out to be such a local hero that President Carter invited him to the White House for a little southern hospitality and a huge thank you for saving all those Georgia citizens. The National Transportation and Safety Board didn't want to ruin a presidentially-endorsed, heartwarming story. Thus, the investigation was closed in two days, and Trans South quickly dismantled the aircraft. To this day, no one knows what happened to the plane's engines or why it went into a nosedive, but Trans South reservation agents received an idiotic request from several customers: "Book me on a plane that Harry Hutter is flying!"

* * * * *

For a second time, Miami Air Traffic Control advised Harry to delay the stormy evening departure, and Harry's reply was, "Is that a suggestion or an order?"

Mustaf Dasani, an old Egyptian fighter pilot, currently the head of air traffic control in Miami, and Harry's golf partner every Thursday at the Doral Country Club put Harry on a private frequency and responded, "Who can overrule Hurricane Hutter? I believe that would only be Allah, no?"

"Thought so." Back on the required public broadcast frequency, Harry adjusted his headset and proffered, "Trans South 256 requesting a thumbs up for departure on Runway 36R."

A second glance at the atmospheric conditions on the tower's weather radar showed severely threatening thunderstorms with lightning bolts, hail, and high whirling winds moving rapidly over land from the Gulf of Mexico, approximately seventy-five miles east of Marco Island. That put the storm front only twenty-six miles from MIA. Mustaf sensed imminent danger lurked to the west but wasn't sure he could wrestle control of TS256 from his stubborn friend Harry while it sat on the runway ready for takeoff.

"Roger, 256. Advise winds swirling in a southeasterly direction between twenty and thirty knots. All inbound flights are now on a holding pattern until the weather relaxes. Bayou 667 heavy has been diverted to Orlando. You're clear for takeoff, but we strongly suggest a temp delay 256."

"Roger, tower. But a little drizzle won't ground this bird. Got ZynzoTech Corporation boys and girls on board who need to make their Frankfurt connection by 10:30. Can't have Big Zee twiddling their thumbs on the Miami runway when the Germans need a little technology on their desks, now can we?" Harry pushed down the throttle, and the turbo engines lurched the jet westward down the barely visible runway. "140 knots, roll back, Johnny."

Johnny Berger was the only copilot who enjoyed riding with Harry. He was a single, recently retired Navy F-16 pilot who thought flying upside-down was the ultimate life experience. Johnny said someday he would ask the passengers if they wanted to try that trick and see if they could all agree! But today, even Johnny was leery about taking off in this weather.

Johnny lowered the flaps while Harry pulled back on the yoke, lifting the nose off the runway. Ominous black clouds blanketed the horizon with frequent lightning bolts illuminating the night sky. Harry radioed Mustaf as the back wheels lifted off the concrete. "Miami Tower, this is Trans South 256 requesting a radar lock to get us through the burnt marshmallows up ahead. Can't imagine any other brave soul trying to fly in this weather, though."

"Roger, 256. We detect a small northbound aircraft about fifty miles south-southwest at 3,000 feet and heading in your direction. It appears to be gaining altitude to try and get above the weather. We're attempting to hail it as we speak."

"Roger, Miami. I see a bleep on our screen, too. I'll go with your lock."

Wind shear caught the jet's right wing and caused the airplane to dip during its incline, which of course, caused hands to be folded on the passenger's laps. The all-powerful ZynzoTech execs who control most everything that exists in the modern technological world were suddenly at the mercy of one Harry Hurricane Hutter. But a little turbulence is Harry's joy in life, and all he could do was chuckle at the utter quietness that had engulfed the passenger cabin as the plane soared towards the heavens. He thought about doing a little shaky-shake, rock and roll maneuver, but didn't really want the smell of vomit penetrating into the cockpit. Thus, he stabilized the jet back on track and radioed to Mustaf.

"Miami Tower, what's the status of that small plane?"

"Trans South 256, hold your course. We haven't been able to reach the plane, but at this point, your flight path will take you well over the top. Doubtful if that plane will go above 6,000 feet. Advise you to ascend to 12,000 and wait for instructions."

"Roger, Miami. We're pulling up hard as we speak."

Trans South 256 reached the billowy black clouds, and raindrops were scattering over the cockpit windshield and passenger portholes. Creaking noises could be heard throughout the cabin as wing and fuselage metal stretched and retracted into place in unison with the violent wind. From the back of the plane, a faint "Oh Lord Jesus" could be heard. Many of the travelers tried to focus on a page in their paperback to keep their minds off Harry's thrill ride.

"Trans South 256, our little buddy has changed course again. Please set a new course heading to—" The voice in Harry's headset went dead. He quickly looked over to Johnny Berger, who could only shrug his shoulders.

"Did you get that heading, Johnny?"

"Negative, Harry. It cut off."

"Trans South 256, this is Miami Tower. We cut you off because our radar is dead. We're trying to switch you over to Sarasota Tower, but they're not responding. Can you see the plane on your screen?"

"Negative, Miami. The turbulent weather is sending up white blotches all over our screen. Can't tell if any are small planes or just big birds."

"Hold tight on your heading, 256, we're also requesting assistance from Fort Lauderdale. Can't seem to get ahold of anyone!"

"Damn it, Mustaf, we can't see a thing, and I got a bad feeling about our present course!"

"Relax, Harry, we're working on it as quickly as possible." So much for FAA regulations and proper radio communication protocol. Harry and Mustaf were friends, and things were becoming serious. They both needed the comfort of calling each other by first names.

Although the wind didn't want to cooperate, Harry was masterful at keeping the metal bird on course. However, with every screech, cabin prayers were bountiful, trusting that God would make sure the wings didn't fall off.

"Mayday, Miami Tower. This is PanMexico 441 requesting immediate landing clearance. We have a rupture in our fuel line, and we'll be running on fumes soon!" The PanMexico jet from Cancun had been in a holding pattern over the

Everglades with twelve other planes waiting for the weather to clear when the pilot noticed a rapid drop on his fuel gauge. A warning light alerted the rupture.

"Roger Mex 441, however, you probably heard we have no radar capacity at the moment to bring you in. Are you able to reach Sarasota or Fort Lauderdale Tower?"

"Roger, Miami, but they are having the same problem you are. Seems the radars are jammed!"

"Do you have any visual, 441?"

"Negative, Miami. No visual for your runways. There is a slight break in the clouds just ahead, so I'm requesting a manual approach that will bring us in under the clouds."

"Hold on 441. You have a Trans South on departure with no radar assistance."

"No can do, Miami! My warning light is flashing red. I can't keep us up here any longer!" With that, the PanMexico pilot began his rapid, blind descent into Miami.

"Trans South 256, we have an emergency on approach. Can't advise, Harry, because I can't see either of you!"

"Oh shit, Mustaf! I'm coming back in! No choice if I don't know what's up here keeping me company!"

"Your call, 256. Good luck, Harry."

"Let's go, Johnny. Let our ZynzoTech folks know what's happening and prepare to break out the diapers!" With that, Harry made a sharp bank southward while the wind monster grabbed and yanked on both wings. Harry could barely see a small crack in the clouds just above as he tried to level off amidst severe turbulence that shook his bird silly. But he didn't see the PanMexico jet soaring through the break at 350 miles-per-hour.

The blast could be heard up the coast to Stuart, and the ground shook with earthquake type tremors. Metal and luggage and shoes and body parts showered on to the sugar cane fields below.

"Trans South 256, can you read?! Harry, are you there?! Damn it, Harry, come in! PanMexico 441, can YOU read?!"

Mustaf repeated the request several times, each shout out more intense and desperate than the previous one. Finally, discerning the obvious, Mustaf took off his headset and dropped his head into his hands. The entire Miami tower became eerily silent. Mustaf fought back the anguish from the loss of his friend and those onboard both aircraft and forced himself to call nine-one-one.

As red lights and sirens converged from all directions to the outskirts of Miami, a small unidentified floatplane crossed northward over Lake Okeechobee, turned off its signal lights, and began an approach to land on the swamp adjacent to Roy Jackson's ranch. Just before the pilot landed, he reached over to hit the switch that would turn back on the jammed radar controls in Miami, Fort Lauderdale, West Palm Beach, and Sarasota.

The lights flickered on the screens in the Miami tower, and Mustaf quickly locked in the positions of the commercial aircraft that were holding over the Everglades. He radioed Fort Lauderdale to request that the planes be diverted there and then called the head of Miami operations to advise a shut down until emergency crews could secure the crash area.

Mustaf rolled his leather chair back from the screens and folded his hands in deep thought. Cal Swenson, the second in charge in the Miami tower, walked over to Mustaf and pulled up a chair next to him. "Sorry about Harry, Mustaf. It wasn't your fault."

"I could have ordered him not to fly! Damn well was my fault, Cal, and you know it!"

Cal reached out his arm and put his hand affectionately on Mustaf's shoulder. He then scooted his chair in front of Mustaf's and looked him in the eyes. "I know this isn't the best time to talk about it, but something's seriously wrong with our radar unit. This is now the seventh outage we've had in the past two months."

"Yes, I know, but every time the SignalNav boys check it out, they find nothing. And they find nothing in Fort

Lauderdale, West Palm, and Sarasota either, yet we all lose radar at the same time. Fortunately, up until now, nothing's happened. But the FAA needs to shut us all down until they figure out what's wrong."

Cal shook his head. "Too much tourism revenue lost if they do that. The president would never allow it. Florida is a key state for his re-election bid."

"If the country ever found out that the FAA knew we had a problem and just ignored it, thus costing hundreds of lives, the re-election bid would be over much quicker!" Mustaf pushed himself to his feet and walked aimlessly to a window and gazed out on the rain-soaked runways below. He then stared up into the still dark clouds and pondered, "What radar connection do the four airports have in common anyway? We're all on our own frequency, right?"

"Yes, but the echo effect is the same for everyone. We all use the same satellite beacon," Cal replied but was beginning to understand where Mustaf was going with his question.

"So, if there's a break in the radio beacon, it would have nothing to do with our receivers." Mustaf raced back to his own master control station, just about knocking Cal over. He punched in a few keys on the computer keyboard, then pressed *PRINT*.

Cal followed Mustaf to his desk and peered over his shoulder. "What are you thinking, Mustaf?"

"I want to print out the history of the ten minutes before the radar outage and compare notes with the other six outages. Do we have the dates and times stored somewhere?"

"Have to. The NTSB required the logs to be stored in a safe place. They're in the Sentry cabinet in the back room. I'll get them for you."

"How far back can we pull up historical data and screen blimps, Cal?"

"Should be able to go back a year."

"Thanks. Get those dates for me, please."

"You got it, boss." Cal headed for the storage room.

*****

An hour later, Cal laid out the log sheets for the previous six outages on Mustaf's desk. Both he and Mustaf could not understand why the FAA had not examined them for commonalities. No, instead, the FAA would just log the dates of the outages and require SignalNav Enterprises to send service reps to check their high tech pricey instruments for malfunctions. For each outage, SignalNav claimed the problem stemmed from the ZynzoTech mainframe transmitter sporadically shutting down, not with their radar or satellite equipment. ZynzoTech would send service folks to investigate and then claim it was SignalNav's fault. The FAA told both mega-companies to get together and fix the problem, and that was the end of the FAA official report. No follow up was ever assigned. No one compared notes until now, and simple logic would tell you that it shouldn't have been Mustaf and Cal making those comparisons.

The screen dot coordinates of flights in the air over southern Florida were posted on the black printout that looked like an amateur photographer's picture of the night sky with no moon but plenty of stars. There were four pictures of the radar screen on a page, automatically registered every fifteen seconds, and Mustaf had asked for the last ten minutes before each outage. Every dot had a tiny box next to it that listed its coordinates as well as the flight name and number if it were known.

In the early evening, outbound Miami air traffic, for the most part, was headed east over the Atlantic to Europe, or south across the Caribbean to South America. However, inbound flights were arriving from all directions as vacationers packed the clean, white sandy beaches year-round, especially in the winter.

By looking at the printout, Mustaf and Cal couldn't find any glaring evidence of commonalities, then again, they weren't sure exactly what it was they were looking for. Mustaf headed back to his computer and once again punched in a few keys that displayed a spreadsheet of latitude and longitude coordinates, flight names and numbers, and dates and times. He decided to do a search of common coordinates, thinking that maybe an interference associated with an aircraft flying through the satellite beacon was causing the outages by breaking a tracing line. That would be similar to when an object pierces the beacon generated by a police radar that is fixed on an automobile's radar detector, and the reading in the squad car goes blank.

No luck. Mustaf stared at the spreadsheet, then back to the radar screen printouts. Once again, he glanced at the spreadsheet then back to the printout. His eyes noticed something, but his brain wasn't registering it. Then it came to him, and he punched away at his keyboard.

"What's up?" Cal wanted to know.

"Not sure. I'm going to do a search of the aircraft names and numbers," Mustaf replied.

"Doubtful any of the same aircraft were approaching Miami because the times were different," Cal said with a puzzled look on his face. "And even so, what would that prove?"

"I don't know, but I have a strange feeling that I can't pinpoint at the moment, Cal."

The search provided only one match, yet that match was the same for the dates that each outage occurred: UNKNOWN AIRCRAFT.

"Bingo, there's our match!" Mustaf shouted.

"Mustaf, have you lost a few particles up here," Cal said skeptically while pointing at the temples on his own head. "There's always many unknown aircraft flying the skies, primarily the small Cessnas that our air traffic controllers don't bother to log because of time constraints."

"That's not news to me, Cal, but there might be more to this. Call Al and have him come in and cover for me. I'm heading out to the crash site." Mustaf pulled his NTSB pass card from his desk and headed to the door. He paused, then changed directions and walked warily over to the tower's window and saw the burning mass in the distance. The pounding rain had done little to eliminate the flames. The shock and grief finally overcame Mustaf, and he pounded his fists on the glass while tears dripped down his nose. "Damn it," he whispered to himself, "You were the best, Harry."

CHAPTER 25

Friday, February 19, 1982
8:30 p.m.

"Daddy's an asshole."

"Girl, don't look this way for an argument," Tyrone sputtered back at Jenny as he watched the red and white bobber dip under the surface and pop back up. It was early evening, and an incessant chop on Lake Okeechobee made it difficult to know if the wind was the cause of the bobber's movement, or if a baby crappie was nibbling at the nightcrawler dangling from the small copper hook. Tyrone really didn't like messing with someone else's cane pole, but he couldn't pass on a fishing trip, especially with Jenny. It turned out that leaving after Berry's memorial service for an afternoon of fishing was just what the doctor ordered. Tyrone's broken heart was beginning to mend.

Why Roy Jackson would own a worn-out old cane pole was a bit confusing to Tyrone. Plus, Jackson's family pontoon boat was nothing special either, which made it hard to believe that Roy Jackson possessed it. With all his dough, it should be lined with sparkling diamond studs embedded in gold railings. Instead, it was constructed of faded pink two-by-fours tied together by a rope that rested on top of two, long aluminum pontoon floats. The captain's wooden steering wheel was connected to what looked like a college professor's lectern on the twelve by eighteen-foot platform boat. A bar stool was placed behind the wheel, and a cushioned bench seat ran along the aft rail. A hand-made canvas canopy covered just a small portion of the boat and was used for a shade break from the intense Florida sun. The vessel was powered, if you could call it that, by a single, fifty horsepower Mercury outboard motor and a propeller that was drastically distorted from its run-ins with shallow water, gravel, and sand. But dang, you can't catch a largemouth bass anywhere except along the weedy shoreline, so a banged-up prop was nothing but collateral damage.

Dark clouds and lightning flashes appeared in the distance to the southwest, and gusty winds blanketed the lake. Tyrone had steered the pontoon from its dock in the Angler's Delight marina to the weed patch at the mouth of the Kissimmee River. He slowly maneuvered the boat southward and hid behind a mass of swamp grass stalks eight feet high, not so much because that's where the fish were biting the best, but because Jenny had a bad habit of topless sunbathing, day or night, whenever she boarded a boat!

"Tyrone, I've got to tell you something," Jenny murmured hesitantly.

"What's up, babe?"

"I think Daddy may be up to something. Jimmy and me have never been allowed to go in or even near the migrants' cottages that are way out back behind the barn on our ranch. He said the workers need privacy, and we should never, ever bother them. When we were little, and Daddy wasn't looking, we'd sneak out to the cottages, but the doors were always locked. Anyway, the night you beat Martin Park, you know, the night Coach Berry and his wife were killed, I was putting on my cheerleader dress for the game, and I happened to notice out my window that four or five migrants were dragging something to a pickup truck that was parked next to the cottages. I thought it was an alligator they killed, and they were going to haul it to the DNR or the dump. Well, I noticed the same truck was in the school parking lot when we left after the game. Nobody was around it, and the cheerleaders were the last to leave. It crossed my mind that I recognized the truck, but at the time, I couldn't place where I had seen it. Not surprising, after all, we were all wrapped up in celebrating your big win."

"So what's the big deal? You got a bunch load of gators out your way, and maybe the migrants went to the game after they were done hauling one of them away." Tyrone was puzzled as he glanced over at Jenny.

"Yeah, but like I just said, we, the cheerleaders, were the last ones out of the parking lot because we were the last to leave the school. Remember, we waited 'til you boys were all showered so we could give y'all hugs without being drenched in sweat! Anyway, I didn't think about it until Daddy asked me and Jimmy to give him a ride to school on the way to the memorial service this morning. He wanted us to drop him off at the school office cuz he said he had business to attend to. We told him no one was going to be in the office cuz they would all be going to the service. He said it was none of our concern what he was doing. We asked him if we should pick him up when the service was over, and he said no cuz he had a ride. I couldn't figure out why he wanted to go to the school office, seeing everyone was at the service in the gym anyway. And I was a bit ticked off that he didn't want to go with us out of respect for the Berrys. After we dropped him off, I noticed the pickup truck was still in the parking lot, and then I realized that the truck was the same one that was parked outside of our migrants' cottages the night of the game."

"So your dad was just picking up the migrants' truck. Who cares?"

"Why didn't he tell us he was picking up the truck when he asked for the ride? And by the way, our migrants don't own a truck. They have a rusted out Ford Pinto that hasn't been driven since the muffler fell off a couple of weeks ago."

"Would your rich old daddy have bought them a truck?" Tyrone was searching for a common-sense angle.

"Maybe, but I would have known cuz I would have seen it there before. The only time I ever saw it was that night. Just one time, Tyrone."

"So you got some sort of theory or something, Jenny?"

"Heck, no, Tyrone, but it sure seems strange, don't you think?"

The bobber submerged, and the cane pole bent like a whip. Tyrone grabbed the pole and snapped it upward, then pulled the one-pound speckled perch up by the nylon filament line. "The key is to break its neck. This poor crappie never had a chance!"

"I probably should get back, Ty, or Daddy will break your neck."

CHAPTER 26
Friday, March 5, 1982
9:00 a.m.

Bob Cummings was a handsome man in his mid-forties. His hair was dark brown, but it was beginning to show slight signs of gray around the sideburns. He was a fighter pilot and a crash survivor during the early stages of the Vietnam War. Today, when he's asked if he was shot down during a mid-air dogfight or trying to dodge Viet Cong ground missiles, Bob shrugs his shoulders, and his face turns a bit red. You see, with no enemy in sight, Bob accidentally crashed his multimillion-dollar F-102 Supersonic Interceptor into the Bay of Burma, trying to fly low upon a night return to his base. He was able to discharge his life raft into the water and climb on board moments before the jet sunk to the bottom of the bay. Bob received the Purple Heart, awarded to servicemen who are wounded by an instrument of war in the hands of the enemy, for what happened next.

Bob was struck by a Viet Cong guerrilla's stray bullet meant for a high flying seagull. The North Vietnamese sharpshooter was bored and decided to amuse himself by taking potshots at birds for target practice. One stray bullet that missed its target wandered back down to earth at missile speed and embedded in the bone, flesh, and muscle of Bob's left shoulder. A few moments later, his life raft ripped apart on a coral reef, and he was forced to swim the final seventy yards to shore with just his right arm. Bob was sent back to the States and received an Honorable Discharge from the Air Force in 1970.

The day after he was discharged, Bob filed a complaint with the Department of Defense claiming that the F-102 was unsafe for flying because it had a built-in altimeter error of up to 500 feet and was also underpowered for combat. He had compiled data charts and aeronautical engineering design flaws associated with the F-102. And to help summarize his report, he blamed his own accident on those flaws. To keep his story from reaching the press, which would have resulted in another blow to Richard Nixon's handling of the war effort, the DOD thanked Bob and recommended his appointment to the National Transportation Safety Board, a government organization still in its infancy. The NTSB was formed three years earlier to investigate all types of aeronautical accidents. Ten years later, Bob headed up the Miami Region of the NTSB but spent way too much time and taxpayer money trying to overcome the challenges from aircraft manufacturers' lawyers in civil court cases. Those lawyers always did their homework, and they knew Bob never flew commercial planes, which meant he could hardly be used as an expert witness against them. Meanwhile, the ambulance-chasing class action attorneys were bribing him with personal yachts and Lear Jets if he testified on their behalf. But Bob demonstrated stalwart integrity during testimony, and he never cracked while presenting his accident reports in court.

Two weeks to the day following the midair collision of Trans South 256 and PanMexico 441, Mustaf Dasani was summoned to the Miami regional office of the NTSB. Bob Cummings had gathered a dozen investigators as part of his "Go Team" and assigned his number one man, Jake Tassett, as the Investigator-in-Charge. Two Bayou Airline Pilots, two HoftanJet engineers, and Mustaf were asked to provide consultative information to the Go Team. For the past thirteen days and nights, the investigators researched the history of events leading up to the accident and every crewmembers' duties for a month before the crash. They examined the remains of the engines and attempted to calculate the impact angles to help determine both planes' pre-impact course and altitude.

The HoftanJet engineers provided a functional status report for all components of both planes' hydraulic and electrical systems, together with instruments and elements of the flight control system. Mustaf was asked to reconstruct the historical air traffic data communicated verbally to both planes, including the acquisition of ATC radar data and transcripts of controller-pilot radio transmissions. He was a wee bit worried, considering that his voice conversations with Harry Hutter were recorded for all to hear and examine.

"I knew the odds were pretty damn good that we'd be investigating another one of Harry's accidents," Bob Cummings professed while shaking his head. "The SOB wouldn't listen to anyone, and now he's responsible for 322 lives."

"There's absolutely nothing in our investigative research that would indicate that anything mechanical went wrong in either aircraft," Jake Tassett inserted. "Mustaf advised Harry to wait out the storm, and Harry being Harry thought he was invincible and ignored him. I've got to say though, Mustaf, you lacked a great deal of professionalism in your ground to aircraft communications. In fact, it bordered on several violations of FAA code."

"Yes, sir, and I apologize, and I am fully willing to accept the consequences for my actions. Nothing, however, will replace the loss of my close friend. Say what you want, but Harry was a very good pilot."

"A good pilot's skills go beyond knowing how to handle the controls; he must know how to use good judgment. I'm sorry about your friend, Mustaf, but Harry's sagacity is questionable. Now, tell us about the pattern of radar blackouts at Miami International and your theory."

"We've had seven radar outages in the past two months. The outages at Miami have coincided with outages at Fort

Lauderdale, West Palm, and Sarasota. Upon tracing the blip history of aircraft flying within our radar lock shortly before each outage occurred, we found one gigantic commonality: there was an unknown small aircraft flying precisely at 3000 feet bearing a five-degree northwesterly course from Homestead. Most unknown aircraft blips can be traced back to registered flight plans, but not one of these seven blips had filed any flight plans."

Jake Tassett glanced over at Bob Cummings, but Bob had his head down, and he was rubbing the back of his neck. There was no doubt he was deep in thought. Jake looked back at Mustaf as the two questions on every committee members' mind rolled off his lips: "Is it your belief that the same unknown aircraft was responsible for each outage? If so, how was it done?"

"It's only a theory, Mr. Tassett, but I do believe the same aircraft was responsible for jamming our radar equipment. Are you familiar with light-emitting diodes, or LED?"

"I think so, Mustaf. Isn't that what is better known as laser technology?"

"Yes, sir. Well, I believe the unknown aircraft scatter-fired invisible infrared pulses that confused our radar instrumentation device by providing false signals, thus causing the computer system to temporarily crash."

"Oh, come on, Mustaf. You've been watching too many *Star Trek* reruns!" A few chuckles could be heard from the normally serious committee. Mustaf wasn't laughing. He didn't like Jake Tassett's comments about his friend Harry's intelligence, he didn't like being reprimanded in front of the entire Go Team, and he didn't appreciate the sarcastic remarks related to his theory. Mustaf sat straight up in his chair and glared directly at Jake. Jake tried to maintain eye contact, but it was difficult.

"SignalNav has checked, rechecked, and checked again both our ATC instrumentation devices and those on both planes, at least what they could put together from the wreckage," stated Mustaf matter-of-factly. "All their tests were monitored by the FAA, and all came back clear. There was no detected internal electrical problem, which means something interrupted the tracking transmissions between the Miami, Fort Lauderdale, Sarasota, and West Palm towers and all of the aircraft that were in flight at the time. The failures occurred seven times in the past two months. Lastly, one constant remains the same; the projected flight path of the suspected unknown aircraft leads directly over Lake Okeechobee. Coincidence? I doubt it. You have a problem, folks. You obviously have no more need for my services. Have a nice day." Mustaf abruptly stood up, nodded at the stunned committee members, and swiftly exited the conference room.

Bob Cummings' nervous expression turned to confusion. "Jake, your report indicates that there was no engine malfunction in either aircraft other than the sputtering PanMexico jet that was running out of fuel. Although the weather was terrible, wind shear or turbulence did not cause the crash. We can't label it pilot error when ground and cockpit instruments were not functioning correctly. Is it—could it be possible that something might have jammed the radar transmissions?"

"Well, Bob, we can label the cause of the crash either a malfunction of radar equipment or laser warfare originating from Unidentified Flying Objects, as Mustaf would have us believe. I guess that means either SignalNav faces a gigantic lawsuit—or you and I live out the rest of our lives in the funny farm. What's your preference?"

"Jake, I've been flying for over twenty years and have seen some incredibly strange sights in the night skies," interjected Cal Cooper, a captain for Bayou. "I don't believe in UFOs, but a laser jamming device isn't beyond my level of comprehension."

Bill Turloney, a HoftanJet engineer, added, "None of our findings indicated a problem with SignalNav's equipment. How can we hang the blame on them?"

"We spent too damn much money on this investigation to label the cause of the crash 'unknown,'" Jake stormed back. "The newspapers would hang us! I say let SignalNav fight it out in court, they probably would win so they would only be out legal costs. A couple hundred thousand dollars is a drop in the bucket to them. Us trying to fight for a UFO theory would make headlines in the National Enquirer every week for the next two years!"

"One thing you may be forgetting," Cal exclaimed, "is if someone did intentionally jam the radar devices, then it becomes a criminal investigation for the FBI. It's the NTSB's responsibility to invite them in if we deem the cause intentional."

Bob Cummings was now pacing while scratching the back of his head. "I think we all know that, Cal. Let's not jump the gun. We need to think logically."

"For the sake of argument, let's assume Mustaf's theory is correct," chimed Bill Turloney. "NASA sent a man to the moon in less than ten years, so it's conceivable to John Q. Public that laser jamming technology is a possibility."

"But futuristic weaponry in the hands of civilians? You'll cause a major panic from coast to coast!" Jake was starting to believe he was about to get into the debate of the century.

"If the public believed that bad folks were doing something to crash jets and kill people, they'd demand solutions immediately," Bob added. "Jake's right, a panic could not be averted."

"Well, dang it, Bob. If the laser story could possibly be true, we damn well better do something about it—and now!" said Cal. "I say we call the FBI."

"Slow down, Cal. You're the one panicking." Bob paced towards the window, paused a few seconds, and then turned to the committee. "The bottom line is this: we don't have enough evidence to say for certain that a laser jamming device caused the accident, and we don't want our agency to look stupid by labeling the cause as 'unknown.' I'm going to officially designate the cause of the accident as 'unavoidable pilot error' on both captains. I personally believe that to be correct. We will then send the entire report to President Layman's staff, and if they wish, they can ask the FAA and FBI to reopen the case. At that point, we will work with NASA engineers and try to investigate Mustaf's theory in depth."

Cal was exasperated but realized that changing Bob's mind was futile. "Okay, Bob, I'm with you, but you know as well as me that the president isn't going to reopen the case. He's already busy trying to convince the American people that the Soviet Union won't nuke our country with mid-range missiles. I shudder to think what type of panic he would create if he announced that we may have UFOs bringing down passenger jets! Can you imagine his approval rating if the citizens that he promised to protect were too afraid to take to the skies for travel? Well, anyway, thank goodness I don't work for Trans South or PanMexico or their insurance companies. I better get going so I don't drown in lawyer saliva before I get home!"

CHAPTER 27

Monday, March 8, 1982

10:00 a.m.

"Lew Berry, please." Seminole Bend County Coroner Cliff Sutton wasn't looking forward to making this call.

"This is Lew. What's up?"

"Lew, Cliff Sutton down in Florida. Sorry this has taken so long, but we had to be certain before contacting you. For the record, I need to officially verify you as the next of kin. Please confirm that you are Sheryl Berry's closest living relative."

"Damn it, Dr. Sutton, I confirmed that to you already. Sheryl's parents and brother were killed in a head-on crash two years ago, and we have acted on her behalf since that time. Now, get to the point. You told me you would call back within forty-eight hours, Dr. Sutton. It's been over two weeks. I've made and canceled plans three times to transport what remains of Sheryl's body to Pennsylvania. Just what the hell is going on down there?" Lew Berry still hoped that there was a possibility that the burned victim of that horrible crash after the basketball game might not be his daughter-in-law. He and his wife assumed that could be a possibility based upon Dr. Sutton's explanation of the bone length theory from the body found in the pickup truck. A week ago, the coroner released Brett Berry's body for transport, and the Berry's held a funeral for their son instead of waiting to bury both of them at the same time.

"Sorry, Lew. We ended up bringing in medical experts from John Hopkins up in Maryland, who, in turn, called in the FBI. They wouldn't let me give you any information." Cliff knew the conversation was long from over.

"FBI? Why is the FBI involved?" Lew's voice sounded puzzled, but Cliff was almost sure the question was rhetorical.

"Lew, the body in the truck was not Sheryl's. It belonged to someone approximately six feet tall. Based on the bone width and composition, it is most likely a male. The FBI was called in because we suspected a possible kidnapping occurred, and the medical experts thought they had evidence that Sheryl may have been transported out of state."

"Kidnapping? So you're saying someone removed Sheryl from the accident scene and placed someone else inside the truck before it burned?" This time, Lew was perplexed.

"No, Lew, there wouldn't have been enough time. Sheryl may or may not have even gotten into the truck. It's probable that the kidnapping coincided with the theft of the pickup. Whoever drove it was in a hurry to get away and lost control on the slippery road."

"So, do you know where Sheryl is? Is she alive? Why couldn't you have told us sooner?! If this is true, my son did not have to die!" Lew was doing his best to keep control, but his anger began seeping through the cracks of his raised voice.

"I was under strict orders from the FBI not to divulge any information until today. I'm sorry, Lew, I really am. My only hope now is that your daughter-in-law is alright. The FBI would like for you and your wife to meet them at their Miami office as soon as possible. There is a US Air flight leaving Pittsburgh in four hours. They're flying you first-class and will pick you up at your doorstep in an hour." Cliff was told by the FBI to say no more, so he apologized a second time and reluctantly hung up. He knew he hadn't provided any consolation for the Berrys, who were agonizing more than ever over the tragic loss of their children.

Five seconds after Cliff Sutton had hung up with Lew Berry, his phone rang. Cliff really didn't want any incoming calls for a few moments following his poignant conversation with Lew. A phone call to a coroner was usually not happy news.

"Cliff, this is Sheriff Bonty. Hey, when are you planning on releasing Sheryl Berry's body? I'm sure Coach Berry's parents want to know. They already had the coach's funeral, so it's just not right that her burial can't be done quickly. You know what I mean?"

Cliff Sutton was not one to interfere with the law, but he damn sure was not going to let the law interfere with him. And Cliff wasn't all that sure Sheriff Bonty was on the right side of the law anyway. For someone who was supposed to be a cooperative partner with the medical examiner, Al Bonty had a bad habit of questioning all of Cliff's findings recently. Cliff found it very strange that Bonty called him about virtually every death that occurred in the county. Granted, Cliff had jurisdiction over all Seminole Bend deaths that were supposedly suspicious, unusual, or from strange circumstances, but the sheriff's inquiries seemed inexplicable. There's no doubt that an officer of the law needs to investigate homicides, but what baffled Cliff was why Sheriff Bonty was so overzealous with accident victims. Bonty had listed the cause of death on the original traffic report as a "possible accident due to speed deemed too fast for existing weather and road conditions."

"Al, I can't give you any information on the victim's release date." Cliff struggled trying not to tell Bonty more than what was absolutely necessary.

"Why are you being so cold, Cliff? We all knew and liked Sheryl, so you can at least call her by name instead of calling her 'victim.'" Sheriff Bonty paused momentarily for a reply, but Cliff said nothing. "So, is it that you 'can't' give me any information, or that you 'won't' give me any information? Keep in mind that I am the duly appointed officer whose job it is to uphold the law and protect our citizens. You have no legal right to hide information from me if I'm investigating the possibility that a crime has been committed."

"What makes you think a crime was committed, Sheriff? I thought you said it was an accident, pure and simple."

"I said 'possibility,' dang it! And I don't have to tell you nothing cuz you ain't no law enforcement officer. Now tell me what you know, Cliff, or I just might arrest you for withholding evidence." Sheriff Bonty was losing what little composure he had.

"Aw, go to hell, Bonty. You'd have quite a lot of explaining to do if you threw the 'duly' elected coroner in jail. All I'm going to tell you is the body can't be released until the FBI gives the okay. That's my orders."

Cliff was about to hang up the phone, or more specifically, slam it or ram it, when he heard Bonty shout into the receiver, "Why is the FBI involved? Who asked them to investigate anything? If you or them think some sort of interstate crime has been committed, then dang it, I can figure it out just as well as them suits from DC!"

Cliff decided to just lay the phone receiver down gently on the table without hanging up. That way, he wouldn't need to field any calls for a few moments while he got his thoughts together. Bonty had a reputation for blowing smoke to anyone who would listen, so as long as he thought Cliff was still on the line, he would continue to vent. It took the sheriff ten minutes of a nonstop diatribe about FBI agents before he realized that no one was listening.

CHAPTER 28

Monday, March 8, 1982

6:00 p.m.

The US Airways flight touched down twelve minutes ahead of schedule in sunny Miami, which was a minor accomplishment considering they departed thirteen minutes late in an early March snowstorm that was blanketing eastern Ohio and western Pennsylvania. March had come in like a lion, and the Quaker State folks were looking forward to the lamb. Lew Berry was met at the gate by three young, well-built FBI agents, all wearing the trademark dark blue suit and spit-shined black shoes.

"Mr. Berry, this is Agent Tecka and Agent Johnson. My name is Agent Jones. Where is Mrs. Berry?"

"So, how did you know who I am?" Lew said, a bit startled. He was wearing a Penn State sweatshirt and cap while carrying a ski jacket in his arms. His brown leather carry-on was nearly worn out, laced with scratches and scuff marks.

"Mr. Berry, your picture is part of your daughter-in-law Sheryl's file. Please, sir, where is your wife?"

"She's had enough pain and suffering for this lifetime. I decided it was best for her to stay in Pennsylvania. So, where are we going?"

"Please follow us. We have a car waiting out front that will take us to FBI Headquarters just a few miles east of here," Agent Jones stated matter-of-factly. "We'll brief you there."

"So you folks work late hours, eh Jones? It's past six o'clock. When do you go home?"

"We're not on a clock, Mr. Berry," said Agent Jones with no apparent emotion.

The twenty-minute drive to FBI Headquarters in Miami was accomplished with nary a sound. Lew stared out the window at the late rush hour traffic moving slowly on the Dolphin Expressway. His thoughts turned to Brett and Sheryl's wedding day just a few years ago and how blissfully happy they both appeared, knowing they would be spending the rest of their lives together. Lew also remembered the close relationship that had emerged between his family and Sheryl's parents and brother before they perished in a car accident. It was difficult now to conceive that four kith and kin were no longer here on earth, and Sheryl could very well be dead, as well.

The black Mercury Marquis pulled into the parking lot of a concrete and steel-reinforced building that couldn't seem to hide the wear and tear from years of constant humidity, rain, and sunshine beating down on it. The new FBI headquarters would soon be in North Miami Beach, but for now, wearing crisp blue suits and riding around in fancy cars were the only perks given to the federal law enforcement agents in this area. Agent Tecka parked the car and immediately exited the vehicle to open the door for Lew, who was sitting in the back seat. The four men walked quickly through the front doors, past the security desk, and down a long hallway. Many more blue suits could be seen milling about in the labyrinth of cubicles scattered throughout the building.

The FBI agents and Lew entered a small interrogation room on the left. There were no windows except for a smoked-glass reflective pane on the wall around the corner, which was to the right of the entry door. Lew had been a big fan of *The FBI* television series in the early seventies, and he could picture Efrem Zimbalist Junior listening carefully behind the fake mirror that was no doubt a hiding place for investigators. But he wondered why he would be led into a cross-examination room when he was only in Miami to get information on Sheryl's death.

Agents Jones, Tecka, and Johnson motioned for Lew to have a seat on a fold-out metal chair that was tucked underneath a square metal table, which was probably used for agents to play poker on in their spare time. Agent Jones then sat down across the card table from Lew, while agents Tecka and Johnson leaned on the wall by the door. Lew was beginning to feel paranoid, trying to speculate what the conversation was going to entail. He placed his cap and ski jacket on top of the table and folded his hands in nervous bewilderment.

Leaning forward on his elbows, Agent Jones spoke first. "Mr. Berry, when was the last time you spoke to your daughter-in-law?"

"Please, Agent Jones, call me Lew." Lew wanted this conversation to become a whole lot less formal.

"Okay, Lew, and you can call me Jack if you wish. Now, when was the last time you spoke to Sheryl?"

Jack Jones. Yep, Lew could picture that name for him. The agent was tall with a muscular body, dark complexion, blue eyes, and dimples that would make the ladies wobbly if he looked at them. Lew thought that Jack could easily be the little brother of his wife's favorite singer, Tom Jones.

"I spoke with Brett every week. He would give me updates on his basketball team frequently. I can't remember the last time I spoke to Sheryl, though. I know that sounds rude, sorry."

"You are aware from Coroner Sutton that the FBI is involved in this investigation because we suspect that Sheryl was kidnapped," stated Agent Jones rhetorically.

"Yes, I am. But I thought a kidnapping had to cross state lines before the FBI was called in."

"That's correct, Lew. We got involved when the medical experts who investigated the remains in your son's pickup truck found some evidence."

"What the hell does some unknown dead body in Brett's pickup have to do with Sheryl's kidnapping? And what makes you think she was transported out of Florida?" Lew was losing his cool and his patience.

"I can't give you that information right now, Lew. We are still early in our investigation," Agent Jones said calmly.

"Okay, Jack, if you say so. But a lot of things simply don't add up. For instance, if Sheryl didn't get into Brett's truck after the game that night, where did she go? From what I understand, there was quite a crowd in the gym because the teams were arch-rivals. How could someone not see her get forcibly taken away? She's well known in town, feisty enough to put up a struggle, and seven months pregnant! Hard to imagine there weren't any witnesses. And also, does anyone know who that man in Brett's truck was and how he got there?"

"Lew, I understand you are upset, and I apologize for not being able to divulge any more information. We brought you here to ask some questions, and I'd like to get on with that if you don't mind?" Agent Jones' tone of voice was turning a bit more serious.

"Fine. Then, get on with it," said Lew insolently. Lew wasn't about to hide his frustrations with this inquiry. His son was dead, his daughter-in-law was missing and might be somewhere outside of Florida, and his questions were unrequited.

Agent Tecka walked out of the interrogation room for a long moment while Agent Jones kept silent. Jones snuck a quick glance over at Lew, then folded his hands on top of the table and twiddled his thumbs, a sign, perhaps, that he was a bit nervous himself. Agent Tecka returned with a small, black plastic pill box sealed with two narrow strips of clear tape. After placing the box on the table, he took out a pocketknife and slashed away the tape.

Agent Jones then looked up at Lew and asked, "Is there any chance that you saw Sheryl's wedding ring, either before or after they were married?"

"I didn't see it, but I remember they exchanged rings right after their vows were said. I guess most couples do. Why? So, is that what you think is in that box, Sheryl's wedding ring?" Lew's curiosity was sparked.

"Well, quite frankly, Lew, that is why we wanted your wife to come along on this trip with you. Women usually enjoy examining a wedding ring more so then men, and chances might be better that Janet knows if this is Sheryl's ring or not." Agent Jones then opened the lid. The ring was large, especially the band which was made from silver, or so it appeared that way. The stone itself was enormous, perhaps four or five carats.

"That ain't Sheryl's," Lew said without really taking an in-depth, hard look at the jewelry.

"You didn't look very close, Lew. Are you sure it's not hers?"

"I don't have to look very close. That ring is humungous! It must have cost a fortune! Brett was a school teacher and coach. Ain't no way he could have afforded that thing without robbing a bank!" Lew caught himself a bit too late—not the best choice of words to share with FBI agents, he thought!

"Lew, this ring appears to be very beautiful. In fact, our jewelry expert verified that it's a replica of Queen Elizabeth the Second's engagement ring that she received from Prince Phillip in 1946."

"Well, there you have it. Brett would have been extremely lucky to make that kind of money in his whole career, say nothing of having it laying around before the wedding." Lew was once again on the brink of full sarcasm.

Agent Jones paused a few seconds to make sure Lew was listening carefully. "The stone on this ring is made from cubic zirconia, not pure diamond. The band itself is sterling silver.

The total cost is estimated under $100." Jones didn't ask a question; he didn't need to.

Wrinkles appeared on Lew's forehead as he tilted his head up, opened his mouth, and squeezed his chin with his thumb and forefinger. He was now in deep thought but keeping silent. Finally, he needed to know.

"Why do you think this is Sheryl's, Jack?"

"Take a look at the engraving on the inside of the band." Agent Jones placed the ring in Lew's palm.

Sure enough, there were two initials, "SB" and "BB," separated by a heart. Sheryl's maiden name was Babbitt.

"Where did you find the ring?" Lew asked, not sure if he wanted the answer.

"The ring was found in a marsh just west of Miami International Airport during an investigation into the crash of those two jets a couple of weeks ago. A human finger, severed from a hand at the knuckle, was found a few feet away from an unidentified body, and this ring was lying on the ground next to it. Because there was red nail polish, the finger most likely belonged to a female. Forensics said the dried blood on the finger was type AB positive. We checked Sheryl's birth records, and she is AB positive. Sorry, Lew, there was no easy way to tell you." Agent Jones' face was melancholy as he locked eyes with Lew.

"Are you saying Sheryl was on one of those flights? Oh my God! Could there be another explanation? She and Brett can't be the only SB and BB to ever get married! And plenty of other women have AB positive blood type!" Lew's voice was transitioning from angry to panicky.

Agent Jones reached across the table and patted Lew's wrist. His serious nature was beginning to melt. However, he quickly regained his professional composure despite his somewhat demure disposition. "Your absolutely right, Lew. The ring and blood type match could be purely coincidental. But there's one other thing. The Trans South Airlines flight manifest listed a Susan Blanchard sitting in seat 14C. A travel agent in Orlando made the reservation on the agency's Sabre computer system but claimed to not know the lady. She was a walk-in, first-time customer. The agent asked the lady for a driver's license to complete the reservation so her home address would be correct on the ticket. Susan Blanchard provided her Florida license with an address listed in Winter Haven. We checked that address. There is none, not even an actual street with that name in Winter Haven. And no, there is no Susan Blanchard living in Winter Haven, either."

"Okay, but I'm not following you. What does a Susan Blanchard, fictional or not, in Winter Haven have to do with Sheryl Berry in Seminole Bend?"

"The Trans South customer service rep who checked in Susan Blanchard at the airport remembered her very clearly. Usually, people remember other people and events more vividly when something out of the ordinary happens. The rep described a few strange incidents that he remembered about this girl Susan. He claims Susan's traveling partner was leading her, well actually somewhat pushing her, to the counter, and then the partner provided driver's licenses for both himself and the lady. According to the rep, Susan was wearing an obvious wig tucked underneath a loose scarf. When she reached the counter, she put her head down with her chin literally touching her chest, and she never looked up at him. After checking in at the ticket counter, the traveling partner tugged her around and yanked her towards the gate. But the rep especially remembered her name because of another oddity," Jones paused for a moment. "The traveling partner's name was John Smith."

"So you think Susan may have been Sheryl with a fake ID? Come on! That's simply spontaneous and fluky, just like the ring with the initials on it." Lew was even more puzzled but determined to contradict the agent's speculation. "It's time you tell me what you're thinking, Jack! As I remember from the newspapers, the Trans South flight was going to Atlanta, right? Why would an incognito Susan Blanchard be traveling to Atlanta? How does that play into your theory?"

"The travel agent in Orlando provided a description of Susan Blanchard to one of our artists. Here, take a look." Agent Jones nodded to Agent Johnson, who removed a manila envelope from inside his suit coat and placed it on the table. Agent Jones opened the envelope, slid out the artist's sketch, and offered it to Lew. Lew laid the picture on the table, and a startled look appeared on his face. "Now, here is an artist's sketch of the gal the Trans South rep at the Miami airport described." Agent Jones removed a second picture from the envelope and placed it on the table so both sketches were sitting side by side. Lew was dumbfounded.

"They look like the same girl, and they appear to be pregnant." Lew's voice was quiet, almost incoherent. "Yes, they both look a bit like Sheryl."

Lew was dazed, and Agent Jones got to the point. "Could Sheryl have been in Orlando on February 11th, the date the airline ticket was purchased?"

"Absolutely not, Jack! During the basketball season, neither Sheryl nor Brett traveled anywhere except for out of town games. They looked forward to Spring Break when the basketball season was over, and they could finally relax. You guys are investigating on a wing and a prayer!"

"I'm not saying those pictures are Sheryl, Lew. As a matter of fact, because we're pretty sure the lady at the airport was wearing a wig, someone went to a great deal of trouble to look like Sheryl. I had to ask the question about the date to help confirm our suspicions and check that off our list. Now, only one item remains on that list, and that's the wedding ring. Would you mind calling your wife and find out if she has ever seen Sheryl's diamond?"

CHAPTER 29

Tuesday, March 9, 1982
8:00 a.m.

On Monday night, Lew attempted three phone calls to his wife Janet in Pennsylvania to inquire about his daughter-in-law's wedding ring, but each time the call went to her answering machine. On Tuesday morning, he phoned his neighbor Ralph Kline and asked him to check on Janet. Lew waited as patiently as possible in his hotel room for Ralph's return call.

Ten minutes later, the phone rang. Ralph said he knocked on the door and waited for five minutes, but no one came. He checked the door handle and found it unlocked, so he went into Berry's home and looked around. On the kitchen table, he found a note written by Janet. Ralph asked Lew if he should read it to him over the phone, and Lew said, "yes."

Dear Lew,

I needed to get away for a few days to clear my head. I've tried everything to get over losing Brett and Sheryl and can't do it. Going up to the Poconos and hoping the fresh air will help. Sorry, I was going to call your hotel but couldn't remember where you were staying. Can't wait to hear what the FBI said. Be back soon.

Love, Janet

The airline ticket issued to Lew in Pennsylvania had an open-ended return. He threw his clothes and personal belongings into his carry-on suitcase and checked out of the

Holiday Inn. The FBI had set up direct billing, so Lew dropped off his key at the front desk and ran for the Yellow Cab that was parked outside the lobby. "Airport, fast, please."

"Sure. What airline, sir?" replied the cabbie.

"Allegheny, I mean US Air, and please step on it!"

The cab driver was used to dealing with rush hour in Miami, and amid a flurry of honks and middle fingers being flashed his way, he cut, swerved, and battled Lew to the airport in twenty minutes flat. The smallest bill in Lew's wallet was a twenty, so he threw it in the cabbie's lap and told him to keep the change. The fare was $8, and the big tip was much appreciated by the driver. He could now head to Denny's for a Grand Slam breakfast.

US Airways Flight 450 was departing Miami in fifty-five minutes for Pittsburgh. Lew wanted to be on it, and there were plenty of open seats. However, the counter agent noticed that the open jaw return had been stamped "Compulsory Approval Needed by Procurer," so the agent advised Lew that he would need to call the phone number written on the ticket before he could reserve a seat. Lew tapped his fingers on the counter while the US Air agent called the FBI. Five minutes later, Lew was told that his return to Pennsylvania had been denied.

Lew was furious. The US Air agent didn't want to cause a scene, so he invited Lew to step into the supervisor's office and use one of their company phones to call the FBI back. A secretary looked up the number and dialed while Lew fumed in a cheap metal folding chair. After waiting on hold for fifteen minutes, the secretary was finally connected to Agent Jones, and she handed the receiver over to Lew.

"Jones, just what the hell is going on? I need to return to Pittsburgh, and my return ticket was denied! Who the hell denied it?"

"I denied it, Lew. You need to at least tell us why you're going back. The last we spoke yesterday, you were going to call Janet and find out about the wedding ring."

Lew explained his unanswered phone call attempts and the note found on the kitchen table by his neighbor.

"Lew, I understand how you feel. But please let me make some calls to our office in Pittsburgh and see what I can find out. It won't do you any good to go looking for Janet without knowing exactly where she went."

"Janet wouldn't just get up and leave like that without talking to me first," countered Lew. "I can't explain her letter, but I'm worried something happened. Could you call the police up in Uniontown and start an investigation?"

"Lew, I will make the call, but legally Janet will be considered a 'Voluntary Missing Adult' because she wrote a note explaining her absence. They probably won't even file a report for a week, but I'll see what I can do. Hang tight at the airport. I'll call you on this line as soon as possible."

The flight to Pittsburgh had just departed when Agent Jones called back. "Lew, I talked the Uniontown PD down to a forty-eight hour waiting period, and they will open a file first thing on Thursday if you don't hear from her first. It's best if you stay in Florida until we know where she is. Once that happens, we can either fly you back to Pittsburgh or wherever she is staying. Please take a taxi back to the Holiday Inn and kill some time by the pool or something. Or we could pick you up and take you back there if you wish. I'll call and let the hotel know you'll be returning. One thing, we would like to accompany you when you return to Uniontown. Not really a request, I might add."

Lew wasn't sure why the FBI wanted to go to Pennsylvania with him, but he assumed it had to do with Sheryl's wedding ring. He also knew it wouldn't do much good to argue with Agent Jones.

"Alright, fine, Jones. I can get my own damn ride back to the hotel. But I'll be at your doorstep first thing on Thursday morning. And then I want some action, got it?" Lew was determined to get the last word in and make sure it was hammered home.

"Sure thing, Lew. But call me immediately if you hear from Janet before Thursday."

Lew hung up the receiver without responding. He thanked the US Air folks for their hospitality, grabbed his bag, and headed for the car rentals. He had no plan to spend the next two days hanging loose by the Holiday Inn pool.

CHAPTER 30
Tuesday, March 9, 1982
10:30 a.m.

Lew gave the Hertz agent his MasterCard and opted for the collision damage waiver because he planned to test the limits of the accelerator and his own common sense all at once. He inquired as to the fastest route to Seminole Bend, and the car rental rep cracked a smile and replied, "We're *Number One*, but we don't rent helicopters!"

When the rep noticed Lew staring blankly at him, he added, "Just kidding, man." The rep then pulled out a large paper with a map of Florida on one side and boxes with blown up diagrams of major cities on the other. With a yellow transparent marker, he highlighted the route.

"Take the 836 to the 826, head north to Highway 27 and turn right onto US 98 in Okeelanta. Highway 98 winds around the big lake and takes you right to Seminole Bend, can't miss it. You know, Lake Okeechobee is the second largest freshwater lake totally enclosed in the United States. Lake Michigan is the biggest, but the other Great Lakes are partly in Canada, so they don't count." The Hertz comedian and trivia expert was really getting on Lew's nerves. He had no time for a geography lesson.

Lew upgraded to a black Pontiac Trans Am with a detailed painting on the rear spoiler of Smokey, Sheriff Buford T. Justice, chasing the Bandit. He adjusted the mirror, glanced at his reflection and thought, "I see a little bit of Burt Reynolds in this face." Moments later, the Hertz check-out security guard cautioned him, "Be careful with this baby, sir.

This here car's our pride and joy." An hour later, Lew turned onto Highway 98 and headed north. He completed his first eighty miles in a mere sixty minutes, passing twelve slow-moving semis hauling sugar cane in the process.

Thinking he had finally reached a mild form of civilization, Lew pulled into Bennett's Airboat Palace, a decrepit shack that was located just a few feet from the rim canal that looped around Lake Okeechobee. Like many other tourists, he was looking forward to seeing the expansive lake, but the US Army Corps of Engineers ruined that hope back in 1928 when they constructed the thirty-foot-tall, hurricane-taming, Herbert Hoover Dike, which separated the rim canal from the Big "O." As he got out of the rented Pontiac, Lew noticed a weather-beaten, middle-aged, tall man hosing down an airboat just off the dock behind the shack. Too many years in the Florida sun had turned his skin into wrinkled leather.

Lew walked up to Phil Bennett and offered his hand for shaking, "Excuse me, sir. Sorry to interrupt your business, but I was just wondering if you could give me some directions?"

"Penn State, eh?" Phil said while pointing at Lew's Polo shirt with the Nittany Lion emblem on the pocket. "You a graduate or just a fan?"

Lew glanced down at the pocket and smiled, "A big-time fan. Thanks for noticing."

"So, you must be another one of them lost snowbirds, huh?" Phil uttered sarcastically. "Northern folks been moving out of here lately, so it's nice to have one come in."

"Moving out? Why's that? I thought this lake was an angler's paradise for us Yanks. Can't catch big bass like you got down here back home in Pennsylvania."

"Got nothing to do with the fish. Them flapping little critters are still here and hungry. You must not read the newspapers up north."

"I'm not following you, sir. By the way, the name's Lew Berry."

"Howdy, Lew. I'm Phil Bennett, and you're standing at the gates to my palace." They shook hands a second time. Even Phil could joke about the shabby framework of the business he so deliberately misnamed. "What I meant by the news is we've had a bunch of killings here the last month. An old lady named Potts was murdered in her home when some guy smashed a pot over her head, no pun intended. And just minutes later, her husband was killed in a traffic accident. Then some dude slips and falls over at Elmer's Hardware Store, killing himself, and about the same time, an old man is run over by a car in the BoldMart parking lot. But worst of all was when our basketball coach was killed trying to save his wife who died after crashing into a culvert up on Highway 441."

Lew dropped his chin down to his chest, and teardrops were forming in his eyes. Phil abruptly stopped his narrative of the recent tragic events in Seminole Bend and, with a hint of compassion, said, "Hey, what's up, man? Was there something I said?"

Lew regained his composure and replied, "Sorry, Phil. Need to tell you something. That basketball coach, Brett Berry, well he's my son. I'm here to gather some of his belongings."

"Oh my God, Lew. I humbly apologize. I need to just shut my trap sometimes." Phil gave Lew a sympathetic pat on the shoulder. Lew wiped his face with his shirtsleeve.

"It's alright. You didn't know. Anyway, I haven't seen Brett and Sheryl's new house that they built in December and actually don't have a clue how to get there. Any chance you could help me?"

"Yep, I know they built a new home up on the golf course. I hate to say it, but town folks and me found that awfully strange, you know. Please don't take this the wrong way cuz we all respected your son, but he wasn't making much coaching, and she wasn't working. No one could figure out how they got the money to buy a new house, and it's a dandy I hear."

"I'm not sure how they afforded to buy one either, Phil. Just assumed they had been saving up, I guess. They didn't ask me for any cash. Anyway, you think you could give me directions to their place?"

"Would love to, Lew, but not many folks know where they lived. Heard it was kind of hidden behind a bunch of trees on the seventh hole. None of my gossiping friends have ever even seen it."

"Can you show me the way to the golf course then?" asked Lew. "Somebody should be able to help me from there."

"Maybe I can do better than that. Ever been on an airboat, Lew?"

"No, why?" replied Lew with a puzzled look.

"Back when the golf course was being built, they dug an irrigation canal right off the Kissimmee River all the way up there, about fifteen miles I'd say. The golf course is owned by a rich rancher named Roy Jackson, so it must've set him back quite a penny digging it. People around these parts found that building a water trench was a bit peculiar, seeing we get plenty of rain down here. Anyway, the canal is pretty much hidden from the river, but I know how to find it. If the Taylor Creek locks are open, I can get ya up there faster on my airboat then you probably could do driving."

"Wow, sounds like a plan. But don't you need to stay here in case someone wants to rent a boat?"

"Naw. This here's my only airboat left, and if we's driving it, ain't no one gonna rent it. I had four airboats, but some snowbirds already rented two of them for the week, and the third one was destroyed a few weeks ago by a couple of deputy sheriffs."

"Deputy sheriffs? What happened?" Lew inquired.

"Deputies Willy Banks and Sam McCormick went out fishing one night and busted up my airboat. Willy said he was going to pay me double the cost of buying a new one in a few months. Ain't seen Sam since the accident, but I figure he's alright or Willy would've told me different. Willy's a good man, though; in fact, his nephew played on your son's basketball team. His name is Tyrone, and he's only a sophomore. Great athlete, he is! Well, then again, his daddy, Tyrus, was one of the best back in his time, too."

"Do you think this Willy Banks knows anything about my son and his wife's accident?"

"He sure oughta. This here county ain't that populated, so I'm assuming most everyone in the sheriff's department knows most things that happen to everyone round here."

"When we get back, can you point me in the direction of the sheriff's office," asked Lew. "Just would feel better if I knew exactly what happened that night, you know."

"Sure, don't blame ya, Lew. I'd want to know myself iffin it was my kids. Say, you hungry, by the way?"

"Well, as a matter of fact, I'm starving. You know a good place to eat, Phil?"

"After we cross the lake, there's a place called the Angler's Delight restaurant right on the Kissimmee River. They got great catfish caught on the river and deep-fried with the best cornmeal batter round these parts."

"Let's do it, Phil. My mouth's watering just listening to you."

* * * * *

The Taylor Creek locks were the northernmost entrance to the lake, and the rear access was open to the canal when Phil and Lew arrived. Phil guided his craft into the confined caisson carefully with five other boats of various sizes, grabbed the frayed rope that was hanging from the lip, and waited for the steel gate to close behind them. As the water level rose, Lew looked around and was amazed by the engineering feat that surrounded him. But when they reached the level of Lake Okeechobee, and the top gate opened to allow the boats to exit, Lew was stunned. He thought the airboat was about to enter an ocean. Nothing but water lie straight ahead all the way to the horizon. A flock of Florida mottled mallards rested in the spikerush and water reeds off to the right. Lew could imagine native alligators moving in with only their snouts showing ready to gobble up an unsuspecting fowl luncheon.

Phil's twelve-foot airboat installed with an opposed six-cylinder Piper aircraft engine clipped across the eight miles of choppy water to the Kissimmee River's mouth in about ten minutes, give or take a few seconds. Moments later, they docked at Angler's Delight Marina and made their way into the restaurant. They sat in a booth by the window overlooking an array of watercraft, everything from aluminum rowboats to mid-sized cabin cruisers.

A young man wearing a Seminole Bend High School Warriors t-shirt was talking to a well-built, gray-haired, lanky giant of a man wearing a University of Florida Polo shirt in the booth across the aisle. Listening intently to the conversation with their elbows on the tabletop sat a middle-aged man and woman who didn't say much, but kept nodding their heads in affirmation. Phil glanced over, noticed the group, did a double-take, and then stared at the man in the Polo shirt. "Well, I'll be damned! If it ain't Martin Woods sitting there chatting to Kenny Gormon and his mom and dad, Maxine and Marvin."

"Martin Woods? You mean the Martin Woods who played on a couple of championships for the Boston Celtics? That Martin Woods? He's the Florida Gator's coach now, ain't he?"

"Sure is. Damn good player in his time. Played with Russell and Havlicck on Red Auerbach's teams in the sixties. He must be here recruiting Kenny."

"Kenny must be a good player. I don't remember Brett mentioning his name, though."

"Kenny pretty much single-handedly ended Martin Park's seventy-three game winning streak last month. Helluva player, yep, helluva player!" Phil boasted.

"Didn't know about Kenny," Lew said while looking away and out the window. Another teardrop had begun to trickle down his cheek, and he wiped it away with the back of his closed fist. Phil knew immediately that he had brought up a heart-wrenching topic and wished he could take it back.

"Sorry, Lew. I just remembered that was the same night Lew and Sheryl were killed. There I went and done it again to you cuz I can't keep my dang big mouth shut."

"I thought I was over it, but I'm feeling like a miserable grown-up baby," Lew responded as the waitress placed two glasses of water and a couple of menus on the table.

"Be back in a few minutes to take your order," interjected the waitress and then hastily headed off to the kitchen. Angler's Delight was starting to get crowded.

Phil couldn't think of anything to say that would make Lew feel better, so he said nothing. They both grabbed their glasses and took a sip of water.

A few minutes later, Lew broke the ice, "So, do you think Kenny is good enough to make it at Florida?"

"Sure do," retorted Phil confidently. "The kid hustles and never misses. Best shooter I've ever seen, and that includes high school, college, and the pros! Only one problem is that Kenny wasn't a starter on the Warriors team. Rarely do bench players get a shot at the SEC or any other big school conference, you know. Heck, most don't even get to play in a small college."

"If Kenny was that good, why did Brett not start him?" Lew asked.

"Not sure, but probably had something to do with Jimmy Jackson getting most of the playing time. Remember I mentioned that rich rancher named Roy Jackson who owns the golf course where we're headed? Anyway, his kid is Jimmy Jackson and—" Phil caught himself in mid-sentence and paused. He wasn't going to upset Lew again. "Well, nothing. I'm wrong to even bring it up."

"Bring what up?" quizzed Lew. He had a perplexed look on his face.

"Aw, nothing, Lew. Brett was a great coach and a good man. You had quite the remarkable son. Should be very proud of him." Phil was ready to change the subject, but his diversion only made Lew more mystified.

"Tell me, Phil. If you're hesitant to say something bad about Brett, don't worry. I'm fine. What's this about Jimmy Jackson and his dad?"

"No big deal, ya know. But rumor has it that Roy Jackson throws his money around quite liberally to get what he wants. Didn't want to tell you, but some folks round here think he paid for Brett's new house so Jimmy could play. I'm not so sure, though, cuz as I told ya, Brett was a good man. A really good man."

Lew took another sip of water and sat in momentary silence, gazing out the window. He was trying to process the implication that Phil had just presented. He had a hard time believing Brett could be bought and his integrity be compromised. Phil was eager to switch the conversation away from sports. "So, you gonna have the catfish for lunch, Lew? I highly recommend them!"

During lunch, Lew and Phil chitchatted small talk in every colloquial direction that avoided basketball: types and sizes of fish in Lake Okeechobee, the scale of unfriendliness posed by native alligators, the power of hurricanes in South Florida, and the amount of sugar production in the area. But throughout the sea of prattle, Lew couldn't keep from thinking about his son taking kickbacks from a wealthy rancher.

Noticing that Coach Woods and the Gormon family had finished eating and were now involved in a serious discussion at their table, Lew handed the waitress his MasterCard and asked her to put the check that was lying in a leather binder in front of the coach on his own tab. The waitress walked over to the Gormon party, pointed to Lew, then explained to Coach Woods that he would like to pay their bill. The Gormon's and Coach Woods all turned to see who the generous man was who had picked up the check, but none of them recognized him. But Marvin Gormon spotted the other man and said, "Well, dang if it ain't Phil Bennett sitting with that man. Wonder if he's giving the guy an airboat tour or something."

Coach Woods got up and walked over to thank Lew. He reached out his long arm for a handshake, and Lew stood up to greet him. Phil watched in awe.

"Do I know you?" asked Woods.

"No, sir, but my son, Brett Berry, was the basketball coach here in Seminole Bend before he died in an accident," replied Lew.

"Sure thing. I never knew him personally but heard tremendous things about him. Very sorry about your loss."

"I appreciate that, Coach. I remember watching you compete when you were with the Celtics. You had some great teams! Do you miss your playing days?"

"A little bit," offered Woods. "But I miss smelling Red's cigar smoke during practices even more!" His reference to Red Auerbach caused a chuckle, and the ice was officially broken. Phil then stood up and introduced himself.

"Well, I just wanted to express my appreciation for picking up the check. It certainly wasn't necessary." Woods patted Lew on the shoulders.

"Happy to do it, Coach. From what Phil tells me, Kenny Gormon is quite a player. I'm assuming you're trying to sign him?"

"Not only a good player, but a terrific kid. High GPA and marvelous attitude. He's got the whole package."

"Well, good luck snagging him, Coach, and good luck on a winning season. A championship year ahead, what do you think?"

Woods pointed to the embroidery on Lew's shirt pocket and said, "As long as we don't have to mess with Penn State, we should do just fine."

The men shook hands again, and Coach Woods went back to his booth. The waitress brought the credit card slip. Lew signed it and added a big tip. Lew and Phil waved at Coach Woods and the Gormon's as they exited Angler's Delight and headed back to the airboat.

Sitting on a stool in the bar at the back of the restaurant, unnoticed by everyone except the bartender who was serving up shots of Southern Comfort to the angry-looking man, Roy Jackson stared intensely at the Gormon table. He was plotting how to put an end to the Florida Gators' newest recruit.

CHAPTER 31

Tuesday, March 9, 1982

1:30 p.m.

About a quarter-mile upriver from Angler's Delight was a man-made tributary that dumped into the Kissimmee. Mangrove tree roots extended out into the river and disguised the nine-foot-wide entrance making it look like swampy backwater instead of access to a canal. To get through the thick shrubs, someone sitting in the bow had to separate the brush and push it off to the side while the boat gently floated in. Usually, that was done with the front passenger's arms and an oar, and that passenger had scabby scratches for a few days. Many times the boat captain gave a shove from the stern then ducked his head, lest he took a branch to the eyeball.

Phil Bennett learned from his bloody mistakes and had a better idea. He rigged a protective shield for the airboat that would guard his weathered face from the arms of nature, otherwise known as tree branches. Phil put the shield to good use as he'd been up the canal to where it entered the golf course property many times. He was lured there by cash, plain and simple. Phil knew that at the edge of the golf course sat a pond covered with tropical reeds, lily pads, and Titleists. Once a month, he went up there with a long pole attached to a fine mesh net and sifted out a paint bucket worth of golf balls. He usually earned about $50 at the Saturday swap meet peddling those little buggers.

Phil told Lew to lift up the four-foot square plywood plank that was lying on the floorboard and slip it in the manmade slots that he had welded onto the aluminum base for just these occasions. The plywood was an inch thick, plenty strong enough for pushing aside the shrubbery, and wide enough to cover the front passenger and driver, too. That is if his arms were long enough to grab the throttle while reaching backward.

"Now duck down behind the shield, Lew. Keep your arms tucked in, too."

When Lew was safely sheltered behind the new bulkhead, Phil crawled on the floorboard behind him and reached back to the steering handle. He guided the airboat straight at the canal, then reached for the throttle and gave the big fan just enough gas to delicately penetrate the bushy area. The shrubs at the entrance had been moved so many times that they offered little resistance, and eight feet later, the canal opened up into a boulevard of scrub pines, cypress trees, and brown reeds. The irrigation canal made a beeline northward to the horizon, and after laying the bulkhead shield back on the floorboard, Phil climbed into the pilot's seat and opened up the engine full blast.

As Lew checked out the swampy surroundings, he understood why the townsfolks were puzzled at the dredging of a canal through wetlands. It made no sense. Water was abundant in all directions and could easily be channeled to irrigate fairways, greens, and lawns for the golf course residents. He turned around in the boat and put up a hand, signaling Phil to stop. Phil slowed the engine and then killed it.

"What's up, Lew? Peaceful country, huh?" stated Phil rhetorically.

"Yep, sure is. Is that one of those sonar fish finders next to you by any chance?" asked Lew.

"Dang tooting it is. I can find schools of fish easier than those pro bass guys! Why? Do you want to do some fishing right here? I thought you were in a hurry to get up to your boy's place."

"Yes, I am Phil, and no, I'm not interested in fishing right now. I'm just curious as to the depth of this irrigation canal."

"Why's that?"

"Something's not right about this ditch. I can't place it, but it doesn't make sense. So I was just wondering what the depth was."

"I can turn on this thingamajig, but it ain't always perfect. Lots of wiggles and lines show up on the screen." Phil flipped the switch and waited for a few minutes to warm up the meter. Seconds later, the screen read a depth of thirty-three feet.

"Says it's thirty-three feet, Phil. Does that mean anything to you?"

"Well, why would an irrigation canal need to be thirty-three feet deep? Most irrigation ditches I've seen are shallower than they are wide."

"Don't know. Hmm, does make you think." Phil scratched his forehead.

"Who'd you say owns this land, Phil? You know, the man who supposedly paid off my son so his kid could play hoops."

"Not sure he really did that, Lew, just rumors you know," replied Phil, still embarrassed that he even mentioned it. "Anyway, his name is Roy Jackson. Not liked much around these parts. Can afford to buy damn near anything his heart desires, he can."

"Including millions of dollars to dredge a needless thirty-three-foot deep irrigation canal for fifteen miles?" retorted Lew shaking his head. "He must be involved in something more than breeding Brahman cattle."

"That's what most people round here think, Lew, but no one can seem to prove anything. Mind if I head up to the golf course now?"

"Sure thing, sorry about holding you up," responded Lew.

A short time later, the airboat reached the golf course property line. Phil shut off the airboat's loud engine and started up an electric trolling motor attached to the stern.

With minimal wake to ensure the folks teeing off weren't disturbed, he quietly maneuvered the winding canal as it snaked through the course. Approaching a widespread pond that was an ominous water trap for the fifth hole duffers who sailed their balls over the green, Phil noticed a small dock with a canoe roped up next to it. He cautiously jockeyed the airboat to the opposite side, where Lew hopped out and wrapped the mooring line to a steel cleat on the sturdy pier.

The dock led to the backyard of a two-story Spanish Mission estate home hidden behind a smattering of Laurel Oak and Mahogany trees. The house had a plantation look with six white marble columns, a never-ending porch with old antebellum furniture, and a red brick façade with a creamy antique texture. Whoever lived here paid more in real estate taxes than most folks in Seminole Bend earned in a year. Lew and Phil both hoped the security system wasn't of the canine variety.

The Saint Augustine grass that covered the backyard was damp, spongy, and needed a haircut. Thinking the Dobermans would be released any second now, Lew and Phil huddled nervously close to each other, searching in all directions as they plodded uphill to the porch. Had they not been middle-aged men with graying sideburns and wrinkled, sweaty foreheads, they probably would have held hands so the boogeyman wouldn't eat them.

"Disculpe, señor y señor. Esto es propiedad privada!"

Miguel, a groundskeeper, was running towards Lew and Phil with one hand above his head, motioning them to stop, and the other hand grasping a steel blade by his waist. They froze and stared at the blade. Death by Doberman or death by slash—neither sounded appealing.

"Okay, okay," shouted Phil at the skinny Hispanic man in the worn-down blue jeans, muddy canvas Converse tennis shoes, and sweaty teal and orange t-shirt with a faded emblem of the Miami Dolphins on it. "We were just about to leave."

As they turned to head back to the airboat, Miguel stopped running, peered at Phil, and said, "Señor Bennett? You Señor Bennett?"

Phil and Lew both turned back around, glancing first at Miguel's face, then down to the blade he held in his left hand. It was then they saw the blade was from a lawnmower.

Miguel noticed the men staring at the blade, and he realized why they looked so frightened. He lifted it up slightly and said, "Sorry, sorry. Lawnmower blade. I sharpen blade so I can mow yard." He tossed it on the ground. Miguel's command of the English language was marginal, but Lew and Phil got the message. Needless to say, they were relieved. There was still a chance their bodies would walk out of here with their heads attached. Phil looked closely and pondered who the gardener could be. He recognized the face but couldn't place his name.

"Sorry, I know you, but I can't remember your name," said Phil. "Where have we met?"

"My name is Miguel. Mi amigo Pancho and me, we fish in river at your place year ago. You give free ride on lake with airboat." Miguel smiled and moved closer with his arms spread wide ready to hug Phil, but Phil reached out and shook his hand first. The grass clippings on Miguel would just have to remain stuck to the perspiration that was serving as an ocean for the Miami Dolphin.

"Ah, yes, I remember now," said Phil. "I felt bad you boys weren't catching any fish, so I thought we could have some fun. Anchored and did a little swimming, too, 'til we saw those gator snouts coming our way."

"Si, si! Fun, yes! What you here for?" asked Miguel, trying his best to speak English.

"We're looking for Coach Berry's home. The basketball coach and his wife lived out here somewhere. You happen to know where?"

"Si, yes. But coach and wife killed in car accident and no one home," replied Miguel.

"Yes, we know that. My friend here, his name is Lew, and, well, he is Coach Berry's dad. He's never been to his son's house because it's new and Coach had just moved there. He just wants to take a look."

"Okay, si, okay," said Miguel, pointing back toward the estate and motioning beyond the property. "Coach's house, it is across street. On hole siete, no, sorry, mean hole seven. Can't get there by water, so leave boat and walk. Come, come, I show you."

Miguel started towards the side of the estate home and waved for Lew and Phil to follow. He wanted to settle up with Phil for the kindness he had shown him and Pancho last year, so he walked the men across the front yard and to the street.

"Can't see from here. Go down path and you come to house." Miguel pointed at a long, cobblestone driveway that began underneath a brick archway, which led to who knows where. A redwood fence connected to the arch was supposedly meant to delineate the property line. A sign on the fence read *Private Property, No Trespassing*. There was no indication as to who occupied the home, just a fancy black mailbox with the reflective street number emblazoned on the side. Lew and Phil sauntered down the meandering driveway until they reached the house, a spacious two-story, charming European wood frame design with elegant, seamless connectivity to the large pool in the back. The landscaping was consistently sub-tropical, dotted with Queen palms, palmettos, and hibiscus shrubs. You couldn't see the seventh fairway, but you knew where it was from the sounds of projectiles slicing through tree branches, and newfangled cussing linguistics echoed simultaneously by the duffers who launched the dimpled warheads.

Lew placed his hands on his hips and shook his head. "My son didn't buy this home on his coaching salary. Ain't no way, Phil."

"Yes, I see what you're saying. Strange, huh?"

They walked up to the massive oak front door and tried the latch. It was locked, which surprised neither of them. Lew expected entering the home to be a challenge. They walked around the house to the pool and found a fifty-pound plastic bucket of chlorine tablets lying next to a decorative wooden shed that housed the pump, filter, gas heater, and a variety of pool supplies. The bucket hadn't been opened, so the fifty-pound capacity was still intact. Lew grabbed the wobbly grip strap and headed towards the sliding glass door on the patio. A small decal next to the handle warned that Buttress Home Security was monitoring the Berry's estate. Chances were that no one had paid Buttress since Brett and Sheryl's death. Thus the protection service had ended. At least that's what Lew was hoping. He guessed right.

Tossing the bucket at the reinforced glass did no damage. So together, Lew and Phil tilted the container, stepped back from the door about twenty feet, then strutted awkwardly but quickly and rammed the bottom of the bucket hard into the glass, shattering it into large, jagged shards. Their momentum carried them headfirst into the family room where they lay scraped and stunned on the ceramic tile floor.

Seconds later, as Lew and Phil were rising, being careful not to step on the sharp pieces of tempered glass, they heard noises directly above them. Something had been slammed shut, a door or a dresser perhaps, followed by the sounds of footsteps scuttling down a hallway. Lew and Phil paused a moment and looked up at the ceiling, then nodded at each other and ran towards the staircase that led to the upper floor. At the base of the steps, they realized they had no weapon or way of protecting themselves, so Lew ran to the nearby fireplace and grabbed a brass poker. Side-by-side, they slowly ascended the stairs, leading with the pointed end of the metal rod. The sounds had ended. They peeked their heads in unison around the corner and saw an open window at the end of a long hallway and dashed to it. Both men glanced towards the yard and saw the unknown intruder wearing a full-length raincoat with the hood up and tied tightly around the head. The person was limping briskly towards the seventh fairway carrying a container the size of a shoebox.

"Damn, it's a good fifteen foot drop out of this here window, Lew," exclaimed Phil as he looked down at the grass below and then to the trespasser who was now out of sight. "I don't think we're gonna catch him. Better call the cops."

"Hold on, Phil. We just busted up the patio door. I'm not in the mood right now to explain how or why we did that. Even though the property is my son's, it's still breaking and entering. I think we need to check out the house quickly and then just get out of here."

"Miguel, over yonder, where we docked the boat, saw us and knows me. If cops come investigating, we're screwed!"

"We need to take that chance now, Phil. We can deny it later, and they would have to prove we were the ones who smashed the glass. And being it was my son's house, I can probably talk my way out of it. Come on, let's take a quick look around and go."

Lew dropped the fireplace poker, and the men walked into the master bedroom where they had heard the intruder's footsteps from the first floor. The drawers to a dresser next to the bed were closed, but a framed picture was lying on the floor face down. Most likely, it fell when the person slammed the drawer shut. The protective cover over the print was made of plastic; thus, it was still intact, but the edge of the wooden frame had split, and the casing was ruined. Phil picked it up and flipped it around as Lew glanced over his shoulder.

"Who are those boys with Brett?" asked Lew as he looked at the picture of his son standing in the middle with his arms around three players. The boys were in uniform, dripping with sweat, and were standing in the high school gymnasium. The crowd of people in the background were frozen in time hugging and slapping hands, obviously celebrating some sort of victory.

"See the sign on the wall. Says *Beat Sebring*. Must be after that game a few weeks ago. It was the last game before they beat Martin Park, you know the game where, well, you know." Phil dropped his head down, not wanting to look at Lew. Lew nodded and patted his new friend on the back.

"It's okay, Phil. I know, Martin Park was Brett's last game. So who are the boys he's with?"

Phil looked up empathetically at Lew and said, "That's Kenny Gormon, Tyrone Banks, and Jimmy Jackson. Kenny's the young man we saw in the restaurant earlier today with Coach Woods. Tyrone is the nephew of that sheriff's deputy I was telling you about. And Jimmy Jackson is Roy Jackson's son, ya know, the guy who owns the golf course."

Lew stood up and paced slowly around the room. There were framed pictures of Brett and Sheryl everywhere he looked. All were photos of a young couple clearly in love. In the top drawer of the nightstand was a Polaroid instant picture of a very pregnant Sheryl lying on the beach stretching her bikini to the limit. It was apparently hidden in the nightstand for private enjoyment only, unlike the others that were displayed prominently to be appreciated by all. Lew put the picture back in the drawer and closed it. His eyes were watering once again.

"Mind if you take me back to your shop to get my car, Phil? I think I've seen all I care to see right now. I want to get over to the sheriff's department to talk to that deputy before I head back to Miami. You said his name was Willy Banks, I think?"

"Sure thing, Lew, and yep, his name is Willy Banks."

Lew and Phil secured the upstairs hallway window, then swept up the shards in the family room and tossed them in the trash can by the garage. A refrigerator-sized cardboard box had been unfolded and placed on the floor of the garage to soak up any oil that might leak from a car parked above it. They took the cardboard and covered up the patio door frame using duct tape to keep it in place. Barring any more trespassers, the home would be left as is until Berry's estate had been probated. At this point, that could be quite some time in the future. The FBI had placed a legal hold on administering the assets until they had completed their case.

Lew and Phil strode back down Brett's long driveway, crossed the street, and snuck along the shrubbed edge of the Spanish Mission estate's property line to the airboat. Moments later, they fired up the engine, reversed course, and headed back down the water route they had come in by. The noise angered both the golfers and residents who were enjoying drinks on their patios. From the guest room window on the top floor of his estate home, Oliver Harfield watched them depart. When they were out of view, he picked up the phone next to the bed and dialed a number.

Oliver was a man of few words, and he only needed four to let the person on the other end of the receiver know there was a problem.

"We may have trouble," said Oliver simply. But he needed seven words to solve the problem: "You need to take care of it."

CHAPTER 32

Tuesday, March 9, 1982
6:05 p.m.

Lew and Phil tied up to the dock at Bennett's Airboat Palace a few minutes past six. Lew made a call to the sheriff's department from the payphone and was told that Willy Banks was on duty, but couldn't be "bothered." Lew offered to meet the deputy anywhere in the county, and the response was, "Not today, sir." Lew detected a tone in the receptionist's voice that something was going on with Willy Banks, and it was none of his business. Lew wasn't about to fight the law, but his curiosity had just peaked.

"They won't let me talk to Willy Banks," declared Lew. "You got any options, Phil?"

"Won't let you talk? Strange, being he's a public servant, wouldn't you say?"

"Very strange, indeed. You know where he lives by any chance? Maybe I could visit him at home."

"Not sure, but I do know that his brother's girlfriend, well, ex-girlfriend, works in the photo department over at BoldMart. Her name's Abby Charles. She's Tyrone Banks' mama. Nice gal, but not sure she works this late. The store's open 'til nine if you want to check it out. She lives with Willy, so she should know how to get ahold of him."

"How do I get to BoldMart?"

"Go left out of here and at the stoplight turn right. It will be a couple miles up on the right. Can't miss it."

"Thanks so much for everything," said Lew as he shook hands with Phil. He took out a piece of gum and unwrapped the tin foil, then scratched his phone number onto the inside of the wrapper. “Here’s my phone number. Keep in touch. Let’s do some fishing next time I come!”

“Dang tooting, Lew. Be much obliged to find you a whopping big bass!”

*****

There were plenty of parking spaces at BoldMart, which was the case most Tuesday nights. Folks in Seminole Bend wouldn’t miss *Happy Days*, *Laverne and Shirley,* and *Three’s Company* back-to-back unless there were a Warriors basketball game in town. Thus, BoldMart used Tuesday nights to run inventory on its stock. That was the reason Abby Charles was working late. The photo department had processed 137 rolls of film the previous week, but the credit card slips and cash in the till amounted to 124 rolls, and someone had some explaining to do. Abby was visibly stressed when Lew came up to her counter.

“May I help you?” uttered the attractive clerk with a hint of anxiety in her voice. She didn’t look up at Lew. She was busy examining the spreadsheet in front of her hoping to find the source of thirteen errors she was tasked to find.

“I’m looking for Abby Charles. Is she working tonight?”

Abby glanced up and replied sarcastically, “Working would be a mild term used in this labor camp. I’m Abby Charles. How can I help you?”

“Actually, I’m looking for Willy Banks. Can you help me?”

“Try the sheriff’s department. He’s working the noon to eight shift.”

“I did try to call down there. They wouldn’t let me talk to him. Phil Bennett told me you worked here and could find him for me.”

“Why wouldn’t they let you speak to him? Are you some sort of hitman?” Abby was back to her sarcastic ways. She was busy and needed this conversation to end.

"No ma'am, far from it. My name is Lew Berry, I'm Coach Brett Berry's dad. I'm just in town for a short time and wanted to ask Willy some questions about my son's accident, that's all."

"I'm so sorry," apologized Abby. "I didn't mean to be rude, just have a lot of stuff to finish here tonight. Your son and daughter-in-law's accidents, well, they were just terrible. My son, Tyrone, played for Coach. Loved him! He was a good man, Mr. Berry, a really decent man!"

"Thank you. That's much appreciated, it really is. So any chance you could hook me up with Willy?"

"Sure thing, but he usually heads down to Nubbin Slough for some night fishing after work on Tuesdays and gets home pretty late. Are you staying in town tonight? Willy will be heading for work 'morrow before noon. You can catch him before he goes."

"Guess I'll stick around for one more day. Can I get your address?"

Abby wrote her address with directions down on a notepad and handed it to Lew. Lew thanked her and started to head off when Abby called for him. "Lew, hey, want to see a great picture of your son in action?" Lew turned around and came back to the photo counter.

"I just processed this picture today, and I know I'm not supposed to show folks someone else's private photos, but I thought it was fantastic. I'm thinking about making a copy for Tyrone, so don't tell anyone you saw it." Abby reached in a drawer and pulled out an envelope that contained a pack of pictures and six strips of negatives. She opened it carefully, flipped through several prints, pulled one out, and handed it to Lew. The image was of Brett standing by the bench with his arm raised high and displaying four fingers. He was calling out a play. Standing next to him, his faced beaded with sweat and looking rather nervous about the game situation, was Tyrone Banks. It appeared he was taking a short breather.

"Very nice," commented Lew with little emotion. He enjoyed seeing a picture of his son but was once again overwhelmed with grief at his loss. "So, who took the pics? He or she is a fine photographer."

"Well, as I said before, I'm not supposed to tell you this, but they were taken by some cowboy named Danny Martin. Don't know the man, but he printed his name and phone number on the label. The dude was huge, Lew, all muscles and such. He didn't look like no photographer. Sorry, I know that's a stereotype, and I shouldn't be talking that way."

"Did he take any other pictures at the basketball game? I wouldn't mind seeing them before I leave."

"That's the strange thing. This was the only photo from the game. Most folks will shoot a whole roll for a sporting event. Also, I know all the boys on the team, and none of them have the sir name Martin."

"When was the picture taken?" asked Lew.

"It was right in the middle of the roll of film, and I'm guessing it could have been during the Sebring game. They played them at home a week before your son's accident. I processed prints that your daughter-in-law Sheryl took from that game, and there were some great pictures. She bought a frame for one that Brett was in while he was celebrating with the boys. Sheryl was a good lady, too, Lew. I'm so, so very sorry for your loss."

"Thank you, Abby," said Lew as he was glancing back at the picture of Brett and Tyrone. Who are the other boys on the bench? I really only heard about the starters from Brett."

Abby pointed at the photograph and said, "That's Willis Mann, Amos Carnes, Tony Rambus, and Tim Carter behind Coach and Tyrone. I recognize Norma Foss sitting behind Brett, she was the boy's fifth-grade teacher who just took a leave of absence to have a baby. Nice gal, they all loved her back in elementary school. And over on the left is Gordon Timkins, probably Seminole Bend's biggest fan! He always sits right behind the players' bench so he can hear what

Coach is saying in the huddle. There on the right is Bard Smith. He's a sport's writer for the *Miami Sentinel*. And up on top of the picture is Marvin and Maxine Gormon, Kenny Gormon's mama and daddy. You can barely see them."

"Yes, I recognize them. I saw them briefly at Angler's Delight earlier today. The coach from Florida was recruiting Kenny."

"No kidding?" asked Abby with a surprised look on her face. "Well, I'm happy for Kenny, but I'll bet Roy Jackson would have a shit fit, oh, sorry 'bout my language, Lew, if he knew Florida was recruiting Kenny and not his son Jimmy."

"I've heard about this Roy Jackson. Phil Bennett told me. He sounds like some pompous ass if you ask me." Lew paused momentarily. "Oh, now I'm sorry for my language, Miss Charles."

Abby chuckled, and Lew smiled.

"By the way, Abby, I heard Willy was involved in quite an airboat accident a couple of months back. Phil Bennett told me that, too. Was he injured badly?"

"Quite frankly, my friend Willy is crazy! He smashed into something and flew headfirst into the river bank. Almost got eaten alive by a gator. Some Mexican dude saved his butt, thank God!" Abby shook her head as she remembered how close Willy had come to dying.

"Who's the Mexican man? I'll bet he's Willy's best friend, huh?"

"Don't know. He disappeared after dropping Willy off at Angler's Delight."

"Why would a town hero disappear?" asked Lew. "Saving the life of a sheriff's deputy could be legendary around here."

"You would think, wouldn't you?" replied Abby. "Well, I don't mean to rush, but I best be getting back to work, or I won't have a place to work come tomorrow."

Abby began to place the pack of photos into the package, but several of the prints on top slipped out and fell to the floor. Lew bent down to pick them up and noticed there were eight photos of a Mexican man taken at a convenience store. Six of them were of him chatting with some other folks, perhaps co-workers, and two were of the man munching on a Hostess Twinkie.

Lew stood up, handed the pictures back to Abby, pointed at the top one, and asked, "Who is this guy? The photographer must have found him pretty interesting to take eight shots, wouldn't you say?"

Abby looked closely at the first picture, then shuffled through the other seven. "Don't know, but the picture was taken at Quick Stuff. That rusty Chevy van in the background hauls migrants over to the orange groves on the coast. I've seen them many times early in the morning getting junk food."

"Well, I don't know what you think, but taking eight pictures of that Mexican guy seems kind of suspicious to me," said Lew. "You sure you don't know this Danny Martin fella that took the pictures?"

"Nope. Ain't never seen him before he dropped off that roll of film a couple of days back. Maybe the guy is a friend of his, that's all."

"You said Danny is a big, muscular cowboy. Ever see cowboys hanging around with migrant workers?"

Abby shook her head no.

"What's on the rest of the pictures in that pack," inquired Lew. "Would you mind if I took a look?"

"Absolutely not, Lew! I could get in big trouble as it is looking through private pics. But showing those pics to someone else is terribly wrong." Abby stacked the photos into a neat rectangular bundle and placed them back into the package.

Lew glimpsed down at the spreadsheet on the counter in front of Abby and recognized that it was a cash flow statement. Abby had been stressed about something on that balance sheet when he first arrived, so he thought he would take a guess. "How much are you off today?"

"What?" replied Abby.

"I noticed you were a bit anxious when I met you, so I was just assuming the balance sheet was off."

"Yes, you're right, Lew, but it's really none of your business. I like you, but I think you should go now. I'll see you tomorrow at the house if you stop by."

"Please, Abby. Don't get me wrong. I was just curious and making small talk, that's all."

"Well, if you think you must know, I'm missing sixty-five dollars somehow. But that's not your problem, so I'll just deal with it."

Lew reached for the wallet in his back pocket and pulled out four twenty-dollar bills and handed them to Abby. "Here's eighty bucks. I would just like to rent those photos we just saw for one day. They'll be as good as new when I get them back to you tomorrow night, no finger smudge marks or anything. What do you say, Abby?"

Abby stared into Lew's eyes and was stunned. She glanced away and shook her head no, but with little emphasis. She didn't have enough money of her own to cover the loss, and she feared losing her job if the balance sheet wasn't equalized. Seconds later, Abby stopped shaking her head, and her red, tired eyes locked again on Lew's.

"One day! One day only I'm telling ya! I'm working only until four tomorrow afternoon. Don't be a minute late, and don't you dare tell a soul, you hear?" Abby took the pictures out of the package and placed them in a manila envelope. That way she could keep the negatives at the store. If for some reason Lew didn't get the photos back, Abby would have to make reprints. But before handing the envelope over to Lew, her curiosity peaked, and she decided to skim the pics for herself. The last three photos were of a man fishing in the distance. Abby recognized the location as Nubbin Slough, and then she thought she knew the man in the picture holding a cane pole and staring intensely at a red and white bobber that was floating on the water. She pulled a magnifying glass out of the drawer and maneuvered it over the fisherman's head. Abby looked up at Lew with trepidation.

"What's the matter, Abby?" asked Lew.

"It's this guy fishing," Abby replied as she pointed to the distant face in the picture. "It's Willy."

CHAPTER 33

Tuesday, March 9, 1982
8:30 p.m.

"Seminole Bend," sighed Lew to himself from the practically empty BoldMart parking lot as he scanned the surrounding concrete block houses hidden in nighttime shadows. "I've got a bad feeling about this place." In the course of just a couple days, he learned that his daughter-in-law was not killed in a horrible accident, but rather kidnapped by unknown persons, and his son may have been taking money under the table from a notorious local pain in the ass named Roy Jackson. And who was in Brett's house searching his bedroom? Lew was pondering the circumstances of recent events from the bucket seat of his rented Pontiac Trans Am. He could not seem to organize his thoughts as he flipped through the eight pictures of the Mexican man at Quick Stuff and the three photos of Deputy Willy Banks fishing on a riverbank. Perhaps there was somehow a link between the Mexican man and Willy Banks? Lew knew bizarre things were happening in this small town, and he had a gut feeling that Brett and Sheryl were at the center of the strangeness. But he couldn't place his finger on it. He needed to find out more before heading back to the FBI office in Miami on Thursday. Lew got out of the car and walked over to a nearby phone booth and dialed "O."

"May I help you?" asked the operator in a southern drawl that reminded Lew of his all-time favorite movie, *Gone With The Wind.*

"I'd like to make a collect call to 412-687-2211. My name is Lew Berry."

After eight rings, the operator said gently, "Sorry, sir, there doesn't appear to be anyone at home."

Lew thanked the operator and hung up. What was his wife, Janet, doing in the Poconos? It had been a very long day, starting with the FBI refusing to allow him to board the flight home to Pittsburgh. And although he was thoroughly exhausted, he wanted to find out if there was a connection between the mystery Mexican in the pictures and Deputy Banks, even though he had never met either one. Abby had mentioned that Tuesday night was Willy's fishing night, usually at Nubbin Slough. Maybe he could find him there.

Lew checked the Seminole County road map he purchased on the way out of BoldMart and found Nubbin Slough. He fired up the Trans Am and squealed rubber as he left the parking lot. It was going on nine when he pulled the nocturnally concealed black car well off the road near the marsh.

Lew carefully moved along a trodden path to an embankment overlooking the watershed. Cricket frogs and cicadas chirped madly in melody with the hoots from a Barred Owl. He began to descend down towards the water but stopped suddenly as a long, shiny silver snake slithered through the weeds in front of him. It appeared to be an Eastern Ribbonsnake or some type of racer, but with Lew's limited knowledge of herpetology, for all he knew, it could be a Cottonmouth that despised Pennsylvania-bred snowbirds. From where he was frozen in his tracks, Lew surveyed both banks to see if anyone was fishing. No one, he was sure of it.

Lew backtracked the path to his car, his sleep-deprived mind nervously searching for man-eating salamanders or killer terrapins along the way. In the safety of his bucket seat, Lew contemplated his next move. He remembered that the gardener he and Phil met earlier while docking the airboat mentioned that he enjoyed fishing. Could there be a chance that he's fished with Willy Banks?

"Was his name Miguel?" muttered Lew thinking aloud. "Or did he say his name was Pancho? No, I think he said his friend was Pancho, and they rode with Phil on his airboat. It's either Miguel or Pancho. I'm sure of it. Maybe. Why am I talking to myself? I'm losing it."

With nothing but time to kill, Lew decided to drive back to the golf course estate and see if he could find the Mexican. He remembered seeing an oversized utility shed hidden from sight near the dock, and Lew thought at the time that the gardener probably lived in it. Perhaps a hundred-dollar bill might entice the man to lead him to a fishing hole where Willy might be. Lew pulled out on to the road and made a U-turn. He entered the Seminole Bend Golf Course Estates a half-hour later, and according to the bronze sign attached to a security guard post at the entrance, the development was a *Division of Harfield & Jackson Enterprises*. The guard slid open the Plexiglas window and grabbed a clipboard and pen.

"Yeah, where to?" asked the disinterested guard. He was in a hurry. Lew could see a portable thirteen-inch Sony television on the counter next to the guard. The Knicks and Celtics were in overtime.

Lew thought for a moment, then decided to tell the truth, well, sort of the truth. "Brett Berry's house."

"Know you're coming?" replied the guard without looking at Lew. His focus was entirely on the Sony. Larry Bird just hit a three-pointer from the corner. "Damn it, Holzman! Campy Russell can't guard Bird. Put Maurice Lucas on him!"

"Sure, he's been expecting me for a while now. I'm running a bit late." Lew lied. He decided to take advantage of this well-timed NBA advantage to distract the guard. "So, you a Knicks fan?"

"No, not really. Just sick of watching the Celtics win every year. Okay, let me see. You said Brett Berry's house. What's your name?"

"Lew Berry. I'm his father."

The security guard wrote down Lew's name and time of arrival in the column next to Brett's name. If he had checked the restrictions list as he was required to do, the guard would have noticed that no visitors were allowed to Brett Berry's estate without permission from Sheriff Al Bonty. But if he had taken the time to check that list, he would have missed Micheal Ray Richardson's three-point swish from the top of the key to tie the game back up.

"Yes sir, that was big time! That kid from Montana is clutch!" The security guard waved Lew in without looking at him.

Lew drove around the dark asphalt streets that wound around the estate homes. The only time he had been here was earlier in the afternoon, but he had arrived by boat. The dim street lighting was practically useless, and the homes themselves were set back from the road and obscured by foliage. When he was about to give up and head back to Seminole Bend, Lew noticed the brick archway and cobblestone driveway that was unquestionably the entryway to his son's house. He parked the Trans Am just off the road in front of Brett's *Private Property* sign. As Lew was about to lock the door, he paused as he glanced at the envelope lying on the passenger side seat. Not really knowing why he opened the door and grabbed the pictures that Abby had given him. He locked the door and crossed the street.

Oliver Harfield's mansion was too big to hide behind trees, so the wealthy owner hadn't bothered to even try. A thick layer of lush, green, Saint Augustine grass ran from the street to his front door, a distance of a hundred yards or so. The driveway was made of white brick and curved near the entrance to the estate so those arriving by limos or other luxury vehicles could simply continue around the circle without shifting into reverse. Good thing, too, because backing up may have resulted in destroying the newly planted cypress trees that lined the driveway. Oliver had returned recently from a vacation in Italy, and he decided his Florida mansion needed a little taste of Tuscany.

The Harfield property line was separated from neighbors by a neatly trimmed row of podocarpus shrubs accented with allamanda bushes that ran from the street all the way to the canal. Near the dock, the shrubbery branched off and formed a rectangular box that neatly hid the utility shed from sight. Lew ducked and treaded softly alongside the natural barrier until he reached the shed. On the side facing the water, a small pushout casement window was open, and a light showed inside. Lew peeked through the window and saw Miguel, or was it Pancho, sitting at a card table reading a book. Deciding he had a fifty-fifty chance at picking the right name, he reached up, tapped on the glass, and whispered, "Hey, Miguel. Miguel, over here."

Miguel jolted from his seat and jumped back to the wall opposite the window. He had never had a visitor, and this could only be trouble. The only entry into the shed was by a roll-up door that he never locked while he was in it. Next to the door was a rake. He dashed over and picked it up, then rolled up the door and held the rake like a baseball bat.

"Quien esta ahi!" shouted Miguel, looking at the corner of the shed but afraid to go any further. Lew stepped around the edge and stopped in his tracks when he saw Miguel ready to swing the rake.

Lew raised his hands high in the air. "Hold on, son! It's me. I met you earlier today with Phil Bennett, remember?"

With the rake ready to strike, Miguel leaned in to get a closer look at the intruder's face. "Si, yes, you with Señor Bennett. I remember." He laid the rake against the side of the shed. "Why you come back?"

"Do you know a deputy sheriff named Willy Banks?"

"No, sir. Por que?"

Lew pulled out the envelope with the photos from his jacket pocket and held the bunch up for Miguel to see. "Can I show you a picture of him?"

"Si, entra, por favor." Miguel pointed at the shed door.

Lew followed Miguel inside the combo utility shed and home. Half of the space was taken up by yard maintenance tools, a well-used riding mower, and a non-motorized reel mower. The other half of the shed was what Miguel called home: a folding card table with one chair, a portable cot with a pillow and a thin blanket, and a small dresser with multiple scratches. On top of the dresser was an old AM-FM transistor radio, Miguel's only form of entertainment besides the book he was reading. Lew noticed the book was *The Family of Pascual Duarte*, written in Spanish by Camilo Jose Cela. By the looks of the torn cover and ripped pages, Miguel most likely found it in someone's trash. Lew was appalled that someone so rich couldn't provide better living quarters for his groundskeeper.

Miguel had survived three scorching, humid Florida summers without air conditioning in this shed and was just happy to have a job. He drank water from the garden hose and used a portable Coleman cooking stove behind the shed to fry up the fish he caught in the canal. On the nights the fish weren't biting, Miguel sautéed earthworms with carrots and butter, a delectable meal rich in protein! Cleaning the one plate and one fork he owned, along with the two t-shirts, two pairs of underwear, and a pair of faded Levi's was done during his daytime break. The canal was his washing machine, sink, fresh fish market, and latrine all combined into one.

Miguel motioned to the cot and said, "Sit, por favor."

"Thanks, but I think I'll stand," answered Lew graciously. "Here is a picture of Willy Banks fishing down at Nubbin Slough. Do you recognize him?" He handed the three pictures over to Miguel. Miguel studied them closely.

"Sorry, no," replied Miguel. "Don't think I know him."

Lew decided to sit down on the cot. He wasn't sure what to do next. After a few moments of awkward silence, Lew stood up and placed the rest of the pictures on the card table so he could take the wallet out of his pants pocket. He reached into a hidden compartment behind his driver's license, unfolded a hundred-dollar bill, and handed it to Miguel.

Miguel's face looked puzzled, and he didn't know the English language well enough to ask what Lew was doing. He opened his hand to receive the money, and a wide grin appeared. "Gracias, gracias. Thank you, thank you!"

"Bienvenido, Miguel. My Spanish isn't the best, but I'm very happy to help you out. We just met, but I can tell you are a good man."

Miguel bowed his head several times to show his gratitude. That's when he noticed the other pictures that Lew had placed on the card table next to the three of Willy Banks. He stopped bowing and picked one up.

"Señor, where you get pictures of my amigo, Pancho?" He flipped through the eight photos of his friend at Quick Stuff.

"Those are pictures of your friend?" asked a perplexed Lew Berry. "Is this your fishing buddy? The one you were with at Bennett's Airboat Palace?"

"Si, yes. Pancho," replied Miguel. He pointed to the picture. "He at Quick Stuff in the picture. Eats breakfast there before work."

"Where does he work?"

"Picks oranges near Fort Pierce. Stop at Quick Stuff each morning on way."

"What time does he stop at Quick Stuff?" asked Lew.

Miguel shrugged his shoulders and said politely, "No understand. Sorry."

Lew was trying to extract the correct Spanish words from deep within his gray matter, but he had last taken Spanish as a senior in high school, and the extraction was difficult. He failed the course his junior year, and his mother forced him to retake it and pass or no playing football.

"Uh, que hora at Quick Stuff?" asked Lew while pointing to his watch.

Now Miguel understood and responded, “Early. Six or seven in morning.”

Miguel handed Lew the photos of Pancho, and Lew scooped up the remaining pictures and placed them back in the envelope. He thanked Miguel several times and then departed, once again following the hedge to his rented Trans Am. A few minutes later, he was back at the security guard’s hut.

“Who won?” Lew asked the security guard.

“McKale tossed in a baby hook at the buzzer. Celtics won in the third overtime.” The security guard logged Lew’s exit time and waved at him. It was eleven o’clock. The Suns and Lakers were just getting started at the Forum in LA.

CHAPTER 34

Wednesday, March 10, 1982

12:10 a.m.

Lew drove around Seminole Bend until he located Quick Stuff, the twenty-four-hour convenience store that catered to the rancid coffee-by-day and malt liquor-by-night crowds. Actually, you could find stale coffee day or night at Quick Stuff. What wasn't sold stayed in the glass pot until it was sold, perhaps a day or two later. The store owner made sure the pot was cleaned out each winter. Nice of him. Cellophane wrapped sandwiches that hadn't sold by the expiration date at Dixie Food and Drug were sent over to Quick Stuff at a deeply discounted wholesale rate. The various shades of bologna hoagies decorated the cooler better than Christmas ornaments.

Lew decided to park the car in the lot, as far away from the security lighting and the store as possible, and try to catch up on some needed sleep. He wanted to be there when the migrant's van pulled in. Lunch at Angler's Delight had been his last meal, so he walked into Quick Stuff and bought a package of Little Debbie donuts and a Yahoo for dinner. Healthy eating had eluded Lew his entire life. He wasn't about to start now.

At 6:20 a.m., a rusty, one-ton, Chevy cargo van rolled into the parking lot. The raucous noise from the muffler that was partially dragging on the road awakened Lew abruptly. He looked in the rearview mirror and watched as fifteen Latino men hurried into the store. Lew grabbed the photos and walked over to the van, waiting for the workers to exit the store with their Hostess Twinkies and liter bottles of Coke. It was too expensive for each migrant to buy their own individual bottles, so they pitched in for the big size and passed it around on the way to the coast.

Minutes later, the men came out of Quick Stuff laughing and chatting with each other. They obviously enjoyed the brotherhood of migrant workers. Lew took out the most explicit photo of Pancho and waited for a group of four men to approach him while he stood at the side door to the van.

"Hello, fellas," greeted Lew with a smile. He handed a picture to the nearest worker. "This man's name is Pancho. Do you know him?" They all glanced at each other and nodded to Lew.

"Yes, sir," said the migrant worker who was holding the picture. "Pancho works with us." The group looked around the lot and towards the store. "Don't see him here today. Probably out fishing again." The men looked at each other and chuckled.

Lew handed the three prints of Willy Banks fishing at Nubbin Slough to the group of workers. "How about this man? Ever see him?"

Seeing the picture of Pancho and then the one of Willy Banks caught the attention of the group's spokesman. "Can't see too well cuz the man's so far away, but maybe that's that big ass black guy that Pancho claims to have saved a few weeks back!" The migrants high-fived each other amid loud laughter. "Pancho be bragging he freed some dude from being eaten by a gator."

"You're saying this guy Pancho saved the life of this man fishing?"

"Si, yes. That's what he say alright."

That would undoubtedly confirm Abby's story about Willy being in an airboat accident and being saved by a Mexican man who strangely disappeared afterward. Could it possibly be a coincidence that this cowboy dude, Danny Martin, took spy-like pictures of both Willy and Pancho without knowing that the two were connected somehow? "Doubtful," thought Lew.

Lew still wasn't sure Pancho or Willy had any information about his son's death and daughter-in-law's kidnapping, but now he was curious why Brett's picture was in the cowboy's pack of photos with the others. He needed some answers. Finding Pancho may be next to impossible, but Willy Banks is a sheriff's deputy and public servant and Lew wasn't leaving Seminole Bend without speaking to him. Lew thanked the migrant workers as they loaded up the van. They were packed like sardines, sitting cross-legged on the metal floor for the forty-five-minute ride to Fort Pierce.

Lew reached into his pocket and pulled out the address Abby had written on a notepad. She said Willy would head off to work before noon, so Lew decided to try and catch him at home before he left. Abby would be back at BoldMart, hopefully with the books all straightened out and the boss happy. He decided to drop off the photos on the way to Willy's house even though he was plenty of hours ahead of the four o'clock deadline she had imposed. Lew was ready with one hand on the steering wheel and the other on the gear shift when he paused momentarily. He wanted to take one more look at the picture of Brett with Tyrone and the other players on the bench. Lew flipped through the prints until he found the photo, then stared at it until teardrops once again rolled down his cheeks. He dearly missed his son.

Lew wiped his cheeks on his shirtsleeve and determined that he needed to regain his composure before seeing Abby. He went into Quick Stuff and bought a small cup of old coffee to wash down the last Little Debbie leftover from dinner, and off he went. Lew had barely pulled out of the Quick Stuff parking lot when he slammed on his brakes and sat motionless in the middle of the highway. A blurred image passed through his fatigued mind, and he made a swift U-turn, utterly oblivious to the traffic coming from both directions that swerved into the ditch to avoid the maniac in the Trans Am. With a little luck, the highly torqued V-8 engine would have Lew back at the Seminole Bend Golf Course Estates in a few short minutes.

CHAPTER 35
Wednesday, March 10, 1982
7:30 a.m.

The security guard working the entrance to the Estates was not the NBA aficionado of the previous night. Lew would have to come up with a new plan. If push came to shove, he still had three more folded up Benjamin Franklins tucked neatly into a hidden compartment of his wallet. That could very likely be a couple of week's wages for the security guard.

The new security guard was a well-groomed young man still in his teens and trying desperately to grow some dark hair on his upper lip. Lew figured him to be either a high school dropout wanting to turn his life around or the son of a wealthy Seminole Bend Golf Course Estate owner waiting out the years to become the CEO of his dad's company. Lew was hoping he was a dropout.

The young man put down his orange juice on the counter, and the glass window slid open. That was a good sign. It was early morning, and the guard wasn't drinking coffee. The insalubrious consequences of caffeine had not infiltrated his youthful mind, and Lew was confident the jolt he himself received from the corroded Quick Stuff java would be enough to persuade the innocent young fella to let him enter the Estates.

"May I help you, sir?" smiled the security guard.

"Ah, yes, you can, son," grinned Lew back at the window. "I was here visiting last evening and forgot my camera. I'm heading back home to Pennsylvania and just wanted to pick it up on my way to the airport. If you check the sign-in sheet, you'll see I was here around eleven. Name's Lew Berry."

The boy pulled off the clipboard that was hanging on a nail and glanced at the names of visitors from last night. Sure enough, Lew Berry had logged in and out. There was no need for him to check the restricted list because that should have been done by the night guard.

"Okay, Mr. Berry. According to the vehicle make and license plate, I see you're driving the same car. I'll go ahead and sign you in. Have a nice day!"

"Thank you, young man," said Lew. "I'll be out in no time flat." Lew entered the gate and tried to remember how he found his son's place last night. It was much easier in the daylight.

* * * * *

The cardboard covering the patio door had been removed and was lying against the stucco wall a few feet away. Someone was either inside the house now or had been inside the house since the time Lew and Phil left yesterday. Lew went back to his rental car and grabbed the crowbar from the trunk. He wasn't going to take any chances.

Lew quietly entered the house through the broken glass and crept into the family room. Under the paddle fan, he stopped, looked around, and listened for sounds. Nothing. He found the first picture he was looking for on the fireplace mantel. He removed the photo from the frame and headed towards the stairs.

Lew froze as he entered the master bedroom on the second floor. The king-size mattress was lying upside down next to the box spring, every drawer was open, and all the clothes in the closet had been ripped off the hangars and were lying in piles on the floor. Whoever broke in was in a hurry and seemed to be looking for something specific.

The next picture Lew was looking for was right where Phil put it yesterday. Encased in a chipped wooden frame, it was a picture of the celebration in the gym after the Warriors beat Sebring. It had been lying on the floor when they first came into the bedroom, but Phil placed it on the window sill after showing it to Lew. Lew again took the photo out of the frame and put that and the print from the fireplace temporarily on top of the dresser, then went to the nightstand drawer to get the picture he wanted most - the Polaroid shot of Sheryl pregnant on the beach. It was gone.

"Why would an intruder want a Polaroid picture?" whispered Lew to himself. "This doesn't make sense."

Lew checked every shelf and drawer in the bedroom, closet, and master bathroom, but couldn't find the other item he was trying to find. There was no jewelry box anywhere in sight. He remembered seeing something the size of a shoebox tucked into the trespasser's arms yesterday as he and Phil gawped from the hallway window where the intruder had jumped and run out on to the golf course. Lew surmised that the burglar made off with Sheryl's jewelry and most likely had returned to find more valuables. But still, why snatch the Polaroid from the nightstand?

Knowing his fingerprints were everywhere, Lew elected to clean up the bedroom mess to avoid raising suspicions to law enforcement personnel who would return once the estate was released from FBI possession and could finally be probated. He lifted the mattress back on the box spring, hung up the clothes, and shut all the drawers. Lew grabbed the two pictures he had removed from the frames and exited the master bedroom. He moved about the house, scanning each room from top to bottom, arranging items as he went along. Everything was back to neat and tidy, except for one thing: the patio door needed to be fixed. Miguel's handyman skills appeared to be quite admirable, and Lew speculated as to the Mexican man's ability to replace a patio door. Might as well find out, seeing his new friend was right next door and could certainly use some extra cash.

Lew replaced the cardboard covering over the shattered glass door, then drove to the end of the driveway where he parked the car. Before getting out, he looked closely at the two photos he took from Brett's house. Lew needed the missing Polaroid picture to confirm his theory, but that wasn't going to happen. He laid the prints on the dashboard and got out of the Trans Am.

As he was about to follow the hedge to Miguel's shed home, Lew stopped and watched two men exit the back seat of a black Lincoln Continental and enter the front door of the mansion. That normally wouldn't have surprised Lew, except one of the passengers was wearing a sheriff's uniform. Lew wondered why an officer on duty would be riding in a civilian car and not in a police vehicle.

The shed door was open, and Miguel was replacing the sharpened blade onto the push mower. "Hi Miguel," said Lew in an unruffled voice. He didn't want to startle him again this morning as he had last evening.

Miguel jumped up and gave Lew a big hug when he saw him in the doorway. "Hola Señor Lew, mi amigo! You come back, why?"

"Come with me, please," motioned Lew using hand gestures to point in the direction of Brett's house. He pulled out another $100 bill from his wallet and used it as a carrot to intrigue Miguel to follow him.

Miguel looked up to the windows of the Harfield estate to make sure no one was watching, then said to Lew, "Okay, okay. Pronto! Señor Harfield fire me if he sees me gone."

Lew and Miguel slithered alongside the shrubbery at the property's edge, pausing at times to check for unsuspecting onlookers. When they were certain no one was watching, they ran across the road and up Brett's driveway to the house. Lew stopped and bent over, his hands firmly placed on his waist. Sweat was beading from his forehead, and his Polo shirt was drenched. Both his clothes and heart chambers were getting quite a workout on this short trip to Seminole Bend!

Lew led Miguel to the patio door and, using hand gestures combined with short English words, asked him if he could fix it.

"Si, yes! I fix it, but need glass," answered Miguel as he nodded and pointed to the frame.

"Yes, okay. I'll get the glass and come back." Lew was happy to know Miguel could do the job but realized the next two problems might be difficult to overcome. He would need a pickup truck to transport the glass, and then find a way to get past the security guards for a third time. Lew wondered if Phil owned a pickup truck.

* * * * *

Lew got back into his car while Miguel bustled along the hedge back to the shed. The Lincoln was still parked in the driveway circle near the entrance to the Harfield mansion. He was about to turn left and head toward the exit to the Estates when he noticed something peculiar in Harfield's driveway, a few feet from the *No Trespassing* sign posted on the property fence. Lew shifted the Trans Am back into park and got out. He stood in the middle of the road trying to figure out why there was a rectangular metal grate set into the decorative path to the house. Lew had seen it before but thought it was a drainage trench for rain runoff. Now with a second look, he noticed it was actually a solid four-by-six-foot iron hatchway with no slots to drain water. Odd.

Lew ignored the warning sign and walked up to the hatch. It was fastened shut with a two-foot sliding cylindrical bar and two locks, one at each end of the rod. Someone was going to great lengths to keep people out of this vault. Lew looked up. He heard chatter coming from the mansion's front door and noticed the two men from the Lincoln were just about to leave. They were shaking hands, but apparently the noise level was high, and Lew guessed the men were arguing about something. He ran back to the Trans Am, fired it up, and hurried toward the security gate. The young guard checked the clock and wrote the time on the clipboard next to Lew's name.

"Thanks," said Lew. "Hey, by the way, my son was looking at putting in a new sliding glass door. I may be back with a pickup truck to deliver it. That okay with you?"

"Thought you said you were heading to the airport?" replied the guard. "Don't matter, though, cuz I'm done working in a few minutes. Sheriff Al himself will be on duty after me."

"Sheriff Al? Is he the sheriff of Seminole Bend?"

"Yep. One and only."

"Why would a sheriff work the security gate out here at the Estates?"

"Good question, Mr. Berry. Not sure, and I don't ask cuz it's none of my business."

"How long will he be working?"

"Noon to one. Then George Dellon comes in and replaces the sheriff."

"He works for just one hour? How many days a week?"

"Oh no, not each week. Sheriff Al only works one day a month."

"You're saying the sheriff works as a security guard here only one day a month and for only one hour at a time?" Lew had an incredulous look on his face. "Okay, well, thanks again. It's much appreciated!"

Lew waved at the guard and drove away. He pulled off the road about a quarter-mile from the guard post, got out, and locked the doors to his Trans Am. He then snuck back towards the guard post behind a line of palm trees and hid behind a hibiscus shrub about twenty feet from the hut.

With his nose firmly planted between two pink flowers while thorn scratches were slicing up his face, Lew watched the Lincoln Continental that had been at the mansion stop next to the security gate. Exiting from the back seat was the man with the uniform. He slammed the back door shut, and the Lincoln continued down the road away from the Estates. Sheriff Al Bonty opened the door to the guard post and entered. A few minutes later, the teenage boy left and walked up the road into the Estates.

"Well, I'll be damned," breathed Lew to himself. "The kid lives out here. So much for my dropout theory."

Five minutes later, an eighteen-wheeled semi drove up and stopped at the guard post. Lew examined it carefully but could find absolutely no markings on it whatsoever. No letters, no numbers, no logos, nothing! The truck driver conversed with the sheriff for a minute or so, then proceeded to enter the Estates. Lew checked the license plate: *RJCorp*, registered in Florida.

Lew scampered over a couple of property fences and followed the slow-moving semi up the road, keeping out of sight. The last wall Lew climbed was his son Brett's, and he hid behind the arched entrance as he watched the truck pull into the Harfield mansion across the street. The trailer stopped directly over the iron ingress, and the driver stepped down from the cab and crawled underneath his vehicle. Moments later, he wormed his way out with the cylindrical metal bar, two locks, and a key in his hands. He placed the objects on the ground and walked back to the cab.

Lew peered under the truck and noticed the two doors of the hatch were propped open to a vertical position instead of being laid flat on the ground. The bald, bulky truck driver went back to the cab but then disappeared, most likely through a connecting door from the cab into the trailer. Lew guessed that the floor of the trailer must also have an opening, and odds were that it was located directly over the underground vault. Who builds a truck like that?

The rear doors to the trailer remained closed. Because they were sealed, and the fact that the iron hatches to the underground compartment were opened at a ninety-degree angle to the truck, whatever was being moved in or out of the subterranean vault was shielded from view. Lew assumed that was the plan.

Well, shields work just fine in both directions, so Lew crouched down and tepidly crossed the street to the truck. Surveying all around him and seeing no one, he rushed to the side of the trailer, picked up one of the locks, and yanked the key out of the keyhole. He hoped the burly truck driver wouldn't notice the key missing when he re-locked the vault doors. Lew then hustled back to his hiding place across the street and held his breath. After a minute, he stuck his head around the corner and exhaled. No one had seen him.

Lew could hear clanging and assumed something metal was being moved either into or out of the truck. It was closing in on one o'clock when the hatch doors closed, and the truck driver slid the rod back into place. The locks were in the open position, and the man clicked them shut on both ends. He first placed his hands in his jeans pockets, then patted his shirt pocket. He then squatted down and looked under the truck and around the hatch. Lew knew the driver was looking for the missing key.

The driver glanced at his watch and decided it was time to hit the road. He climbed into the cab, shifted the semi into reverse, and carefully backed out into the street. When he was out of sight, Lew sprinted across the street and to the iron covering. He knelt down and unfastened both locks, then slid the rod out of the slots. Lew surveyed the area for any onlookers, and when he was sure no one was watching, he lifted one door to the hatch and flapped it over onto the driveway. What he saw next was very puzzling. About thirty feet down was a water channel that either started or ended right below him. Lew could see that the canal seemed to veer towards the mansion, but his vision was limited. However, he clearly saw a floating vessel directly below the entryway.

The vessel appeared to be a five-by-eight-foot rectangular watertight container that was as high as it was long. The top of the container was the point of ingress, and the entry was similar to the driveway hatch: two metal doors that swung open on hinges. However, there were no locks anywhere in sight. There was a nine-inch propeller coming out one end of the container attached to a mechanism and bracket. Inflatable floatation devices were wrapped around the box, mainly for damage control, but could also raise and lower it in the water. Barely visible to Lew were two rails on the bottom of the canal. Obviously, the propeller generated thrust while the tracks guided the vessel through the water. Lew wondered what was in the container, or what had been in the container that was now being trucked away. The hatch was too far down to reach, so a ladder must have been used to move the items from the container to the truck, or vice versa.

Lew closed the driveway hatch and locked it. He tossed the key on the ground to avoid suspicion in case the truck driver told someone it was missing, then ran across the street to his son's property. He hurried back to his car the best he could while dodging bushes and climbing fences. Lew slowly pulled out onto the Estate's entrance road, trying not to attract attention from the security guard, aka sheriff. But as he was attempting a Y-turn, he stopped directly in the middle of the street and gazed at the hut. It was empty!

Lew remembered the teenage guard saying that the sheriff was on duty for only an hour when he worked a shift, but why would he leave before the next guard showed up to relieve him? It was just a few minutes past one, so it was possible the next guard was a bit late, especially if the guard was another youngster who had spent Tuesday night fishing and cuddling up with a six-pack. And where did the sheriff go? He arrived at the post in the Lincoln Continental, but who picked him up? Lew was puzzled. Is it possible the sheriff caught a ride with the semi driver?

Lew completed his Y-turn and gunned the Trans Am back down the road to Seminole Bend. By now, Willy Banks would have reported for duty so he couldn't catch him at his home. He would try again at the sheriff's office, this time in person. Lew couldn't pin it down, but something was fishy—and it wasn't coming from bass boats on Lake Okeechobee.

CHAPTER 36

Wednesday, March 10, 1982
2:00 p.m.

"Deputy Willy Banks is no longer employed by the Seminole Bend Sheriff's Department," said Johnny Murphree with a solemn tone. "That's all I can tell ya."

"How's that?" asked Lew Berry. "I just talked to his brother's ex-girlfriend yesterday, and she told me I could find him here."

"Just happened. If you've been talking with Abby, I'm guessing this here's a personal request. Maybe you can find him at home."

"It's both personal and professional, sir. My name is Lew Berry, and I'm the dad of the basketball coach here at the high school who was killed in an accident. I believe some strange things are going on regarding his death, and Willy might have some answers."

Johnny was about to respond until he noticed an overweight man with a felt cowboy hat emblazoned with a five-star badge appear from the men's room next to the reception desk. The sheriff approached Lew and shook hands.

"And what makes you think Willy Banks would have any information about your son's accident?" questioned Sheriff Al Bonty. "Oh, pardon me. I'm Al Bonty, sheriff of Seminole Bend County. And I'm sorry about your son's death and that his wife is missing."

Lew and Johnny Murphree simultaneously looked at the sheriff and hesitated a moment. They must have been thinking the same thing. Could it have been a slip of the tongue or an honest mistake? Lew was about to find out.

"Wife missing?" inquired Lew with a raised eyebrow. "I thought Sheryl died in the accident?" Only the FBI had information that Sheryl was possibly kidnapped, or at least that's what they told him.

Sheriff Bonty's face turned bright red as he stammered through his explanation. "Well, of course, she died in the accident. Did I say missing? No, I mean that she definitely was killed along with your son."

Johnny Murphree turned his face away from Al Bonty and rolled his eyes. Lew noticed. And then Lew noticed something else.

"I feel bad about you good folks working down here at the sheriff's department," uttered Lew sarcastically.

"Why's that?" inquired Sheriff Al.

"I mean, you all must not get paid much for all the hard, dangerous work you do, right?"

"We get paid just fine, sir," replied Bonty sharply. "What makes you think we don't?"

"Oh, I'm sorry to upset you," said Lew smugly while shrugging his shoulders. "I just figured that if you have to moonlight, you probably aren't getting much of a salary, that's all."

"I don't think any of my deputies are moonlighting, but if they are, it's really none of your business or any of our taxpayer's business what they do after hours." Sheriff Al was becoming feisty.

"I'm not talking about your deputies, Sheriff. I'm talking about you." Lew poked his finger at Al Bonty's face, stopping just millimeters from his big nose. Johnny Murphree was now watching the two men with awe. Lew had broken no laws so he couldn't be arrested, but Sheriff Bonty didn't take well to being disrespected. This was getting interesting!

"What do you mean 'me'? I'm not following you, Mr. Berry." Feisty to angry in a few short seconds, Al was losing control.

"Don't you work as a security guard at the gate to the entrance of Seminole Bend Golf Course Estates?" Lew locked eyes on his victim. Sheriff Al's mouth dropped open, then closed. He obviously had no response.

"Didn't I see you there just a few minutes ago?" egged Lew relentlessly. "Could have sworn you rode to work in a Lincoln Continental and left in a semi-truck. Interesting combination for a commute, wouldn't you say?"

Sheriff Bonty looked at Johnny Murphree and then noticed two other deputies had heard the conversation and were standing in the hallway listening to every word.

"You need to leave now, Berry." The conversation had disintegrated from politeness to contempt in a few short minutes.

"Yes, I believe I do. Have a good day, Sheriff." Lew exited the building with a smile and a nod to Al Bonty and his deputies.

Sheriff Bonty glanced ungracefully at his deputies and ordered, "Get back to work, y'all! That whole conversation was just a bunch of horse manure. That old man's just seeing things, that's all."

Johnny Murphree wasn't quite so sure.

CHAPTER 37
Wednesday, March 10, 1982
2:15 p.m.

Lew made the decision not to bother Willy today. If he just lost his job, he would be in no mood to answer questions. Instead, Lew drove his rental car to Bennett's Airboat Palace to see if his new buddy had a pickup truck. He needed to fix Brett's patio door before heading back to Miami.

Phil Bennett was gassing up an airboat at the dock when he looked back and saw Lew's Trans Am pulling into the parking lot. He replaced the nozzle onto the rusty pump and walked over to greet him.

"Decided to take me up on that fishing proposal after all, eh Lew?" teased Phil as he gripped Lew's hands to welcome him back. "Well, as luck has it, I hear they're biting big time today!"

"Would love to, Phil, but I have a favor to ask."

"Shoot. I'm happy to help whatever you need, friend."

"Do you own a pickup truck?" inquired Lew. "I think I better fix that patio window we busted up before heading out."

"You know anything about fixing windows?" asked Phil skeptically.

"No, but remember Miguel, that gardener across the street?"

"Yep, sure do."

"Well, he said he knew how to fix it. Just need to get him the glass."

"When did you see Miguel?"

"This morning," replied Lew. "Let me show you something, Phil." Lew reached through the open passenger window of the Trans Am, grabbed the envelope of pictures, and pulled out the photos of Pancho. "Do you recognize this guy?"

Phil studied the pictures closely then glanced precariously at Lew. "Yep, I sure do. That's that Mexican man I told ya who went fishing with me and Miguel. Where did you get these?"

"You got any Coke in your palace and a place to sit and chat?" asked Lew. "It don't have to be a throne either."

"Yep, got both," answered Phil. "Please enter my kingdom!" Phil pointed to the door, and the two friends walked in.

Phil reached for two Cokes from a mini-fridge and then sat down in one of two brown, ripped, and patched with strapping tape leather chairs in the customer's lounge. Lew collapsed in the other one, then for the next half hour, told Phil about everything that had happened since yesterday when he left to see Abby Charles at BoldMart. Phil sat in stunned silence. Thinking about all the mysterious deaths in recent weeks, he wasn't sure he wanted to tag along with Lew, but he could see the man needed him. Although he only knew Lew for a little more than a day now, he felt like they had been friends since childhood. Phil wasn't about to abandon a comrade in need. Friendship is unconditional.

"My pickup's in the shop getting a new transmission," said Phil. "But we can take an airboat back to the Estates. I can secure the glass with a couple of ratchet straps. Just a mile down the road is Gibby's Glass Warehouse. Buck Gibson, the owner, is a friend and will deliver the glass over here. Getting the damn thing from the dock up to Brett's place could be a challenge, though."

"If Buck could get the glass here this afternoon, we could ride up there after dark, and then Miguel can help us."

Phil nodded. "Let's see if he has it in stock. What are the dimensions?"

Phil called up Buck, who was thrilled to have some business today. Nary a customer had stopped by the entire morning, and Gibby was about to close early when the phone rang. He had the type of glass they were looking for but would need to cut it down a bit to meet the specs. Buck said to give him a couple of hours.

CHAPTER 38

Wednesday, March 10, 1982
4:00 p.m.

The Florida Department of Public Safety Internal Affairs investigation into the death of the old man in the BoldMart parking lot was complete. Deputy Willy Banks' "reckless behavior unbecoming of an officer" was listed as the primary cause of the accident, and Internal Affairs recommended his immediate dismissal. Willy was notified of his discharge via a certified letter addressed to his home. Sheriff Al Bonty didn't want to explain the reasons for firing him face to face. Willy knew the sheriff wanted him gone, but how could Internal Affairs conduct a reliable investigation without even speaking to him?

No matter. Willy was fed up with the system. He was ready to wash his hands of the corrupt law enforcement administration and also the likes of Roy Jackson. Willy thought about becoming a bass fishing guide, and perhaps with just the right amount of marketing to those snowbirds up north, Willy could make plenty of money. However, although he had a unique talent for finding the ten-pound largemouths and hauling them in with his secret lure (a crankbait with a tiny piece of a nightcrawler attached for scent), creative advertising for a guide service was not his forte.

But every time that Willy thought about doing something different, he remembered his near-death experience at the hands of Roy Jackson. A month had passed since that night he lost his partner, Sam McCormick, and he had been left for dead to be eaten by swamp critters. Willy also knew that Roy was just waiting for the right moment to strike again, and this time Jackson wouldn't rely on an alligator to finish the job. Willy thought he should try starting up his own private detective agency with himself as his first client! Unfortunately, Willy hadn't accumulated or saved much money during his time with the sheriff's department, and commencing any kind of business would be more than he had ever put aside for this "rainy day."

It was time to relieve some stress. Willy put on his workout shorts and went outside to lift weights in the front yard of his inherited, two-room, concrete block house that sat smack dab in the center of Yardlyville, a section of Seminole Bend that didn't attract many visitors. Yardlyville really wasn't the official name, but those who lived there didn't know it by any other name. The white folks just called it the ghetto. Willy paused a moment before gripping the barbell to remember his best friend Bo Yardly.

"God rest your soul, my main man."

Droplets of sweat beaded up on Willy's forehead. The temperature in southern Florida was hovering in the mid-seventies, and the humidity was less than forty percent, a perfect day by both local folk and snowbird standards. But Willy always pushed himself to the breaking point while working out in his front yard, and his perspiration puddles could water the lawn on any day, mild or muggy. His mind had wandered away from proper weightlifting and breathing techniques as he reminisced about the days of his youth. It was twelve years ago since he last fooled around with Bo and he missed him dearly . . .

* * * * *

Willy had spent a week fishing, jawing, and playing checkers with Bo from sunup to sundown and well into the midnight hour back in March of 1970. Bo was on a short leave after completing basic training in Fort Sill, Oklahoma. Willy was pissed that the Army had stolen Bo away from the NFL after a sensational rookie season, and Bo was pissed that Coach Bear Bryant hadn't offered Willy a scholarship to Alabama so he could have blocked for him in college. Just for the hell of it, they drove down to Hudster's Hardware Store and bought two new transistor radios to break apart and put together again like the good old days when they were kids. Bo was excited to be joining the Signal Corp and heading to Colorado for specialized training the next week.

"Willy Boy, watch this." Bo had taken a blue wire from his transistor radio and attached it to some metal gadget he had in his pocket. Willy had never seen a device like it: a small, cylindrical silver widget with a green wire sticking out both ends. Bo tied the green wire to the blue wire in the radio, then took out a fine point needle nose pliers and wound the wires onto the base of the antenna. He replaced the batteries and flipped the switch. A few minutes later, Willy could hear a garbled, static-laced sound that he recognized as a communication's transmission from a pilot to an air traffic controller somewhere on the ground. Willy shot a look at Bo, raised his eyebrows, and smiled.

"Where did you learn that one, Bo?"

"Not much else to do up in Green Bay after the first Wisconsin snowfall. Half the bars close down because the owners go out deer hunting, and the ones that stay open can smell an enemy a block away, and they ain't too friendly. The night before we were smoked by the Packers, I was tinkering around with the clock radio by my bed, and I noticed something curious. There was a Radio Shack next to the hotel that was open 'til nine, so I bought me some doodads and just started messing around with the radio. Bingo, this is what I discovered."

*****

A few tears fell from Willy's eyes as he remembered that great week with Bo. Back then, he had no idea the next and last time he would see him would be during Bo's funeral over at Calvary Baptist.

*****

Willy dressed for the funeral in his finest military décor, including insignia and the service ribbons that displayed his Purple Heart and Medal of Honor. After the burial, when everyone had gone back to the church for refreshments, Willy walked over to the casket of his best friend and knelt down. The coffin had been partially lowered into the burial vault, but the grave would not be filled until later that evening. The funeral home's staff were fans of Bo's, too, and they were back in the church sharing memories with the others. Willy unpinned his two priceless medals and laid them gently on top of the casket. He tossed a handful of dirt over them, whispered a final prayer, and left for home. Willy didn't feel like socializing. Even after surviving four bullets in the back, the pain of losing his buddy was the worst torture he had ever endured. Abby and his four-year-old nephew Tyrone gave him a long, well-needed hug when he had returned to the house.

CHAPTER 39

Wednesday, March 10, 1982
4:30 p.m.

Willy went back into the house and took a shower. Abby would be home from work in a couple of hours, and Willy would have to find a way to tell her that he was fired from the sheriff's department. Willy let Abby and Tyrone move into his mama's house with Otis back in the fall of 1966 while he was stationed in Orlando. He served two more years, then came home to Seminole Bend in the fall of 1968.

*****

Abby thought Willy would make a fine husband and daddy. He was kind, respectful, heroic, and shoot–pretty dang good looking! But Willy refused to start up a romantic liaison with the girlfriend, or fiancé, of his older brother. Abby was dazzling and quite the catch for any bachelor, but there was something wrong about stealing Tyrus' gal even though he had walked out on her. Regardless, Willy promised to take great care of Abby and Tyrone until Abby could find a more permanent relationship.

Through the years, Otis, the youngest of the Banks brothers, kept moving in and out of the house. Each time he found a job, he would go rent a room at Duff's Motor Lodge for three dollars a day. Albert Duff was spending life in prison for murdering a customer who he caught fooling around with his wife Gertrude. Meanwhile, Gertrude took over the motel operations, but business came to a standstill after the trial. She wasn't liked much by most folks around Seminole Bend. Citizens were mad at the jury for siding with Albert's adulterous wife. Gertrude was forced to drop the rent to a measly three bucks a day just to get someone to stay there. Otis Banks was her best customer, that is, when he had a job. Otherwise, Otis spent his nights on the couch at Willy's house.

* * * * *

The workout had cleared up Willy's angry and confused mind, and now his head and heart were filled with determination. Whatever Roy Jackson was doing out on his estate was illegal, and the SOB had Sheriff Al Bonty and most likely other high-ranking law enforcement folks playing the crooked game with him. Willy and Bo had risked their lives in Vietnam for a better America, and Willy decided that ending the corruption in Seminole Bend was his next mission. It could be his last.

It was late afternoon when Otis got up off the couch to make himself breakfast. He was working nights down at Mucker's Produce and slept most of the day. Abby would be home any minute now and plop down on the couch Otis had just relinquished. She worked six days a week developing thirty-five-millimeter color prints on a fancy new photo processor at BoldMart. Her job was to remove the film from the cartridge using a picker and place it on the leader card. She did this with her hands in a dark box to prevent light from exposing the film. One mess up, and Abby could lose her job. Handling film all day long, together with the stress of perfection, meant her daily collapse onto the couch was justifiably warranted.

Tyrone usually got home from school shortly after his mama's afternoon nap began. His promising basketball season came to an abrupt end after the horrible deaths of Coach Berry and his wife. The last two games of the regular season had been forfeited, and the Warriors lost in the first round of the regional tournament to Clewiston, the same team they had beaten twice by over forty points back in December and January. Team spirit and energy died on the highway that fateful night, right alongside their beloved coach. Tyrone planned to start looking for a job that would keep him busy and put food on the table until football practice began in August. He still used Abby's bedroom to store his clothes and stuff, but he slept in a pup tent in the backyard. Somehow, sharing a bedroom with your mama when you're a sophomore in high school didn't sound too cool.

"Hey, Otis," Willy interrupted his little brother as he was making a peanut butter and jelly sandwich, "I need to ask you a question."

"What's up, bro?"

"You ever drank any Mad Dog Twenty?"

"Dang tooting, every chance I can get." Otis smiled at the thought as he smeared strawberry jam over his colossal mound of peanut butter.

"Where did you buy it, O?"

"Can't afford to buys it, even though it is dirt cheap. But I got a friend who will share a gulp or two on my way home from work."

"Your way home from work? Otis, you come home way past midnight. Who you meeting at those hours?" Willy wasn't sure he wanted his little brother messing around with winos in the middle of the night.

"Dude's homeless, bro. Dang sure likes me for the company. But some nights I can't find him, so I thinks he's got some woman stashed away somewhere."

"What's the dude's name?"

"I think he said Lars or Lance or something like that. I knows its starts with an L. At least, I'm pretty sure. Why's you asking me all these questions, Willy?" Otis shoved a double-wide portion of his sandwich creation into his jowls and began chomping loudly.

"Just curious about the MD Twenty thing. I called down to Mel's Spirits Shop and found out that Mogen David doesn't have a distributor in southern Florida. And the gal working there said you can't find it in any of the liquor stores in Seminole Bend."

"Well, that there friend of mine dang sure got it somewhere, Willy!"

"Are you planning on seeing him again anytime soon?"

"You betcha! I stop by his place every night, so I sees him tonight if he ain't with that lady friend."

"Where's his place? I thought you said he was homeless?"

"He is, but we all got a place to call home. That dude's place is in the telephone booth down by Dixie Food and Drug."

"You mind if I meet you there tonight, Otis?"

"Why? You got a hankering for some cheap wine, Willy?"

"You might say that."

CHAPTER 40
Wednesday, March 10, 1982
5:00 p.m.

Lew dozed off in the leather chair while Phil prepped the airboat for the night journey across the lake and up the canal. He attached a high-powered spotlight to the top of the propeller cage and rigged two long ratchet straps to eye bolts on the front and rear of the boat. Lew then went out back to the dumpster and pulled four, seven-foot metal support frames from two beds that had been tossed in the refuse bin a few nights ago. At the time, Phil was upset that people were using his dumpster without asking permission, but now he had a creative thought that might just work as a way of holding the glass on the airboat. He carried the supports back to the watercraft and grabbed his arc welding kit from the garage. It took an hour to vertically weld the support frames to the floor, one on each corner of the boat. On the six-inch by four-inch bolt plates that were now sticking straight up seven feet from the floorboard, Phil slipped on several layers of hot pads he had stored in the gas grill cabinet that was outdoors next to the garage. That would provide protection for the glass during transport. He went back into his store and sat in the chair next to Lew, who was snoring so loud that Phil worried the fish in Lake Okeechobee would be scared and go into hiding in the weeds. Soon, Phil was singing the same tune. Lord help the crappies!

Buck "Gibby" Gibson delivered the newly cut glass at five o'clock on his way home from work. He woke Lew and Phil from their stupor, and the three men carefully placed the glass onto the modified bed frame supports, then ratcheted the glass tightly to the eye bolts. The glass was now a clear boat canopy, and Phil thought that maybe this could be a get-rich invention someday. The ride up to Seminole Bend Golf Course Estates would be a good test for the new contraption.

At 6:30 p.m., as the sun was setting on a cloudless night in southern Florida, Lew and Phil fired up the engine and navigated the rim canal slowly. The glass canopy could be heard rattling on its steel posts, and both men hoped it would survive the journey. They were the only boat in the locks, and operator Ernie Hyle barely noticed them enter. When he did see them, he jumped off the stool and dropped his Double Whopper on the Playboy magazine he was reading and walked outside the booth onto the ledge.

“What the hell is that?” shouted Ernie as he peered through the canopy. “Phil Bennett, is that you down there under that glass roof?”

Phil looked up and waved. “Yep, Ernie, it’s me and my friend Lew here. Like my newly redesigned boat? Just invented it and am trying it out tonight. What d’ya think?”

“Glass top boat in sunny Florida is going to roast all your customers. Have ya turned crazy on me or something?”

“Nope. This here’s a ‘moon roof’ canopy for night fishing, my man. During the day, you can cover it with a piece of canvas to keep the sun out.” Lew was doing his best to keep a straight face as Phil poured out the lies.

“Okay, guess that makes sense. Well, are y’all fishing tonight?”

“No, not tonight. Just testing out my new invention, that’s all.”

“Well, I’ll be here when you come back. Damn Gordon Finch called in sick again. I’ll be working ‘til midnight. You boys are lucky you weren’t trying to come through a half-hour ago. I had to close it up for an hour to get me a couple Double Whoppers over at Burger King.”

Lew and Phil grabbed the hanging ropes as Ernie closed the gate behind them. They emerged onto Lake Okeechobee as the moon was rising over the horizon in the east, and the sun was vanishing below the skyline in the west. The result was radiant illuminations dancing around the surface of the big lake, which was serenely calm in the gentle wind.

The crossing to the mouth of the Kissimmee River was effortless, and the men reached the camouflaged entrance to the man-made irrigation canal as the last traces of sunset vanished. Phil turned on the spotlight and aimed the beam at the mangrove roots, then at the shrubs that covered the tributary. The glass canopy on the airboat prevented the men from inserting the plywood shield that they used yesterday to keep from scratching their arms and faces.

"I ain't gonna lie to you, Lew. This probably ain't gonna be pretty. You need to hold the front edge of the glass in place while I try to get us through this mess. Put your back to the bushes so they don't hit ya in the eyeballs."

"I'll do my best. Got any Neosporin lying around? I got a feeling I'll be needing some once we get to the other side!"

"Ain't got none of that, but I got some first aid spray in a can. Stings a bit, that's all." Phil winked and smiled as Lew shifted into position, facing backward on the bow. Lew grabbed the edge of the patio glass with both hands and ducked his head down the best he could.

"Okay, I'm as ready as ready gets," said Lew tentatively. "Onward, Captain!"

Phil lowered his body and gripped the controls, then gave the aircraft engine just enough gas to penetrate the thick foliage. Branches scraped across Lew's back, but he held firmly onto the glass. A tree limb struck the spotlight, causing it to turn sideways. Seconds later, the airboat emerged blindly onto the irrigation canal. Lew dropped his hands down from the glass and rubbed the myriad of abrasions on his arms. His Penn State Polo shirt was torn in multiple places on his back, and blood was soaking into the cotton fabric. But the glass was intact, and that's all that mattered.

"Perhaps a first aid spray break is suitable and proper at this time. What do you think, Phil?" Lew was applying a layer of humor to his pain. "Drop anchor here, okay?"

"What do you mean, drop anchor here?" asked Phil with a puzzled look. "I can spray your back without dropping anchor!"

"I'm kidding about spraying me. I'll live without antiseptic. Remember earlier today when I told you about the underground storage compartment in the driveway of that mansion across the street from Brett's house? There was some sort of rails that guided the chamber along the waterway."

"Yep, I remember. But what does that have to do with dropping anchor here?"

"Yesterday you said the depth of this canal was twenty to thirty feet, which seemed bizarre considering it's supposed to be used for irrigation. And why anyone would feel the need to irrigate a swamp is beyond me. I just want to check and see if there are rails on the bottom of the canal right here. If there are, then that canal goes under the mansion and all the way to the Kissimmee River."

"But why would anyone want to transport something underwater to some guy's driveway?" inquired Phil while Lew dropped the anchor off the bow of the airboat. "Wouldn't it be much easier to drive the truck from the factory or warehouse instead of dragging it through the bottom of an irrigation ditch?"

"I'm guessing that's a rhetorical question, Phil?"

"Don't know what kind of question it is, but if this here canal is being used as an underwater transport system, something illegal is going on." Phil straightened out the spotlight and then surveyed the area. The swamp was an eerie place at night. "How are you planning on finding out if there are rails in this canal?"

"Thought I'd dive down to the bottom and check it out," replied Lew as he lifted off his bloodstained shirt, then stood up and dropped his shorts to the boat's deck. Phil stared at him a moment inquisitively, then began to chuckle. Lew was standing in his royal blue and white checked boxers with an image of a lion climbing a mountain with the number 1855 etched below it. A Penn State fan to the bitter bare necessities!

"You can't be serious, my friend? You'd be gator bait this time of night if the water moccasins didn't get you first! Do you even know how to swim?"

Lew looked sadly at Phil and nodded. He was about to speak, then held back a moment, apparently trying to gain some composure. He squatted, turned his head, and focused on a ripple in the canal. Then Lew said quietly, "Navy. World War Two. I was stationed on the *USS Vestal* in Pearl Harbor on December 7th of '41. We were moored with the *Arizona* when the Japs bombed it, and the explosion blew our commander, Captain Young, right off our deck into the water. A couple of my comrades tossed a life ring buoy, but the captain began to sink. We were in about forty feet of water, so I dove down to try and save him, but instead of returning with our captain, I returned with the body of a dead sailor. No head. Just the body."

Phil sat cross-legged on the floorboard, dumbfounded as he listened to Lew. Neither man spoke, nor did they look at each other. Phil's cousin was killed aboard the *USS West Virginia* when an explosion ripped a three-inch, fifty-caliber gun barrel from its turret, flung it across the deck and slammed into his cousin's chest, crushing every rib and shredding the heart chambers. Memories of the Pearl Harbor tragedy consumed their thoughts as both men silently reflected on the massive loss of lives that day. Then Lew stood back up and dove into the canal before Phil could stop him.

"Wait!" screamed Phil as he tried in vain to grab for any of Lew's limbs he could latch on to. He crawled back to the spotlight and swiftly irradiated the water where Lew had entered. The muddy water and dark of night made it impossible for Phil to see Lew, but the beam of light illuminated the canal just enough for Lew to see a few feet ahead of him. He descended rapidly and within seconds came face to face with the whiskers of a freshwater channel catfish. The catfish had no fear, and if you could read his mind, he thought that Lew might pose significant competition to his bottom-feeding efforts. But Lew found what he was looking for: iron railings used to guide a small craft through the canal. With his lungs beginning to burn, Lew surfaced quickly. Phil reached his arm over the side of the airboat and supported Lew as he climbed aboard. A fourteen-foot confused alligator watched nearby with glowing green eyes perched above his snout. If only he hadn't just filled himself up on a wonderful egret dinner. Hmmm.

"Rails are down there," said Lew as he wiped himself off on his bloody Polo shirt. Phil had no idea this trip would involve swimming and diving; thus, he left towels back at the shop. "I'm guessing this irrigation canal runs from the Kissimmee River all the way to the driveway next to the mansion. It must have been dug deep to get that cargo hauler back and forth underwater. But why? The only possible answer is whatever is being hauled is a secret for somebody. Who lives in that mansion up in the Estates anyway, Phil?"

"His name's Oliver Harfield, that's all I know," replied Phil. "And the only reason I know that is Governor Daughtry had his picture taken with Harfield at his mansion a month or so ago, and it was plastered all over the *Seminole Bend Journal*."

"But how do you know that it's the same mansion we were at yesterday?"

"Cuz the picture was taken down by the street at the end of the driveway, and the photo was aimed opposite the mansion."

"What the heck does that mean, Phil?"

"In the background, you can see the archway that marks the entrance to your son Brett's house."

"Come on, Phil, those types of entryways can be found in a bunch of places," declared a frustrated Lew as he shrugged his shoulders and raised his hands in a gesture of uncertainty. "I need more evidence than that!"

Phil hesitated for a moment or two, opened his mouth to say something, and decided against it.

"What is it?" asked Lew. "What were you going to say?"

"Aw, it's nothing," replied Phil. "It's just that, well, aw, nothing. It's best we get moving on, what d'ya say?"

"Tell me, Phil. What aren't you telling me?"

Phil looked at his friend, paused, and shook his head, then said, "Oliver Harfield is on one side of the governor, and, well, Brett is on the other side. The caption read, *'Governor visits with millionaire Oliver Harfield and Brett Berry in Seminole Bend Golf Course Estates.'* Caused quite a ruckus in town, especially during morning coffee time with the old retired folks who knew Brett was the basketball coach. They assumed their taxpayer dollars had made him a millionaire."

"How could anyone believe that, Phil? Coach's salaries are public knowledge, right?"

"Yep, that's right, Lew. And that's what calmed things down in town. Several of the old fogies marched down to the school board office, and they were proven wrong."

Lew mulled over what Phil had told him, but he was still befuddled. "So the question is, how DID Brett afford that house in the Estates? It sure wasn't on his teaching and coaching salary." Phil nodded and shrugged. Lew continued, "Any idea what Oliver Harfield does for a living?"

"Can't say. Like I said, the first I ever heard of him was that picture with Brett and the governor."

"Well, he knows the sheriff pretty good, too. He greeted him at the door to his mansion after the sheriff got out of that fancy car. Remember me telling you that when the sheriff left, he spent an hour in the Estate's security hut?"

"Yeah, that's awfully strange, it is. You said you think this here irrigation canal ends at Harfield's driveway? What d'ya suppose is being hauled through this here water?"

"All I can tell you right now is this ain't no damn irrigation canal. I figured that out yesterday when we saw the depth and the fact that a swamp needs no irrigation! Let's get this glass up to Brett's place while it's still dark. Maybe Miguel could shed some light on who his boss Oliver Harfield really is."

Phil crawled under the glass canopy back to the airboat's controls while Lew positioned himself at the bow and yanked on the anchor, trying to free it from the bottom of the canal. The spotlight was fixed straight ahead as Phil patiently waited for his buddy to loosen the submerged mooring hook. It was lodged on something, and it wouldn't budge.

"It's caught on something," shouted Lew. "Can you reverse backward to try and unhook it?"

"This here's an airboat, Lew. They don't do backwards. Let me try a hard forward throttle and see if that does the trick. I'm planning on driving right smack dab over the anchor chain, so this could get rough. Lay down and hold on tight to one of them bed frames."

Lew grabbed the nearest post and gripped mightily. He thought he saw the glass slide a bit on the support, but he wasn't sure. Phil throttled down, the propellers vigorously churning inside the cage, but the boat wasn't moving forward one bit. Instead, the stern was oscillating left and right while Phil tried to maintain control. But then the anchor rope and eyebolt it was attached to snapped viciously off the floorboard and into the water. The airboat jolted forward with tremendous thrust, causing the patio glass to slip back under the ratchet straps and launch into the canal behind the craft. Within seconds it sank to the bottom of the channel.

Phil shut down the engine, and both men looked dejectedly at one another.

"I need to go down there and get that glass, you know," said Lew matter-of-factly. "Now don't try and talk me out of it, you got that?"

"There ain't a fiber of buoyancy in that thing! How do you think you'll get it back to the surface?" It was too dark for Lew to see how red Phil's face had turned.

"I'll get the anchor first. It was probably hitched onto one of those rails. Then I'll come up for some air, then go back down and see if I can hook the anchor to the side of the glass. We might be able to pull it up using the rope. You can pull while I guide it through the water from down below."

"You are absolutely crazy, Lew, you know that? Oh, what the hell, you're more dang stubborn than my ex-wife, so just do your thing and be careful. Let me swing the boat around."

This time Lew eased himself into the water, hoping to locate the anchor before he needed to resurface for air. Phil once again shined the spotlight in the canal where Lew was descending, but the murky water prevented him from seeing clearly. Directly below the boat, Lew found the iron rails that lay on the bottom of the canal, and only a few feet away, he noticed the end of the anchor rope, still attached to the eyebolt. He reached for the line and guided himself towards the anchor. Lew was almost out of breath when he came upon the grapnel and discovered the source of its impasse. It was wedged firmly under the base of the same container he saw at the Harfield mansion yesterday. The rope had snagged onto a propeller sticking out of the submerged vessel.

Lew hastily surfaced and gasped for air as soon as his head popped out of the canal. He treaded water and turned until he noticed the airboat about fifteen feet away. Phil was moving the spotlight in all directions on the surface, trying to locate Lew.

"Hey, over here!" shouted Lew. Phil swung the light to his right and shined it on his buddy. Lew swam to the boat, grabbed the aluminum siding, and looked up at Phil. "I found the anchor. It's stuck under a steel box container that's sitting on the rails. Phil, it's the same damn container I saw under the driveway in the Estates! I'm going back down to see what's in it."

"Going back down to see what's in it? Are you nuts? Forget about the anchor and that dang container. Did you find the patio glass?"

"Nope, but this is more important."

"I'm sure it's bolted shut. How you plan on getting inside?"

"I remember from seeing it yesterday that the container isn't secured. The top opens up with two flaps. But it must be sealed somehow to keep the water out."

"So how did that truck driver open it up underwater without getting everything all wet?"

"I noticed the container has some sort of buoyancy compensator device that is embedded into its walls. It probably was floating on the surface while the truck driver was loading or unloading it, then became negatively buoyant so it would sink to the bottom. The container could then be propelled and guided along the rails."

"You sound like James Bond," said Phil sarcastically. "Well, it obviously can't be opened underwater, so how do you plan to get it to the surface?"

"The buoyancy compensator must have an external switch, or how else could the truck driver make it rise and sink?" pondered Lew.

Just then, the five by eight-foot container emerged and bobbed on the surface of the canal. Phil saw it first and pointed. "What the hell?"

Lew released his grip on the side of the airboat and spun around in the water to see what Phil was pointing at. His feet were kicking, his arms were splashing, and his heart was beating madly! Then the flaps of the container opened, and a shadowy figure of a man appeared. He was waving his hands back and forth in the direction of Lew and Phil.

"Look out! Look out behind you!"

Phil turned and saw what the mystery man was indicating, but Lew was obstructed by the airboat. Phil dove to the floorboard, reached over the side, and clamped on to Lew underneath his armpits. With pure adrenaline giving him a mighty boost, Phil scrambled to his knees and then to his feet, all the while with Lew's backbone braced to Phil's chest. One final, fierce yank later, and both men stumbled backward, Lew pinning Phil to the deck. Both men stretched their necks and glanced overboard in time to see the giant, formerly confused gator kick his tail and dive under the boat. Surely frustrated to have just missed out on Lew à la mode, he would have to find a new dessert to compliment his egret dinner.

Lew and Phil sat up to see who had warned them about the gator. The skinny figure was standing in the container looking back with both hands nervously grasping the hair on his head. He had watched intensely as the gator lunged for Lew's foot, and was frightened by the near-miss.

Phil reached for the oar and paddled slowly to the floating container. It was submerged about six feet, while two feet of its sides rose forth from the surface of the water. From close up, both men noticed an inflatable bladder attached to all four sides of the container's walls and a sealed, watertight air hose running from the bladders to the interior of the vessel. The unknown man was holding a remote control device in his left hand that was attached to two waterproof electric wires. One was affixed to a gas cylinder tank and the other to a small motor. The gas cylinder was connected to the hoses running from the bladders, while the motor was used to engage the propeller. But the most amazing contraptions were two large video cameras tightly secured to the front and rear walls. They were each aimed at a two-inch convex lens embedded into both ends of the metal box. A small screen was attached to the cameras that displayed a wide-angle view of the canal. The hungry alligator could be seen on one camera, apparently circling the container, hoping to find some careless human appetizers out for another swim. It was now clear how the vessel was navigated and how the navigator saw the gator moving towards Phil's airboat.

Lew grabbed the side of the container with his left hand while extending his right arm to shake hands with the pilot of the floating box.

"Thank you, sir, you may have saved my life," said Lew, staring directly in the man's eyes with a most appreciative look. "What is your name, if you don't mind me asking?"

The brown-skinned man with a weather-beaten face clutched Lew's hand, then smiled and replied, "Pancho. My name is Pancho."

CHAPTER 41

Wednesday, March 10, 1982
8:00 p.m.

"Pancho?" inquired Lew and Phil at the same time as they shot a stupefied glance at each other.

"Are you by any chance the same Pancho who has a friend named Miguel?" asked Lew. Pancho looked at Lew, then to Phil, and then back to Lew.

"Yes sir, Miguel is my best friend. But how do you know Miguel?" Pancho took a step back in his vessel and had a guarded look on his face.

"Please don't worry," said Phil as he waved his hand to indicate he wasn't going to hurt Pancho. "Take a look. Do you remember me?"

Phil ducked and turned his head so the spotlight would remove the silhouetted mug that Pancho was trying to decipher.

"Hey, you the man who runs that airboat store," declared Pancho as he pointed his finger at Phil. "You took Miguel and me out fishing in your boat, right?"

"Yep, that's right. I'm the same guy. And this here's my friend Lew. But Miguel said that you are an orange picker. What are you doing in this contraption?"

Pancho stayed silent, so Lew asked, "Pancho, are you the man who saved the life of a deputy sheriff named Willy Banks?"

Pancho's eyes opened almost as wide as his mouth. He glanced again at Lew and Phil but remained mute.

"I know you're wondering how we know about this and why we're asking," said Lew. "I understand you may be confused, but we believe evil things are happening in Seminole Bend. What is this submarine container, and why are you in it?"

Pancho paused a moment to think. He was still not sure if he could trust Phil and Lew, but he badly needed to release his burdens, so he decided to take a chance. "If I tell you, you can't tell anyone. Please, it's very important, sir." Pancho's pleading eyes were a dead giveaway that the Mexican man feared something or someone.

"Pancho, we are on your side. If you are worried about something, we will try our best to help. May we come in your vessel and have a look around?"

Pancho motioned to Lew and Phil. The two men climbed onto a rope ladder that hung inside the container, and then entered the underwater craft. Phil had grabbed a mooring line from his airboat, and once inside the container, he secured the vessels together. Lew and Phil quickly skimmed the contraption and were curiously stunned by the sophisticated video navigation, propulsion, and buoyancy systems on board.

Pancho interrupted their perusal of the container. "About once a week, Miguel's job is to take Mr. Harfield's speedboat to the Kissimmee River and tie it up to a huge old oak tree on the shore by where the river and canal come together. Right there, under the water, is this here box we're in. Miguel then dives down and presses a button on the outside of the box, and that air tank over there fills up those balloons that are stuck to the walls. The balloons make the box rise up so it floats and Miguel can get in it."

Pancho handed Lew and Phil the remote control. "Then he uses this thing to make the box sink back under the water, and he steers it down the canal to Mr. Harfield's house. And you can see all around with these cameras, too. The canal goes underneath Mr. Harfield's house to his driveway where it ends. Then Miguel unloads a few crates up into a truck that's parked in the driveway. When he's all done, he drives the box back to the river and gets into the speedboat and goes back to the house. Then, about a week later, he does it all again."

"So, why are you here tonight?" asked Phil while Lew nodded. "Why isn't Miguel here?"

"Truth is, Mr. Phil, that I ride along with Miguel and help him out most weeks. Mr. Harfield doesn't know about it. Miguel is afraid of Mr. Harfield, and he feels safer if I come along with him."

"Where is Miguel now? Why isn't he with you?"

Pancho looked down at the floor of the vessel, embarrassed for what he was about to say. "Miguel is tied to a tree out by his shed."

"What?!" exclaimed Lew and Phil together.

"I tied him there to protect him so I could take this underwater box out to the speedboat. I'm going to steal the speedboat and get way away from here for once and for all. He would want to come with me, but then if we get caught, he would be in big, big trouble. I don't want him in trouble cuz he's my best friend. When Mr. Harfield sees him tied to a tree, he will think someone did a bad thing to him, and he won't blame him. Miguel will still have a job."

"Why are you trying to get away?" asked Lew. "You work picking oranges, which seems pretty harmless. What's going on anyway, Pancho? Does this have something to do with you saving Deputy Banks a few weeks back?" Lew was desperate for answers about his son's death and what Willy Banks may know. The tone in his voice was becoming stressed.

"Yes, I think so. Some friends I work with told me they saw a man taking pictures of me at Quick Stuff. Why would someone take pictures of me? I got no relatives round here, ya know. I just got this funny feeling something bad's going to happen to me."

"Pancho, we're going to help you," promised Lew. Phil shot a puzzled look at his friend. "But first, can you tell us what is in those crates that are loaded onto the truck in Mr. Harfield's driveway?"

Pancho hesitated, not sure if he should reveal his secret.

Lew prodded, "You know, don't you, Pancho? Please tell us."

Pancho remained silent.

"Pancho, you were right. You are in danger. I saw the pictures that the man took of you."

"What? Where?"

"I'll tell you all about it later," said Lew. "But you need to tell me what is in those crates."

Pancho dug into his pants pocket and pulled out a cylindrical object with green wires coming out both ends. He handed it to Lew. "Here, I took this out of a crate. I thought it was a battery I could use in my flashlight for some night fishing, but it didn't fit. Those green wires are really strange."

Lew and Phil examined the object closely. It was a bit wider, longer, and heavier than a D cell battery. The green wires were baffling.

"You say that Miguel makes a run in this vessel once a week with crates of these?" asked Lew.

"Yes, sir."

"Does the same truck pick up the crates, or is it a different truck each week?"

"Same truck and same driver."

Lew remembered the license plate number for the semi that was parked in Oliver Harfield's driveway. He turned to Phil and asked, "Do you have any idea how we can track down the owner of a license plate without raising suspicions?"

Phil replied, "Nope, not really. Why ya asking? Do you know the plate number of that truck?"

"Yes, I saw it clear earlier today. The plate was *RJCORP*, registered in Florida."

"Well, I ain't no Dick Tracy, but I'll bet your bottom dollar that the truck is owned by Roy Jackson. RJ is a dead giveaway. And I'll double that bet that this here battery ain't something that should be going places by that truck!"

"I think you're right, Phil. Roy Jackson has gone to great lengths to build this canal to obviously hide the transport of whatever these dang things are." Lew turned the object around in his hand, trying to find a way to open it and get a better look. Then he gazed back at Phil. "We need to find Miguel before Oliver Harfield does and get him out of there fast."

"What makes you think Harfield suspects Miguel of anything? He's just his gardener."

"Someone tying him to a tree will be very suspicious, and when he finds out his speedboat is missing, I don't think he'll mess around long with a Mexican laborer. You said yourself that Seminole Bend has suffered some shady deaths lately, and no one will miss Miguel when he's gone."

"Nobody 'cept me," interjected Pancho.

"Except Pancho, of course," nodded Lew in reply. "We need to find Willy Banks. Why was he fired? He must know something we don't. He must! Let's get Miguel untied and go find him."

"What about fixing your patio door?" asked Phil.

"The glass is gone, so the damn door will just have to wait. We need to move this container back to where it's supposed to be down at the Kissimmee so no one suspects anything. Pancho, you take it down there, close it up, and wait for us in the speedboat."

"But you said it yourself. If the speedboat is missing from Harfield's estate, that will be a problem," stated Phil.

"Hopefully, he won't notice it missing until we're far enough away. But Harfield will certainly suspect that Miguel stole it and call the police. I think it's best we drive it a long way from here and ditch it so it looks like Miguel was escaping to somewhere else, which will lead the police on a wild goose chase. Any idea, Phil?"

"Well, we could drive it across Lake Okeechobee to the Caloosahatchee River and dump it somewhere in Fort Myers. Then, we could send Miguel somewhere up north in the opposite direction."

"How long would it take to get the boat to Fort Myers?"

"Let's say the boat's got an average-sized motor. Guessing it cruises around forty miles per hour. Probably 'bout a hundred miles to the Gulf, so should take about three hours, four if we need to stop along the way for gas. We need to bring the airboat to get us back, so I'll need to fuel up, too."

"Well, times a wasting, my friend. Let's get moving!"

Lew and Phil boarded the airboat, fired up the powerful engine, and gunned it towards the Seminole Golf Course Estates. Meanwhile, Pancho sealed up the container and submerged Harfield's vessel. Using the remote control and peering at the video screens, he navigated the boxed craft to its destination at the end of the canal. With excitement, fear, determination, and adrenaline flowing through their systems, the three men were intensely focused on their new mission.

No one noticed the Piper seaplane descending below the dark, cumulonimbus clouds a few miles away. Nor did they see it land momentarily on Roy Jackson's swampland, and then take off again heading northwest into the thunderstorm that was brewing up on the Gulf coast.

CHAPTER 42
Wednesday, March 10, 1982
9:30 p.m.

A grass-stained, low-top, Converse tennis shoe attached to a bloody brown foot and hairy fibula was all that was left of the twenty-three foot, 200-pound Burmese python's dinner. The scaly carnivore appeared very content as each swallow moved his human feast closer to his stomach, and the breaking of bones could be heard from the dock on the other side of the shed. Lew and Phil thought the sounds were twigs being snapped, and they guessed that Miguel must be loose from the tree and getting ready to start a fire. The men crouched and skulked one-by-one quietly around the back of the shed, trying to ensure that Oliver Harfield, or anyone else in the mansion, would not see them.

Lew saw the repulsive spectacle first and froze in his tracks. Phil accidentally bumped him from behind, sending both men face-first to the muddy ground. They scrambled to their knees and gaped at the reptile six feet in front of them that was trying to dislodge a rubber tennis shoe sole stuck in his curved fangs. When the python opened his mouth, Lew and Phil gazed terrifyingly at the shredded remains of Miguel. The Miami Dolphins t-shirt had been regurgitated and was lying on the ground trapped under the nightmarish slimy skin of the massive snake.

Slowly, Lew and Phil rose to their feet and crept gently away from the beast, carefully eyeing the python with each vigilant step. Although not Catholic, Phil nonetheless made a sign of the cross to ensure that he and his buddy were not the next course on the reptile's banquet menu. But just as they were about to make a mad dash back to the airboat, Lew caught a glimpse of something hanging from a large hook on the exterior of the shed, and he grabbed Phil's arm.

"Wait," whispered Lew. "Look at that." He pointed at a long, sturdy rope hanging from the hook.

"Yeah, it's a rope," replied Phil. "So what? Let's get the hell out of here." He started to move again towards the boat, but Lew wouldn't let go of his arm.

"Pancho said he tied Miguel to the tree with a rope, and I didn't see another one near the snake, did you?"

"I wasn't looking for a rope, Lew. I was looking for a fast exit, and we found it. Now let's get the hell out of here!"

"I think that must be the rope that Pancho used to tie Miguel to the tree."

"And who cares if it is, damn it! Come on, let's go, man!"

Lew turned Phil around so he was staring directly into his eyes. "Think about it, Phil. I seriously doubt a Burmese python is skilled enough to untie a human from a tree, and I know the slimy thing isn't considerate enough to tidy up before devouring whoever the rope was tied to!"

"Are you implying what I think you're implying, Lew?"

"Someone untied Miguel from the tree and fed him to the snake. It's the only explanation I can think of."

Phil was shocked and scared. "But why Miguel? He was just a nice, quiet gardener. That doesn't make sense."

"Miguel drove the underwater container back and forth from this mansion to the Kissimmee River for Oliver Harfield. He was more than just a gardener, and he had to know that something deceitful was happening."

Lew motioned for Phil to step inside the shed so they could talk safely. The python's mouth was now closed, but the men could make out Miguel's frame inside the snake's overstretched digestive innards. They peered out the shed's door and gasped in horror, then turned their heads away from each other and puked.

"The snake doesn't appear to want anymore to eat," murmured Phil, still nauseous from the gruesome scene in front of him.

Recovering a bit, Lew replied bluntly, "Probably not hungry. Most likely will take a month or so to fully digest Miguel."

"So, you think Oliver Harfield killed his own gardener?" asked Phil.

"Seems rather likely, don't you think? And by feeding him to a python, all the evidence would be lost."

"Lew, I got a bad feeling inside my brain. Remember I told you 'bout Governor Daughtry in the same newspaper photograph with Harfield and your son?"

"Uh-huh, and I know what you're thinking, Phil. You think that Oliver Harfield, my son Brett, and the governor may have all been in cahoots and did some unlawful things, right? And that means the sheriff and this asshole Roy Jackson are also involved."

Lew wiped a tear from his cheek with the back of his hand. "Brett was a good boy, Phil. I know I'm biased, but I still can't see him involved in something so wrong."

"We don't know that yet, my friend," said Phil as he gave an affectionate pat on Lew's shoulder. "Let's pick up Pancho and get going down to the Caloosahatchee. I don't know how we're going to tell him 'bout his best friend Miguel. Maybe we should just say he's missing, what d'ya think, Lew?"

"I think he needs to know the truth, Phil. I'll give him the bad news."

* * * * *

"Where is he, dang nab it?!" exclaimed Phil as he navigated the airboat back and forth along the foliage that separated the irrigation canal from the Kissimmee River. Lew and Phil located the underwater container but could not find Oliver Harfield's speedboat, or Pancho.

"Pancho must be in trouble," declared Lew. "You think Harfield got to him?"

"Well, he sure ain't here. What do we do now?"

"We must find Willy Banks. And we must tell the FBI what we know."

"The FBI? You think that's the best thing, Lew? They ain't got no FBI office anywhere near Seminole Bend, ya know."

"I'm meeting with the FBI in Miami tomorrow. I wish we had a camera to take a picture of that container, though."

"I got a camera back at the shop. Should we get it and come back?"

"Too dangerous, Phil. But let's get back to your store so I can pick up my car. Maybe Deputy Banks is at home now. We need to find him!"

Phil maneuvered the airboat slowly through the shrubs and mangroves out onto the Kissimmee while Lew struggled to keep branches away from his face. Once on the river, they gunned the engines to full throttle and headed towards the lake.

Just past Angler's Delight Marina, at the mouth of Lake Okeechobee, they heard a deafening explosion in the skies above them. Phil disengaged the throttle, and both men looked up in time to see an enormous flash blasting through the rain clouds. They knew it wasn't lightning.

CHAPTER 43
Thursday, March 11, 1982
12:30 a.m.

Otis met Willy around 12:30 a.m. at the phone booth in the Dixie Food and Drug parking lot. No one was in or near the phone booth, and an old Buick with a flat tire was the only car around. But Willy noticed that the Buick was rocking a bit, which was unusual because the winds were calm.

Willy wasn't planning on giving back his forty-five caliber Colt M1911 pistol that was issued to him by the sheriff's department until Al Bonty came and got it in person. He wanted to look the sheriff in the eyes while giving him a final piece of his mind! Willy rarely even carried the sidearm along with him. He knew his massive biceps were a deterrent to most criminals, and he really didn't have much love for guns after four bullets were removed from his body in Vietnam.

Willy decided to bring his weapon with him to Dixie Food and Drug after carefully considering the rampage of deaths in Seminole Bend that had occurred over the past three months. After telling Otis to wait by the phone booth, he pulled it out of his belt holster and gradually shuffled up to the parked car. Willy could not see through the back windows as they were covered in fog, and it didn't take a detective to know what was going on in the back seat of that decrepit Buick. Willy tapped on the window with the barrel of his Colt. The rocking stopped. He tapped again, this time a bit harder. Nothing.

"Police officer. Get out of the car with your hands up!" Willy exclaimed, even though the small lie about being a police officer rattled his moral fiber a bit.

The door of the Buick slowly creaked open. Willy pointed his pistol at the emerging couple who were both naked as jailbirds. A tall man with a long, scraggly mane and nose hairs about down to the top of his lips came out first. He raised his left arm at Willy's request while his right hand was clasped with a lady's left hand, and the man gently pulled her out of the back seat. When they had fully materialized outside the car, they raised all four hands high towards the sky. Willy bit his lip to keep from laughing. What a sight! But he did detect a whiff of cheap wine on their breaths.

Willy motioned with his gun for the couple to move away from the car. After they shuffled sideways a few feet, Willy reached in the backseat, grabbed their clothes and tossed them to the embarrassed duo.

"Get dressed," Willy said, then put his gun back into the holster. He leaned on the car hoping this wouldn't take too long. "What's your names?"

"Lance Billips, and this here's my lady friend, Ev Pritchard." Lance was thinking about bolting now that Willy had holstered his gun. But he wasn't sure if Willy would chase him or Ev, and he didn't want to risk being the one wrapped up in those monstrous black arms.

Willy looked over towards the phone booth. "Otis, come on over here now," Willy shouted. Otis started trotting to the car.

"What the hell," exclaimed Lance as he noticed his drinking buddy coming at him. "What's going on?"

"Hey, dude," Otis uttered as he reached out to shake Lance's hand. "I see you met my bro Willy!"

Lance was too startled to return Otis' handshake offering.

"You boys are brothers?" asked Ev.

"Yep, and have been ever since birth, I reckon," Otis announced proudly.

"What you want with us?" Lance looked back at Willy.

"Just would like to ask you some questions, if you don't mind?" Willy was still leaning on the car trying to get Lance and Ev to become a bit more relaxed. That may not have been the best strategy. Lance was now transforming back to his old self: belligerent and uncooperative.

"So you says you's a copper. Well, then, I want to see my lawyer." Lance glared at Willy with hands on his hips, trying to portray a stubborn stance.

Willy chuckled at the thought of Lance hiring a lawyer. He pointed at the phone booth and snickered, "There's the phone. Be my guest."

"My brother's an ex-cop. He just wants to figure some stuff out so there's no more killing in Seminole Bend," Otis revealed, hoping to break the ice.

"Well, if you're no cop, then I need to get back home to my husband," Ev announced as she started to walk away. "I told you, Lance, we should've waited until Friday night to do our business. It's bad luck changing up things."

Willy's eyes and mouth gave him away. He was stunned. So Ev Pritchard has a hubby at home, and she's out fooling around with this loser? He shook his head and smiled again.

"I sees you again tomorrow night, Ev?" Lance asked in a pleading tone of voice. Ev was moving away quickly from the parking lot. Willy assumed that she either walked here or parked a car somewhere hidden, probably so her husband wouldn't catch her.

"Maybe, Lance, if my husband don't catch me sneaking in the back door tonight and tear my head off my neck!" A few seconds later, Ev began to jog slowly and awkwardly away. She was obviously not a fitness guru, but it didn't take too long for her to go around the corner and out of sight.

Lance looked back at Willy, then at Otis, and again to Willy. He was becoming angry. "See what you's done now, you has-been cop?"

"Okay, sorry 'bout that, Mr. Billips, but I need your help. Can you give me just a few minutes to answer a couple of questions?" Willy had become serious. It was time to find out if Lance could help him with information about the piece of glass found at Elmer's hardware store.

"My father's name was Mr. Billips. You best call me Lance if you wants me to talk to you." Willy thought he could detect a distraught tone in Lance's voice, and perhaps that meant he wasn't too fond of his father. Most likely, Lance had asked his father for some help getting off the street and was turned down.

Willy thought it would be a good time to patch things up. Clearly, Lance would need a bit of anger management so that Willy could get some information from him. Although never claiming to be a psychologist, Willy quickly thought up a plan that he was sure would work with Lance. First, start by formally reintroducing himself with a gentleman's modus, then get a little help from the sixteenth president of the United States. Yep, a firm grip of the hand was one thing, but Abe Lincoln's face on a five-dollar bill would go much further in softening up the heart and attitude of Lance Billips! Willy rolled the paper money into a cylinder and stuck it between the middle and forefinger of his right hand. He then leaned forward and offered his hand for a shake. "I'm Willy Banks. I was just fired from the sheriff's department for stirring things up during an investigation. There's a bad dude who lives just outside of Seminole Bend that has corrupted our county, and I'm determined to stop him. Will you help me?"

Lance snatched the five-dollar bill from Willy's fingers, pocketed the cash, and then grabbed the huge black hand and returned the greeting. However, Lance's wimp grip was no match for Willy's steel vice, and he gritted his teeth—what was left of the rotting choppers!

"Yeah, man. What's up?" Lance was willing to talk, hoping to collect more of that green paper treasure. And Otis was delighted that he could help out his older brother.

"First things first. Is this your car?" Willy slapped the roof of the old Buick.

"No, man," Lance responded, but then paused and reconsidered. "Well, kinda. You see, it was a gift from my cousin, Lenny. He hotwired it from some guy's driveway down in Stuart. He got 'bout ten miles from here when the tire went flat. Drove it anyway and parked it right here at my home."

"Your home?" Willy looked around and saw nothing even resembling a house for a block or two. "Where's your home, Lance?"

"Over there." Lance pointed at the vacant telephone booth.

"So you say cousin Lenny came up here to give you a stolen car as a gift? Was it your birthday or something? How did he get back home?" Being Lenny was a car thief, Willy figured that was a rhetorical question, but he wanted Lance to answer anyway.

"Lenny didn't go back home. He stole a big old Chevy van and drove it up to Tampa with the stuff he had in the car. I know what you thinking, man, that Lenny peddles them cars to people who sells them, but that ain't right. He ain't got no transportation to call his own right now, and he needs something to carry his products with him. He does that every week—goes from Stuart to Tampa and back. That there is his job, ya know."

"What kind of job requires you to steal cars each week?"

"Lenny is a hauler. But a year ago he rolled his station wagon and trailer just north of here on Highway 441. Didn't have no insurance. Just like most people, couldn't afford it."

"What does Lenny haul?"

"He done haul pita bread from some guy he knows in Stuart up to some grocery store in Tampa called Molly's International Foods. That place sells a bunch of strange foods, I guess. Pita bread is some kind of Arab round crap that's baked in a brick oven. It ain't bad, though, if you smear it with orange marmalade. Anyway, he takes the money he gets from Molly's and stops at a big warehouse owned by some company named Tampa Liquor Distributors. He loads up with as many cases of Mad Dog Twenty as can fit in his car and takes it back to Stuart where he sells it on the street. Ya can't buy that stuff down in Stuart or even around here, ya know."

Lance's mouth was running more than it should, seeing Willy was an ex-cop and still had connections in the law-abiding world. But with the mention of Mad Dog Twenty, Willy perked up.

"Has Lenny ever sold any Mad Dog Twenty while passing through Seminole Bend, by any chance?" Willy thought he may be on to something.

"I don't think so. But he stops by my phone booth and gives me a bottle each week, along with a package of that pita bread stuff. I shoplift the orange marmalade from Dixie Food and Drug. I think they sees me, but let me do it anyway."

"Have you ever been drinking that wine over by Elmer's Hardware store, Lance?"

Lance was taken aback with the mention of Elmer's store. It wasn't but a month ago he grabbed a plumber's wrench off Elmer's shelf and whacked that big old cowboy dude after he had caused an accident that injured Ev and busted up his MD20 bottle. But why was Willy asking if he'd ever been drinking at Elmer's? Lance reckoned he shouldn't have spilled the beans about his cousin stealing cars and him shoplifting, so he decided it was best to shut up and not declare his lethal actions at the hardware store.

"Nope, only drink wine right here in my own domain."

"Look, Lance, I need the truth here. They don't sell Mad Dog in Seminole Bend, but you say you get a bottle each week from your cousin. About a month ago, a big guy had his brains extracted from his skull in Elmer's. So far, there are no leads in his murder, at least that's what those who will still talk to me down at the sheriff's department are saying. But I found a small piece of glass on the floor, and our lab said it had traces of MD20 on it. Interesting, eh Lance, that MD20 would be found in a town that doesn't sell it, but a homeless guy living only a couple of blocks from Elmer's drinks it damn near every night?"

"I ain't no homeless guy, Mr. Willy! I just choose to live in small quarters, that's all."

Otis piped in, "Lance, one night when you and me was guzzling those Budweisers, you told me 'bout seeing that car crash that lit up the whole county. You talked 'bout some knucklehead escaping the crash and hiding out in Elmer's, you did. You said that same knucklehead had done broke your bottle of MD20, so you done broke his neck. When I asked what the knucklehead looked like, you was going to tell me something, but then you shut up and walked away. Said you needed to pee, so I left."

"Yep, I needed to pee. We all need to pee sometimes, so is that a crime?"

"The big dead dude and your knucklehead are one and the same. Right, Lance?" Willy stared directly into Lance's bloodshot, cavernous eyes.

"Could be, I guess," said Lance with a tone that couldn't seem to hide his guilt.

"Are you saying the man in the crash got out alive?" Willy couldn't believe it! He remembered the volunteer firemen talking about the gruesome scene. They watched in horror as Calvin Potts' face melted right before their eyes. The Ford LTD that hit Calvin's Chevy became a terrific fireball, and they said no one in that car could have survived. But they never found any remains, and the sheriff's report indicated that the driver had most likely burned to ashes. Could it be possible that the driver did escape and dragged himself over to Elmer's? If so, and Lance saw him go into the hardware store, well, he had a motive for killing him. That is if breaking a bottle of Mad Dog is grounds for murder.

"Okay, okay, I sees him alright. I sees him go into Elmer's. But I don't think he was in the crash cuz he wouldn't have survived. No way, man! I think the asshole opened the door seconds before it collided with that Chevy, and he rolled out onto Main Street. The car was moving pretty dang fast, so I knows he couldn't have jumped out without scraping up his body pretty bad."

"Then what? So you saw him go into Elmer's and you followed him? What for, Lance?"

"Now, this here's the part where I may need a lawyer, Mr. Willy. Can you find me one of them public defenders?" Lance was still not sure about confessing to a murder, but he was beginning to trust Willy.

"Look, Lance. If what I'm thinking is right, the big ox driving the LTD was a bad man. An evil man, in fact. He may have been a hired killer, which means you could be a town hero instead of a future felon."

"Does he have a reward on his head, Willy? I mean, panhandling is a good career and all, but I sure could use a few extra bucks."

"Don't know about no reward, but could be. Anyway, what happened after you followed him into Elmer's? Did you kill him over a broken bottle of Mad Dog, Lance?"

Lance didn't say anything for a long time. He put his hands in his pocket and stared down at his feet. Willy didn't want to lose him, so he pulled out another five-dollar bill, rolled it into a ball, and then tossed it at Lance's shoes. Lance reached down and grabbed the money, then stood up and gazed at Willy.

"I didn't mean to kill him, Willy. I just wanted to hurt him for hurting my Evie. You see, on the day he crashed himself up, he and me had had a little turf war over using my phone booth. Fortunately for him, I slipped and fell outa my booth, or I woulda kicked his butt right then and there. That's when my bottle of MD20 broke when I slipped. He called someone, slammed the phone down, then drove like a bat outa hell outa the parking lot. Evie was just coming outa Dixie Food and Drug, and the crazy SOB caused a young boy driving a Pinto to lose control and ram into Evie's shopping cart. Evie had to dive to the ground to avoid being dead, but she scraped herself up pretty good. I was mad, so I followed him, and that's when I seen the car crash. Then after the crash, I sees him go into the bathroom in the back of the hardware store, so I picked up a wrench and hit him in the head when he came out. He fell backward and smashed his skull into the sink, and then I ran outa there fast as bees chasing honey!"

"Wait a minute. You said this same dude you hit had earlier tossed you out of the phone booth to make a call?"

"No, no, no! I slipped and fell. Ain't no way nobody gonna force me outa my domain!"

"Okay, Lance, you slipped and fell. But did you hear any of the man's conversation on the phone?"

"Not all of it. But I did hear him say two words."

"Well, what did you hear?"

"Not sure I want to say it to your face, Willy, cuz it's kinda offensive, if you know what I mean."

"Lance, don't mess with me," Willy growled. "What did that goon say?"

"Something about a Buckwheat, and he called the person he was talking to Roy."

Suddenly, an intense flash of light lit up the western sky, followed by an enormous boom like that of a cannonade. Willy, Lance, and Otis all turned and looked up.

"Wow, big storm must be brewing," announced Otis. "Never seen thunder or lightning like that. Best be moving on before we get wet!"

CHAPTER 44

Thursday, March 11, 1982

1:00 a.m.

The large, heavy, blunt object torpedoed directly through the middle of Phil's airboat, slicing it neatly in half and sending both ends of the boat upside-down into midair. Lew and Phil saw the article coming seconds before it hit and dove overboard. Sharp, metal fragments rained down from the sky. One piece, a foot in diameter, struck Phil below the calf, and his ankle was dangling from severed gastrocnemius and soleus muscles that had been sliced away from his Achilles tendon. Lew was an accomplished swimmer, and with his right arm, grabbed Phil under his armpits and elevated his head. While treading water and weeds with his left arm, Lew dragged his friend to the grassy shore. Phil was losing blood rapidly and passed out the moment he was placed on the ground. Lew tore off his shirt and quickly wrapped it around Phil's lower leg, then tied it tightly.

Out of the corner of his eyes, Lew noticed something bobbing on the water. It was the object that had capsized their boat, and it appeared to be an airline seat. Lew peered through the darkness of night and spotted what seemed to be two legs sticking out from the seat. He patted Phil's shoulder and said, "Hang in there, buddy, I'll be right back." Phil didn't hear him. He was out cold.

Lew splashed through the sawgrass and lily pads drudging as fast as he could for the seat. The water depth was about five feet, so Lew was able to swim and totter back to the floating chair swiftly. Lew reached and grabbed the seat by the arms, and spun it around. For the second time tonight, Lew vomited what little was left in his stomach. Strapped into the airplane's seat by a safety belt was likely an elderly man or woman, based upon the wrinkled skin and gray hair on his or her arms. The person's head had been decapitated. His or her legs were crushed beneath the knees, and there were no shoes to be seen. He or she had folded his or her hands in his or her lap, and Lew knew there had been a desperate plea to the Lord for help. Nearby, drifting peacefully away in the choppy waves, Lew sighted a skull whose skin had vanished, burned to the bone. Only a pair of wire-rim spectacles remained oddly in place covering the eye sockets. The intense heat had fused them to the cranium.

Still tucked into the back pocket of the seat was the airliner's signature magazine. The cover had a picture of a jet flying through puffy clouds with now ambiguous words lithographed in the middle: *Fly Safe Fly Jubilant Fly Heartland Lakes.*

Lew was dizzy as he trudged back to the shore. The shock of seeing Miguel devoured by a Burmese python was now distant in his mind. He was beginning to believe this trip to Seminole Bend was a death trap that he couldn't escape. Phil was still unconscious as he knelt down beside him. Lew needed to get Phil to a hospital soon, but dragging him through the swampland would only injure his foot even more. And who knew how many startled alligators awakened by the explosion were now suffering from hunger pains.

Lew decided his best chance was to swim across the Kissimmee River to the marina and call an ambulance from Angler's Delight. It was just past midnight, and the restaurant would be closed, but there was a payphone out front. Lew tightly refastened the shirt that was tied around Phil's leg and waded out into the water. He could hear sirens approaching from all directions, including a marine patrol boat coming in over the lake from the east. The news of the plane crash had finally reached authorities, and the rescue had just begun.

Lew was halfway across the Kissimmee when a runabout appeared out of the darkness moving slowly, but its bow heading straight for him. Strangely, the boat was operating without its running lights. Just as Lew was about to dive to avoid a collision with the hull, he could hear a reverse thrust coming from the engine. The bow flattened, and the boat came to a stop. A person on board rushed to the front and switched on a spotlight, shining it directly in Lew's face, blinding him.

"Señor Lew, Señor Lew! Is that you?!" came the voice from the boat.

"Pancho?"

"Si, señor, it's me!"

"Get that damn spotlight off me so I can see!" shouted Lew. "Where can I board?"

"Over here," replied Pancho. He attached an aluminum ladder to the side of the boat and shined the spotlight on it.

Lew swam over to the ladder and scrambled into the boat. It was Oliver Harfield's. Lew grabbed Pancho by his arms and shook him.

"Pancho, what happened? Why did you leave us, damn it?!"

"I wait for you, Señor Lew. But four hombres in big speedboat crash through trees and tie up their boat to this one. They had guns, Señor Lew. I was scared. Two of them got on my boat. One hombre pointed gun at my head, and the other, he drive off to the lake."

"What happened to them? How did you get away?"

"We stop out in lake and drop anchor. One hombre, he talk on a walkie-talkie. Then they go up in front of boat and look up at sky. Forgot about me, I guess. I sit up and sees airboat coming this way, and I know it's you cuz I sees those four steel braces sticking up. Then, big boom in sky, and I sees something crash into your airboat. Our boat start rocking, so

I grab oar and hit hombres on back of head, and they fall in water. They grab anchor rope and hold on, so I start motor and go backward real fast, and anchor get loose. I take knife and cut rope, and hombres sink down underwater. Then, I get away fast."

Lew nodded, then said, "Let me take the controls, Pancho. Phil is badly injured, and we need to get him to a hospital." Pancho moved aside as Lew fired up the Johnson outboard, then guided the boat back towards Phil. Weeds became tangled in the propeller, but the motor hung tough, and Lew beached the hull onto the shore. As carefully as they could, Lew and Pancho lifted Phil into the boat and laid him on the deck. Phil winced in pain for a short moment, then fell back into oblivion.

Pancho slashed away the weeds from the prop and climbed back into the boat. Lew shoved the bow off the white sand and grassy landing, then climbed aboard and used the oar to guide the boat away from the lily pads before restarting the motor. He needed the propeller free and clear to maximize speed across the lake to the Taylor Creek locks and back to Bennett's Airboat Palace. From there, he would use the rental car to transport Phil to the hospital. Lew wasn't sure when he would tell Pancho what happened to his friend Miguel.

CHAPTER 45

Thursday, March 11, 1982
3:00 a.m.

Lew paced restlessly in the waiting room at Gregorson General Hospital while Pancho snoozed in a fake leather chair. No one could answer any questions because the hospital was on full alert and panicking, thinking about the arrival of the airplane crash victims. Doctors and nurses were scampering from room to room, and all three ambulances had been dispatched to Angler's Delight, which would be the staging area for the tragedy. Lew wasn't sure how much care his buddy Phil was getting, if any.

There was a payphone in the hallway, so Lew decided to try and call his house in Pennsylvania to see if his wife had returned home. He was shocked that someone picked up on the first ring, seeing it was in the middle of the night.

"Berry's house!" declared the agitated voice on the other line. "Lew, I hope that's you?!"

"Ralph, is that you?" inquired Lew. He recognized the stressed and nervous tone of his neighbor, Ralph Kline. "Why are you at my house?"

"Man, oh man, Lew. Bad news. I don't want to tell you over the phone. Where are you? Can you come home?" Ralph was firing out sentences without stopping for a breath of air.

Finally, Lew interjected, "No, I can't get home. What is it, damn it? Tell me, Ralph!"

"Janet knocked on my door yesterday. She said she just returned from the Poconos and was leaving for Florida in a couple of hours. She said she couldn't get ahold of you and asked me to keep trying to call you because she was heading to the airport. She wanted me to tell you she was coming to meet up with you. Dang, dang, dang it, Lew!"

"Calm down, Ralph, you're not making any sense. So my wife came home from the Poconos and is headed down here. That's great, so what's the problem?" Lew was wiping the sweat that had formed on his forehead. He wasn't sure he wanted the answer to that question.

"Lew, she couldn't get a direct flight, and she said she would be transferring planes in Chicago. Oh damn nag it, Lew, dang it, dang it, dang it!" Lew could hear Ralph pounding his fist on the countertop.

Lew was becoming irritable. "Ralph, damn it. Get yourself together and tell me what you want to tell me!"

"Lew, she said she was flying Heartland Lakes, and there was a midair plane crash an hour or so ago, and I'm worried Janet was on the plane! Oh man oh man oh man! News is reporting that one plane that crashed was flying from Chicago to Tampa. There is no news about the jet they hit. Oh God, Lew!"

"Hold on, Ralph. Janet thinks I'm in Miami. She wouldn't be flying into Tampa."

"Lew, the plane was scheduled to stop in Tampa, then fly on to Miami, its final destination. Oh man, oh man!"

Lew dropped the phone and began banging his head on the wall. The voice coming from the receiver that was hanging by a cord was shouting, "Lew, Lew, what happened? What's the matter? Lew?" A nurse rushed over to Lew and sat him down on the floor. Lew had made quite a dent in the sheetrock, and his forehead was bleeding and bruised.

An orderly came rushing in to help the nurse get Lew to a vacant room, but Lew put his hand up and motioned them to stop. "I'll be okay, don't take up any bed space for me. You're going to need all the beds you can get real soon." He stood up and grabbed the receiver that was still hanging from the phone. "Ralph, I've got to go. I'll call you later." He hung up the phone and started pacing in the waiting room.

Pancho was still asleep on the chair as Lew turned on the TV that was fastened to the wall. Every major network was now reporting live from rain-soaked Angler's Delight. They had dispatched news helicopters from Sarasota and West Palm Beach and were jostling in the storm for the best filming position. The World Broadcasting Network decided to commandeer a large pontoon boat whose owner had left the key in the ignition. The news giant was now broadcasting via satellite to locations all around the globe from the deck of Lake Okeechobee's largest party boat.

A cluster of marine rescue boats could be seen with their flashing blue and white lights reflecting off the lake while raindrops pounded the surface. The camera panned to an assortment of ambulances lined up from the boat ramp back to the marina's entrance. They had come from Moore Haven, Belle Glade, and Clewiston to help out. Gregorson's three ambulances were the first in line.

"This is Jessica Hoyt reporting live from our WBN studios in New York. At approximately one a.m. Eastern time, a Heartland Lakes Airway's flight from Chicago destined for Tampa, collided in midair with a Sky Tropic Airways jet from Kingston, Jamaica. At this time, there is no report on how many passengers were on board, or if there are any survivors. Authorities at the FAA office in Florida are confirming that both aircraft were circling Tampa in severe weather waiting to land, but were on a holding pattern due to a radar malfunction in the control tower. John Merrick, our local correspondent, is at a marina on Lake Okeechobee, where marine patrols and local fishermen are ramified in a furious attempt to find live bodies. John, what do you have for us?"

"Jessica, this is a terrifying picture from south-central Florida. An intense storm is dumping rain on Lake Okeechobee as we speak, seriously hindering rescue attempts. Although it is very dark, we can make out shadows of floating objects in the distance, most likely debris from the airplanes. We are on a pontoon boat and will be moving onto the Kissimmee River shortly for a better view."

"John, according to the FAA, the cause of the Trans South Airlines and PanMexico jets that collided in midair about a month ago over the Everglades was due to "unavoidable pilot error," however, unconfirmed reports are saying that there was a radar malfunction at the time of that accident, too. Wasn't that correct?"

"Yes, Jessica, at least those are the rumors that have contradicted the initial findings reported by the FAA. Interesting, though, there were severe weather conditions in Miami as there was tonight in Tampa, and planes were placed on hold prior to both midair collisions. Seems this is a horrible and highly improbable coincidence for the state of Florida. But it's also difficult to understand why the jets were so off course, even during a holding pattern. Tampa International is about 150 miles from Lake Okeechobee. My guess is they were trying to avoid the storm as much as possible."

"Yes, that's the most probable conclusion. Thank you, John. We will be returning to you in a moment. We are now cutting to Chicago for a live statement from Ted Banner, Heartland Lake's director of public relations who just arrived at his O'Hare office."

Without finding fault with his company's disintegrated airplane, Banner did his best to comfort family members with compassion and even a few tears of his own. He ensured listeners that Heartland Lakes Airways would comply fully with the FAA, and would demand that a thorough investigation be conducted.

Bob Cummings, director of the Miami office of the National Transportation Safety Board, had been rudely awakened at 3:15 a.m. from an incredible dream. But reality hit him like a slap on the face.

"What?!" exclaimed Bob into the bedside telephone. "You've got to be kidding me! The damn radar malfunctioned? Okay, I'll head up to Tampa right away." He slammed the phone down and walked groggily to the master bathroom and turned on the shower. An hour later, Bob's red Corvette was blazing across Alligator Alley with a portable flashing red light magnetically clamped to the roof.

While Bob Cummings was blistering northward, Lew Berry was scarpering southward in the Trans Am rental back to FBI headquarters in Miami. He had made umpteen calls to Heartland Lakes Airway's customer service number, but every call rang busy. Lew needed to find out if Janet Berry's name was on the flight manifest for the downed jet. If he couldn't get through to Heartland Lakes himself, he guessed Agent Jones at the FBI might have better luck. With the accelerator floored, he would be there when they opened for business.

CHAPTER 46
Thursday, March 11, 1982
4:00 a.m.

Willy couldn't sleep. He tried, but all he could do was roll left, roll right, and then stare straight up at the ceiling. Those two words were causing an anxiety outburst in his mind: "Buckwheat" and "Roy." It was four o'clock in the morning, but Willy knew the night was over. He got up and went to the bathroom, splashed some water on his face, and headed to the kitchen to make a pot of coffee. It was going to be a long day.

Folgers or Maxwell House? Both revived the comatose early morning risers equally well. Willy mixed the two coffee brands together and put fifteen heaping tablespoons into the basket of his eight cup percolator, then placed it on the gas stove. Nothing better than strong coffee to stimulate the brain cells.

When the percolator stopped bubbling, Willy poured a large cup of joe and headed for the porch. He took a sip, stared up to the eastern sky where dawn was about to break, and then sat down on the folding chair. He had claimed the chair a couple of years ago from the sheriff's contraband warehouse that was connected to the jail. The chair had fallen out of the bed of a pickup truck whose driver was being chased for allegedly stealing property from a pawn shop. Willy was on duty and picked up the chair to keep it from being a roadway hazard, then brought it to the warehouse. No one from the pawnshop came to retrieve it, so after a year, Willy asked if he could keep it. The chair was the one and only perk he ever received from Sheriff Al Bonty. The legs were bent a bit from the fall off the truck, but it had nice padding and could hold up well to the bulk of big fellas like Otis or Willy.

Willy took a second sip, and the miracle drug caffeine kicked in. A game plan was beginning to form as his mind began to rouse. His first task must be to explore the recent puzzling deaths in Seminole Bend and connect the dots. There was no doubt in his mind that the "Roy" that Lance overheard the man in the phone booth mention was Roy Jackson. But who was the "Buckwheat"? Despite Martin Luther King's mortal efforts to end racism, white folks in the south still used racial slurs to demean the black folks. Many blacks lived in or near Seminole Bend, but Willy knew of only two that Roy disliked. Willy's nephew, Tyrone, had become a sophomore star on the Warriors basketball team, pushing Jimmy Jackson a notch further down on the prodigy list of local athletes looking for a full ride to a top tier, Division I college. Then there were Roy's suspicions that Tyrone was secretly dating his daughter Jenny. Neither reason seemed like a good motive for hiring a hitman to kill Tyrone, but then again, Roy Jackson was not a reasonable person. The other black that Roy disliked was Willy, and that was the obvious logical explanation for sending a goon out on a murderous mission. Roy needed to remedy some unfinished business. Willy had been left for dead in his swamp, but that hadn't worked out as planned.

Willy's thoughts took another turn. He remembered his chat with Ernie Hyle, the obese Taylor Creek locks operator, the morning the Potts' were killed. Ernie was almost certain that he saw a Mexican male go through the locks with Calvin's boat that same morning. If that Mexican man had either borrowed or stole the boat, perhaps it was the same Alumicraft vessel that was used to rescue Willy.

But how could Roy Jackson's goons know that the boat belonged to Calvin Potts? "That's it!" Willy's coffee was again working miracles. He was now talking aloud to himself. "The thugs that chased me and that Mexican dude out on the Kissimmee must've seen the boat number. If they tracked it and knew the boat was owned by Potts, they must've figured it was Calvin who saved me. They probably didn't see that is was a Mexican guy driving! Damn!"

It was now a little bit after five o'clock, way too early for anyone in Seminole Bend who wasn't fishing to be awake. But Willy couldn't wait for business hours, so he went to the phone book and found Deputy Johnny Murphree's home number. He dialed and let it ring sixteen times, and finally, he heard a voice on the other end mutter, "This dang well better not be a wrong number, or I'll deal with you later in hell!"

"Johnny, it's me, Willy. Sorry 'bout the early call, but I need an answer fast. My life may be on the line here."

It took Johnny a few seconds to get his bearings and shake out the grogginess. "Willy, you doing okay, man? Still can't believe Bonty let you go, dude. You was the best dep we had. You say your life's on the line? What's going on?"

"I'll tell you later, but I need to know something. You remember 'bout a month ago, the day the Potts' couple was killed?"

"Never forget that day, Willy. Potts, they was killed first. You was recouping from that gator bite but still managed to yank that goon through the window of his car down at BoldMart. That same car hits that old man and kills him, which is why you ended up fired and all. Ain't right they blame you, man!"

"So, do you remember if Jackson called Sheriff Bonty the afternoon before the crash? I'm talking 'bout the day before?"

"You mean the day they found you out at Angler's Delight? No man, can't say that I do, but that doesn't mean he didn't call him. Why you asking, Willy?"

"Just wondering if Roy got a boat license number from your office, that's all."

"That wouldn't have happened, Willy. We don't keep records of boats. The DNR down in Homestead keeps all them records."

"The DNR? Who down at the DNR would give Roy Jackson that information if he asked, Johnny?"

"I believe his name is Sam Dulie. He's the South Florida DNR supe."

"Can anybody just call and get that stuff? Is it public record?"

"Don't know. But not many folks working in public offices round here wouldn't give old Roy Jackson anything he asked, now would they?"

"Okay, Johnny, thanks, man! You've been a big help, now go back to sleep."

"You think I can get back to sleep now? I'll be wide awake trying to figure out the puzzle you just laid on me. Tell me what you're doing, Willy."

"Later." Willy hung up the phone. The first of the dots had just been connected. Willy guessed that Jackson's assailants who chased him in the boat saw the license number and called Roy. Roy then made a call to Sam Dulie, who must have provided him with the owner's name from the registration information. Roy assumed that Calvin was Willy's rescuer from the swamp, and he feared that Calvin was a witness to his goon's actions. And Roy didn't want to risk that Calvin had said anything to his wife, so he had Agnes silenced, too.

It was now making more sense. Willy figured the hitman in the phone booth saw Calvin go into the sheriff's office, and he needed to kill him before any investigations took place, so he rammed him with the Ford LTD. The goon escaped, ran into Elmer's Hardware Store, and his life ended when his skull met head-on, literally speaking, with a plumber's wrench and a porcelain sink.

Jackson's thugs had shot Sam McCormick with a twelve-gauge and killed both the Potts. That meant the only person left to testify to the illegal activity at the Jackson ranch was Willy himself. Roy tried to finish the task that the gators couldn't seem to accomplish, so he sent his goons out to follow him when Willy left the hospital, and then kill him at the first opportunity. They had their chance in the BoldMart parking lot but didn't get the job done, even though Willy was damaged goods at the time. There was no doubt Roy would continue his lethal efforts until Willy was silenced forever.

Willy knew his assassination would be imminent unless Roy could be stopped. But no one else had a close encounter with Jackson's gangsters and lived to tell about it. Then again—Willy had forgotten about the Mexican who saved his life. And Roy Jackson had no knowledge of the man because he assumed Willy's swamp liberator was Calvin Potts. Could he find the Mexican guy? And if so, would he testify? Living a comfy life in the Witness Protection Program might appeal to him.

Willy could hear the sound of several sirens in the distance. "Must have been quite a car wreck," he thought. He went back into the house and woke Otis up from a snore-filled serenade on the couch. Willy's new detective agency was about to hire its first employee.

CHAPTER 47

Thursday, March 11, 1982

5:30 a.m.

"Willy, I was dreaming 'bout them Lula girls in Hawaii, so why's you messing with my sleeping?" Otis awoke slowly with one eye looking straight up at Willy, while the other one was still rolled halfway up in his eyelid.

"They called hula girls, Otis, not Lula girls. Sit up a sec, I have an offer for you." Otis was reluctant to let those grass skirts fade from his memory, but he begrudgingly forced himself into a sitting position on the couch. Willy sat down next to him and offered a swig of his coffee. Otis took a gulp, and his eyes bulged. The coffee expelled from his mouth onto the floor, and spittle flew onto Willy's face.

"Holy crap, Willy! Is that rattlesnake venom you be drinking?"

"Relax, O, just wanted to wake you up."

"Well, I be good to go nows, for God's sake!"

"I have a job for you, Otis," Willy said while staring candidly into Otis' bloodshot eyes.

"Pay more than Muckers, Willy?"

"Can't say right now. When I get some cash on hand, I'll make sure you're well compensated."

"What's a cumsated?"

"Compensated. That means you'll get money to work for me. Only thing is you may have to wait a while to get paid."

"What I be doing, Will?"

"Detective work, Otis. You'll be a chief detective in my new agency. And do you think your buddy, Lance, might want a job, too?"

"A detective, just like in the movies?"

"Yep, but this work is going to be riskier than the movies, O."

"I think Lance could be talked into it. Will he get cumsated, too?"

* * * * *

"What you want? You said you was done with me last night, Willy Banks." Lance rubbed his eyes and sat up in the car. He had been sleeping in the back seat of the Buick with the flat tire, the one his cousin Lenny had stolen. Lance knew the cops were too busy with local killings to bother looking for filched cars from the coast. He figured he had another good week or so to sleep and fool around with Evie in the back seat before somebody hauled it away.

"I'm gonna cut right to the chase, Lance. You want a job?"

"Hmmm. Gee, I don't know. Does it have a better retirement plan than my panhandling career?" Lance had no idea what Willy wanted, but getting up and going to work wasn't exactly appealing to him at this moment of lassitude.

"Funny man, ain't you, Lance? Okay, here's the deal. I've decided to be a private investigator, and I need your help locating someone. You'd be working with Otis." Willy gestured to Otis, who had both hands stuck in his front pockets and was standing behind Willy. Otis smiled at Lance.

"I ain't much good at answering no phones, Willy. Best you let Otis do that part. I could be your limo driver, though. What's you paying?"

"My limo is that there 1958 Nash Rambler with three hubcaps missing." Willy pointed to the car that he and Otis drove to the Dixie Food and Drug. "It was a gift to me from the Yardly family after Bo's funeral. We was best friends, and he was killed in Nam. Bo's parents gave the Rambler to him when he graduated from high school as a way to get to Bama and back during college. I guess he forgot to change the oil cuz it ain't running too great. Thing is, Lance, I don't need a driver or even a secretary to answer phones. I need investigators."

"I hears about your buddy Bo. Played in the NFL, huh?" Willy nodded, then Lance continued. "Investigators? Yep, that's right up my alley. Been telling Evie I'd make a good professional sleuth, ya know. Sure the pay will be perfect for my 'bilities, too, right Willy?"

"Right now, I ain't got no money, Lance. You and Otis will have to wait a while to get paid. I'm hoping there might be a reward out some time for finding Agnes Potts' killers. Any money we scrape up from rewards, we split equally three ways."

"Ya think there's any reward on this old Buick yet? Maybe we could call them police over in Stuart and tells them we beat up a car thief over here in Seminole Bend and confiscated his car. Bet they make us some kind of heroes over in Stuart and give us some big bucks! Probably want our pictures on the front page of the news, too. Good free advertising for our new business. What you think, Willy?"

"Ever heard of fingerprints, Lance? May not work out the best for your cousin Lenny if they find his in the car. But I have something to get us started. Ever run into a loner Mexican dude around here who likes fishing?"

"Who don't like fishing? And them Mexicans are geniuses at catching speckled perch with nothing but a cane pole and a hook. Don't even need no bait. They wiggle that copper hook until them fish get hypnotized and bite down on it!" Lance and Otis looked and nodded at each other.

Willy had no plans to keep Lance and Otis on a permanent payroll for his new business. But he thought they might be able to track down one of their own: an insignificant resident of Seminole Bend with pitiable income. He didn't know how he would end the working relationship if and when they located the Mexican man, but he didn't have time to worry about that now. Willy wouldn't lose sleep over putting Lance back to unemployment status, but Otis was his brother, and that would be a different story.

"We need to patch up that tire on Lenny's Buick so you and Otis can have some wheels." Willy had always been an honest man, and just the thought of using a stolen vehicle for this operation was causing him genuine anxiety. Sheriff Bonty would like nothing better than to catch Willy red-handed and book him with grand theft auto. They needed to locate the Mexican quickly and return the car back the way they found it to the Dixie Food and Drug parking lot.

"What we do, bro, if cops stops us for auto robbery?" Otis wanted nothing to do with being a felony thief. Spending a night or two in the jailhouse for stealing sardines off the shelf at the grocery store was one thing, sitting in prison for five years was another.

"Tell them you saw the car parked at Dixie Food and Drug for a few days, but no one ever drove it. You were just turning it into the sheriff's office because you are both proper citizens doing your civic duty." Willy couldn't look at Otis or Lance directly in the eyes when he said it, but he hoped they would buy his story.

Otis glanced over at Lance and nodded in affirmation, "I was planning on telling ya, Lance, that Willy is dang smart at figuring things out. That's a great plan, bro." Looking at the expression on his face, Willy could tell that Lance wasn't so sure. But he nodded back, then looked at the Buick.

"How we fix that dang tire, Willy?"

"Check the trunk for a spare. That's all we need to drive it. Do you have the keys, Lance?"

"Yep, Lenny left 'em with me.

"Good, we best get started fast."

Lance jacked up the rear end while Willy unfastened the lug nuts. The donut spare tire had been used already, and it needed air, but Willy thought it might last a couple of days. Otis' job was to be on the lookout for a police or sheriff's cruiser. They finished up in fifteen minutes, then Lance got in the driver's seat and turned on the ignition. Surprisingly, there were no issues with the battery or plugs. Lance revved the engine several times while Otis got in the passenger seat.

Willy leaned on the driver's side door, and Lance rolled down the window. "Start looking over at Taylor Creek and ask people fishing if they ever seen a Mexican round there. Park the car in a place that it won't be noticed for a while. I can't give you much of a description of the Mexican dude other than he was about five foot seven or eight, skinny with black hair. Then tonight, get down to McDonald's and make sure you are there at sunset. Most of the Mexicans in Seminole Bend are migrants who pick oranges in the winter. They work for a place called Gold Coast Fruit Company down in Fort Pierce, but most of them live here cuz it's cheaper. They got some old rusty van that picks them up every morning where they lives and drops them off at night, but they always stop at McDonald's for a burger before heading home. They will be in a hurry, so you two need to be there to ask all of them questions before they leave."

"What we supposed to ask 'em when we sees 'em, Willy?" Otis was a bit confused with this new detective vocation of his.

"Just plain ask them if they was the one who saved a big ass black man on the Kissimmee a few weeks ago. Look them straight in the eyes when you ask. If you find the one, you'll see him get panicked and scared cuz he won't know what you want with him. Otherwise, you'll just get a confused look."

"You should give us some cuffs, Willy. That way, when we catch him, we can keep him in one place 'til you get there," declared Otis proudly.

"No, Otis, you're not putting cuffs on him. We can't arrest him cuz we're not the police. Besides, the man saved my life, and he ain't broke no law."

"So, how do we get him to talk to you? What if he takes off running?"

"Tell him I just want to give him some cash and take him to dinner for saving my life. Be nice. He probably will want to know who you two are, so tell him you're my brother and that Lance is a good friend."

"But how do we find you after we finds him?"

"I'm going down to the Department of Natural Resources office in Homestead. Probably won't be back until seven or eight. I need to talk to the director, Sam Dulie. He's got some connection to Roy Jackson, and I ain't leaving 'til I find out what it is. If I ain't back yet, I will call Lance's phone booth around eight o'clock to give you an update 'bout where I am. If you can talk the Mexican dude into meeting up at Sal's Steakhouse around nine, then I would buy you all a juicy sirloin. He should be back from picking oranges by then."

Otis smiled again at Lance and winked. "See, I told ya that Willy is pretty dang smart. Runs in the family, ya know!"

CHAPTER 48

Thursday, March 11, 1982

7:55 a.m.

Lew screeched into the FBI parking lot at 7:55 a.m. and pounded on his brakes. He had made good time despite the traffic woes. His Trans Am had to pull off to the shoulder of State Road 710 several times to keep from being a hindrance to the multitude of emergency vehicles heading from West Palm Beach to the airplane accident staging area at Angler's Delight Marina. Lew slammed the transmission into park and sprung from the car, leaving the driver's side door wide open as he sprinted to the front door of the building. He collided head-on with two blue suits coming out while he was going in. One of the suits belonged to Agent Tecka.

"Sorry, sorry!" exclaimed Lew as the three men tried to regain their composure. "Agent Tecka, right? I have a meeting with Agent Jones, and I was running late. Sorry again!"

"You won't find Jack here," said Tecka shaking his head. "He's gone to Tampa. Emergency meeting with the FAA and NTSB about the plane crash this morning. He left an envelope for you inside and said to meet him tomorrow morning at eight o'clock."

"My wife! What about my wife? Did he find something out?" pleaded Lew.

"Don't know, but maybe there's some information in that envelope. We've got to go, Mr. Berry. Sorry, but I'll be at that meeting with you tomorrow. Excuse us, please!" The two FBI agents dusted themselves off, straightened their ties, and walked to their car. Lew was losing it. He watched the agents for a few seconds and tried to relax before going inside.

"May I help you, sir?" asked the front desk receptionist.

"Yes, my name is Lew Berry, and I understand that Agent Jones left an envelope for me.

"Oh, yes, I have it," replied the receptionist. She opened the middle drawer and took out a manila envelope with Lew Berry's name written on the front. "And Agent Jones asked me to tell you how sorry he was for canceling your meeting and wanted to reschedule for tomorrow morning. Is that possible, Mr. Berry?"

"I don't believe I have much of a choice," replied Lew sarcastically. "Okay, what time?"

"How about the same as today, eight o'clock?"

"Yes, yes, I'll be there." Lew took the envelope and jogged out to the Trans Am. From his front bucket seat, he unfastened the bronze metal clasp and pulled out a grainy photograph printed on regular typing paper. It was a picture of his wife sitting in a café talking to a man whose back was towards the camera. Lew didn't know when or where the photo was taken, or who the man was that was sipping coffee with Janet.

Lew was overcome with emotions as he drove back to the Holiday Inn he had checked out of a few days earlier. He was holding out hope that Agent Jones had received encouraging information from the FBI in Pennsylvania, and he would know tomorrow morning. Optimism was a virtue he had instilled in his son but was rapidly fading from his own existence.

CHAPTER 49

Thursday, March 11, 1982

12:05 p.m.

The distance from Seminole Bend to Homestead was about 150 miles. Willy's Nash Rambler topped out at sixty-two miles per hour. If he got it up to sixty-three, chances were good the head gasket would blow. Willy guessed the trip would take him about four hours to complete because maneuvering around traffic in Miami was painstakingly slow. It was still early when he left Seminole Bend. He hoped to arrive at the DNR by noon and chat with Sam Dulie.

When he was done with Sam, Willy planned to drive to Miami and camp somewhere outside the barbed wire fence that surrounded the FBI's automobile impound lot. While still working at the sheriff's department, he had read an addendum to Sheryl Berry's accident report that stated what remained of her truck was being towed to the Miami lot for further examination. Willy wanted to know why, and he knew the FBI had no plans to tell him. On the passenger seat of the Nash Rambler were a pair of wire cutters for the fence and a crowbar for Berry's pickup truck. And in the back seat was a full-face ski mask. The FBI was sure to have a security camera somewhere on sight.

Willy pulled the Rambler into the DNR lot a few minutes past noon. He parked near the entrance next to a newly washed, forest green, 1980 model Ford pickup truck that had the *Great Seal of the State of Florida* emblazoned on both the driver's side and passenger doors. Stenciled above the seals was *State of Florida – Department of Natural Resources* in black, block letters. An identical truck was parked near a side entryway, but that truck was covered with mud, likely from a romp through the nearby Everglades National Park.

Willy exited his vehicle and was heading to the front door of the building when he noticed something in the open bed of the DNR truck. Willy walked over and glanced in. It was a cigar box with no lid that was being used to store several small, cylindrical silver widgets with green wires sticking out the ends. Willy thought he remembered seeing objects such as those cylinders somewhere before. Then it dawned on him that the cylinders were similar to the one that Bo Yardly had used to rig a transistor radio while on leave from the Army back in 1970. Bo had manipulated the radio so it could intercept communications between pilots and air traffic controllers.

Willy entered the DNR and noticed that there was a reception desk, but no one there to answer the phone or greet visitors. Next to the phone was a notepad and a pen, and dust covered the used and abused Formica top. Obviously, not much customer service action happened at the DNR.

"Anybody home?" Willy spoke just loudly enough to get someone's attention without sounding rude.

A moment later, a good-looking young man with dark skin and curly black hair came out of an office and approached Willy.

"May I help you?" asked Sam Dulie as he offered his right hand to Willy. Willy shook his hand and paused a moment, not sure if he wanted to say what he was thinking.

"Ah, sorry, yes, I'm looking for Sam Dulie," stuttered Willy.

"I'm Sam Dulie. May I ask who you are?"

"My name's Willy Banks. Pardon my words, but you don't look like a Sam Dulie."

"And exactly what does a Sam Dulie supposed to look like, Mr. Banks?"

"Well, you look like you hail from somewhere in the Middle East, like an Arab or something. But I've never heard an Arab named Sam or Dulie, and pardon me again for even mentioning it." Willy wasn't prejudiced, but he did want to see how Sam reacted to this.

"How about we skip the cheap talk and get down to business. How can I help you, Mr. Banks?"

Willy had made no game plan on how he was proceeding with his questions. He thought of some options while driving to southern Florida, but none seemed to work in his mind. So he had decided to just wing it, not the best strategy for a private investigator, to be sure. Willy resolved to first find out about the box of tubes in the pickup truck parked out front.

"I happened to notice you had a cigar box with some cylinders lying in the bed of your truck." Willy purposely did not ask a question. Once again, he wanted to see Sam's reaction to that statement. But Sam was no fool, and he remained impervious to Willy's comment.

"Okay, that's great. You have extraordinary vision, Mr. Banks," Sam uttered back calmly. "What is your business today with the Department of Natural Resources, sir?"

"Please, no need to call me Mr. Banks or sir. I'm just Willy."

"Okay, Willy, let's go back to square one. I am the supervisor of the South Florida region for the DNR. I'm assuming your visit today involves the department, no?"

"Actually, Sam—I may call you Sam, right?" Dulie smiled and nodded back. "Actually, I'm here to ask you some questions about a man named Roy Jackson." Willy could detect a faint startled expression on Sam's face, but he hid it well.

"Roy Jackson? And does this man have business with the Department of Natural Resources?" Sam wasn't about to give an inch.

"Not sure, but guessing he does seeing he called you a couple of weeks back."

"Let's not play games, Willy. Why are you here? This man, Roy Jackson, may or may not have called a few weeks back. We don't keep phone logs here. But now you need to explain who you are and what your visit is about because I need to get back to work."

"I'm a private investigator, Sam." Willy was stretching the truth a bit, but then again, he was the only one seemingly interested in putting Roy Jackson's ring of terror to an end, even if that meant telling a fib or two here and there.

"Can I please see your credentials then? Some sort of identification." Sam didn't miss a beat, and now Willy had to think quickly. Willy's mama always said that when in a bind, the truth was always the best option, and you should give it a chance.

"I'm an ex-cop from Seminole Bend's sheriff's department. I'd show you a badge, but it was taken from me when I was fired. I was fired because I had a mission to stop this man Roy Jackson's criminal dictatorship. People are getting killed, good people, Sam. And the sheriff's department is covering it up and protecting Jackson. I became a deputy to stop crime, not to light the flames of corruption like those people I worked for. And to be quite blunt, Sam, I believe you gave Roy the name and address of a boat owner a couple of weeks ago that resulted in his death and the death of his wife. So you want to see my credentials? Perhaps you can read them in my eyes."

Sam paused for a moment to gather his thoughts. If he felt a bit of responsibility or remorse for the deaths of the Potts', he didn't show it. Willy knew it would be difficult to make him talk. Sam was intelligent and calculated, a tough nut to crack.

Sam coolly declared, "I'm sorry you drove all the way to Homestead, Deputy Banks. As I mentioned, we don't keep call logs, so I can't confirm or deny speaking to this Mr. Jackson. I can assure you, sir, that even if we did speak to him, we would not have provided the boat owner's name or address. That information is not public record."

At that moment, the phone on the reception desk rang as did a phone in Sam's office. Instead of picking up the nearby phone that was within arm's reach, Sam excused himself and went back to his office to answer the call. Willy found that a bit strange. Calls to the DNR should be about hunting licenses and boat registrations, things like that. Why would Sam seemingly need privacy to answer a simple call to the agency?

In his haste, Sam left the door to his office open, and Willy could see him pick up the phone and then slink down into his chair. Willy couldn't make out the conversation because Sam's back was to him, and he was basically whispering to the person on the other end of the line. But Willy noticed an electronic gadget that looked like a sizeable two-way radio with the microphone missing sitting on top of Sam's desk. And glancing beyond the desk, outside the office window, he saw a very unusual contraption. It looked like a giant bowl with a metal rod protruding up from its center. Willy decided he may have to sharpen his private investigator skills and give it a closer look before leaving. How he could do that without Sam noticing was yet to be determined.

Willy took a few steps toward Sam's office door and decided to try and listen in on his apparent covert conversation. Sam's whispers were indeed suspicious, considering he worked for a government agency that was dedicated to the great outdoors.

Sam must have sensed Willy nearby as the whispers suddenly changed to a regular voice to whoever was listening on the other end. "Yes, I will be happy to send out a replacement fishing license. You should receive it in the next couple of days. If there is anything else I can do for you, please don't hesitate to call."

Then Sam hung up the phone and faced Willy. "Sorry about that, Deputy Banks, but that was someone who lost his fishing license yesterday and needed a new one. Now, where were we?"

Willy looked at his watch and noted the time. He planned to find out who made the call.

"Well, I guess seeing you have no information that is useful, I will be leaving. I'm sorry I was a bit obtrusive. You're obviously a good man, Sam, just doing your duty for the state of Florida." Willy thought buttering Sam up may work to his benefit. He started away from Sam's office but then turned back abruptly, causing Sam to accidentally stumble into him. "Oh, I'm sorry, Sam. I just wanted to ask you about that big old radio thing you got on your desk. Radios are a hobby of mine, and I ain't never seen anything like it. Mind if I sneak a peek?"

"I'd love to show it to you, Willy, but I have a meeting soon. You were right. It's a short-wave radio that I use to call my officers who are in the field. It has a range of about a hundred miles. Perhaps if you visit again, I can show you how it works."

"Sure, no problem, Sam. By the way, I noticed you don't have a microphone attached. Is it broken?"

"Yep, that's it. We overuse the mics, and they need to be replaced. I'm planning on stopping over at Radio Shack in Miami first thing next week."

"Oh, okay. Well, thanks for your time, Sam."

"My pleasure!" Willy shook hands with Sam and headed out the front door. Sam stood at the doorway and watched him leave. It was apparent that Sam intended to keep a close eye on Willy until he was back on the road and heading towards Miami. Willy fired up the Nash Rambler and pulled out of the parking lot, turning right onto the Ingraham Highway. About a mile down the road, when he knew he was no longer in Sam Dulie's line of vision, Willy pulled over and parked his car next to an overgrown Sabal palmetto tree. He ambled back to the DNR alongside the highway, keeping out of sight by treading just inside the line of tropical woodland that ran next to the roadway. A half-hour later, he was hidden behind the foliage that covered the fence separating the DNR's back courtyard area from the building. He now had an excellent view of the giant dish with the metal rod, and through the window, he could see Sam Dulie holding the telephone to his ear. So much for that meeting he was in a rush to go to.

Sam's back was turned in his chair while talking on the phone, and he was staring at a wall in his office. That meant if Willy was careful, he could approach the dish without being seen. The fence was chain link, so Willy had no problem climbing over it and into the open courtyard. He ducked down and moved quickly to the dish, then laid down underneath the curved lip so he was out of sight from Dulie. The first thing that Willy noticed was a small cable running from the dish to a hole in the concrete frame underneath the office window. He glanced up to the window and could see the same cable connected to the short-wave radio, or whatever it was, on Sam's desk.

Willy estimated the diameter of the dish was about fourteen feet, and it was made of fiberglass. The metal rod or antenna protruding from the center was about eight feet long. Willy had seen pictures of these contraptions and knew they were called satellite dishes. They were used to transmit data, and even television signals, from a satellite to Earth and vice versa. So why in God's name did the Florida Department of Natural Resources need a satellite dish? Willy was now convinced that Sam Dulie was more than the boss man who ruled over flora and fauna of southern Florida. As he turned to make his way back to the fence, he noticed an embossed design on the side of the dish. It was plain old gibberish to Willy, but he touched it with his fingertips anyway:

Just like any good private investigator worth his salt, Willy had a small, spiral notepad and a pencil in his back pocket. He tore out a sheet and placed it over the raised characters, then traced the markings with his pencil. After tucking the etching back in his pocket, Willy hightailed it to the fence and climbed over, then jogged the mile back to his car. He half thought that Roy Jackson and Sam Dulie would be waiting for him at the Nash Rambler with loaded weapons pointed at his face. He was wrong, but he wasn't about to take a leisurely drive through the countryside as he made his way up to Miami.

Willy checked his watch. It was almost two o'clock. He figured it would take about forty-five minutes to get to the FBI's automobile impound lot that was located west of the city on Highway 41 in Tamiami. He turned left off of US 1 onto Florida Route 821 in Cutler Bay and headed north. A mile or two later, he noticed a payphone attached to the side of a post office. He made a U-turn and pulled into the parking lot. He didn't have any change, so he dialed the operator.

"I would like to make a person-to-person collect call to a Johnny Murphree," said Willy to the operator, then gave her the number in a loud, clear voice. The phone rang at the sheriff's department in Seminole Bend, and sure enough, Johnny was working the front desk, as usual. He hesitated a few seconds, but then accepted the call.

"Dang it, Willy Banks, you're going to get me fired! I can't be accepting no collect calls from anyone, let alone you. If the taxpayers don't get me, Bonty will. Now, what's up? And make it fast! The phone's been ringing like crazy all morning, everyone wanting information about that jet crash, you know."

"Sorry 'bout that, Johnny." Willy paused and thought for a moment. "What jet crash?"

"You ain't heard. Where you been, man?" Johnny was dumbfounded that Willy hadn't heard about the second midair collision over Florida in the past month. It was on every news channel around the globe.

Willy thought about the giant flash of light and loud booming sound he and Otis and Lance had heard last night. They assumed it was thunder and lightning. "Haven't been listening to the news, Johnny. But now I know what all the sirens and ambulances were about that I passed this morning. What happened anyway?"

"Don't know too much yet, so best you turn on a TV or something. But I got to go, so what do you need? And I ain't making no guarantees!"

"You know I wouldn't be calling if it wasn't important. And if you do get fired, I got a job waiting for you in my private detective agency." Willy smiled as he could picture Johnny rolling his eyes. "Okay, what I need for you to do is track down a phone number for me."

"A phone number? What kind of phone number, what do you mean?"

"A phone call was placed to the South Florida Department of Natural Resources around one this afternoon. Can you find out who made the call?" Willy decided to cross his fingers. He wasn't much for believing in luck, but if it could help, he had nothing to lose.

"Well, sure, Willy. I'll get Sheriff Bonty on it right away," replied Johnny with more than just a hint of sarcasm.

"Come on, Johnny. An official call from you to AT & T down in Miami might do the trick."

"They ain't no fools, Willy. I would need some sort of search warrant to pull that off, and you know it. Only a judge or the governor can do that stuff."

Willy thought for a moment and then said, "Carla Evans?"

A touch of anger was apparent in Johnny's voice as he replied, "What about Carla?" Carla Evans had been a paralegal in a local Seminole Bend law office and used to be Johnny's fiancé. She was offered a career move to Tallahassee to work as a staffer for Hank Daughtry after he was elected governor. Johnny asked her to choose between a life married to him or a life working in politics. Two weeks later, Carla was pulling a U-Haul truck to the state capital.

"Would Carla be willing to make a call to AT & T to find out who called the DNR?" Willy crossed his fingers again.

"I don't speak to Carla anymore, Willy, and I think you know that!" Johnny was getting upset. If Willy weren't a good friend, he would have slammed down the receiver.

"Johnny, I understand, and I wouldn't be asking if it wasn't important. But I'm on to something, and I can't tell you over the phone just what it is. Trust me. I need this one favor, and maybe we can rid the world of Roy Jackson."

"Your favors are adding up, Willy. I plan to cash in on some of them some time, you know." Johnny had lightened up a bit. Deep down, he thought this could be a good excuse to reunite with his ex-lover. He decided to give it a try. "Okay, I'll make the call, but obviously, there are absolutely no guarantees! Now, how do I get ahold of you?"

"I'm at a payphone in Cutler Bay, but I am heading home. I'll call you back in a few hours if that works for you?"

"Remember, Willy, no guarantees." Johnny hung up on his friend without saying goodbye. Willy took a deep breath and kissed his crossed fingers.

CHAPTER 50
Thursday, March 11, 1982
2:30 p.m.

A half-hour later, Willy approached the FBI's auto impound facility in Tamiami. It was set back about a hundred yards from US 41, and the entrance was a white sand and seashell driveway that led to a motorized, chain link gate. The entire fence around the perimeter, including the gate, was about eight feet high with rolled razor wire affixed to the top. A guardhouse was just inside the entrance and was manned twenty-four hours a day, 365 days a year. If somehow someone were able to get inside the yard, then he or she would need to deal with a dozen German shepherds whose bite was worse than their bark. The facility itself was massive, approximately 90,000 square feet. But because homeowners in the area didn't want a view from their picture window of an impounded vehicle lot, the FBI had planted queen palm trees twelve feet apart around the entire fence and patched hibiscus shrubs in between the tree trunks, so the fence was barely visible.

Willy decided his only option was to wait until dark and hopefully be able to sneak close and hide between a hibiscus shrub and the fence. He decided to call Lance's phone booth in Seminole Bend to let him and Otis know he wouldn't be able to make a dinner meeting tonight as planned with the mystery Mexican man. Willy wasn't sure if Lance and Otis had located him anyway.

Willy drove to a nearby convenience store to buy bottled water and some junk food to hold him over until dusk. He needed change for the phone booth, too. The convenience store had three payphones attached to the building just outside the front entrance. He tried calling Lance's phone booth, but no one answered. By four o'clock, the sunny Florida sky was being replaced by several layers of black cumulonimbus clouds. Thunder crackled in the distance.

Willy opted to keep his car parked at the convenience store and walk the half-mile to the perimeter fence. An empty Nash Rambler parked next to an FBI impound lot could be very suspicious, so there was no need to risk it. The sun wouldn't set until around 7:30, so Willy had three and a half hours to kill. He climbed over into the back seat to catch a nap. The rain began to dance on the roof, and the soothing noise put him to sleep within minutes. He awoke to a loud tapping on his side window and blinding light in his eyes. Willy shaded his eyes with his right hand and squinted to see who was making all the racket outside. It was two men with flashlights, and they each had a badge pinned to their navy blue shirt pockets.

"Tamiami police, sir, can you please step out of your vehicle?" asked the tall, stocky officer in a stern voice. Willy unlatched the door and exited the Rambler.

"Hands where we can see them, sir." It was a direct order, one that Willy had made many times during traffic stops in Seminole Bend. He knew the routine. Willy lifted his arms a few inches away from his pockets.

"Driver's license and registration, sir. Is your registration in the glovebox?"

"Yes, sir. Here is my driver's license, and I will get my registration."

"Please, sir, stay where you are. We will locate your registration ourselves." The tall officer nodded to his partner, who walked around the car and opened the passenger door. Inside the glovebox, the registration was attached by a paper clip to a proof of insurance document. When the officer closed the compartment, he glanced at the floor mat.

"Mel, I think you should come over here and see this," the officer told his partner, who was still examining Willy's driver's license.

"What is it, Todd?" replied Officer Mel.

"You need to see it," said Officer Todd.

Officer Mel looked at Willy and said, "Walk with me and place your hands on the hood of the car." Willy did as he was told, and he knew exactly what the officer named Todd had found.

Mel grabbed the wire cutter, crowbar, and ski mask off the floor and walked back over to Willy. "What exactly are these for, sir?" inquired Officer Mel as he held out the objects for Willy to see.

Instead of lying to the officer, Willy shrugged his shoulders and didn't reply.

"Cuff him, Todd," Officer Mel ordered his partner.

"Why? What crime have I committed?" Willy asked without losing his temper. He knew anger never worked when confronting an officer about to make an arrest, and quite frankly, Willy would have done the same thing.

"You are suspected to be in violation of Florida Penal Code 810.06, possession of burglary tools, which is a third-degree felony. You have the right to remain silent. From this point forward, anything you say may be held against you in a court of law. You have the right to an attorney. If you cannot afford an attorney, one will be provided at no cost to you. Sir, do you understand these rights?"

Willy affirmed with a nod and said, "Yes, sir. I understand." There was no use trying to negotiate a Miranda Warning.

Officer Todd led Willy to the police vehicle and locked him in the back seat. Officer Mel noticed a piece of paper with nonsense writing scribbled on it that was laying on the passenger side front seat. He placed it in the black evidence bag along with the wire cutter, crowbar, and ski mask. A few minutes later, the police car was speeding east on Highway

41 with the roof-mounted light bar flashing, but no siren. Another criminal apprehended before the crime was committed. A great day for the Tamiami PD.

CHAPTER 51

Friday, March 12, 1982

12:30 a.m.

It was half past midnight when Tamiami PD's night desk officer, Jerry Shubert, escorted Willy from his nine-by-nine-foot cell to a payphone located in the hallway. For his one allotted call, Willy wanted to contact Johnny Murphree to help get himself sprung in some sort of police courtesy to another police kind of way. But Johnny doesn't work the night shift in Seminole Bend, and Willy didn't know his home phone number.

"Mr. Banks, you have one free call, so best you make it a good one," said Officer Shubert respectfully. Willy knew he should be contacting a lawyer, but he didn't have time for the legal system to work its way through the dawdling court system. He gambled that Johnny Murphree could take care of this right away, but he was skeptical that he could find a way to get ahold of him this late at night. Shubert called the operator and gave her an account code. The one free call from the payphone was automatically charged back to the Tamiami PD. Willy dialed the phone booth in the parking lot at Dixie Food and Drug. For the third time today, Willy crossed his fingers.

Lance picked up the call on the fourth ring. "Yep, who's calling?"

"Lance, it's me, Willy. I need a big favor."

"Willy. Where you at, man? Otis and me been waiting for you over at Sal's Steakhouse. Said you be there at nine."

“Did you find the Mexican?” Willy asked impatiently. He needed a quick response from Lance because he had only three minutes allotted for the call.

“No, man. But we think his name is Pancho. When we asked the Mexican orange pickers up at Quick Stuff if any of ‘em saved a ‘big ass black man’ on the Kissimmee, a couple of ‘em chuckled and told us that this skinny dude they work with named Pancho told ‘em some tale like that. They also said some older white dude come down to Quick Stuff looking for him just last Wednesday morn when they was being picked up. Even called him by his name. Kind of a coincidence, wouldn’t you say, Willy?”

“Okay, Lance. I need you and Otis to do two things for me. First, go to my friend Deputy Johnny Murphree’s house and wake him up. He lives on Second Street, two houses up on the right from the auto parts store. Tell him I’m in jail in Tamiami, and I need him to call me right away. Don’t know the number, but tell him to call directory assistance. Then, keep looking for this Pancho dude. Go over to Quick Stuff this morning before sunrise and see if you can get a description of the white dude that was asking ‘bout Pancho. Then check every fishing hole around.”

“What you doing in jail, Willy? Dang man, you’re a cop, not a robber.”

“Long story, Lance, and I ain’t got much time left. Please, you’ve got to convince Johnny to call me right away.”

“Hey, me and Otis are the best damn employees you got. If we can’t get the job done, nobody can!” Lance was beaming with pride at his newfound PI career. Soon he could move out of the phone booth into a comfy apartment. He went over to the stolen Buick and woke up Otis, who was curled up on the back seat and snoring so loud it was driving the mallards back home to Minnesota. “Wake up, Otis, my man. We back on the clock!”

*****

Officer Shubert escorted Willy back to his cell. Willy told him that he couldn't reach the person he tried to call, but left a message for the man to call him at the PD. Shubert was working alone tonight because the other night officer had called in sick, so he had no problem allowing an incoming call put through to Willy Banks. Willy had been very respectful, and Shubert was willing to reward him for his consideration. He didn't observe many courteous behaviors from criminals while working the night shift.

An hour later, Shubert returned to the cellblock and ushered Willy to the phone on his desk. "You got a call from some guy named Murphree. Is that who you were expecting?"

"Yes, sir, that's him. Thank you." Willy took the receiver but didn't turn his head away from the night cop. He wanted Officer Shubert to hear. Shubert took a seat in the lopsided desk chair and went back to working on a report he was filling out.

"Hey, Johnny. Sorry 'bout the late call. Need your help again, buddy."

"Well, I dang near shot your brother and his friend! They come pounding on my bedroom window a few minutes ago. What the hell are you doing in jail, Willy?"

"Long story, Johnny, but trust me when I tell you I ain't done nothing illegal. At least not yet." Officer Shubert, who was pretending not to be listening, glanced up. Willy looked at him and whispered, "Just kidding!"

Johnny hadn't heard the whisper, but he was trying to process what Willy had just said. "What do you mean by 'not yet'?"

"Johnny, can you please tell Officer Shubert that I am a Seminole Bend sheriff's deputy?" Willy again looked directly into Shubert's eyes. Now the desk officer's entire face contorted into an incredibly puzzled expression as he fixed his gaze right back at Willy.

"Put him on," replied Johnny with a tone of disgust in his voice.

Willy handed the phone to Officer Shubert. “Would you mind speaking to my friend?”

“This is Officer Jerry Shubert of the Tamiami Police Department. How can I help you?”

“Hi, Jerry. My name is Johnny Murphree, and I’m a deputy sheriff for Seminole Bend County. I understand my friend Willy has found his way into your nice abode?” Johnny purposely said “friend” instead of “colleague” because he was trying to be very careful with his words. If he claimed that Willy was still working for the sheriff’s department and Bonty found out, he would be looking for a new job, too.

“Yes sir, deputy, he has been booked on possession of burglary tools, which is a third-degree felony in Florida, as you know.”

“Hmmm. What exactly was in his possession, Jerry? You don’t mind if I call you Jerry, do you? And please call me Johnny.” This was Johnny’s way of softening up the conversation and assuaging the predicament Willy was in, whatever that may be. He had no idea what type of tools Willy had, or even why he had them.

“No, sir, Johnny, I don’t mind. You can call me Jerry. So, Mr. Banks had a pair of wire cutters, a crowbar, and a ski mask on the floor of his vehicle.”

After a moment’s pause, Johnny said, “Well, there’s an easy explanation for that, Jerry. Willy was sent down there to recover those tools from the home of a man we recently booked on a breaking and entering charge up here. We need them for evidence in a case we’re prosecuting in a few weeks.”

Like Willy, Johnny despised lying. But after speaking to his ex-fiancé at the governor’s office earlier, Johnny knew Willy was on to something, and he needed to talk with him soon. A white lie here or there for the good of the order wouldn’t be so bad.

“Okay, that makes sense. But why was he driving an old Nash Rambler instead of a sheriff’s vehicle, and why hadn’t he put the items in an evidence bag?”

"Our vehicles were all being used, Jerry. We offered to pay Willy the going mileage rate to take his own car down there. Why he didn't put the items into an evidence bag is beyond me. That is certainly not acceptable here, and he will be reprimanded for it." Johnny was hoping Jerry was buying it. He wished he could see his face.

"Johnny, this all sounds credible, seeing that Willy has been nothing but respectful since he was booked. But we are planning on sending him to the courthouse for a hearing by a judge in a few hours. There's nothing I can do to change that."

Johnny was desperate. It was time to mix a bit of truth into his batch of lies. "I understand, Jerry, but I'm three or four hours away, and quite frankly, we need Willy back here as soon as possible. He's working on a crucial case that needs immediate closure. I know this is a strange and unethical request, but if you could simply tear up the police report and let him go, perhaps you would be doing a huge favor for the people in our county and even yours. The case he is working on involves a series of murders in the Seminole Bend area. If Willy's suspect is not caught, every citizen in southern Florida is at risk. Have you been following the news, Jerry? You may have heard about the deaths here last month."

"I read about a basketball coach and his wife died in a weird accident. Is that part of it?"

"Yes sir, Jerry. And it is much more complicated than that. So, what do you say?"

"I would need to contact the arresting officers and tell them your story. I also need for you to verify that you work in the sheriff's department at Seminole Bend. Sorry, Johnny, but I'm just doing my job."

"Of course, Jerry. My badge number is 461385, and my name is John Murphree. That's Murphree with two e's at the end, not a y. You should have a reference book that lists all police and sheriff's officers by name and also by badge number."

"Yes, we do, Johnny. Give me a minute, okay?" Officer Shubert pulled out the reference book from the middle drawer in his desk and found Johnny's badge number. It correlated correctly with his exact name and spelling. Then he flipped back a few pages and found a William Banks registered as a deputy in Seminole Bend, too. The reference book was a year old, and Willy hadn't been fired until recently. "Yep, found it, Johnny. You check out okay, and so does Willy. Now let me get ahold of Mel and Todd. They were the arresting officers and are working until six."

"Thanks, man. I'll hold." Johnny was beginning to think his story may work. Willy, listening nearby, had a mild clue what the conversation between Johnny and Jerry had involved when he overheard Officer Shubert mention the burglary tools not being put in an evidence bag. Willy guessed that Johnny's story made it look like Willy found the tools on someone he was investigating. He wasn't sure how Johnny responded to him driving his own car or why he was sent to Miami, so if asked, Willy would have to play it by ear. He likely would need to corroborate the story somewhere along the way, but he was starting to feel some hope.

Officer Shubert went over to the desk by the window and pushed the button on the two-way radio. "Eighty-seven, this is base. Do you read?"

"Go ahead, base. What's up, Jerry?" Officers Mel and Todd had just parked their squad car at Yummy's, the all-night donut shop on Highway 41.

"Please come to the base as soon as possible. No emergency."

"No emergency? Does that mean we can have a donut and coffee first?"

"Negative, eighty-seven. But if you want to bring a dozen back with you, it would be much appreciated."

"Okay, base, we'll be right there. Chocolate frosted or blueberry?"

"Both. See you soon. Over." Officer Shubert hung up the mic and went back to Willy, who had been standing by the front desk the entire time.

"Willy, take a seat, please. It will be a few minutes, but I think there's a chance we could release you tonight."

"Thanks, Jerry. Any chance I could speak to Johnny while we're waiting?" Officer Shubert nodded and handed the receiver to Willy.

"Hey, Johnny, thanks, man." Willy was careful not to say much or ask what Johnny had told Shubert. He hoped Johnny would divulge what he said to get Willy released, but Johnny never did.

"Okay, Banks, you owe me even more. That there detective agency of yours best be hiring because I truly believe my job's in jeopardy now thanks to you. But listen closely. I made the call to my ex, you know Carla Evans up in Tallahassee, to check out that phone number you gave me. By the way, that may have been a good thing cuz I think we're getting together in a few weeks. Anyway, she checked it out and get this, the only call to the South Florida DNR during that time frame you were there was from the governor's office. And listen to this, it originated from the private executive phone line. Yep, you guessed it. Daughtry himself made the call."

"You don't suppose the governor lost his hunting license and needed a replacement, do you?" The race of neurons was firing up again in Willy's brain.

* * * * *

Officers Mel and Todd were none too happy that all their paperwork may have been for naught. But on the other side of the coin, they wouldn't have to waste time in Judge Platt's courtroom for an inquiry examination. Judge Platt could never try a case or conduct a hearing without babbling on about something insignificant, and it was difficult to stay awake. Many a police officer, juror, and even defendant had been reprimanded for dozing during a trial. Mel and Todd liked the idea of one less Platt parable to capitulate.

"So you're one of us, huh Banks? Why didn't you tell us that when we arrested you?" Mel had a natural curiosity that complimented his investigative skills.

"During the arrest, it really didn't matter. You did the right thing by booking me, regardless if I was a cop or not." Willy was walking on thin ice, and he needed to extoll some charm.

"When I asked what the wire cutters, crowbar, and mask were going to be used for, you didn't reply. Why not?"

"Any police officer knows at that point it is time for some legal representation. I didn't think that if I told you the truth, you would believe me."

"So, what is the truth, Willy?" Mel was a good cop. He wasn't going to release Willy until his curiosity was quelled.

This was the make or break point. The right answer could get him released. The wrong one, and Willy would be attentively focused on Judge Platt's anecdotes in the morning. "I was gathering evidence from a criminal investigation in Seminole Bend. I believe my colleague clarified that with Jerry." This was the extent of what Willy perceived based on what he overheard between Johnny and Officer Shubert. Willy thought about crossing his fingers again.

"He's right, Mel," said Officer Shubert. "He's needed back in Seminole Bend with that evidence, so let's get him back on the road." Mel paused and said nothing for an uncomfortable minute or two. He was thinking about the ramifications if anyone found out. Freeing a possible felon without going through the proper procedures could be a career-ending mistake for all three officers.

"Alright then, Jerry, shred the report." Mel glanced over to Willy. "Best be on your way, deputy. We towed your car over here, and it's parked out back by the dumpster. Here are your keys. For our sake and yours, go directly home, okay?"

Willy took the keys and said, "Yes, definitely, and thank you. Someday, I hope to repay the favor. Any of you like to fish for speckled perch? I'll show you where to find the big and tasty ones out on Lake Okeechobee, and you'll have piquant memories to write home about."

"We'll take you up on that offer, Willy," replied Jerry with a smile while Mel and Todd nodded. "Been longing for some time away from the hustle and bustle of the city."

"You are always welcome, my friends. Now, any chance I could get those items I need for evidence in my case?"

Officer Todd handed over the evidence bag, and Willy carefully removed the wire cutters, crowbar, and ski mask. A piece of paper also came out of the bag and fell to the floor, but Willy didn't see it. Mel picked it up and said, "Deputy, you dropped this." He reached his hand to offer it to Willy, then stopped just before Willy could get ahold of it.

"By the way, what exactly is the scribbling on this paper all about?" Mel asked. He then gave the paper with the etching from the satellite dish to Willy.

"Not sure, Mel. I found it with the other items and wasn't sure if it was important. I plan to send it to our lab when I get back to Seminole Bend. Thanks again, guys!"

Willy turned and walked through the front doors as the three Tamiami police officers watched him leave. He went around to the back by the dumpster, unlocked the Nash Rambler, and turned on the ignition. There were still a few hours of darkness to work with, so he turned onto Highway 41 and headed west. He knew he would have to find a good hiding place for his vehicle while he was snipping away at the FBI's fence. Mel and Todd were still on duty until dawn.

CHAPTER 52
Friday, March 12, 1982
3:00 a.m.

At the western edge of town, a new housing development was under construction. Everglades Estates was literally where humanity met the swamp. There were three completed homes, each one a model for the types of houses that would be built in the ten-acre development. The sign at the entrance said:

Everglades Estates
Be one with nature
Track homes from the $90s

Willy wasn't sure what was meant by a track home. None of the lots appeared to have enough room for sprints or running long distances in the backyard. A swimming pool, maybe, but certainly not an oval track. No matter, Willy found this area perfect for hiding his car. The model homes were empty, and eight new houses were just being framed up. He had scoured the area around the FBI's auto impound facility, driving his Rambler back and forth on Highway 41 and Coral Way, plus north and south on several city streets. Everglades Estates was about two miles from the FBI's lot, but he could reach it with a twenty to thirty-minute jog. He backed the Rambler into the unpaved driveway of the furthest house that was being constructed from the entrance.

Willy left the crowbar in his car so he could run faster, then jogged down the shoulder of Highway 41. He knew his own strength very well, and he figured he could rip the door off Berry's truck by hand if need be. With nervous adrenaline pumping through his veins, Willy began to run faster. When cars approached, he ducked down behind shrubbery or trees in the ditch. Not many cars were out and about at four in the morning, and there were only a small amount of scattered, ramshackle concrete block homes in the area. Doubtful the folks inside them were business executives that would commute to Miami during the six o'clock rush hour. Anyone heading west on the Tamiami Trail, the nickname for US 41, wouldn't see civilization again until they arrived in Naples, which was ninety miles away. Venturing through the Everglades at night wasn't recommended as there were only a few places to pull a car over should it break down, and AAA offered no towing service in or out of the infamous swamp.

Willy arrived at the northwest end of the perimeter fence at 4:15 a.m. and quickly hid behind a large hibiscus. He wanted to move several more yards down the fence line to make a faster approach to the impounded autos, but when a car approached driving slowly west on the highway, he decided to make this his point of entry. He wasn't going to chance getting back on the road after he noticed the occupants of the slow-moving vehicle. It was Mel and Todd.

Willy snipped a three-by-three-foot gap in the fence using his wire cutters, then placed the ski mask over his face and squeezed through the hole. Once inside, he noticed the facility had thirty-five to forty cars slotted in numbered parking spots on well-worn asphalt. He thought he would recognize Berry's truck even with its damage, but he carried the license plate number in his wallet just to be sure.

Willy crouched down and took two steps forward towards the cars. That's when the first bark vibrated his eardrum. Within seconds, two more barks, then every hound in the confines of the lot were singing their egregious melody. Willy hoped they had recently been fed. Willy wished he had brought his crowbar.

High School football is demanding and an excellent test of stamina, especially for athletes that compete in the Deep South. Temps in the nineties and humidity to the max during August workouts build determination, and now Willy was about to see if all those sweaty high school days carried over to real-life situations. He tore off his ski mask, shifted into his best linebacker athletic stance, and studied the entire field of play, which of course, was dotted with dusty and damaged automobiles instead of running backs and wide receivers.

Only one German shepherd was coming his way, and he appeared fixated on tearing Willy to shreds. NFL announcers would have nicknamed him Canine Express, a shoo-in for the Pro Bowl. But as Willy darted his eyes left and right to locate the rest of the hounds, strangely, the other dogs had stopped running and stayed within a predetermined area, almost like they were playing a zone defense. The barking continued, but Willy, fortunately, had only one pooch to manhandle.

During his days in Army boot camp, Willy learned the choke-out maneuver: a chokehold that would cause syncope and render an opponent unconscious. He didn't want to kill the dog, so he hoped he could grapple him into a temporary coma. The German shepherd was sprinting Willy's direction at about thirty miles per hour. If Willy tried to run, he would be torn apart, so he maintained his defensive stance and readied himself for impact.

From five feet away, the shepherd leaped at Willy's chest, fangs glittering in the moonlight. Willy caught him in midair around the neck, but the dog's momentum had driven him to the ground. With all the strength he could muster, Willy kept the jolted dog at arm's length from his face. Quickly, he rolled over and trapped the shepherd between his massive muscular body and the soft, sandy earth below, then moved his biceps into position under the hound's chin. One swift snap upward and Canine Express was fast asleep.

Willy loosened his clamp around the dog's neck and left him lying in the dirt. He was still breathing and would probably be unconscious for only a few seconds. Willy hastily got up, dashed onto the asphalt, and hid behind the first car he could see: a black limousine with license plate number *BADASS77*. Didn't take much thought to picture why that car was impounded in the FBI's lot. The other German shepherds were barking incessantly, but none had moved out of their zone. Excellent trainers, questionable security procedures.

The nineteen-inch diameter, four and a half million candlepower searchlight attached to the roof of the guardhouse fired up, and the beam moved in a clockwise revolution slowly around the parking lot. The guard on duty heard barks from every direction so he couldn't pinpoint the actual location of an intruder. He carefully swept the entire facility with the stream of light. Willy was sure the guard was trained to press an alert button to call for backup, and he knew FBI agents would be swarming soon. He had about ten minutes to work with before the G-Men would be arriving from Miami in their patented black sedans.

Three vehicles down from the limo was a charred and semi-flattened Ford L-series pickup truck. All four wheels were crammed with a bulk of dried sludge. Willy didn't need to check a plate number to know this was Coach Berry's truck. He remembered the fire department talking about the accident and the difficulty they had putting out the fire on the truck's rubber tires. They ended up packing the tires with mud to cut off the oxygen and reduce the smoke.

The searchlight beam was in the opposite direction, and amid nonstop howls and woofs from the watchdogs, Willy scurried to the truck's passenger door and climbed through the narrow, glassless window frame onto the charred, but intact front seat. The roof had caved in only slightly, thanks to a heavy-duty roll bar installed on the bed behind the cab's rear window, and the bench seat was in relatively fair condition due to fibers infused with asbestos, a flame retardant. Willy didn't know exactly what he was looking for, but he hoped the penlight attached to his keychain would shed some light as to why the FBI wanted to impound the vehicle.

Except for globs of dark gray muck stemming from the mixture of ash and the water used to douse the flames, there wasn't much to see. The truck and everything in it, apart from the scorched front seat, had obviously been torched beyond recognition, and there was a good chance that Willy was now defiling Sheryl Berry's cremated remains. While lying face down on the seat, he flickered the penlight's narrow ray of light all around the cab, from the roof to the floorboards. Nothing. "What in the world does the FBI think they will find in this incinerated mess?" muttered Willy to himself.

Willy's line of vision was hampered by the uncomfortable position of his body, so he rotated his substantial frame awkwardly onto his back to have a better angle to shine the light at the driver's side door. He unclipped the penlight from his keychain to make it easier to maneuver. Willy's extra-large hands didn't do well with small objects, and the tiny flashlight fell to the floor and rolled under the bench. He again clumsily turned back onto his stomach and tried unsuccessfully to grab the light with his outstretched arms. Springs from the seat had broken off and were preventing a clear path to grasp anything beneath him. And to top it off, the damn barking mutts were still protecting their areas but remained relentlessly growling in the direction of Berry's truck. Willy was becoming especially nervous. He didn't have much time.

Willy stuck his head down and peered under the seat. He grabbed the penlight then heard sirens in the distance. Willy shifted into a position to exit the truck through the same window he came in.

At that moment, the watchtower searchlight was sweeping towards him, so Willy ducked back down. As the beam glimmered through the interior of the truck, Willy noticed something attached to the bottom of the steering column. It was a small, rectangular box with a concave fitting that set perfectly on the cylindrical support. Willy wiggled and waggled down to the floorboard to get a better look. The box had loosened from the fire, so Willy clutched it with his fingers and yanked hard. It detached from the steering column, but two wires remained connected from the box to another gadget inside the metal tube. Willy would need to dismantle the steering support to extract the internal device, and he didn't have time. With one powerful jerk, the wires from the box dislodged from whatever they were attached to inside the steering column. The box was too large to put in his pocket, so he tossed it out the window for the moment. He stayed low as the searchlight continued its clockwise sweep away from the truck.

Flashing red lights lit up the night sky as three FBI vehicles screeched to a halt at the front gate. The watchtower guard pressed a switch, and the gate swung open. The FBI cars entered quickly, then slammed on their brakes. Leaving their cars running and ready, six agents ran towards the watchtower. A few minutes later, they returned to their vehicles and took off slowly and deliberately in different directions through the lot, with driver and passenger side floodlights scouring the facility.

Willy tried to budge open the passenger door, but it had been fused to the chassis from the blaze. Even his muscular mass couldn't force it to dislodge. With no other option, he squeezed his body through the window and tumbled onto the asphalt. He picked up the box and sprinted towards the hole he had made in the fence. The German shepherds were still barking wildly, but miraculously they did just what they were trained to do: stay put and guard their assigned area.

Willy was twenty-five yards from the hole when the FBI agents in the closest car spotted him. They locked the passenger side floodlight on him and floored the accelerator. A few seconds later, a piercing whistle blew from the watchtower, and the dogs were on the chase. The other two sedans abruptly U-turned and raced towards the gate, heading for Highway 41. "So this is what it looks like when all hell breaks loose," mumbled Willy to himself as he ducked and dove through the opening in the fence he had created a few minutes earlier. His back was skinned from his fall to the asphalt while exiting the truck, and now his head was bleeding as the hibiscus bush scraped his scalp. No matter, he pushed away from the branches and moved towards the road.

The FBI agents slammed on the brakes a few feet from the fence, opened their doors to use as a shield, and pulled out their weapons. They had assumed that Willy was armed. "Halt, or we'll shoot!" Willy wasn't about to take their advice.

The agents began rapidly firing their semi-automatic Smith and Wesson 459s into the bushes, but by that time, Willy had reached Tamiami Trail and was sprinting towards Everglades Estates. The two other FBI cars had just fishtailed out of the impound lot onto the highway and were speeding towards Willy with lights blazing and sirens wailing.

Across the road, Willy noticed a small, shabby concrete-block house set back about seventy-five yards into a sprinkling of palm trees and palmetto bushes. The driveway was white sand and seashells, and the entrance was marked with a tin mailbox hanging by its last thread on a well-worn wooden post. It was Willy's only hope for escape. He hurried across the road and dashed down the driveway clutching to the box he found in Berry's truck. Willy's destination was the thick mangrove swamp behind the dwelling that could lead to a promising, yet boggy escape route. But when he came up to the house, he noticed a paltry wooden shed in the back with a 400cc Kawasaki motorcycle leaning up against it. The sirens were getting closer, so Willy darted towards the end of the shed, slipped on a patch of soggy grass, and slid into a pile of mud.

The FBI sedans zipped past the driveway and continued west down Tamiami Trail. They hadn't seen Willy cross the road. However, the first German shepherd that hurdled through the hole in the fence had locked on to Willy's scent and was now bolting down the driveway towards the shed. Willy dropped the box into the sludge and readied himself for another attack. There was a bizarre smell that was making him gag, but he couldn't think about that now. He assumed the linebacker stance and was about to turn to face the oncoming aggressor, but his feet gave way, and Willy stumbled and fell flat on his face, his eye sockets, nose, and mouth filled with muck. That's when he realized that the shed was not a shed, it was an outhouse, and the sludge he was wallowing in was waste overflowing from the holding tank.

A split-second later, the vicious canine leaped and landed on Willy's back, his claws penetrating both skin and muscle tissue. The trained-to-kill beast then dug his fangs deeply into Willy's neck, and Willy was trapped. The dog's jaw was clamped firmly into the trapezius tendons of his helpless victim, and then the shepherd began rapidly shaking his head back and forth. The pain was unbearable, and Willy had resigned himself to believe this was the end. He closed his eyes and prayed for a better life in heaven, one without the likes of Roy Jackson.

Suddenly, Willy's neck was liberated from the razor-sharp fangs, and the claws ripping into his rhomboid tissue were swiftly retracted. But as Willy tried to rise, he was driven back down into the muck by what seemed like a 1,000-pound sledgehammer. He could hear a whining whimper coming from the attacking watchdog, then a crunching sound, like bones being snapped. Willy rolled his head to the side and glimpsed out his feces-slathered eyeballs in time to see the German shepherd's carcass fall headless to the ground. A fourteen-foot gator was chomping away at the canine cranium, and it appeared he was taking deep pleasure in his furry feast. Willy's backside was a perfect banquet table for the king of the swamp. He hoped the mammoth reptile would pass on dessert.

CHAPTER 53

Friday, March 12, 1982

7:55 a.m.

Although trying to appear calm and collected, Lew Berry didn't hide his anxiety well. He'd been waiting since seven at the FBI's headquarters, and it was now five minutes to eight. Lew opened the envelope that Agent Jones left for him yesterday and glanced at the picture again. He still didn't recognize the man, nor did he know why Jones had given it to him. The same front desk receptionist he spoke to yesterday told him that Agent Jones was due to report for work at any minute, but Lew was on the verge of a panic attack.

At 8:25 a.m., Agent Jones walked into the waiting area at FBI Headquarters. He extended his arm and shook hands with Lew, who stood up and greeted him with sweaty palms and apprehensive eyes. "Sorry about yesterday, Lew. I was called over to Tampa by the FAA regarding the air disaster. And I'm sorry I'm late today, but we had a problem earlier this morning over at our auto impound lot. There's something I need to tell you."

"What is it, Jack? This photo you left for me—have you got news about Janet? Have the Uniontown police opened up an investigation yet?" Lew's angst was getting the best of him. He didn't want to tell Agent Jones what his neighbor Ralph Kline had told him for fear of the answer he was hoping to avoid.

"Don't know yet what's happening in Pennsylvania. That photo I gave you was wired from the FBI office in Pittsburgh.

It's from a security camera at Burns Coffee Shop in Harrisburg. Our men had put out a tracer on your bank accounts and credit cards. Janet used a credit card at Burns on Tuesday to pay for coffee and a roll. They rolled back the tape from the security camera and located Janet. Do you have any idea who the man sitting with her could be?"

"No idea, Jack. And the most direct way to the Poconos doesn't go through Harrisburg. Was her credit card used somewhere else in Pennsylvania?"

"Not sure what the FBI may have found yesterday while I was in Tampa, but I'll call again. What I needed to tell you, though, is rather strange—and just coincidental, I hope."

"Can't it wait?" replied Lew irritably. "You need to make sure the FBI and police are looking for my wife, damn it!"

"Yes, I'll call. But you should know that Brett and Sheryl's truck was broken into last night at our impound lot in Tamiami."

"Broken into? How does someone break into an FBI secured area? Can you explain that to me, Jack?" Lew was beside himself with anger. "What did they take out of the truck? I thought everything in it was burned to a crisp."

"Yes, everything appeared to be incinerated except for the front bench seat, which was protected somewhat because it contained asbestos fibers. As for what was taken, we're not sure yet. I was there when our boys went through it looking for prints. We were able to get some clear ones, by the way. Whoever broke in didn't bother to wear any gloves."

"Okay, that's great, Jack," replied Lew with a hint of sarcasm. "But you didn't answer my other question. What did they take?"

"Lew, what I'm about to tell you is highly classified information at this point in our investigation. I'm only telling you this in the hopes that you will begin to fully cooperate with us. I asked you to stay here in Miami, and you disappointed me by renting a car and driving to Seminole Bend." Agent Jones stared stoically into Lew's eyes.

"I'm not your little baby boy, Jack. What I do on my own time is my own business. So you had me followed?"

"No, but you used your MasterCard to rent the car at the airport, and four hours later you bought lunch at the Angler's Delight restaurant."

"You are tracing my credit card, too? Unbelievable! What crime am I suspected of, Jones?" Lew was seething. His hands were firmly on his waist, and his red face revealed a rapidly advancing fury.

"You are not a suspect, Lew, so please relax. It's standard procedure to monitor all parties when investigating a possible kidnapping, which is what we are doing with your daughter-in-law."

"You said you were going to give me some classified information. What is it?" Lew responded harshly.

"I told you on Monday that we had found some evidence while searching Brett's truck. We gathered several pellets that were scattered under the seat. The lab concluded the pellets were from a 12-gauge shotgun shell."

"So you're saying someone shot whoever the man was that was driving the truck? Is that what caused him to lose control?" inquired Lew.

"Well, that would certainly be one theory. The problem is that for a shotgun to be effective killing a human, it must be fired at a fairly close range. The autopsy showed significant damage to the upper portion of the parietal bone, meaning whoever—"

Lew cut him off tersely, "I'm not a doctor, Jones, speak English, okay?"

Agent Jones replied, "The top of the skull was torn open, meaning whoever fired the shot did so from close proximity and a position above the dead man. That would seem impossible considering the victim was driving the truck. Unless, however, he noticed the gunman from a distance of no more than fifteen feet outside the windshield and ducked his head at the last minute."

Lew thought about that for a moment. Half to himself, half to Jones, he said, "Meaning the gunman would be standing in the middle of the road, right? That would be taking quite a risk with a pickup truck barreling full speed down the highway. And if he waited until the last second to fire the weapon, the truck would have been unable to avoid hitting him."

"Yes, you are absolutely right. It's improbable that the truck ended up in the culvert by accident. The autopsy shows damage to the top of the skull, which could have happened in an accident. That's what Seminole Bend's sheriff wants us to believe. But we made a call yesterday to Cliff Sutton, the county coroner up there. He says the damage to the cranium is more consistent with a close-range blast from a shotgun shell than blunt force trauma, which would have occurred in a vehicle accident. When I asked why that wasn't in his report, he said it was originally, but had been redacted by a court order. So, that leaves us with a different theory that is, quite frankly, inexplicable."

"Well?" asked Lew curiously. "What theory do you now have?"

"The man driving the truck was already dead."

CHAPTER 54

Friday, March 12, 1982
8:10 a.m.

The German shepherd's brain was soft, spongy, and very tasty, and its eyeballs were a sheer delight. The alligator wanted more of that delicacy. The dog's torso was lying in the muck just a few feet away, and the gator opted for a canine dessert over the human variety that he had pinned underneath his belly. As he crawled off Willy with his giant webbed feet, the gator's claws dug deeply into Willy's posterior, puncturing the hulking man's thick skin and muscular trunk. But Willy was relieved to have the immense weight of the reptile off his back, and now he could finally lift his face out of the moist feces that had spilled over from the outhouse.

Willy scrambled awkwardly to his knees and cleared the feculence from his mouth with his equally filthy hands. The detestable stench made him dizzy, and the repulsive taste made him vomit. The gator was contently chomping down on his furry pabulum. It was time to go. Willy searched in the sludge for the metal box he had stripped from the steering column of Brett Berry's pickup truck. It was now lying next to the mighty tail of the beast.

The scrapes from the hibiscus shrubs combined with the claws of both the German shepherd and alligator had butchered Willy's ebony skin raw, so he figured he had nothing to lose, except perhaps his life. He grabbed the box and ran down the seashell and white sand driveway, across the road, and all the way back to Everglades Estates. He didn't stop until he reached the Nash Rambler, where he collapsed onto the back seat and fell asleep. The blood, sweat, and feces slowly dried and clung to Willy's ripped clothing and frazzled epidermis. The connective tissues and lymph vessels beneath the skin were shredded, and bacterial infection was rapidly cultivating. Willy would need antibiotics very soon.

*****

"How does a dead man drive a truck?" inquired Lew with a look of skepticism. "What you really mean is that someone shot the man immediately after the accident, right?"

"Think about this, Lew. First, as I mentioned earlier, a shooter wouldn't be trying to kill the driver of a moving vehicle with shotgun spray," replied Agent Jones. "If that were the case, the shooter would have to be close to the truck to penetrate the windshield, and then the vehicle would most likely run the shooter over. Second, if the man had just been involved in a spectacular fiery crash, why would anyone bother to stick around and light up his body with shotgun pellets?"

"What are you getting at, Jack?" Lew wasn't connecting the dots.

"Lew, I need to say this one more time. This is highly confidential. The only reason I'm telling you is because of your personal losses and to secure your complete cooperation. But you must not tell anyone, got it?"

"Yes, yes, come on, Jack. What are you trying to say?"

"Whoever broke into your son's truck at our impound lot this morning either unscrewed or yanked a metal box that was attached to the steering column. We compared pictures of the truck's interior that were taken immediately at the scene of the accident with those taken today. Our lab processed the film as fast as possible, but that is what delayed me, which was why I was late this morning. Anyway, the metal box was in the pictures taken at the scene, but not in the pictures from this morning."

"I still don't get it," said Lew anxiously. "What is in the metal box?"

"We're not a hundred percent sure, but we believe it's some sort of radio receiver that was used to drive the vehicle from a remote location."

"This sounds like science fiction if you ask me!" exclaimed Lew shaking his head. "How does it work?"

"Radio waves are transmitted from a controller to the box by way of an antenna. A circuit board inside the metal box receives signals from the transmitter and activates electrical impulses that can turn the wheel left or right."

"But how can the person controlling the truck see the road?"

"That's a great question, Lew. Our theory is that whoever installed the box to the steering column also installed a video camera to the front grille, which allowed the controller a clear view. However, the entire front end was demolished, and the sheriff's department didn't find any remains of a video camera at the site. But in all honesty, they weren't looking for a video camera. They found broken glass and plastic that they assumed came from the headlights, grille, and windshield."

"How do you know the sheriff's investigators weren't looking for a camera, Jack?"

"What do you mean by that, Lew? Why would they be looking for a video camera at that moment? The radio transmitter theory is ours, and no one but us and you know about it." Now Agent Jones was confused and curious. What was Lew thinking?

Lew didn't think now was the time and place to discuss his hunch about Al Bonty and the Seminole Bend sheriff's dereliction of duty. He needed more proof that Sheriff Bonty was involved in illegal activity, and he needed to find Willy Banks to make that happen. But first, he frantically needed to know if his wife was on the downed Heartland Lakes flight.

He decided to tell Agent Jones about his conversation with next-door-neighbor, Ralph Kline.

Perhaps the FBI would have more luck getting through to Heartland Lake's customer service than he had.

CHAPTER 55

Friday, March 12, 1982
12:00 noon

Gray saliva drooled out of Willy's mouth onto the back seat of the Nash Rambler. He lifted his head slightly off the vinyl and tried to recall where exactly he was lying. Until he noticed clumps of dung driveling onto the worn-out carpet of the car, he had assumed it was all just a dream. Unfortunately, that was not the case.

Willy could feel the sting of the now healing claw marks on his back. He sat up in the car seat, reached his arm around, and touched the base of his neck. When he brought his arm back, there was a gooey, yellowish-brown substance on his fingers. Pus was oozing from his wounds. That could be a good sign, Willy thought. The discharge was now engaged in a fierce battle with bacteria, and perhaps he would avoid a lethal infection.

Willy picked up the metal box he had ripped off the steering column of Brett Berry's truck and tossed it in the front passenger seat, then he slowly moved into the driver's seat. He bent forward to keep his posterior wounds from rubbing against the back support. He needed water to rinse out his mouth and clean up his filthy body, but he didn't know where to go. Willy's clothes were grungy and torn to shreds, and the smell of his body was outright obscene. He needed to find a place where no one would see him.

That's when Willy noticed a sign in front of a model home a few houses down that gave him an idea:

Flamingo Model: Four Bedrooms and Three Baths (A Touch of Paradise in Paradise)

Willy looked up and down the street and could see no vehicles anywhere in sight. He drove slowly and parked in the model home's driveway. It was noon on Friday, the height of business hours, and he could see no salesperson or realtor around. He assumed the model homes were not ready for sale yet. But was the plumbing installed and ready to go? Willy grabbed his crowbar, walked around to the patio door in the back, and smashed the pane of glass into a thousand pieces. He paused for a moment to listen. No security alarms. Willy reached through the broken glass and unlatched the sliding door. He tried the light switch, but nothing happened. He moved into the house and tried another switch. Nothing again. The electricity had not been turned on.

Willy went into the kitchen and tried the sink. The water was on and flowing smoothly. He turned it back off and looked in the cabinet under the sink. There was a plastic pail, a sponge, paper towels, and Formula 409 Carpet Cleaner spray. Willy put the items in the bucket and headed for the master bedroom.

The marble-tiled shower area was colossal and had two shower heads: his and hers, Willy guessed. He turned the faucet handle on one of them, and water gushed out from the spout. With no electricity, the water was cold, but Willy didn't care. He ripped off his clothes and stepped underneath the showerhead, filling up his mouth with water, swishing it around, and spitting it out. He repeated that several times. It was better, but Willy couldn't completely clear the aftertaste of feces.

Willy then grabbed the carpet cleaner and sprayed his entire body from his forehead down to his toes. Using the sponge, he rubbed the degreaser deep into his pores. It wasn't soft and pure like bar soap, but it did the trick.

Willy then made a spot decision and ran with it. He pointed the nozzle of the Formula 409 sprayer into his mouth and squeezed, using his tongue to block the liquid from seeping down his throat. Willy swished the putrid and poisonous solvent around his mouth and spat it out. He repeated it several times, then filled his mouth with water and rinsed the disgusting, vile substance from the soft tissue of his cheeks and gums. Then Willy stuck his forefinger into the back of his mouth until it made contact with his uvula. He vomited, clearing whatever toxic waste remained in his stomach. After a few more mouth rinses, he stepped out onto the tile floor.

Willy unwrapped the paper towels and dried himself off. He left the grimy clothes and used paper towels on the floor in the master bathroom. It was doubtful anyone would bother trying to figure out who broke in, and the realtors would naturally assume it was a local vagrant. They would have to draw straws to see who got clean up duty.

Willy entered the Nash Rambler wearing only his birthday suit. He knew going into a clothing store or a restaurant would be out of the question. Just the vision brought new meaning to "no shirt, no shoes, no service." He turned on the ignition and started to pull out of the driveway when something caught his eye. Willy picked up the metal box he had tossed in the front seat and looked closely. Engraved on the side was:

صنع في آل القادر

The characters, symbols, or designs were just gobbledygook to Willy. But he swore he saw the same markings somewhere else. Then it hit him.

"Sam Dulie," muttered Willy to himself. "The satellite dish. That's it. Where did I put that paper I etched? Shoot, what did I do with it?!" Willy thought about the last place he saw the paper and remembered dropping it on the floor at the

Tamiami Police Department, and Officer Mel handing it back to him. He had stuck it in his pants pocket.

Willy ran back into the house and up to the bathroom where he had left his pants. He reached into the sordid right pocket and pulled out the piece of paper he had etched the markings from the satellite dish. The paper was wet, and the pencil lead had faded into a gray smudge making it impossible to discern what was written.

It was time to pay Sam Dulie's workplace another visit to inspect the satellite dish and compare the markings with those on the metal box. Newfound torque embedded into the Nash Rambler's gears overcame the rotation resistance, and the old car darted down Tamiami Trail to US 1. The Rambler then maxed out at a personal world record of seventy miles per hour as the floored vehicle raced southbound towards Homestead. If stopped by the police, Willy "Godiva" would have a lot of explaining to do.

Ten miles from Homestead, Willy noticed a Goodwill collection bin inside the boundaries of a grocery store parking lot. He cut sharply across traffic and turned into the lot. Oncoming cars slammed on brakes and honked horns. The middle finger was rather long sticking out of the closed fist of one driver.

There were too many customers going in and out of the market for Willy not to be seen by someone. At this point, he really didn't care. He jumped out of the car, flashing two elderly ladies who covered their mouths in astonishment but stared reverently at his gargantuan naked body. He pushed the bin's hatch open and grabbed the first sack he could find. It was children's clothes. Next, he pulled out a plastic garbage bag and glanced inside. It was men's clothing, but he didn't have time to be picky about fashion. He climbed back into the driver's seat and quickly sifted through the clothes. He found a pair of thirty-four by thirty-two-inch blue jeans, faded quite a bit, but in good shape. Willy's size was forty by thirty-four, but these would have to do. With all the strength he could muster, he yanked the pants up. But his massive thighs posed a huge problem, so Willy took the car keys and ripped the jeans open from mid-thigh to the knee, and then from below the knees to the ankles. That worked, but the pant legs came up to his calf, and the waist was too tight to snap shut. It would just have to do. He found a large t-shirt with a stenciled drawing of an angry Elmer Fudd emblazed on the front. Elmer had one finger raised high in the air, and inside a cartoon word bubble, it said: *Just wait 'til I get my hands on that scwewy wabbit!* Willy ripped off the short sleeves from the shirt and pulled it over his head. It was tightly drawn over his muscular frame and reached only to his belly button. He didn't have time to see what else was in the bag, so he punched the Rambler's accelerator and continued on to Homestead.

Willy slowed down and parked a half-mile away from the DNR parking lot. He exited the Rambler and snuck alongside a hedge of bushes until he saw the building in the distance. The two DNR pickup trucks were nowhere to be found, meaning the field rangers were most likely working the swamps freeing egrets from discarded monofilament fishing lines.

Willy crept slowly towards the satellite dish in his taut blue jeans and t-shirt, holding the front of his pants closed with his left hand. He wanted to make sure the marking on the dish was the same as the metal box before confronting Sam Dulie. When Willy was close, he crawled on all fours and scrooched behind the dish so he was blocked from Dulie's window. He peeked his head around the vast saucer and didn't see anyone in the administrator's office, so he began searching for the embedded inscription.

But as Willy stood up, he froze in place and stared at the front door of the DNR headquarters. He couldn't believe his eyes. Exiting the building were three men, all casually dressed in blue jeans and khaki button-down shirts carrying what appeared to be heavy boxes and walking to the center of the parking lot. With Sam Dulie was Governor Daughtry, which was in itself somewhat unsettling. But the third man drew Willy's undivided attention and complete bewilderment. It was his older brother, Tyrus.

CHAPTER 56
Friday, March 12, 1982
1:30 p.m.

The sheriff was becoming frustrated as Oliver Harfield leaned back on his brown leather rocking recliner and read another article from the latest issue of *Time Magazine*. Bonty could tell that Oliver Harfield was paying no attention to him. He glanced out the window and noticed a silver DeLorean DMC-12 sports car buzzing up the driveway, then slamming to a halt near the front entrance to the mansion. Two gull-winged doors opened, and the Jackson brothers emerged from both sides of the vehicle. The Jackson collection of expensive automobiles seemingly had no end, nor did the Jackson collection of wealth.

Ray and Roy Jackson entered Harfield's home without knocking and moved directly to the study where Oliver seemed to be in deep thought.

"The Gormon boy is going to get a scholarship," blurted Roy, not bothering with any pleasantries. "Jimmy has no chance at Florida. Brett shouldn't have let Gormon play the second half against Martin Park. That's what started it all, you know."

"So, your answer was to have Brett killed after the fact?" replied Oliver. Then he pointed his finger and waved it back and forth. "Not a smart move, Roy!"

"I didn't want to kill Brett! I just wanted him to think Sheryl died in the crash. His death was an accident when the truck overturned on him. But Brett defied me, Oliver! I told him at halftime to bench Gormon. We made life good for him out here, and he tested my authority. He knew we needed Jimmy playing basketball for the Gators so we could bring him into the circle. Only Florida men's basketball players and coaches have access to the men's locker room at the O'Sullivan Center. It just made sense to have someone who could come and go without raising any suspicions."

"Who's to say Jimmy would have come on board with us?" asked Sheriff Bonty. "From what I know of him, he's a good kid. I can't picture him being part of this mission or any criminal mission, as far as that goes."

"Jimmy wouldn't have any choice," replied Roy. "I'm his daddy, and down here in the south, you do what your daddy asks." Roy glared at the sheriff, and Al glared right back at him.

"You ain't been no daddy to that boy, and you know it," stated Bonty angrily, then walked away to avoid a further confrontation.

"Alright, that's enough," said Oliver. "But now we need a Plan B. For our mission to work, gentlemen, Raymond will need some assistance up there in Gainesville."

CHAPTER 57
Friday, March 12, 1982
1:45 p.m.

The Sikorsky CH-53E Super Stallion helicopter hovered momentarily while Sam Dulie, Governor Daughtry, and Tyrus Banks shaded their eyes with their hands. The huge and powerful military aircraft then landed gently onto the DNR parking lot. Willy crept up and hid behind a dumpster to get a better look. There were a United States flag and a Marine Corps symbol embossed on the body of the chopper. The cargo hold was enormous, and as soon as the helicopter landed and the seven blades attached to the main rotor were shut down, a dark-skinned man wearing blue jeans, a green t-shirt with Arabic writing scripted above a sword, and a red and white checkered kufiyah wrapped around his head emerged. The man walked over to Sam Dulie, and they embraced, then kissed each other on both cheeks. Willy was aghast. "What the heck?" he muttered to himself.

"As-salamu alaykum, Abdul," said the man from the chopper.

"Wa-alaikum-salaam," replied Sam Dulie.

Willy was clueless as to what was being said, but it certainly looked to be some sort of greeting. He was no linguist, but he thought the words could be Arabic. The unidentified man then shook hands with Governor Daughtry and Tyrus. The boxes they had carried out from Sam's office were loaded into the Sikorsky with the help of two more Arab men; obviously, workers hired to handle the cargo. Then, the workers went back into the DNR building five more times and returned each time with boxes the same size and shape. The DNR supervisor, the governor, and Willy's older brother watched closely, and as soon as the chopper was loaded, they walked up the ramp and disappeared into the cabin. A short time later, the Sikorsky lifted off as gently as it had landed, then turned towards the south and was soon out of sight.

Willy walked around the dumpster with his hands on his waist and stared perplexingly at the sky. What just happened? He was certain Sam Dulie and Governor Daughtry were up to no good, but how was his brother involved. Willy thought back to the day Tyrus' son, Tyrone, was born back in June of 1966. While recuperating in a Vietnamese Army hospital, Willy received a letter from Tyrus' girlfriend, Abby Charles, claiming Tyrus had mysteriously disappeared the night Tyrone was born. That same night, Tyrus had proposed to marry Abby, and she had accepted. After Willy was discharged from the Army, he moved in with Abby and helped raise his nephew Tyrone. He couldn't believe Tyrus would abandon his own son and wife-to-be, but here he was, only a hundred or so miles from Seminole Bend and had never tried to even make contact with his family in the past sixteen years.

Willy was determined to find some evidence of wrongdoing in Sam Dulie's office, so with a sore shoulder, cut up backside, and a skin-tight Elmer Fudd t-shirt, he launched a cement block that had been lying in the parking lot through Sam Dulie's office window and climbed in.

CHAPTER 58

Friday, March 12, 1982

3:00 p.m.

Lew nervously watched footage of the airplane crash site from a television in Agent Jones' office. Seldom seen in church since Brett's death, Lew's hands were folded in his lap, and he was now pleading with God that his wife was not on that flight. Jones had noticed Lew's lips moving and could guess what he was thinking, but he also knew that the past couldn't be changed regardless of the prayers being offered. At least he didn't think it could. Jones had been on the phone continuously for the past few hours talking with other agents in Tampa when Agent Johnson walked into the room.

"Jack, I need to interrupt. It's important." Agent Johnson looked over to Lew and then lowered his head, not wanting to make eye contact with Lew.

"Should I leave?" asked Lew.

"No, you need to hear this, too," replied Agent Johnson.

Agent Jones hung up the phone and looked up from his desk at Agent Johnson. "What's up?"

"We just got word from Heartland Lakes Airways." Johnson paused momentarily, then continued. "Janet Berry was on the manifest list. I'm so very sorry, Mr. Berry."

Lew dropped his chin down to his chest, and tears welled up in his eyes. Agent Jones moved from his chair and stooped down in front of him. He softly patted Lew on the thigh and said, "I'm sorry, Lew, I really am. I hope you know if there's anything I can do, I want you to ask."

Lew looked up, and with a faint smile, he choked out the words, "Thanks. I will." However, the reality of losing his only son, his daughter-in-law, and now his wife was too much to bear.

"We will issue you a plane ticket back to Pittsburgh. There's a flight from Miami at 8:20 if you can be ready. It's almost three o'clock now, so you have a few hours."

"Thanks," breathed Lew in a barely decipherable tone, but he shook his head no. "I need to go back to Seminole Bend. I left some unfinished business there."

Agents Jones and Johnson looked at each other inquisitively.

"Well, okay, Lew," said Jones. Because of Lew's apparent dysphoria, he was going to leave it at that. But before Lew left, he wanted to give him assurance that the FBI was going to continue their efforts to find answers in Brett's case. "When we find out more information about Brett's truck and the man who was last seen with your wife, how can we contact you?"

Lew stood up and shook hands with both agents, then headed to the hallway. As he exited the door to Agent Jones' office, Lew turned back and said, "Don't call me, I'll call you."

A minute later, he was back in the Trans Am headed for Seminole Bend.

CHAPTER 59

Friday, March 12, 1982

3:15 p.m.

Willy examined every inch of the Department of Natural Resources building as any good private investigator would do. He found boxes of blank fishing and hunting license applications in storage closets. The file cabinets were full of reports on alligator migrations in the Everglades and bald eagle sightings in Wekiwa Springs State Park. But he found no evidence of Sam Dulie's wrongdoings.

Willy stood in front of Sam's desk and examined the communications contraption that had a cable wire running from it attached to the satellite dish outside. Sam had said it was missing a faulty mic that he had planned to replace at Radio Shack. But as Willy looked closer, he could tell there was nowhere for a mic to be attached. Strange!

Willy started to pick up the contraption, but it wouldn't budge. Something was holding it down on the metal desktop. Willy looked under the desk for a nut and bolt but didn't see any type of coupling. He was about to stand up when he noticed a one-inch-square plate fastened onto the underside of the desk with two tiny screws. It was so small he almost missed it.

Using a micro-sized Phillips head screwdriver and a flashlight he found in Sam's top drawer, Willy unscrewed the plate and peeked inside. Another cable was coming from the bottom of the electronic gizmo and being routed through a gap in the desktop to the left rear leg of the escritoire. Because of the tiny opening, Willy couldn't see far, but he assumed the cable was running inside the leg and down to the floor. He looked at the floor and couldn't see the cable, which could only mean that the cable ran underneath the linoleum tiles and possibly through the concrete slab foundation. But how could that be? There are no basements in southern Florida. The Atlantic Ocean would wreak havoc on one.

Willy stooped down and noticed the desk's legs did not sit on the floor, but descended entirely through the linoleum tiles and were fastened somehow underneath the concrete. That way, the desk would never move from its spot by the window. Although his arms and shoulders were sore, Willy grabbed the backside of the desk near the leg with the cable and yanked mightily. He heard a screeching sound and then a snap. The desk rose about an inch, then Willy put it down. He knew he couldn't have damaged a solid slab of concrete with that jerk regardless of how vigorous it may have been. That snapping sound must have been wood.

Willy was puzzled. Could the linoleum have been laid over lumber? Willy wasn't much of a scientist, but he knew that a wood floorboard existing in the extraordinarily high humidity and intense rain of southern Florida would be a feast for termites.

Willy wrestled with his tight blue jeans and dug into a pocket to pull out his Swiss Army knife. He sliced into the linoleum near the leg of the desk, cut a two-inch strip, and jimmied one end so his fingers could find a grip. With a pocket lighter he found on Sam Dulie's desk, Willy heated up the tile until the glue underneath softened, and he could pull back the strip. Sure enough, the linoleum had been laid on plywood coated with a thin layer of plastic to keep moisture out.

Willy found a toolbox in a storage closet and returned to the desk with a hammer and coping saw. He pounded the one-inch-thick plywood until it fractured enough to allow the coping saw an entry point. Then he chiseled out a two-foot-square chunk of pulp and plastic, making sure he left enough support to keep the desk from collapsing on top of him.

Willy shined the flashlight into the hole. Directly under the desk was a basin about eight-feet-by-six-feet wide and three-feet deep. A concrete slab foundation surrounded the vault and was protected on all sides with very thick plastic material to make it moisture-proof. Fitted neatly into the vault was an electronic box with wires and cables running in and out of it, one through the leg of the desk that Willy assumed was attached to the contraption on top. A series of blinking blue, red, yellow, and green lights assured Willy that the box in the hole was currently switched on and functioning. Several coaxial cables ran from the back of the box through a polyvinyl chloride pipe conduit that fit snuggly through a hole in the wall of the vault. The cables continued to run underneath the concrete foundation of the DNR building, and Willy was determined to track the PVC conduit and locate its origin.

Willy walked out the back door of the office and traced his steps along the DNR's foundation line. Moments later, he noticed a bare stretch of earth that began near a utility shed that was connected to the building. It appeared to be a very long and narrow trench that was covered by dirt and seeded with ryegrass. The trench line was easy to follow because the ryegrass was a lighter shade of green compared to the Saint Augustine turf surrounding it. Willy grabbed a shovel out of the utility shed and dug down. Sure enough, the PVC conduit was running about a foot underneath the ground and heading west beyond the DNR property line.

Willy dusted off his hands and went back into the storage room next to Sam Dulie's office. He remembered seeing several dark green shirts with a *State of Florida Department of Natural Resources* logo embossed on the shirt pocket. They were hanging over a cardboard box full of khaki shorts. The shirts had large numbers on the back and a picture of a cartoon alligator swinging a bat. The taxpayers of Florida were supporting the DNR's local softball team and according to the plaque on the wall in the lobby, the winners of last month's beer trophy in the Florida City Invitational.

Willy found an extra-large shirt and shorts that fit him, albeit snuggly, so he exchanged his unsnappable blue jeans and Elmer Fudd t-shirt for number twelve and walked back to the trench. He climbed over the chain-link fence that marked the DNR's boundary and followed the line through a thick patch of Brazilian Pepper trees until he came to a small orange grove about a mile away. Peering through the trees, Willy noticed a cement block structure in the distance. The trench line ran from the DNR office and ended in that building.

The structure appeared to be a house with the citrus grove being used as a backyard. Willy thought it was strange that the back of the house had no door and no windows. Who would live in a home without doors or windows? Willy glanced beyond the side of the house and saw a gravel road that ran perpendicular to a seashell and sand driveway. He started to walk around the corner to the front yard but froze in place when the barrel of a Colt 9mm submachine gun rammed into his chest.

"Halt!" said the gunman, who was dressed in a National Guard uniform. "Who are you, and what are you doing on this private property?"

Thinking quickly, Willy responded, "Oh, sorry, sir! I work for the DNR and was looking for our guard dog, Snuffy. He's a German shepherd that started chasing a rabbit this way. Haven't seen him, have you?"

"No, and you need to leave, sir. Use the road this time." The guard pointed to the gravel street with the machine gun.

"Will do, sir. Right away. By the way, who lives here? Just curious. It's not every day the good folks of southern Florida hire a guard to watch their home." Willy pretended to be looking at the guard, but he was actually checking out the house. The front had a metal door, and there was a four-by-five-foot picture window on the east façade with iron bars draping its exterior. That was it, plain and simple, a cheap, but very secure home. Why would a National Guardsman be providing security services, with a machine gun, no less?

"This is Governor Daughtry's winter home, now take a hike!" replied the guard.

"Governor Daughtry? Why have a home here? You'd think he'd want to be on South Beach, wouldn't you?"

"I don't ask questions, and you shouldn't either. Now for the last time, you need to leave." Once again, the guard pointed with the gun.

It had been a very long couple of days for Willy, and he'd heard enough. The governor would not be living in this dump. This is where the trench line stopped, and whatever the electric wires and coaxial cable were attached to was inside. He wasn't about to leave now.

"Yes, sir. Nice to meet you, sir!" Willy reached out with his right arm to shake hands goodbye, and the submachine gun's barrel rose to Willy's forehead. With a mighty force, Willy kicked the guard directly in his groin. The stunned young man lurched backward and dropped the gun to the ground. The helmet he was wearing jerked loose from the chinstrap and slid down his face, covering his eyes. He doubled over and instinctively reached for his crotch wishing beyond hope that the searing pain would subside soon.

Willy grabbed the gun and pointed it at the guard who was in tears, not from losing his defensive position, but from the throbbing misery below his belly.

"Put your hands up," Willy ordered.

"I, I, I can't just yet," stuttered the guard. "Please, just give me a minute." His hands were at his crotch, holding on tight.

Willy pushed the guard to the ground and unbuckled the man's belt. He slid the belt off, then rolled the man over so his face was tasting the white sandy earth. Using the belt, Willy tied the guard's arms behind his back. To buy some time, he used the trusty knockout chokehold that he had learned in the Army, and the guard immediately became unconscious. Willy blasted through the door lock by firing a sustained round of ammunition from the submachine gun. Then he dragged the guard inside the house and shoved him into a cloakroom next to the entryway. Willy blocked the door by shoving a large couch from the living room in front of it, then he pushed a mahogany gun cabinet next to the couch and tipped it over. The guard wouldn't be coming out through that closet door anytime soon.

Willy looked around. The small living room resembled a hunter's man cave. The leather couch that was now blocking the cloakroom door had a matching marshmallow-soft chair placed next to a brick fireplace with an oak mantelpiece. Fastened to the wall, above the mantel, was the mounted head of a red deer. Old *Field and Stream* magazines were spread out on an oak coffee table. But the only window in the entire house was protected by iron bars, and Willy found that very peculiar. Beyond the living room was a simple kitchen with a gas stove and refrigerator, plus a small cheap table with two chairs. Not the type of place you would find a governor of any state calling his "winter home."

Willy noticed a door off to the right that led into the master bedroom. Oddly, considering no one was home, it was locked. Willy gave it a kick, but it didn't budge. Willy saw that there were three deadbolts securing entry into the room. Using the corkscrew on his Swiss Army knife, Willy tried to drill a hole through the door near the locks but found that the wood was reinforced with a plate of steel inside. Governor Daughtry must want to ensure his nights were uninterrupted.

Willy tried to smash through the sheetrock, but that too was steel-reinforced. Then Willy had an idea. He walked outside and around to the back of the house where the trench line came in, then dug down using the fireplace poker and shovel until he hit the PVC pipe. He dug away under the cement foundation, being careful not to dislodge the conduit.

A short while later, darkness set in. Willy went back into the house and located a flashlight in a kitchen cabinet that could shed enough light to keep digging. It was almost eight o'clock when Willy finally came to the spot where the pipe took a right angle upwards into the house. Lying on his back in the cramped hole he had excavated under the foundation, Willy started chipping away at the concrete with the blade of his Swiss Army knife. An hour later, he had broken through, and a few minutes before midnight Willy had produced a hole in the substructure large enough for him to enter the room.

Willy boosted himself up and rested on his knees for a moment to catch his breath, then shined the light around the room. This was definitely the master bedroom because he could now see the inside of the door with the three deadbolt locks. But this master bedroom had no bed, nor did it have a dresser or nightstand. What it did have was twelve television screens, each with a videocassette recorder and a remote control device. The walls were covered with shelves that contained thousands of videotapes, most likely used to record whatever was displayed on the television screens. Eleven monitors were currently active with a black and white view from a live feed. The twelfth was on, but it was showing only the snow of a disrupted signal. Willy stood up and looked for a light switch, which he found next to the door. He turned on the lights and glanced around the room in stunned silence.

In the muffled distance, Willy could hear the guard pounding on the closet door and yelling profanities. The young man would just have to wait.

CHAPTER 60

Saturday, March 13, 1982

12:15 a.m.

Not knowing where to start, Willy took a look at the TV screens. Each was numbered from one to twelve, and they appeared to be sending live signals. Television number one was videoing movement down a highway somewhere. It was difficult to see the location because of the darkness of the night sky. A camera must be attached to the very front of a vehicle, perhaps on the hood or in the grille. Willy couldn't tell what kind of vehicle it was because the camera was forward-facing, and the car, truck, bus, or van was behind it.

Screen number two was also a vehicle moving down a road, but this was very puzzling to Willy. It was in daylight. Thus, if it were a live feed, it would not be in the continental United States, seeing it was just past midnight in Florida. A billboard along the side of the road was in a language that Willy didn't recognize.

Screens three through eleven had no movement, just a still image which Willy assumed was due to the vehicle being parked. However, it was obvious the mode of transport on those screens was airplanes because Willy recognized walkways to the left, buildings with tall glass windows straight ahead, and gate numbers posted above them. Screen number twelve was just television snow, complete interference with the picture display.

Willy noticed that on a desk in front of each screen was a remote control device with a joystick. He picked one up and examined it closely. There were two buttons on top, a green one labeled *engaged,* and a red one labeled *disengaged.* Willy had no idea what that meant.

Out of the corner of his eye, Willy noticed that the vehicle on screen number one had turned and was heading down a service road that was well lit. The car was moving slow enough that he could read the overhead sign. It said *Tampa International Airport* in white letters on a blue background. Willy watched, then the vehicle pulled into a parking lot and stopped in front of a white brick building. The sign above the door read *National Transportation Safety Board.* A few seconds later, a man in a dark blue windbreaker with the letters *NTSB* stenciled onto the jacket unlocked the front door and went in. Apparently, he was the man who had been driving the car or truck or whatever.

Willy glanced at screen number two, where a vehicle was moving rapidly down a four-lane freeway in the daylight. Inquisitively, Willy picked up the remote and fiddled with the joystick. Nothing happened on the TV. Then he pushed the green button, and words flashed on the screen: *Warning – System Engaged.*

Willy's curiosity got the best of him, and he pushed the joystick to the left. The video feed suddenly darted left, crossed a sunken grass barrier, and emerged perpendicular to the road on the other side. Willy knew right then that he had caused the vehicle to go out of control. Quickly trying to compensate, he moved the joystick back to the right, but the turn was too sharp, and the video feed tumbled around and around several times. Then Willy saw that the vehicle was momentarily airborne, and in a matter of seconds, the screen went blank, just like the static on television twelve.

Willy slammed the remote back onto the desk and dropped to his knees, staring dumbfounded at the random dot pixels in front of him. He realized that chances were good that he just killed someone, someone he didn't know. Tears welled up in his eyes. Willy also now understood that Governor Daughtry controlled more than just the budget for the state of Florida. Literally, lives could be destroyed by the elected top official on a whim.

A few minutes later, Willy tried to get a grip and focus on the situation before him. He was upset that his older brother Tyrus was most likely involved in something terrible. Thinking about the scene in the DNR parking lot with the boxes and helicopter, and now this, he needed to contact the FBI. As he turned towards the door, a chilling thought came to Willy, and he froze. Goosebumps covered his body, and he darted back towards the blank screen, then pounded his fists on the desk.

"Oh my God!" uttered Willy out loud. He just remembered that Governor Hank Daughtry was friends with Coach Berry's neighbor out in Seminole Bend Golf Course Estates, who was also friends with Roy Jackson. Then, a couple of days before he was fired, Willy recalled overhearing coroner Cliff Sutton tell Sheriff Bonty that the person driving the pickup the night the Berrys were killed could not have been Sheryl. The length of the charred remains of the bone at the scene determined that the body was over six feet tall.

Willy picked up the remote control device with the joystick and stared at it. Thinking aloud, he said, "Could Brett's truck have been rigged, and Daughtry forced whoever was driving it into the ditch with this damn thing? But why?!"

Willy struggled to remember the name of Brett's very wealthy neighbor. "Harmon. Harper. No, Harfield! That's it! Oliver Harfield. He's that rich cat who lives in that mansion out on the fifth hole!" He remembered seeing a news photo of Daughtry, Harfield, and Brett hugging each other a while back.

Willy noticed that a yellow light on the videocassette recorder beneath the blank TV screen was blinking. He looked closely and saw that the light indicator was labeled *Auto Pause.* Could there have been a recording of the accident he just caused? Willy pushed the rewind button for only a few seconds and heard the tape spin. Then he pushed the play button, and a picture replaced the snow on the TV. It was definitely a replay of the vehicle that had been on the four-lane freeway. Willy held his breath as he watched the car or truck veer ninety degrees to the left and go over the median, then attempt to turn ninety degrees to the right before the camera indicated a series of airborne spins. Once the spins ended, so did the camera feed, and the screen went blank.

Willy stopped the recorder and hit rewind again, this time allowing the tape to go all the way back to the beginning. He pushed play. A digital display on the upper right corner of the screen read *00:00*. On the upper left corner was a twenty-four-hour clock that showed the local time and date. As the tape started up, the TV screen displayed the words *Auto Paused*, but that lasted only momentarily and faded out when the camera feed began to move in reverse. It appeared that the vehicle was backing out of a parking spot. Then suddenly, the camera revealed a forward movement that lasted for ten minutes until the car came to a stop in a gas station. The TV screen once again displayed *Auto Paused,* and the local time indicator became frozen, but the tape's playback continued to roll. A split second later, the vehicle began to move, but Willy noticed that the clock was now revealing a time that was six minutes ahead of what it had displayed when the vehicle had stopped. The car, truck, van, or whatever had filled up with gas in six minutes and was on the move again. Willy realized that the video feed would automatically initiate recording when the vehicle was moving, but would pause when there was no inertia. During playback, the gaps in time simply appeared instantaneously.

Willy guessed that the other screens showing airplanes parked at the gate were not being recorded due to non-motion. Then he looked down at the last television, which also had a blank, snowy screen. He wondered what the videotape had recorded. Willy walked to the desk and sat in a rolling chair, then pushed rewind. The tape spun backward and stopped. The LCD display showed four hours of tape time had been recorded.

Willy pressed the play button, and he immediately knew the camera was affixed somewhere in the cockpit of an airplane as he saw the nose of the craft sticking out. On the bottom of the screen, Willy could just make out that the plane was being pushed back from the gate by a low-rise yellow tractor. As soon as the aircraft turned and began to move down a taxiway, the television flashed a warning: *Jam Disengaged ORD*. Willy had no idea what that meant. A few minutes later, the plane turned onto the runway, then stopped momentarily to wait for ATC clearance as *Auto Pause* flashed on the screen. Seconds later, the aircraft gained speed, rolled back, and thrust skyward.

The plane rose and turned, and that's when Willy could see the Sears Tower and outline of Lake Michigan on the bottom of the TV. He knew the plane had taken off from Chicago. As the plane leveled off, another warning flashed on the screen: *Jam Disengaged TPA*. Once again, Willy couldn't understand what that meant. He fast-forwarded through two hours of tape time, watching carefully for any abnormality of this flight when another warning flashed on the screen. Willy pushed play, and the tape slowed down to real-time. The warning read: *Jam Engaged TPA*.

Willy's eyes were wide open and glued to the television. A few minutes later, he noticed dark skies with flashes of lightning on the left side of the screen. Then the plane did something incredibly bizarre. It turned directly into the storm and Willy could tell it was taking on tremendous turbulence. "Why would the pilot do that?" whispered Willy to himself. The skies were clear on the opposite side of the screen.

Two minutes later, an enormous burst of light illuminated the picture feed for a split second, and then the screen went blank. Willy could tell it was an explosion. He had seen enough of them during his time in Vietnam. With a chill running through his spine, Willy now understood what he had just witnessed: the midair collision of the two passenger jets over Lake Okeechobee.

"Jam Engaged TPA. What does that mean, damn it?!" Willy was speaking aloud to try and talk his way through the disaster. "Tampa, that must be TPA! But what the heck is ORD? The plane took off from Chicago, not Orlando! And jam engaged? Could Daughtry be able to jam airport radars from here?"

Willy glanced over to the other TVs, and a terrifying thought raced through his mind. Are those planes locked and loaded, awaiting another catastrophic episode in midair? And was the man who entered the National Transportation Safety Board a target for Governor Daughtry? Willy looked at the shelves stacked with videocassettes and realized the implausible amount of criminal evidence that lay in front of him.

Willy ejected the videocassette of the doomed aircraft and headed for the door. He needed to get to FBI headquarters in Miami fast! He would give them the tape and the metal box he had extracted from Brett Berry's truck, even though he fully understood that he would be admitting to a felony break-in at the FBI auto impound lot. But he would also be implicating his brother Tyrus in a crime that would no doubt end up with the death penalty. He didn't care. He had to do what was right.

The deadbolts were not locked from inside the room, so exiting it was simplified. Willy turned all three locks and opened the door. He was greeted by the muzzle of a well-recognized submachine gun pointed directly at his nose. The irate-looking guard had one eye shut and was taking aim from a distance of two feet. Willy had no doubt the nine-millimeter bullets would easily find their mark.

CHAPTER 61
Saturday, March 13, 1982
8:00 a.m.

Lew slept restlessly in the front seat of his rented Trans Am. He was parked at Gregorson General Hospital waiting for visiting hours to begin so he could check on his buddy Phil. It was eight o'clock, and the hospital staff was in a tizzy and had been since the mid-air plane crash. The hospital was allowing rooms to be used as a temporary morgue because the county's morgue was designed to hold a maximum of eight bodies, and it was already beyond capacity. Lew went into the lobby restroom, and using just his hands, he rinsed off his stubbly face. His clothes were dirty, and he looked disheveled and exhausted. Lew could use a strong cup of coffee.

"I'm here to visit Phil Bennett," said Lew to the nurse at the receiving desk. "Should I sign in here?"

"Sir, are you a relative of Mr. Bennett's?" asked the nurse hesitantly.

"No, just a friend. Please, I'm in a bit of a hurry."

"Sir, I have some bad news. Mr. Bennett died in his sleep just a few hours ago."

Lew staggered backward, then dropped to the floor and rested his back on the adjacent wall. He covered his eyes with his hands, and the tears flowed down his cheeks. The nurse rushed around the reception desk and stooped down to Lew.

"Sir, are you okay?" asked the nurse. "Do you need some assistance? Let me call for someone."

"No, I'll be okay," stuttered Lew. "Please, just give me a minute."

"Please let me get you to a chair in the lobby." The nurse helped Lew to his feet, put her arms around him, and walked him to the waiting room. The room was packed with visitors, all of them friends and relatives of the passengers on the doomed airplanes waiting for confirmed identifications. A younger man stood up and offered his chair to Lew.

"If you need something, please ask," said the nurse in a kind tone of voice. "I need to get back to my desk."

Lew was distraught and was finding it impossible to get his agitated thoughts together. The lack of sleep combined with the loss of his son, daughter-in-law, and wife had taken a toll on his sanity, and now the death of his new friend had put him over the edge. After several minutes listening to the demons inside, he was considering giving up and ending his own life when an inner spirit slapped him back into consciousness. Lew had never been a quitter and wasn't about to start now. Then, a thought hit him, and he walked back to the nurse's station.

"Sorry to bother you again. I just wanted to thank you for helping me." Lew smiled at the nurse, and she returned the visage with a slight nod. "I should have introduced myself. My name is Lew Berry."

"Are you doing okay now, Mr. Berry? Is there anything I can help you with?" The nurse was remarkably controlled, considering the situation. Cries from loved ones echoed throughout the hallways.

"Yes, would you mind if I looked at your visitor's sign-in sheet? I want to know if any of Phil's friends or family members had visited him before he passed." Lew was hoping to comfort a loved one by providing testimony to Phil's heartfelt compassion for humankind. It was the least he could do for all that his friend had done for him.

"No, certainly, I don't mind. Please, go ahead and look." The nurse pushed the clipboard towards Lew. The visitor log was full of names from yesterday. More than a couple hundred passengers had to have been on those two planes.

Lew carefully perused the list and found only one visitor for Phil. Pancho had signed in and out several times during the day on Friday. However, strangely, he had signed in at nine o'clock last night and never signed out. Visiting hours were over at ten, and nurses were required to check the list to make sure no one was still in the patients' rooms. Whoever was on duty must have missed it, but considering the deluge of friends and relatives checking on the status of their loved ones, that could have been an easy mistake.

Lew was about to hand the clipboard back to the nurse when he noticed another name. Roy Jackson had signed in at 9:30 p.m. and signed out at 10:00 p.m. Under the column labeled *Patient*, Jackson wrote *Mickey Mouse* and room number *zero*.

Lew paused a moment, then asked the nurse, "Does anyone here ask for identification when a visitor signs in?"

"Yes, Mr. Berry. All visitors must show a driver's license. Why do you ask?"

"Do you then check to see that the patient's name and room number are correct on the visitor's log?"

"Well, we may not check too close because the visitor usually asks what room their friend or relative is in, and we assume they write it down correctly. What are you getting at, Mr. Berry?"

"Have you admitted a patient named Mickey Mouse?" asked Lew with a straight face. The nurse looked at him and frowned.

"Please, Mr. Berry, now's not the time for jokes."

"I agree," replied Lew. "Please take a look." He pushed the clipboard back to the nurse and pointed to the line with Jackson's name.

"Huh? Now that's strange. I can't believe a respectable member of the community, like Mr. Jackson, would do such a thing. And he wrote the room number as zero. There is no room zero in our hospital!"

"Respectable? You're kidding me, right?" Lew rolled his eyes and shook his head. "Do you have any idea who Jackson was really here to see?" inquired Lew.

"No, I came on duty at six o'clock this morning. The night nurse would have been here. But because Jackson's on the hospital board of directors, I'm sure she wouldn't have bothered him for any identification, nor would she have checked to see if he wrote the correct name down on the log."

Before Lew could ask another question, a middle-aged man wearing a white shirt, black dress pants, and a beat-up paisley tie underneath a physician's half-unbuttoned coat approached the desk. He handed the nurse a discharge form while interrupting the conversation she was having with Lew.

"Excuse me, please," said the doctor. "Here is the paperwork for patient Bennett. An ambulance is waiting out back to take him to my office."

The nurse glanced at Lew, who now wondered if this doctor was talking about Phil Bennett.

"Is Phil still here?" Lew asked the nurse. "Why hasn't he been sent to a funeral home?"

The doctor looked at Lew, then to the nurse, and then back at Lew. "I'm sorry, are you a friend or relative of Phil Bennett's?" He offered to shake Lew's hand as an offer of condolence, but Lew didn't take it.

"As a matter of fact, I am. May I ask who you are and why you are taking him to some office?"

"I am the county coroner. My name is Cliff Sutton. I need to run some tests on Phil that I can't do here, that's all." Cliff retracted his handshake offer seeing that Lew had no plans to accept it.

"So, you're doing an autopsy? Why? My friend Phil almost lost his leg from debris falling from the sky during the plane accident. I figured he lost too much blood. Was there more to it?"

"I'm sorry sir, I'm not at liberty to give out any information. Do you mind me asking what your name is?"

"Sure, doc. And just so you know, we've spoken to each other in the past. Over the phone a few days ago. I'm sure you will remember our conversation." Lew gave the coroner a hostile stare.

"I'm sorry," Cliff paused and squinted at Lew. "You are who?"

"Lew Berry. I'm Brett Berry's father."

"Would you like a cup of coffee so we can chat?"

"Love one! Thanks!"

CHAPTER 62

Saturday, March 13, 1982
9:30 a.m.

Pancho woke up wearily around mid-morning with a throbbing headache and soreness throughout his body. He opened his eyelids but had difficulty focusing on anything near or far. He tried to stand up but fell down. His legs were weak and wobbly. Then he noticed iron bars and realized he was in a jail cell. Sitting on a bench across the cell was the last man he had seen before passing out. It was Sheriff Al Bonty, and he was spinning a chain of jail keys around on his finger, presumably waiting for Pancho to awaken.

Now it was starting to come back to Pancho. He had been sitting in the hospital chatting with Phil Bennett when a man with a fancy cowboy hat walked into the room. Just as he turned his head around, Pancho was struck in the temple with the butt of the rancher's gun. He was dazed, but still able to see what was happening from where his head was lying on the floor.

Although his eyes were out of focus, Pancho remembered watching the man shove a wad of cloth into Phil's mouth with one hand while reaching for a bottle of nasal spray with the other. While Phil was gagging, the man pushed his head back and sprayed a liquid mist into Phil's nose. In less than a minute, Phil was unconscious, and the man removed the cloth, opened the first-floor window, and tossed it outside. Then he lifted Pancho off the hospital floor and jostled him headfirst out the window.

Pancho laid in the gravel employee parking lot behind the hospital trying to move but kept falling in and out of consciousness. A few minutes later, Roy Jackson appeared from around the corner of the building and handcuffed him. He dragged Pancho by his feet over the rough surface to a sheriff's department squad car, then thrust him into the back seat. A few seconds later, Pancho felt a sharp pain in the back of his leg and realized that Jackson had stuck a needle in him.

Pancho awoke again later, but only for a moment, as he was dragged once again from the car into another building. The skin on his back had been shredded from the gravel, and the pain was excruciating. But before passing out for the final time, he vaguely remembered seeing Sheriff Bonty. That was Pancho's last memory.

"Ready to talk, son?" asked Sheriff Bonty with a rough tone.

"Why am I here?" muttered Pancho. "What did you do to Mr. Phil?"

"I'll ask the questions, amigo," responded Bonty. "Why were you in Phil Bennett's room last night?"

* * * * *

Taylor Creek winds through Seminole Bend as it makes its way to Lake Okeechobee. Hidden behind thick sawgrass and palmetto bushes, it flows directly behind the sheriff's department, unnoticeable by anyone who doesn't know it's there. But hungry bass love to hide in the lily pads, and only the locals know about this fishing hole. Otis and Lance thought they might find the Mexican orange picker Pancho dangling some grub on a hook out there.

An hour or so before midnight last night, Otis and Lance were coming up from the river when they noticed the sheriff's car pulling into the jailhouse parking lot. Not wanting to be seen and questioned by the law, they ducked down in the tall grass. They watched as Roy Jackson pulled what appeared to be an unconscious criminal out of the back seat and drag him feet first into the building. Thinking that was rather inhumane, the two newest employees of the *Willy Banks Private Investigator Firm* slinked to the backside of the office where the cell blocks were located. Lance got on Otis' shoulders and peered through a tiny, barred window and witnessed Jackson propel the lifeless man face-first onto the concrete floor while the sheriff watched. The insentient creature was Hispanic, and Otis and Lance wondered if he could be their man Pancho? They decided to come back in the morning and find out.

CHAPTER 63

Saturday, March 13, 1982

9:45 a.m.

Otis and Lance slept in Cousin Lenny's stolen Buick next to the dumpster behind McDonald's. Lance had dined many a breakfast on someone else's half-eaten Egg McMuffin and hash browns that had been dropped on the dirty floor. Breakfast would be over at 10:30, and Donny Douglas would bring out the morning trash from the inside garbage bins. Donny was a hardworking employee and a Seminole Bend High School freshman who covered his zits with Calamine lotion hoping the girls wouldn't notice. Lance had befriended Donny, and sometimes Donny would sneak out a small cup of hot coffee to wash down the cold eggs and oversyrupped pancakes. But this morning, Donny invited both Lance and Otis into the restaurant. He said the manager had to leave on an emergency and had appointed him in charge for a couple of hours.

Lance and Otis were sipping on hot coffee and eating a complimentary sausage biscuit when Deputy Johnny Murphree entered and walked to the counter. He was stopping by for a quick breakfast before heading to work. Lance and Otis looked at each other and nodded, then Otis got up and approached Johnny.

"Hello Officer Murphree," said Otis shyly as he reached out his arm to shake hands. "Don't know if you 'member me, but I was the one who woke you up soze you could call my brother Willy Banks who was in jail down in Miami. I be Otis, Otis Banks."

Johnny Murphree gripped Otis' hand and returned the greeting. "How could I forget? It was in the middle of the night!"

"Yes, sir. Sorry 'bout that, I really am. Did you talk to Willy? Is he okay?"

"Not sure, but I think so. He hasn't called me back." The deputy picked up the brown to-go bag off the countertop and turned to head out. "So, I have to get back to work, Otis. If you hear from Willy, let me know, okay. I need to speak to him."

"Wait, sir, please. My friend and I need to ask you a question. Just one minute, please. Won't be long, I promise." Otis motioned for Johnny to join him and Lance at the table. Reluctantly, the deputy agreed.

"One minute, that's all Otis. I need to be at work."

Johnny sat down and nodded at Lance. He didn't want to shake his grimy hand before munching down the four Sausage McMuffins awaiting his taste buds. "What can I do for y'all?"

"You ever met the man who saved Willy's life when he was attacked by a gator last month out on the Kissimmee?" asked Lance.

"No, he dropped Willy off at Angler's Delight Marina and hasn't been seen since. Even Willy doesn't know who he is, so why you asking?"

"I think that Mexican man is locked up in your jailhouse."

"That's absurd!" exclaimed Johnny. "All our officers are helping out at the airplane crash site. Sheriff Bonty ordered us to detain any possible criminal in the sheriff's holding van that's out at the marina, and there was no one locked up yesterday. We've only got one officer on duty at the jail, and right now it's Bonty, who I'm supposed to relieve. He won't be happy if I'm late, seeing he worked the whole night shift, so I best be going."

Johnny started to get up, and Lance reached over and grabbed his wrist. Johnny jerked his arm back to release himself from the hold, then leaned down and pointed his finger at Lance. "I am an officer of the law, sir, and you won't be touching me again. Understand?!"

"That rich rancher, Roy Jackson, was driving the sheriff's car last night. He got out and yanked the Mexican man outa the backseat. Poor fella was sure enough out cold, and Roy dragged him over the rocks and into the jailhouse feet first!" interrupted Otis. "We both saw it, and then we snuck up and peeked through the cell window. The Mexican guy had been beaten up pretty darn good, he had."

"Impossible," replied Johnny. "Bonty wouldn't have let Roy Jackson drive a sheriff's vehicle or arrest anybody. Makes no sense."

"We telling ya, Deputy Murphree, it happened just like we say. And we pretty sure he's the Mexican man my brother Willy is looking for."

"Okay, come on over to the jail in a few minutes and wait, but make sure the sheriff is gone. If the Mexican man is in a cell, I'll let you talk to him. But if he ain't, I don't want to hear no more nonsense talk. You got it?"

"Yes, sir! Thank you, Mr. Johnny. We'll be over shortly."

Johnny drove away in the squad car as Cliff Sutton and Lew Berry were just pulling into the parking lot. Lance and Otis got in the Buick and turned on the radio. They needed to kill time for ten minutes or so.

CHAPTER 64

Saturday, March 13, 1982

10:00 a.m.

Lew had driven the rented Trans Am with Cliff riding shotgun. Neither said a word until they had ordered breakfast and found a seat in a booth by the window. Lew wasn't going to speak until Cliff said something, so he took a sip of coffee and glared into the coroner's eyes. With paranoia setting in, Cliff decided to go first.

"Mr. Berry, do you mind if I call you Lew?"

"That's my name. Do you mind if I call you Cliff?"

"No problem. So let me begin by saying how terribly sorry I am for the loss of your son."

"What about my son's wife, Cliff? What about her? Aren't you sorry about her, too?" Cliff looked out the window. If the coroner only knew what other losses Lew had suffered!

"Yes, I am. But as I told you on the phone earlier this week, I know the remains in Brett's truck were not your daughter-in-law's. The bone structure fits a man over six feet tall. I'm hoping the news is good that she is still alive. I haven't heard back from the FBI, so I don't know how your conversation went."

"They think Sheryl was on the flight that crashed in Miami last month." Lew looked away again. Hope was nowhere to be seen in his eyes.

"Really? So why do they think that?" Cliff had a surprised look on his face.

"A severed finger was found at the crash site with a wedding ring on it that had Sheryl and Brett's initials carved on the inside. The blood type was the same as Sheryl's."

"Oh my God. I'm so sorry, Lew!"

"Well, that's not the end of it. Yesterday the FBI confirmed that my wife, Janet, was on the plane that crashed here." Lew began to weep and wiped his eyes with the paper towel on his tray.

Cliff paused for a long time, not knowing if he should say what he was thinking. But this conversation was baffling him, and he wanted answers as much as Lew. "Lew, sorry to say this, but that is quite a coincidence, having two family members killed in airplane crashes within a month of each other. Wouldn't you say? Something's not right about that if I do say so myself."

Lew decided that Cliff could be trusted. He certainly seemed empathetic towards the tragic events of the past couple of months, and let's face it, with Phil Bennett gone, he needed a new friend. So Lew gambled and told the coroner everything that had happened since he arrived in Florida. He left out no details.

When Lew stopped talking, Cliff was staring at him with his mouth wide open. It was an incredible story, so incredible that he, too, believed that something sinister was taking place in Seminole Bend. He had never trusted Sheriff Al Bonty, and now he may have realized why.

CHAPTER 65

Saturday, March 13, 1982
10:30 a.m.

Otis and Lance waited for Sheriff Bonty to pull out of the jail parking lot, then they pulled in and parked near the front door. Johnny Murphree met them there.

"You were right," said Johnny before the door had even closed behind Otis and Lance. "Bonty locked up a Mexican man last night following a citizen's arrest by Roy Jackson. He said the man had been disturbing the peace over at Gregorson Hospital. I went back and asked him his name. He said it's Pancho. He had been roughed up pretty good, just like you said."

"Can we talk to him, Johnny?" asked Otis.

"Let's do it." The three men grabbed plastic chairs from a nearby office and went back to Pancho's cell. They propped themselves down outside the iron bars.

After Pancho was told that Otis was Willy's brother, he figured he could trust all three, including Deputy Murphree. He said he would speak openly, but he was starving and asked for a bite to eat. Johnny unlocked the cell door and said, "Let's go back to McDonald's. I don't think I need to worry that you will escape."

Otis, Lance, and Pancho got into Johnny's squad car and drove back to McDonald's. As they entered the restaurant, Lew Berry noticed him and stood up. "Pardon me, Cliff, I'll be right back."

As Lew approached, Pancho saw him, and the two men embraced.

"Mr. Lew, I'm so happy to see you again!" Pancho wouldn't stop shaking Lew's hand.

"You know this man?" Johnny asked Pancho while motioning to Lew. Otis and Lance looked at each other and shrugged their shoulders.

"Yes, sir. This is Mr. Lew. Long story, Mr. Deputy, please, I will tell you everything."

"What happened to you?" Lew ignored Johnny and pointed at Pancho's injuries.

"Let's get Pancho some food," interrupted Johnny. "Then he can tell us all what happened."

Lew went back to his table and pushed it next to the adjacent one, then pulled up six chairs. A few minutes later, Otis, Lance, Pancho, and Johnny sat down with Lew and Cliff. Pancho devoured two Egg McMuffins and three hash browns in less than a minute, then washed it down with orange juice. Everyone was startled, including Lance, who spent most days hungry himself.

While waiting for Pancho's digestion to kick in, the others introduced themselves. Otis decided to start.

"I'm Otis, Otis Banks." Otis nodded at the group. Then he decided to be polite and introduce Lance. "And this here's Lance Billips, my good friend, and now we's business partners with my brother Willy."

Lew perked up. "Willy Banks? Willy Banks, the deputy? You're his brother?"

"Yes, sir. But Willy ain't no deputy anymore. He got fired this week, and now he's running his own private investigator firm, and me and Lance are his top agents. How do you know Willy?"

"I've been looking for him all week. I met your older brother's fiancé, Abby, at BoldMart. I think he has some information about my son Brett Berry's death."

"You Coach Berry's daddy? Sorry 'bout what happened to him and all. But Abby ain't no fiancé, Mr. Berry. My big brother Tyrus, he ain't never got no plans to marry her. He left the night Tyrone was born. Tyrone is Tyrus' kid, and he be my nephew."

Johnny Murphree interrupted the conversation. "Pancho, perhaps we should start from the beginning. Otis and Lance here think you may be the guy who saved Willy's life last month. Is that true?"

Pancho put his head down and nodded. "Yes, sir. I sorry I didn't tell anyone before now. I was scared to tell." Pancho paused for a few seconds, then told everyone the story about how he had skipped work and gone fishing when he came upon Willy in the swamp. Then he talked about his friendship with Miguel and how he came to operate the underwater shuttle between Oliver Harfield's mansion and the Kissimmee River. He explained that this was how he met Lew Berry.

Lew then told everyone about his week in Florida. Cliff Sutton had already heard the story but picked up on a few more details the second time around. Johnny pulled out a notebook and was taking notes like a good deputy should. When Lew had ended his narrative, Pancho told the story about last night in the hospital and how Roy Jackson had knocked him out, but he was still able to see Jackson spray something in Phil Bennett's nose. Now it was Cliff's turn to pull out a notebook.

Johnny looked over at Cliff and asked, "Were you planning on doing an autopsy, Dr. Sutton?"

"Yes. I noticed several tiny blisters on the cartilage tissue inside Phil's nose that could be a fast-acting form of the carcinogen beta-propiolactone," replied Cliff.

"Now, I pretty sure I was like third or something in my class, which is why I didn't bother to graduate, cuz I figured I was already smart, you know," interjected Lance. "But I don't reckon I done heard them words, car seat bepropiltone, before?"

"Sorry," replied Cliff. "In other words, the spray could be some sort of arsenic, I mean poison. Phil's records didn't indicate that he was being treated for nasal congestion or any other illness that would require a nasal inhalant."

"So what you are saying, Doc, is that it's possible Roy Jackson intentionally tried to end Phil's life?" inquired Johnny. "Perhaps with a bottle of poisonous nasal spray like Pancho claims to have seen?"

"Yes, deputy, that's exactly what I'm trying to say. I believe another term for it would be called murder."

Johnny looked at Otis. "Where is Willy now?" We need him to help us nail Sheriff Bonty, Roy Jackson, and Oliver Harfield. He may know more than we do. Last I heard from him he was trying to get out of jail down in Miami. I know, because I was trying to help his cause."

"We ain't heard from him since we talked to you," replied Otis. "Ya think he could still be in jail down there?"

"We need to find him fast," said Johnny, then glanced over to Cliff. "Dr. Sutton, please do your autopsy on Phil right away, then hang tight at your office. I don't think I need to tell you, but Bonty or Jackson will come looking for you if they know what you're doing. When we know something about Willy, I'll call you. I'm going to park the squad car back at the jail. Lew, you need to drive us down to Miami. We don't have much time. As soon as Bonty figures out that I'm not at the jailhouse, he'll be coming back. When he sees me and Pancho missing, he won't stop looking until he finds us. So let's get moving!"

CHAPTER 66

Saturday, March 13, 1982

11:00 a.m.

Otis, Lance, and Pancho crammed into the back seat of Lew's rented Trans Am, and Lew pushed his personal belongings and pictures onto the passenger side floor so Johnny could get in the front. As Johnny was strapping himself in with the seat belt, he noticed that a picture had slipped out of the top envelope that was lying on the floor. He reached down and picked it up, then did a double-take as he examined the photo.

"Where did you get this picture?" asked Johnny as he handed it to Lew, who had just cranked the ignition.

"FBI in Miami. It's a picture of my wife having coffee with someone in Harrisburg, Pennsylvania, a couple of days ago."

"Do you know who the man is?" Johnny asked the question as though he knew the answer.

"No idea, Johnny. Why?" Lew gave Johnny a speculative glance. "Do you know who it is?"

"Yes, I think so. I'm pretty sure it's Roy Jackson."

"Roy Jackson!" yelled Otis from the back seat. "What's that sonabitch doing with your wife?"

"You think this could be Roy Jackson?" Lew asked nervously again to Johnny.

"Well, it's hard to tell for sure looking at his back. But take a look at that gigantic gold ring he's wearing on the hand holding the coffee cup." Johnny pointed at the ring. "It's a little grainy from this distance, but you can barely make out engraved crossed swords and a huge diamond. Word around town is that a Jasurbian prince gave it to Roy when Roy invited him out at the ranch during a vacation."

"Why would Roy Jackson be having coffee with my wife?" pondered Lew to himself, however, loud enough for all to hear. "She's never met him."

"You told us that she was on the flight from Chicago to Tampa the next morning, right?" Johnny asked hesitantly. "It could be more than just a coincidence that she met up with Jackson shortly before dy—"

Johnny stopped abruptly, trying not to cause any more emotional suffering for Lew.

"Dying," said Lew, finishing Johnny's sentence. "Go ahead, you can say it. But I know what you are thinking, and that's pure insanity! You think Roy Jackson had something to do with that airplane crash, right? How could he have caused that disaster? Impossible!"

"I hope you're right, Lew. Jackson's an idiotic ass, but he's been involved in all sorts of suspected crimes in Seminole Bend. I don't know how he would pull this off, but as an officer of the law, I'm not going to rule out the possibility that he's a terrorist, too."

"He's having coffee with my wife one day in Pennsylvania, and the next day he's killing Phil Bennett in a Seminole Bend hospital! Why is the man not in jail, damn it?" Lew was upset and angry. "If he's been involved in multiple crimes, as you say, why is he still functioning outside the walls of a damn prison?!"

"Sheriff Bonty covers for him. I don't know why, but Willy was close to finding out something when he was fired."

"Yep, sure was!" pitched in Otis from the back seat. "Willy will tell us soon as we find him."

Lew shifted into gear and floored it, squealing rubber from his tires and throwing up gravel at the parked cars. Johnny perked up in his seat and gripped the dash with his fingertips. "Want me to drive," he asked but didn't look at Lew. He was afraid to take his eyes off the road.

"Nope. I can handle it!" Lew replied with a look of determination mixed with desperation. He passed the first car going 104 in a forty-five zone. Otis, Lance, and Pancho felt around for their seat belts. They found them but weren't sure how they worked. They had never buckled up before in their lives.

CHAPTER 67

Saturday, March 13, 1982

11:15 a.m.

"You got a minute, Jack?" asked Agent Tecka as he opened the door to Agent Jones' office.

"Sure, Tom. Come on in. What's up?" replied Agent Jones as he motioned for Tecka to sit down.

"Got a couple of things back from the lab. Strange things, Jack."

"Hit me. What do you got?"

Agent Tecka laid down two manila envelopes, each with a white label stuck on the upper left corner. A case number was printed on each one. He opened the first envelope and took out the report, then slid it across the desk to Agent Jones.

"Remember that finger with a wedding ring on it that was found at the scene of the Miami midair crash?"

"Yep. The finger had AB blood type, and we assumed it belonged to Sheryl Berry. Why?"

"Well, here's the strange thing. The finger belongs to the hand that was found next to it, but the hand doesn't fit the unidentified body nearby."

"Explain, please, Tom."

"The unidentified burned body definitely was missing a hand, but our forensic staff says the severed hand found next to it was too small to come from that body."

"So, there must have been other bodies close by. Could it have come from a different body than the one we thought?"

"No other bodies we found were missing a hand, Jack. That's what's curious."

"Are you saying what I think you're saying, Tom?"

"The hand on the unidentified body was most likely removed after the accident, and the hand with the finger cut off was placed next to it as a set up to lead us on a wild goose chase."

Agent Jones paused a moment to digest what Agent Tecka had reported, then said, "That would mean a crime was committed before the airplane accident."

"Much more than that, Jack." Agent Tecka stared directly at Agent Jones, and both realized the magnitude of the report. "If the hand was placed at the scene, someone knew that there was going to be an airplane crash in the vicinity that night, and most likely knew he could find a body to go with the hand they had just cut off!"

"So you're saying the plane accident may not have been a control tower malfunction mixed with bad weather? You think someone on the ground caused two airplanes to crash in the air?" Agent Jones mulled over the possibility in his mind. "What's worse, the crash over Lake Okeechobee this week was a midair collision, too. Could it be possible the same person or people are responsible for causing that?" Angst could be detected from the voice inflection of both FBI agents. "I hate to ask, but what's in the other report?"

Agent Tecka opened the second envelope and pulled out another report. "We got prints back already from the break-in to Berry's truck at the auto lot. It was an easy search. The fingerprints belong to a man named Willy Banks. No record, but get this. He's a cop in the Seminole Bend sheriff's department. I tried to call up there to verify, but no one was answering. I assume everyone's out at the scene of the crash."

"The prints belong to a deputy sheriff?" Agent Jones considered the unthinkable. "He breaks into a truck belonging to Brett Berry. Why didn't he ask us instead? He's an officer of the law. We would have tried to work things out together with a Seminole Bend investigation, wouldn't we?"

"What are you getting at, Jack? I'm not sure I follow you."

"Coach Berry is married to Sheryl, who was kidnapped at the basketball game, then an unidentified body is found in Brett's truck after it rolls into a culvert. We are guessing someone maneuvered the vehicle using a radio remote control device and video camera. Then we assume Sheryl was on the flight that crashed in Miami. Now we think Sheryl's hand was placed at the scene of what is no longer an accident, but an act of terrorism or mass murder on two passenger jets. Then a Seminole Bend's sheriff's deputy secretly removes something from the steering wheel in Berry's truck and disappears. I think we are dealing with more than a coincidence here, Tom."

"If that was a remote control device in Berry's truck, why do you think Deputy Banks removed it? This is getting quite complex, Jack!"

"I know. Then add the fact that Lew's wife, Janet Berry, was on the flight manifest for the Tampa crash, it becomes way too coincidental. We need to find Banks. What do we know?"

"He escaped on foot and was last seen running down Tamiami Trail. Where to, no one knows."

"Let's go out there and take a look ourselves. Grab your weapon and meet me at my car."

*****

Agents Jones and Tecka began their search at the auto impound facility where they were shown the exit point in the fence that Willy used to elude the authorities. Then they examined the broken down shack with an outhouse that was presumed to be along Willy's escape route. By the edge of the property leading into the swamp was a blood-soaked tail of a very furry dog, most likely the FBI's German shepherd. Jones and Tecka assumed the serial killer gator wanted to leave a trophy behind.

They returned to their vehicle and drove down Tamiami Trail until they reached the new Everglades Estates housing development. They pulled into the driveway of a model home that was being used as a sales office. A middle-aged brunette gal wearing a smart gray business suit was hastily marching around the property. She was madly shaking a heavy object in the air and muttering to herself. "Damn vagrants!" is what Agent Tecka heard as he was opening the car door. Because of her anger, she hadn't noticed the FBI car pull into the model home's driveway, and she was startled to see two men in blue suits approach her.

Jones and Tecka flashed their badges at the same time while introducing themselves to the saleslady. "I'm Agent Jack Jones, FBI ma'am. This is Agent Tom Tecka. We'd like to ask you a couple of questions if you don't mind?"

"Don't mind?" replied Karen Morris, who seemed a bit agitated at the moment. "You came at the right time!"

"Right time?" asked Agent Jones. "What do you mean by that?"

Karen raised a crowbar in her right hand. "Someone broke into our model home with this. Used our shower and left the place a damn mess! I was going to show the house in a couple of hours to a prospective customer. Well, that just ain't gonna happen now, is it?!"

Jones and Tecka glanced at each other, then Tecka asked Karen, "Mind if I take a look at that crowbar?" The saleslady handed it to him.

"It's from an old Nash Rambler," said Tecka to Jones as he pointed at something etched on the iron bar. "Back in the day when American Motors bought out the Nash company, they used to engrave the words *The Kenosha Cadillac* on the Rambler's fenders, mirrors, and even spare tire crowbars. It was some marketing symbol or something."

"On a crowbar, how ridiculous is that?" replied Jones. He looked over to Karen Morris and asked, "Would you mind if we take a peek at the house?"

"Sure, why not?" answered Morris. "But that's not why you're here. What were those questions you wanted to ask me?"

"You may have already answered them. We wanted to know if you had seen someone unusual around here early this morning."

"Well, I just got here a short while ago and was going to prep the house for my client when I noticed the break-in. Didn't see anyone, but I assumed whoever broke in was some homeless guy wanting a shower. Strange, though, he left his clothes on the floor in the master bathroom. They were almost ripped to shreds and all bloody. I wonder what he changed into?"

Jones and Tecka followed Karen up to the house and then into the master bathroom. Jones picked up the abandoned clothing and checked the labels. Size forty waist on the pants and an XXL shirt. "Big fella, this guy."

The FBI agents offered to call the local police for Karen to report the break-in, but Karen said she would take care of it herself. They thanked the saleslady for her time, got into their car, and radioed a request for information back to the office. Jones and Tecka waited in the driveway for a response. It came fifteen minutes later.

"Jack," said the voice on the speaker. "According to the Florida Motor Vehicle Division, there are only a handful of Nash Ramblers still licensed in the state. And yes, one belongs to a man up in Seminole Bend named Willy Banks. Our databank lists him as a deputy sheriff for that county. Hope that helps!"

"Roger that. Appreciate you finding out fast! Over."

Jones hung up the receiver and said to Tecka, "So Willy Banks used his own personal vehicle, which means he wasn't on official business. Didn't think so. Put out an APB for the Nash Rambler. There ain't many down here, so it shouldn't be all that hard to find."

"You think Banks is a good guy or a bad guy, Jack?"

"Someone who breaks into an FBI impounded vehicle lot for the purpose of burglary can't be all that good, now can he, Tom?"

"Where to next, Jack?"

* * * * *

"Hold on, Jack!" screamed Agent Tecka. "Hit the brakes!"

Jones and Tecka were headed for Seminole Bend and traveling north on the Florida Turnpike when Tecka spotted a black car speeding southward on the other side of the divided highway. The FBI agents were in the left lane and boxed in by other traffic to their right, so Jones slammed on the pedal and pulled off into the median.

"That's a Trans Am rental!" howled Tecka as he pointed at the car racing towards them. As the car whizzed by, both agents noticed the yellow and black Hertz plate on the front and saw that the man driving looked like Lew Berry. "The car looks like the one Berry had rented for the week, and it sure looked like him driving."

"I think you're right. But the car was full of people. Lew doesn't know anyone down here since his son died. What's going on? And why is he driving like a bat out of hell?"

"We need to find out. Follow him!"

Jones made a U-turn in the muddy median and pulled out into the southbound traffic, then pounced on the accelerator. "Turn on the flasher. We need to have him pull over."

Tecka placed the blue light on the dash and was about to flick the switch when a thought occurred, and he paused. "Maybe we should just follow him, Jack. If he doesn't know anyone up in Seminole Bend, it's possible he's been hijacked by those other passengers. Let's see where they're taking him."

Agent Jones nodded and slowed to 105 mph, then shook his head and muttered, "Damn!". He calculated that the Trans Am was flying down the road near 120 mph, all while weaving in and out of traffic. It was a Saturday in March, and there were loads of Spring Breakers headed for the Keys. "He's going to kill somebody driving like that! I'm not sure how long we can stay on his tail."

Less than a half-hour later, the Trans Am slowed and exited at the Campbell Drive tollbooth. Three cars back was the FBI's dark blue Ford LTD, and both Jones and Tecka breathed a deep sigh of relief that everyone on the turnpike had survived. Jones flashed his badge at the tollbooth operator, and they pulled quickly out onto Campbell Drive.

Lew and company turned south on the Dixie Highway, then headed west towards the Everglades. A mile before the entrance to America's southernmost national park, Lew turned onto a service road. Jones and Tecka followed and noticed a small brown sign with white embossed letters that was posted next to the intersection. The sign read, *Florida Department of Natural Resources*. Jones looked over at his partner, and Tecka just shrugged his shoulders.

A quarter-mile down the road, tucked behind some shrubs, was an abandoned Nash Rambler. The FBI agents caught a flash of light as the sun reflected off the fender, and they stopped their car to investigate. Moments later, they were barreling down the road headed for the DNR office.

CHAPTER 68

Saturday, March 13, 1982

2:00 p.m.

Willy had been knocked unconscious by the butt of the guard's submachine gun seconds after opening the door to the video room in the small house. The guard struggled mightily but managed to lift the gigantic sheriff's deputy and put him in a wheelbarrow. He then rolled him for a mile back to the DNR office, stopping every thirty or so yards to catch his breath. Once there, he strapped every inch of Willy to a chair with duct tape. Willy looked like a silver mummy that decided to spend eternity in a sitting position.

The guard saw the Trans Am slam on its brakes in the parking lot, and he readied himself by pointing the Colt 9mm SMG at the front door. But no one entered. He walked over to the window and glanced out. For some strange reason, it appeared that there were four bodies slumped down in the seats, all peeking out the back window, while someone dressed in a police uniform was standing in the middle of the lot with a handgun pointed in the direction of the service road. The guard flinched and slid to the other side of the window to get a better view. As soon as he had arrived at the DNR office, he tried to call Governor Daughtry to tell him about the break-in to his video room and that he had the perpetrator tied up, but he got no answer. Should he try to call again?

Seconds later, a dark blue Ford LTD drove up the service road and then slammed on its brakes when the driver noticed a weapon pointed at his vehicle. The man in the uniform approached the car slowly, never dropping his aim, then motioned with his revolver for the driver and his passenger to get out. Both front doors of the LTD opened, and two men dressed in dark suits exited with their hands raised over their heads. The driver said something to the uniformed man, then reached in the pocket of his coat and pulled out a badge. The passenger did the same. The uniformed man holstered his pistol, flashed his own badge, and began to chat with the men. Then, a man wearing a Penn State sweatshirt got out of the Trans Am and walked up to the two men in the suits.

"Jones and Tecka, what are you doing here?" shouted the Penn State man as he approached.

"We were about to ask you the same question, Lew," answered Agent Jones. "We were headed to Seminole Bend when we saw your Trans Am flying down the road like a bat out of hell on the other side of the turnpike. What are you doing at the DNR office?"

Johnny Murphree, who had buckled his weapon firmly in his holster, interrupted. "So you are the FBI agents that are investigating Sheryl Berry's kidnapping?"

"Yes, that's how we know Lew. Why are you with him?" Agent Jones knew Johnny was a Seminole Bend sheriff's deputy after their short introduction, but that was all.

"We're here looking for my partner."

"You're looking for your partner riding with your uniform on in a rented vehicle?" Agent Jones stared at Johnny with a skeptical look. "That sounds a bit strange, wouldn't you say?"

"It's a long story, but never mind that. I noticed you following us as we exited at Homestead. Before we answer any questions, I'd like to know why the FBI would bother to pursue someone speeding? Why not just call the highway patrol?"

"We recognized the car first and then saw Lew driving with a carload of passengers. We didn't think Lew knew enough folks in Florida for a beach excursion to a southern Florida resort, so we were suspicious thinking he may have been apprehended."

"Why were you going to Seminole Bend, Jack?" asked Lew. "Looking for me?"

"Actually, no, and maybe Deputy Murphree here can answer a question for us that will explain the reason we were headed up there." Agent Jones glanced from Lew back to Johnny. "Is there a Willy Banks currently working for the sheriff's department?"

Lew and Johnny shot a puzzled look at each other while Otis, Lance, and Pancho walked up and joined the group.

"Deputy Banks is, or I should say was, the partner I was looking for. We knew he had come down here to talk to the DNR supervisor about something. Think his name is Sam Dulie."

Before Agent Jones could respond, Otis piped in. "Willy Banks, he's my brother." Otis placed his hands on his hips and gave Agent Jones an evil stare. "What you want with him?"

Lance wasn't about to be left out. "Yea, and Willy's my boss. Like Otis say, what you want with him?"

Agent Jones looked over at the skinny Mexican man, Pancho, who had been minding his own business but listening intently and couldn't help himself. "Let me guess, you must be Willy Bank's bodyguard," he said sarcastically as he eyed the Mexican man up and down.

"No, sir, but I did save his life. He be a good man. Sheriff Bonty, now he be a bad man. Real bad man. We need to find Willy cuz he might be in trouble." Jones looked at Tecka, and both were beginning to think that Willy Banks, who had broken into the FBI auto impound lot and stolen a metal box from Brett Berry's truck, may be a good guy after all. They decided the conversation needed to become serious again.

"Does your brother own a Nash Rambler?" Jones asked Otis.

"Dang tootin'! Nice wheels it is, too."

"It's parked down the road behind some bushes."

"What?! Where?!" exclaimed Otis.

"Willy's around here somewhere, and we need to find him." Jones led the seven men towards the entrance. As they opened the door, a Colt 9mm submachine gun was pointed directly at the bridge of Agent Jones' nose.

* * * * *

"Wait! Whoa! Hold on!" Agent Jones exclaimed as he raised his hands high over his head. "I'm FBI, and you don't want to do this!"

The guard moved the muzzle of the machine gun back and forth, catching aim at the whole crowd of stunned visitors. "Come in and lay down on the floor face first and put your hands behind your backs. Do it! Now!" The seven men came inside the DNR office and followed orders to a tee. Seated in a chair two feet behind the guard, wrapped in duct tape with only small slits for his eyes and nose, was a furious Willy Banks.

Knowing he had just one chance, Willy made the best of it. He lurched forward, and the top of his head hit the guard squarely in the back of the legs, buckling the man's knees. Unable to stop his momentum, Willy then smashed his nose on the dirty linoleum floor. Now, he was still bound by the gray tape, but in a most awkward, silly-looking position with his hind end in the air fastened tightly to the seat of the upside-down chair. Meanwhile, the guard let loose the gun to catch his own fall, and immediately Agent Jones scrambled and snatched it.

Jones aimed the weapon at the stunned guard, who quickly raised his hands above his head. "Please, sir, I was only doing what I was ordered. I promise."

Jones gave the gun to Agent Tecka, then with both hands, grabbed the guard by his neck and lifted him off the ground. Tecka reached into his suit pocket with one hand, walked over to the guard, and cuffed him. Jones pushed him to the wall. "Who ordered you?"

The guard said nothing. Tecka lifted the submachine gun and placed the nose of the muzzle directly on the frightened man's temple.

"Listen," stated Jones as he gripped his fingers tighter on the guard's neck. "I've got six witnesses," he paused and looked over at Willy, who was moaning and groaning face down on the floor. "Make that seven, assuming this fella is on our side, and considering you wrapped him up like a roach trapped on flypaper, I'd bet my last dollar he is on our side. Anyway, all these witnesses will confirm that you accidentally shot yourself with this here machine gun and left an awfully bloody mess. So, one last chance. Who ordered you?"

The guard didn't hesitate. "Governor Daughtry."

CHAPTER 69

Saturday, March 13, 1982

2:30 p.m.

Otis pulled out his pocket knife and began cutting through Willy's duct tape. He heard loud groans and thought his brother was in severe pain. After ripping a few shreds of tape off the middle of his back, Otis figured out he should probably cut a hole near Willy's mouth so he could breathe.

As soon as the hole was slit, Willy yelled, "Dang nab it, Otis, sit this dang chair back upright so all the blood in my body doesn't come squirting out my eyeballs!" Otis realized why Willy had been groaning.

Soon Willy was free, as too were his new DNR clothes. While Willy was complaining that the knife was scratching him, Otis told him, "I ain't no tape surgeon, bro, so just be happy I be cutting you out of this mess."

Willy stood up, naked once again, but lost his balance and slipped back on the chair. He had been through the mill the past twenty-four hours and needed a rest, but there wasn't time for that. He stood back up and lumbered over to the storage closet where he found one last size XL t-shirt and shorts belonging to the DNR softball team.

They all sat down in a small conference room with folding chairs and a card table. Poker was no doubt a favorite activity for DNR workers when they weren't freeing herons that were trapped in some careless fisherman's monofilament line. Agent Jones slammed the guard into a chair, but the guard had to bend forward because his arms were cuffed behind his back. Jones stood and hovered directly over the frightened young man.

"Before we start," Agent Jones said as he looked over at Willy. "Willy Banks, you've got some explaining to do. How is it that a sheriff's deputy would break into an FBI auto impound lot, steal something from a truck and then resist arrest to a federal officer?"

Willy didn't respond. Instead, he looked around at the crowd gathered before him. Willy assumed his buddy Johnny Murphree drove his brother Otis and Lance down here trying to find him, but he didn't know who the older gentleman wearing the Penn State sweatshirt could be. Then he looked at Pancho and did a double-take. "You're the man who saved my life out on the Kissimmee, ain't you?" Pancho nodded. Willy carefully stood back up, walked over to the Mexican man, and gave him an awkward hug. Sort of looked like a whale cuddling with a minnow.

He broke the embrace and looked at Lew, who had a lot of questions but was waiting for the appropriate time to ask them. Berry wasn't sure where he stood in the pecking order here.

"And who are you?" asked Willy.

"Lew Berry, sir. I'm Coach Brett Berry's dad. And it was me who drove everyone here."

"Coach's dad? Why are you here?"

"I'm looking for you, Willy. I think you can give me more information about Brett's death and Sheryl's disappearance."

"Yes, Mr. Berry, I think I can now give everyone here some vital information." Willy glanced over at the two FBI agents, then pointed to the back door. "I need to show you something, and the sooner, the better. But first, I want this man to answer a question." Willy leaned over the card table and peered into the nervous guard's eyes. "What exactly is that room in Daughtry's house used for?"

With eight pairs of angry, restless eyeballs staring at him, the guard had no choice but to cooperate. "I don't know, sir.

The governor ordered me never to enter the room. He called it a matter of national security. I was curious, yes, especially when he was talking about United States security, not just Florida's."

"What's in this room you're talking about?" inquired Agent Jones.

"Follow me," replied Willy. "I'll show you. But we must all move quickly. If I'm guessing right, there's something disastrous in the works. I'll explain everything after you see. Take the guard with us, I might have some more questions for him." Otis and Lance decided to do the honors, and they yanked and shoved the guard from the back door of the DNR office all the way to Daughtry's house.

CHAPTER 70

Saturday, March 13, 1982

4:00 p.m.

"This is incredible," declared Agent Jones as he looked around the secret room in Daughtry's house. Willy showed him the video feeds and remote controllers and how they operated. Then he pulled out a videotape for all to see. The room was utterly silent as the jet taxied down to the runway, and the words *Jam Disengaged ORD* flashed across the screen.

As the plane rose above the Sears Tower and turned south, Willy said, "I don't understand what ORD is? I believe it's a code for Orlando, but the plane is obviously in Chicago."

Agent Tecka replied, "ORD is the airport code for O'Hare, which is in Chicago." All eyes were focused on the television.

A few moments later, the words *Jam Disengaged TPA* appeared. Agent Jones interrupted the eerie silence. "Damn. Someone must be controlling the radar functions in Chicago and Tampa. Daughtry, you suppose?" The question was rhetorical. No one bothered to answer.

"Hold on," exclaimed Willy. "It gets worse." They all watched closely as Willy fast-forwarded the video feed. Even the guard was stunned as the warning *Jam Engaged TPA* appeared, and the plane veered southwest towards Lake Okeechobee, turbulently bouncing directly in the path of a vicious storm.

Suddenly there was a flash of light, and the video feed abruptly ended. "Oh my God!" was groaned in unison from the stupefied viewers. Lew Berry walked out of the room quickly and vomited in the kitchen. He didn't make it to the sink. Agent Jones glanced at Agent Tecka, and both ran to Lew, holding him upright as his knees began to buckle underneath.

"I'm sorry, Lew, we simply forgot," said Jones compassionately. "Your wife was on that flight. We are so very sorry." They helped Lew to a chair and brought him a glass of water. The others in the room had no idea that Coach Berry's mother had died in that crash.

"You need to see this," Willy quietly said to the FBI agents as they were comforting Lew. Pancho nodded to Jones and Tecka, and he sat down with Lew so the agents could follow Willy back into the video room.

"I may have accidentally killed a man," said Willy somberly. He showed the replay of the car crossing the median, then changing course abruptly before flipping over. "In front of the televisions are some sort of remotes. They control whatever machine or vehicle is being fed by the video. I didn't know that, and I caused this accident."

"That's exactly how my son's truck crashed, wasn't it?" Lew Berry had reentered the room and was watching from the door. "But you said it wasn't Sheryl in the truck, so who could it have been that Daughtry wanted to kill?"

Now the group was listening intensely as the FBI agents hesitantly gave out information that was classified. "We believe the person in Coach Berry's truck was a man who was already dead, and now the whole thing looks to be a setup. Daughtry wanted to make it look like a simple accident and that Sheryl Berry was killed. Brett died trying to save her in the culvert. We believe she was kidnapped."

"It's not Daughtry, Agent Jones," interrupted Willy. "A rancher named Roy Jackson and the sheriff of Seminole Bend are in cahoots and have been doing atrocious acts for quite some time. I thought it was drug running, but now I think that was a decoy for something even bigger."

"He's right," added Johnny Murphree. "Willy was close to finding something out, so Sheriff Bonty had him fired."

"I know this probably has nothing to do with what's happening here, but it's been bothering me, and I need to know," Lew piped in. "I was on my way back to Seminole Bend after leaving the FBI headquarters to find a picture. You see, a few days ago me and a new friend named Phil Bennett broke into my son's house to check out his belongings. We heard someone scrambling upstairs after we came in through the patio door that we just smashed in, but whoever it was jumped out the second-floor hallway window and ran to the golf course. He was carrying what looked like a shoebox or something. Anyway, we found several framed pictures all over the place. But in a nightstand in the master bedroom was a Polaroid picture of Sheryl, who was on a beach and very pregnant at the time. Something about that picture was bugging me, so I went back the next day. When I got there, the house had been broken into, and the master bedroom was in shambles. There was no jewelry box in the house, so I'm assuming that's what the thief took, but that jewelry box could have been taken by the unknown jumper the day before. Don't really know. Anyway, here's the strange thing. The Polaroid picture of Sheryl on the beach was missing from the nightstand. I can't figure out why an intruder would want a cheap personal picture."

"Why didn't you report the break-ins, Lew?" asked Johnny Murphree. "We should be investigating those kind of things, and you should know that."

"After my little chat with Sheriff Bonty, do you really think I trusted the sheriff's department with an investigation? Come on, you got to be kidding me! And besides that, I had broken in myself and didn't want to be explaining why I did."

"So what's bugging you about the photo, Lew?" asked Willy.

"I don't know, really. Your brother's girlfriend, Abby, showed me some other pictures of Brett coaching the team, you know, just to be nice. She said some guy named Danny Martin had taken them, but she didn't know him. Said he was some huge cowboy dude. Anyway, there was a picture of Brett in the package with some players after beating Sebring."

"So what's the problem? Did Abby identify all the players?"

"Yes, but it's not the players that are confusing me. It's something else in the picture, and I think it's related to that Polaroid in Brett's drawer. I've got the picture Abby gave me in my car. I'd like to take another look at it."

Just then, the video feed from the first television began to roll. It was streaming a live shot of the same man Willy saw earlier wearing the dark blue NTSB windbreaker. He was now leaving the building, and Agent Jones leaned forward, his eyes opening wide. Jones got a close look at the man's face. "Well, I'll be damned! It's Bob Cummings."

"Who's Bob Cummings?" asked Willy.

"Head of the Miami office of the National Transportation Safety Board. He's in charge of both the Miami and Lake Okeechobee airplane crashes. Why is he –" Agent Jones stopped abruptly. "Daughtry is targeting him! We need to warn him."

"I think we're okay," responded Willy. "If this place is the control center, there's no one here to operate the remotes. But I need to show you something else. Do you remember the box I took from Berry's truck?"

"How could I forget?!"

"Well, I think it was the remote control receiver for the truck, but it also had a strange marking engraved on it. That same marking is engraved on a big dish-like thing outside of Dulie's office at the DNR. I think that dish is how Dulie and Daughtry operate those videos and remote controllers. And it may be how they jam those radars, too, I don't know."

"What does this engraving look like?" asked Agent Jones.

"It's hard to explain. I need to show you. The box is in my car. We need to get it and then compare it with the dish."

"Okay. But first I need to call in our tech unit to examine this room. Tom, call Toby and get his team down to the DNR's office right away. They can track all the wiring and stuff from there to here. And Tom, tell Toby this is very top secret. I don't want the newspapers finding out and starting a scare before we know what we have, got it?"

"Got it. Let's move, boys!"

CHAPTER 71
Saturday, March 13, 1982
5:00 p.m.

The men hiked swiftly back to the DNR office, then Willy jogged up the service road and drove his Nash Rambler down to the parking lot. Moments later, he showed Jones and Tecka the etched markings on the metal box, then led them out back to the satellite dish, where they confirmed the markings on the box and the dish were a perfect match. Tecka glanced at Jones and said, "It's Arabic writing. I don't know what it says, but it's definitely Arabic."

"I think maybe the supervisor, Sam Dulie, is from the Middle East somewhere," said Willy. "I noticed right away that he had dark skin and eyes."

"You don't find Sam Dulie's in Arab countries," retorted Agent Tecka.

Agent Jones glanced at the metal box, and then to the writing on the satellite dish. It was evident that something was bothering him. "What is it?" asked Johnny Murphree. Everyone shot a look at the FBI agent.

"This writing. I remember that I saw Arabic writing somewhere earlier today, but it didn't hit me until just now."

"Where did you see Arabic writing, Jack?" asked Agent Tecka. "You've been with me all day. I didn't see anything."

"Yes, Tom, I think you did. Remember watching the playback of Willy accidentally crashing that car by using the remote control? There was a billboard along the highway right at the beginning of the tape. I swear the writing was in Arabic."

"If that's the case, are you thinking the car was in an Arab country?"

Willy interrupted, "That would make sense. It was in the middle of the night here when I was fiddling around with that joystick. It would've been daylight over there in the Middle East, right?"

"Right," replied Agent Jones. "When our specialists get here, we need to go examine that tape again."

*****

Waiting in the DNR's conference room for the FBI techies to arrive, Willy revealed his story as completely, yet succinctly, as possible. He started with his investigation back in January at the Jackson ranch, where he saw a small aircraft drop floating containers on the swamp, and how his partner, Sam McCormick, jumped in to retrieve one and hasn't been seen since. He painted a grisly picture of his encounter with the alligator as he was trying to escape from the ranch, and how Pancho had saved his life. Willy then disclosed the strange circumstances surrounding the Calvin and Agnes Potts' deaths, and his own encounter with Roy Jackson's thugs in the BoldMart parking lot. Sheriff Bonty stated that Willy's handling of the situation was ultimately the reason he fired him.

Willy explained that he hired Otis and Lance to try and find Pancho while he headed to Miami to speak to DNR supervisor, Sam Dulie. He wanted to know if Dulie had provided information to Roy Jackson about the boat Pancho had taken. If he had leaked that information, there would be a possible link that resulted in the Potts' murders. He explained why he broke into the FBI auto impound lot to examine Brett Berry's truck, and how he wound up finding Daughtry's video room.

Lew followed Willy's narrative by replaying his week in Florida and how he met Phil Bennett and became friends. He mentioned discovering Pancho's friend, Miguel, and then carefully detailed the submarine container that ran from Oliver Harfield's estate to the Kissimmee River. Mouths flew wide open as Lew annotated Miguel's murder and subsequent consumption in the belly of a Burmese python. He then explained why he believed Sheriff Bonty was involved in some sort of cover-up and relayed the horrific events the night of the airplane crash.

While Willy and Lew were painting a vivid picture of corruption in Seminole Bend, Agent Tecka was taking notes while Agent Jones was mapping out the chronology of events. He thought about all the people involved and tried to connect the dots. Johnny Murphree was standing next to the FBI agents providing guidance and clarity when needed.

After Lew finished speaking, Otis asked a question. "Mr. Lew, you was telling us 'bout a picture that Abby gave you from some dude called Danny. Can we take a peek at it?"

Lew had the envelope with pictures on the table next to him. "Sure, take a look. I still feel like something's not right, but I can't place it. Maybe all of you could help." He pulled out the photo of the celebration after the Sebring basketball game and handed it to Otis.

"Yep," exclaimed Otis as he smiled proudly while pointing at a figure in the picture. "That there is my nephew Tyrone. Dang good player, he is. He lives with me and Willy, sure does."

"It's not the players or Brett that bothers me," said Lew shaking his head. "It's something else." He was about to spell out his thoughts when six FBI techies entered the room. Jones and Tecka stood up and approached them, said a few words, and then Tecka yanked Daughtry's personal guard off his chair and led him to the door. Jones showed the techies Sam Dulie's desk and pointed to the satellite dish that was outside the window while Tecka locked the guard in the back seat of the FBI vehicle.

“Let’s start out there,” said Agent Toby Brewer as he motioned to the dish. “Whatever else is happening here is being run through that thing. There’s an uplink transmitting antenna in the middle of that damn thing.”

“Speak English, Toby,” replied Agent Jones.

“Well, let’s go take a closer look, but I can tell from here that dish out there is what they call an uplink transmitting satellite dish. It sends electronic signals to a transponder satellite just outside the earth’s atmosphere. Then, it converts those signals to a different frequency and sends it back to earth to some receiver on the ground. That’s what is known as a downlink.”

Lance’s eyes opened wide, and he interrupted, “Science fiction right here where we standing! Wow!”

“Fiction is not the right word, sir,” responded Agent Brewer. “That thing has the capability of doing really bad things. And that’s the truth!”

CHAPTER 72

Saturday, March 13, 1982
6:00 p.m.

"Why did you bring me here?" she asked nervously. "I've done what you asked. You said I could go live a normal life when it was all over."

"Because you messed up! You were supposed to rendezvous back at Oliver's last Tuesday. Where the hell have you been?" barked Roy.

"Someone broke into the house while I was upstairs," she replied. "I grabbed the jewelry box and jumped out the second-floor window and ran out onto the golf course. I hurt my ankle, but I went back later for the picture."

"Lew Berry," inserted Sheriff Al Bonty into the conversation. "He's been snooping around and would be the only one who would break into his own son's house. And the man also embarrassed me in my own sheriff's office, in front of my men, dang nab it! I can arrest him for breaking and entering if you want. That would keep him out of the picture. I think Murphree and Willy Banks are involved with him, too. Those two will probably call in the FBI, if I know them."

They were sitting in Oliver Harfield's private jet on the tarmac at Orlando International Airport.

"Right now, we need to stick to the plan, Al. After Daughtry and Dulie drop Tyrus off at the Nike base in Key Largo, they're meeting us here. They should arrive any minute. Afterward, I'll personally deal with Lew Berry. When I'm done with him, you won't need to take up space in your jailhouse, either!"

"Can't you leave him alone?" she asked. "Haven't you taken everything that Lew Berry cherishes already? Give him some peace. He'll go away eventually."

Oliver had been sitting there mildly listening while looking out the small passenger window. "You're right, Roy. We need to get rid of him. We've been planning the end game for over twenty years, and we don't need to be tripped up now. Put him on a doomed plane back to Pittsburgh if you have to."

"What about me?" she asked with a hint of desperation in her voice. "I gave you the jewelry box and left the master bedroom in disarray so it would look like a burglary. If and when the FBI finds the hand and the ring out in the swamp, and if they are smart enough to figure out some things, they will come looking and notice the jewelry box missing. Here's the picture." She tossed the Polaroid print over to Oliver. "Now, am I free to go?"

Oliver stood up and pushed the lady face-first onto the floor. While kneeling on her back, he pulled out handcuffs and fastened her right arm to a bracket under the seat. Her belly was squished, and she screamed in pain.

"Sorry sweetheart, we have other plans for you now," said Oliver with a wink and a smile.

"Lighten up a bit," said Sheriff Bonty. "Keep her chained, but get off her damned back."

The Sikorsky helicopter touched down gently next to Harfield's jet. Governor Daughtry came out first, followed by DNR Supervisor Sam Dulie and Yussef. Two Arab men emerged out of the cargo hold rolling a huge bronze chest. They needed a small hydraulic lift, which had been tucked away on the helicopter, to boost the chest up to the jet's plug door. When the chest had been loaded, and everyone was on board, the door was closed, and they all took seats on the comfortable leather swivel chairs and gazed at the lady lying on the floor.

“A gift for your father, the prince,” said Roy to Yussef as he gestured at the body weeping below him. “He will soon rule the world.”

“The stolen Soviet MiG-25 Foxbat with the two nuclear warheads should be taking off from the Baku airbase in thirty minutes,” stated Yussef matter-of-factly. He was a scientist and engineer, and now merely spitting out information with no emotion. “The distance of 6,845 miles to our target in Miami can be covered in about three and a half hours flying at the max speed of 2,170 miles per hour. Our pilot will eject near Bimini Island, and the autopilot is programmed to take it from there. The jet will need to slow down to sub-mach speed and descend to 20,000 feet for the ejection to be safe, but at that point, the aircraft is only eighty miles from its target. That will be the start of what my father has dreamed of his entire life.”

“And the remote controllers are in the helicopter?” asked Oliver.

“Yes, there are enough remotes and equipment in there now to reconfigure a much larger new guidance facility in Gainesville.”

“And, Roy, the radar jammers have been moved from your ranch?” Oliver was quizzing the group to ensure there were no leaks in the plan.

“The trucks are on the way to the various airports with the jammers and a bunch of decoy goods, like computers, onboard just for looks. Tyrus shut down the factory in Columbia before he left. As you know, his name is listed on the manifest as being on the Sky Tropic Airways flight that collided with the Heartland Lakes plane so there won’t be any trace of him.”

“Hank, you told your staff that you are on retreat at your hideaway in Homestead, right?” The governor nodded. “And Sam, your crew thinks you are staying overnight at the DNR office tonight to catch up on some work, yes or no?”

"Yes, sir, that's correct," replied Dulie. "The entire state of Florida will be mourning the death of their beloved governor and me very soon." Sam chuckled under his breath.

"Excellent!" stated Oliver. "Tomorrow morning, the United States of America will believe we've been attacked by the Soviet Union following the dropping of a nuclear warhead near Miami. The explosion will destroy all the old evidence in Hank's video room and Sam's office, which is only a mile away from the target. We will set up our new video guidance facility under the O'Sullivan Center in Gainesville next week. The trick will be rigging the air traffic control centers' radar equipment. But Jake Tassett plans to use his NTSB credentials to do a fake routine check of the equipment as he did in all the Florida airports and Chicago. Hopefully, no one will notice him installing the jammers. He should have all the airports ready to go in three weeks."

"Are the Nike bases rigged and ready?" asked Roy.

"As you know, using Prince Adil's generous oil money, we have purchased two Nike locations in the south. The Navy had transferred the Key Largo facility to the Air Force last month, and using Sam's and Hank's authorizations, we offered them several million dollars for it. We claimed the DNR wanted to reforest the location. Tyrus has temporarily relocated there.

"Then up at the old Nike base in Albany, Georgia, we bought the land and built an alcohol and drug rehabilitation center on top of it. Figured that would keep the feds away! Tyrus has a man he employed down in Columbia who seems quite capable of holding down that fort. His name is, get this, Jim Brown. Hasn't rushed for any touchdowns, though, as far as I know!" Oliver laughed at his own wit, and the others smiled.

"I'm assuming the missiles are now locked and loaded?" questioned Roy.

"Yes, and our inside source at the White House will book President Layman for an immediate visit to Miami on

Monday to examine the destruction. We were only able to rig up an old Nike Hercules for the Key Largo site, but it should still be able to take out Air Force One. However, the range is only eighty-seven miles, so Albany is a backup in case Largo misses, and Air Force One turns around and hightails back north to Washington. We've got a Zeus-B loaded up there with Mach four speed and a longer range."

"What if that one misses, Oliver, then what?"

"Won't really matter if the president lives or dies. Either way, the US will assume that Russian missiles were targeting Layman, and it won't take long for the Cold War to become a very hot one!

"And my father?" asked Yussef. "When will he become the new world ruler?"

"As soon as we're done here, you and Sam and I will fly to Al Qadir to set up a communications base with a direct link to our operations center that Ray Jackson has created in Gainesville," replied Oliver. "Chances are minimal that the op center will ever be discovered as it is well hidden under the O'Sullivan Center. Once the jammers are in place, we will create a massive hostage situation in the skies. Ray has hired a staff of operators in Gainesville who will take control of several planes full of passengers, but even if the pilots somehow regain control of their aircraft, the jamming equipment will create havoc in the air and on the ground. At that point, your father will contact Vice President Matthews, who will then be President Matthews, assuming, of course, we were able to take down Air Force One with Layman in it. The prince will demand the immediate release of the USS Halibut that is currently mothballed at the Kitsap Naval Base near Seattle. As you know, we were successful in secretly boarding the submarine and rigging its two Regulus missile launchers with the most powerful and destructive nuclear warheads in the world. Each warhead could destroy a swath of land so large it would wipe out every building from Washington, DC, to Boston, including New York and Philly."

"How long will it take to fire up and deploy the Halibut?" asked Daughtry.

"We have a crew of fifteen men stationed at Kitsap that were supposedly transferred there from other naval bases on the order of Admiral Inman, who happens to be a friend of Ray's. It took the good Admiral a mere five minutes to renounce his patriotism and accept Ray's leather briefcase loaded with cash! The estimated time to board and secure the sub is approximately a half-hour. They will need to diesel through the Puget Sound for another half-hour before they can submerge into the Pacific Ocean. I would expect no orders from the higher-ups to attack and sink the Halibut seeing the two warheads onboard would devastate everything from Vancouver to Portland. Meanwhile, the hijacked civilian planes will all have about five hours of fuel; thus, the president's window to make a decision on the ransom is roughly three hours before the jets come crashing to the ground. Once the nuclear submarine and the fate of the world is under the Prince's control, we will all be headed off to our retirement islands with enough wealth to enjoy each and every day left in our lives!"

Just then, the gal cuffed to the seat bracket began to moan and turn pale. They all could see it was no bluff, she was in deep pain.

Roy knelt down beside her and felt for a pulse on her neck. The lady's skin was cold and her heartbeat erratic. "Give me the keys, Oliver."

Oliver sighed, but then reluctantly handed Roy the keys and he unfastened the cuffs. Roy then rolled the lady over on her back.

"She needs some help," Roy said to Oliver. "We need to get her to a doctor now! I don't care what happens to her, but we need to save the baby. That's my grandson she's carrying!"

CHAPTER 73

Sunday, March 14, 1982

12:15 a.m.

"This is all quite sophisticated," exclaimed Agent Toby Brewer. After the FBI team completed a thorough photo session documenting every piece of equipment and cables in the DNR office, Willy had led the team back to Daughtry's house. "The videotapes are enough to send the governor and Dulie to the electric chair. Willy, show me the playback of the car you were controlling."

Willy reluctantly switched on the second television and rewound the tape to where he began the remote control. He pushed the play button.

"Slow it down to almost nothing," ordered Brewer. Willy held down the slow-motion feed button. "There, pause it!" Willy pressed pause.

"What is it, Toby?" asked Agent Jones. "What do you see?"

"The billboard off the highway to the right. It's in Arabic. I believe it's advertising for a gas station in Fayez in ten kilometers, which is about six miles."

"So, they're on the outskirts of the Jasurbian capital?" asked Agent Tecka.

"That would appear to be the area. Obviously, it's a desert location because you see only brown sand all around."

"Whose car would Daughtry want to control in Jasurbia?" inquired Jones with a puzzled look.

* * * * *

Tyrus Banks was in the living quarters connected to the underground Nike base control center in Key Largo. He had left three messages for Jim Brown, his counterpart in Gainesville, and was becoming very nervous. Jim was flying back from his mission in Baku but should have arrived in Florida by now. It was one o'clock, and he couldn't sleep, so Tyrus switched on CNN to clear his mind. The headlines out of the Middle East were shocking. Crown Prince Hakim's limousine driver had lost control of the royal vehicle outside of Fayez, crossed the median and flipped several times. The crown prince, who was also the Jasurbian defense minister, died instantly.

Tyrus sat up, now fully awake, and stared at the TV to watch the never-ending video feed that was live from the scene. "How could this happen?" Tyrus muttered to himself.

He got on the phone and tried to call Jim Brown one more time. No luck, so he left another message: "Crown Prince Hakim was killed in a car accident. According to the time of death, Daughtry was with me in the helicopter, so it wasn't him who did it. Someone must have broken into the house, but who would know about the video controls? I'm going over there to check it out. I'll call when I find something out."

Tyrus had never seen Daughtry's control center, but Jim Brown had faxed him an architectural drawing of the house with the video room clearly delineated. Brown found the drawing on a desk while meeting with Ray Jackson in the secret facility under the O'Sullivan Center. In a handwritten note faxed with the drawing, Brown spelled out precisely what Daughtry was doing in the country house. The plan was to relocate the control center to the Gainesville location and then destroy all the evidence with the nuclear blast from the Russian MiG-25 Foxbat.

Tyrus got dressed and ran to his leased Jeep Wagoneer. He knew the Russian fighter jet would be crashing down on top of him if he wasn't out of Daughtry's house by four o'clock at the latest. Jim Brown supposedly had dismantled the nuclear warheads on the MiG and replaced them with a series of incendiary bombs, which would be ignited by the explosion from the jet. Those bombs would destroy Daughtry's house and the DNR office a mile away, but keep Miami and the surrounding cities from being leveled.

Thirty minutes later, Tyrus pulled up to Daughtry's country home and noticed lights on inside. He parked behind some bushes a hundred yards away and grabbed his own Colt 9mm submachine gun from the back seat. The assault weapons were standard issue by Oliver Harfield's team, and an abundance of the guns was kept at Roy Jackson's ranch. Everyone on Team Harfield carried one or had it tucked away close by.

Tyrus crept to the house in a slow, sinuous manner. He guessed that Daughtry's guard most likely would be sleeping just inside the locked and barricaded front door, but why would the lights be left on? Tyrus peeked through the window and saw silhouettes dancing on the wall in the back room. He pulled out the architectural drawing and knew that whoever was here was in the video room.

Tyrus crept towards the front door to try the lock, but there was no lock in sight. Whoever was inside had blasted their way in using a powerful weapon. Tyrus pushed on the metal door, and it squeaked open. He aimed his Colt 9mm and walked inside, then moved the gun back and forth while surveying the room. Voices could be heard coming from the video room. Tyrus inched slowly past the kitchen to the doorway.

"Hit the floor, all of you!" screamed Tyrus, then fired a round at the ceiling. "Now! Facedown! Move it!"

Instinctively, the FBI agents and Johnny Murphree raised their arms, then dropped to their knees and finally laid down on their stomachs, noses resting on the linoleum. Otis, Lance, and Pancho dove to the ground, all fearing this was the last minute of their lives. Lew got down on all fours and began having heart palpitations. Willy raised his arms and dropped to his knees, but then paused and lowered his arms. His back was to the armed intruder.

"Hands back up in the air, or you're a dead man!" shouted Tyrus to Willy.

"Tyrus, is that you? It's me, man. Your brother, Willy." Slowly, Willy turned around on his knees to face Tyrus.

Tyrus tossed the gun on the floor and bear-hugged his little brother. Willy rose and squeezed back. Otis popped his head up and said, "Tyrus, you here? You not dead, bro? Man, I ain't seen you in a whole buncha years!"

Tyrus broke Willy's embrace and lifted Otis off the floor, then crunched him to his chest. "Otis, what you doing here?"

Agent Jones pulled a revolver out of the holster that was tucked underneath his windbreaker and aimed it at Tyrus' temple. "Sorry to break up this family reunion, but you are under arrest."

Willy quickly stepped between Jones' gun and his two brothers, then raised his arms up over his head. "Sir, my brother's weapon is lying on the floor, and he's greatly outnumbered here. He isn't going anywhere, so please put your weapon down, and let's get some answers."

Tyrus stepped around his brother with his hands reaching high above his shoulders. Each of the FBI agents now had their weapons drawn. "I don't have time to explain, but we all need to get away from here quickly. This place and the DNR office will soon be destroyed by an aircraft carrying incendiary bombs. I didn't see any cars out front. How did you get here?"

"Not so fast, Tyrus," replied Agent Jones, still refusing to lower his aim. "It is Tyrus if I heard your brother right, correct? But we're not going anywhere until you answer some questions."

Lew interrupted, "Come on, Jack. Put cuffs on him or whatever, but if he's telling the truth, none of us should be here. There's been two mid-air crashes in the last month in

Florida, and you just saw what those remote controls can do. Let's get out of here!"

"Our cars are back at the DNR," said Agent Jones as he pulled out his handcuffs and snapped them on Tyrus' wrists. "How much time do we have?"

"Not enough to get to the DNR. I have a Jeep Wagoneer that seats six, and we can cram another three in the rear compartment. The other two of y'all will have to climb on top and hold on to the luggage racks."

"That'll have to do. Let's go!"

With cuffs tightly grappled to his wrists, Tyrus hustled Willy, Otis, Lance, Pancho, Lew, Johnny, and the five FBI agents to the Jeep. Agent Jones ordered Willy to drive with Tyrus in the front middle seat and Agent Tecka by the passenger side window. Jones offered to ride on the roof with Agent Brewer.

Willy floored the Jeep down the driveway and turned abruptly onto the road headed for the Nike base in Key Largo, then slammed on the brakes. Jones and Brewer slid off the top and rolled onto the hood, while Pancho flew from the cargo hold into the back seat.

"What the hell are you doing?" yelled Tecka as Willy jumped out to check on the condition of Jones and Brewer, who were shaken up and visibly upset.

"The guard!" shouted Willy. "We left the guard locked up inside Agent Jones' car back at the DNR. He'll be killed. We need to get him out of there."

"Collateral damage," clamored Agent Brewer. "We ain't got time, and the man worked for Daughtry. Leave him!"

"No way, man. This is America, and he's innocent until we prove him guilty in a court of law. We're gonna get him, so get back up on the roof." There wasn't time to argue. Jones and Brewer climbed up on the roof, this time grabbing the rack as tightly as possible, and Willy U-turned the Jeep around and bolted for the DNR.

CHAPTER 74

Sunday, March 14, 1982

3:00 a.m.

Years ago, Yussef and Hank Daughtry had enrolled in an elective course at Yale called *Genetic Reproduction*, only because it was held at a time during the day that didn't interfere with soccer practice. The chapter in their textbook that provided an overview of the female reproductive system now came in very handy. Together, they delivered a tiny, red-faced baby boy with a small patch of shiny black hair on the crown of his head. Although he was a month premature, his lungs were indeed in proper working order. Screams were echoing off the cylindrical walls of Oliver's private jet.

"Give that child something to eat, damn it!" ordered Oliver. He was frustrated and anxious. Delivering a baby on board his private aircraft at this critical moment in time was not in his master plan.

The infant's mom held the newborn tightly to her chest, feeding and securing him at the same time. This was her only child, and her motherly protective instinct kicked in. She feared for her own safety but trembled at the thought of what might happen to her son.

"I will take care of my grandson," announced Roy as he stood over the boy and his mother. "As for you, young lady, you were promised to Prince Adil for his harem, so you will be flying on to Al Qadir."

Roy waited for a few moments for the baby to finish his first meal, then tried to lift him off his mother. But mom refused to let go of her newborn son. Yussef pulled back her right arm while Hank clutched her left arm, then Roy picked up his grandson and departed down the gangway.

The boy was wrapped in towels that were stored in the cargo hold, then carried to the airport infirmary. Roy was an expert liar, a grand champion in that arena. He explained to the nurses that the baby was born while in the air, and told them the mother was being cared for by a doctor who was on board. He assured the medical staff that he would reunite the infant with his mom and the doctor as soon as they cleaned him up. The nurses bought the story: hook, line, and sinker.

Meanwhile, Oliver's jet taxied to the runway and moments later was airborne, destined for Al Qadir. One passenger was feeling immense pain, not from the miracle of childbirth, but from a broken heart.

CHAPTER 75

Sunday, March 14, 1982
9:00 a.m. (Baku Time Zone)

Yakov Slivko had piloted the MiG-25 Foxbat for the Russian Air Force many times, but never with a cargo of nuclear weapons. And he certainly never dreamed of betraying his country and stealing one of its most prized military possessions. That was until he met Jim Brown and was handed a check for 800,000 Soviet Rubles written from a Swiss bank account. He would redeposit the check in a new Nassau bank account for a little over one million Bahamian dollars, and then spend the rest of his life fishing for blue marlin in the Bermuda Triangle.

It was 9:00 a.m. in Baku when Yakov achieved Mach one speed on the supersonic interceptor as the mighty jet circled over the Caspian Sea bearing south-southwest towards Baghdad, then in a westerly direction over the Mediterranean Sea. Nearing the Jordan border with Iraq, Yakov pushed the throttle down to provide full thrust, and the plane glided through the thin cirrostratus cloud layers towards the edge of the atmosphere. As the MiG-25 began to level off, Yakov felt an enormous shaking and the shrieking sound of stress on the airframe. He gripped the wheel with all his strength and tried to throttle down, but the controls were unresponsive. The autopilot was always disengaged when Yakov was piloting the aircraft because he enjoyed the thrill of flying the Foxbat himself and performing a few barrel rolls to alleviate boredom. But now Yakov had mysteriously lost all control, yet, the jet was engaging its ailerons and banking back towards the east at a steep angle. He hit the kill switch on engine number one to slow the jet down, but nothing happened. Yakov was much too high and going way too fast to eject now. For the first time in his military life, Yakov was scared.

Jim Brown had his right hand on the joystick while he examined the radar control screen in front of him. With a few strokes of the keyboard with his left hand, he locked the coordinates onto the target. After sneaking on board the MiG, Jim didn't have enough time to reconfigure the fighter jet's auto-guidance system, so he would have to manually guide the plane to its destination.

To ensure that his strategy would work, Jim told no one about his redirected plan. He had even lied to Tyrus, making his colleague think the jet was re-rigged with incendiary bombs and on its way to Florida to destroy the evidence left at the governor's house and the DNR office. Instead, the two nuclear weapons were fully engaged and ready for some massive destruction.

Suddenly, the Foxbat fell into a nosedive. Yakov pressed the ejection seat button, but to no avail. He closed his eyes and said a prayer.

Seconds later, an explosion erupted, sending a dense cloud upward and outward that could be seen for hundreds of miles. The ground shook from Dubai to Tel Aviv. Arab geologists hypothesized that an earthquake of substantial magnitude had just occurred, while newscasters and reporters hustled to their vans to try and find the epicenter.

The video camera that Jim Brown had installed on the nose of the MiG-25 stopped abruptly upon impact, but he could see from the radar screen that the Foxbat had hit its target dead center. Prince Adil's palace and communications center would be no more. Jim lamented for a moment as he pondered the collateral damage that had been done: the Prince's harem and innocent workers from Pakistan being paid slave wages. But he couldn't let that cloud the bigger picture. He turned to the man who was chained and gagged lying on a cot in the O'Sullivan Center control room. Jim pulled out a Gillette safety razor from a sheath attached to his belt and twisted it back and forth inches from the dude's petrified eyes.

The slow, clean slice from one side of Ray's neck to the other was profoundly penetrating and extremely painful. The towering spurts of blood decorated the walls like a splatter paint abstract.

Ray Jackson's brother Roy was now an only child.

CHAPTER 76

Sunday, March 14, 1982

3:30 a.m.

It was 3:30 a.m. when the Jeep screeched to a halt in the DNR parking lot. The FBI agents raced to their cars, Jones and Tecka getting into the front seat while Daughtry's guard sat cuffed in the back. Agent Brewer's team of techies hopped in their vehicle, while Lew, Pancho, Otis, and Lance loaded into the Trans Am. Willy and Johnny both filed into the front seat of the Jeep with Tyrus. All four vehicles spun tires violently, then wildly fishtailed down the service road, kicking up dust and gravel. A rock hit Lew's rental and cracked the windshield, but he stayed with the pack as the four cars screeched out onto the main road.

Willy turned to Tyrus and gave him an inquisitive look. "What are you involved in, Tyrus? What happened to you, man?"

"I'll tell you and the FBI the whole story when we get to the Nike base. Just hang in there, okay, Bro?"

"Okay," replied Willy as he and Johnny braced themselves on the dashboard.

"But Willy, just one question," said Tyrus somberly. "How are Abby and my baby boy? What does he look like now?"

Willy pulled out a cracked and faded picture from his wallet taken two years ago when Tyrone was in junior high. "Abby is as gorgeous as ever, Ty. Never did get married. She never found anyone to love like she did you. And Tyrone, he's quite an athlete. But more than that, he's quite a good man. They live with me, Ty."

Tyrus didn't respond. He held the picture in his right hand and steered with his left. Tears were dripping down onto his cheeks.

After a few moments of complete silence, Tyrus glanced at Willy and said, "Hold the wheel, Willy. I got something to show ya." Willy reached over and placed his hands on the steering wheel while Tyrus took a worn down and slightly ripped envelope from his back pocket. He handed the envelope to his brother, then took control of the wheel. "I've carried this on me everywhere I've been for the past sixteen years, Willy. It's the only thing that's kept me going."

Willy opened the unsealed envelope and pulled out a Polaroid instant photo and a note. The colors had dissolved into a dull reddish-orange tone, but Willy knew right away what he was looking at. It was Abby in the hospital maternity ward with newborn Tyrone. The baby was grasping a miniature cloth basketball with his tiny fingers, and his eyes were closed. Willy then read the note:

bro, yur an uncle and baby name is Tyrone and now yur uncle willy and abby is good and they come home tomoro.

"My God, Ty, why didn't you mail this?!" asked Willy. "I was in Nam at the time, but I still would've gotten it."

"That's where my story begins, Bro. But I need to tell the FBI, too."

*****

The four cars wound through the swampy underbrush path to the hidden Nike base. The men exited their vehicles, and Tyrus motioned frantically with his arms and pointed to the metal door that was built into the ground. "Get in there, fast! Bring the guard. I'm hoping we're far enough away from where the MiG will crash, but I don't want to take any chances."

Everyone climbed into the Nike facility and stood with their mouths wide open. They were marveling at this high tech operations center built into an old, deserted, and dilapidated missile launch site from the Korean War era. The video equipment rivaled what they saw at Daughtry's house. Tyrus flipped a switch on two TVs, then punched in some numbers on a computer keyboard. The video feed began to sweep the skies.

"Something's wrong," stated Tyrus as he glanced at both television screens. "Wait here." Tyrus grabbed a pair of binoculars off the desk and went outside. Everyone glanced at each other, wondering what Tyrus was doing. Two minutes later, he returned.

"There's nothing in the sky. The MiG-25 should have crashed by now."

"MiG-25?" questioned Agent Jones. "MiG jets are Soviet-made. Are you saying the jet is being flown from Russia?" A vision of World War Three was swimming around in his mind.

Before he could respond, Tyrus noticed the red light on his answering machine was lit. He picked up the receiver and hit the play button. Tyrus cranked up the volume. Willy and the FBI needed to be in the loop:

"Tyrus, this is Jim. Plans have changed. Sorry, I couldn't tell you before, but I wasn't sure I could rig the Foxbat's controls before it departed. We need to secure the DNR and Daughtry's control room manually. I'm driving down, should be there by eight. Meet me there. And Tyrus, check out CNN. No need to explain, I think you'll get the picture. Later!"

Tyrus switched on the thirty-two-inch Sony. He didn't need to turn on CNN. Every major network's international affiliate was broadcasting from the Middle East. It was still daytime over there, but the skies were dark. A massive cloud was blocking the sun. On the ground were fire engines, military tanks, police vehicles, ambulances, and hundreds of news reporters, all scrambling chaotically in every which way imaginable.

The byline on the bottom of the screen read:

Soviet military jet on suicide mission attacks Jasurbian palace with nuclear weapons. Death toll not yet available. Prince Adil assumed dead.

CHAPTER 77

Sunday, March 14, 1982

6:00 a.m.

"Wake up, Jenny!" yelled Roy while shaking his daughter. He laid the wicker basket on the floor with the screaming newborn inside so he could use both hands to jolt Jenny from her dream world. Sunday mornings, Jenny usually slept in until noon, so Roy needed both hands to arouse her. "Now, Jenny! Up!"

Jenny and Tyrone Banks spent the wee hours fishing for speckled perch out on the dock that extended about fifty yards from the north shore of Lake Okeechobee. They really weren't hoping to catch any fish, they just wanted some time to talk about things. The second midair passenger plane disaster was in the minds of everyone who lived in and around Seminole Bend, and especially the kids from this small town were frightened by the uncontrollable loss of lives. Tyrone had asked Jenny if she thought her dad had anything to do with all the mysterious deaths in the past month, and Jenny simply shrugged her shoulders. Her brother Jimmy had mentioned the same thing to her the day before, and neither sibling could confirm or deny that Roy might be involved in horrible situations. She had rolled around in bed since returning to the ranch around four in the morning and had just dozed off when her father's shaking began.

"I'm up, dad, okay? Give me a minute." Jenny turned her back to her dad but then heard what sounded like a baby crying, and she sprang to a sitting position. "What's that sound?"

Roy reached down, lifted the basket, and placed it on her bed. "It's your new nephew. Long story, don't ask now. But I need you to babysit for a couple of hours, okay?"

Jenny's mouth dropped wide open as she stared at Roy with moist eyes. "My nephew? But how? Jimmy? Why didn't he tell me?"

"I said I would tell you later. Please, just take care of him. There's some work I need to do."

"What's his name?" asked Jenny. She pulled back on the towel that was covering the baby's face, then lightly touched him on the forehead. The baby stopped crying and smiled. Jenny smiled back, and the connection was made instantly. "He's hungry, dad."

"I woke Jimmy up, and he's out getting some formula now. He'll be back soon."

"Jimmy's a dad? Who's the mom?"

Roy didn't bother to respond. He quickly left the room and headed for his office, which was a converted equipment shed attached to the barn. Hank Daughtry and Sheriff Bonty were waiting for him by a TV watching the live coverage coming out of the Middle East.

"They're saying it was a Russian suicide mission meant to provoke a war between Jasurbia and the Soviet Union," said Bonty.

"There's nothing on the news about a jet crashing in Miami, so that must be our MiG!" added the governor.

"We need to get everyone back here and sort things out. Obviously, someone put the screw to our plans." Roy was furious. Twenty years of planning were not going to waste. He had dedicated his life to this project, and now it would need some immediate adjustments. But that was all, just some tinkering.

Roy sat down by the two-way radio and punched in the frequency. The pilot replied, "Harfield One. Go ahead."

"This is Jackson. Put Oliver on! Make it quick!" barked Roy.

A moment later, Oliver entered the cockpit and put on the headset. The boot of Italy could be seen 40,000 feet below. "What's up, Roy?"

"Change of plans. Prince Adil's palace and the compound have been blown to smithereens by none other than our MiG-25 Foxbat. Meet me back here at the ranch. The landing strip is clear."

The pilot had begun his descent for a planned refueling stop in Athens. Oliver removed the headset and slammed it to the cabin floor. "After we fill it up, make a heading for Seminole Bend. We ain't going to Al Qadir."

The door to the cockpit was open. Sam and Yussef heard Oliver's orders and shot a perplexing look at each other. Oliver returned to his seat and said nothing. His face was bright red, and he was massaging his temples. Oliver's headache was about to get worse.

CHAPTER 78
Sunday, March 14, 1982
6:30 a.m.

Agent Jones was reluctant to let Tyrus go back to Daughtry's control center alone. He still had no clear picture of what was happening, nor did he know what crimes had been committed. Finally, he demanded that Agent Tecka and himself accompany Tyrus, or he wouldn't allow him to leave. Tyrus didn't have the time or energy to fight it, so he agreed.

After Jones, Tecka, and Tyrus had departed in Jones' car, chatter erupted in the Nike base. Everyone was in a state of confusion, each asking questions or giving comments at the same time. Everyone, that is, except for Lew Berry. He was holding the photograph taken after the Sebring basketball game and tapping his forefinger at something or someone in the picture.

Willy noticed Lew staring at the photo and asked, "What is it, Lew? What are you looking at?"

"Probably nothing." Lew paused, then continued. "But I think–" Lew paused again and shook his head. Now everyone in the room stopped talking and looked at him.

"Come on, Lew. What's up?"

"I think I know what has been bothering me since I saw this photo. This gal here, one of the fans at the game that is in the background."

"What about her?" asked Johnny Murphree. Lew was still holding the picture, and no one could see who he was pointing at.

"I found a Polaroid picture in the drawer of Brett's end table up in the master bedroom the first time that me and Phil Bennett broke into the house. Well, anyway, when I went back to the house later, it was gone. The room had been ransacked, and I'm not sure what was taken, but I found it rather odd that someone would want to steal a picture of my son and his pregnant wife out on the beach somewhere."

"So, what does that have to do with the picture you're looking at?" inquired Willy.

"Well, this gal here." Lew tapped the photo once again. "She looks a lot like Sheryl did in that Polaroid print. In fact, now I'm not so sure it was Sheryl in that picture on the beach. I think it was this girl."

"Show us the picture. Who are you talking about?" Lew slid the photo on the table so everyone could get a glimpse, then pointed to a pregnant gal standing next to Bard Smith, the sportswriter for the *Miami Sentinel*.

Otis was the first to speak, and he blurted out, "Well, that there is Miss Foss, it sure is! She be a teacher over at the elementary school."

"You're right, Otis," inserted Willy. "But I believe she hasn't been teaching for a couple of months. She's on maternity leave for the rest of the school year."

Lew looked bewildered as he glanced up at Willy. "If this Miss Foss is pregnant, that's probably her in the picture I saw in Brett's drawer." Lew paused, then added, "With him—on the beach."

Lew shook his head. "Can't be, right? Please, tell me it can't be."

CHAPTER 79
Sunday, March 14, 1982
7:00 a.m.

"The informant is flying on a civilian jet from Chicago to Palm Beach," said Jim Brown from a payphone just off the turnpike in Yeehaw Junction. "The plane has been delayed at O'Hare. Snowstorm. Looks like March is still coming in like a lion. I will make the pickup and transport from Palm Beach to Homestead but will be late. Should be there around four or five in the afternoon. Make sure you erase this message and any other messages from your machine."

The call was conveyed aloud over the speaker on Tyrus' answering machine at the Nike base, and everyone in the room heard it except Tyrus, Jones, and Tecka, who were waiting for Jim Brown at Daughtry's summer house, aka control center.

"We need to let Tyrus and the FBI boys know that whoever this Jim Brown guy is, he will be coming late," said Willy. "Johnny, you and me need to go tell them."

"I think we all need to stay here for now," replied Agent Brewer. "That was the plan."

"If Brown doesn't show up, they might decide to look for him thinking he's in danger. Let's all just go. I think every one of us is too deeply involved at this point to just sit back and wait.

"I guess you're right," stated Brewer. "There's not much we can do here anyway."

With that, they loaded back into their cars and headed for Daughtry's control center.

"Otis and me will keep a keen eye on this here prisoner of ours," boasted Lance proudly as he led the handcuffed guard to Lew's Trans Am. "Make sure he don't do no escaping, you know."

* * * * *

Oliver's jet touched down on the cracked asphalt runway that was built for Jackson's private use and for an emergency getaway if the need ever arose. The constant heat from the sun and intense humidity had taken its toll through the years, and the runway resembled a county road that led to a town dump. The jet bounced twice before the brakes took hold as the passengers gripped the armrests tightly.

Oliver strutted down the ramp and over to Roy's office with a purpose. For the past eight hours, he tried to envision how the plan had gone wrong. There must have been a mole, but who? Every moment of that flight from the Athen's refueling stop had made him angrier, and now he was furious. Sam Dulie and Yussef tried their best, but couldn't keep up with Oliver's rapid pace. The young lady who had just given birth less than a day ago was helped down from the steps by the pilot. She was bleeding, but that took a backseat to her declining state of mind. The gal was an emotional wreck. She had no idea that her newborn son was only yards away in Roy's house and being cared for by his daughter.

When the pilot finally got her to Roy's office next to the barn, the rest of the men were sitting around a table, all with concerned looks on their faces. Oliver Harfield was standing and pounding his fist, using cuss words rarely heard in the Deep South, or anywhere English was spoken. But that didn't faze the young lady. She marched right up to Roy and bent down so close that he could see the capillaries about to rupture in her cheeks. The pilot grabbed her arms and attempted to restrain the woman who was in the midst of a nervous breakdown.

"Where's my baby, you wretched jackass?!" she screamed.

Roy looked up at her and grinned. "Now, what kind of language is that for an elementary school teacher, Miss Foss?" Then Roy looked over at the sheriff and motioned for him to remove the lady. "Al, gag her and lock her in the closet. We've got business to discuss. I'll deal with her later." Sheriff Bonty did as he was ordered.

After a few more minutes of ranting and raving, Governor Daughtry interrupted, "Oliver, calm down. We need to sort through this logically."

"No one in this room is going to tell me to calm down, especially you, Daughtry!" yelled Oliver, who was still in a frenzied state. "I made you governor and arranged the financing for this plan for the past two decades. Now you all listen to me. We have a mole in this organization. I've been thinking about it the entire flight back here. It only makes sense that it must be that Jim Brown guy that Tyrus found. We sent him to Baku to bribe the pilot and rig up the nukes. Who else could it be?"

"We can find out pretty quick," replied Roy. "He should be up in Gainesville with my brother Ray right now. Let me give him a call."

"If he's our mole, then what are the chances that Tyrus is in it with him?"

"Where did we find this Tyrus anyway?" asked Sam Dulie. "What do we know about him?" Sam looked around the table, but no one responded to his question. Sheriff Bonty tipped his head down so he wouldn't have to look at Sam. He knew but wasn't going to say anything.

Roy was at his two-way radio dialing the Gainesville op center and heard Sam's question. "I found him. Tyrus. I took him away from his girlfriend and baby the night the boy was born. He was strong and athletic, and I was ramping up our security team in Columbia, where the radar jammers were being assembled. I had threatened to kill his girlfriend and baby if he ever tried to leave, and I knew he believed that I had the power to do it. He became a dedicated worker, one who I came to trust. So I promoted him to head up the operations in Columbia when the man we had in charge was found dead in his swimming pool. Drowned."

Everyone in the room was silent. They were waiting for Roy's call to go through to his brother, but no one was answering on the other end.

"He's supposed to be there," uttered Roy. "Something's happened. I need to get up there and find him."

"Roy, this Tyrus fella, you said he was a Seminole Bend kid when you kidnapped him, right?" asked Oliver.

"Right. So what?"

"What's his background? What did he do for a living?"

Sheriff Bonty stood up and walked to the door as if he was going for some fresh air. Roy replied, "Don't remember what he did exactly, but his brother is Willy Banks, one of Al's deputies."

"You hired the brother of a sheriff's deputy to head up operations in Columbia?" Oliver's voice was becoming enraged. "What the hell were you thinking, damn it?!"

"His brother was in Nam when I grabbed him. I didn't know Willy would be hired by the sheriff's department. But Tyrus was a good worker, someone I trusted. He couldn't be in on any conspiracy against us. I'm sure of it!"

"You said the man who was in charge of operations before Tyrus drowned in a pool? Was there an autopsy done? Was it a legit drowning?"

Roy didn't respond. He wasn't sure himself. He wanted to ask Sheriff Bonty why Willy was hired as a deputy knowing he was Tyrus' brother, but the sheriff was no longer in the room.

CHAPTER 80

Sunday, March 14, 1982
6:00 p.m.

Agent Brewer and his crew offered to escort Daughtry's guard back to FBI headquarters in Miami for further questioning. Agent Jones said that would be fine, but to be ready to come back quickly, if needed.

At six o'clock, Jones, Tecka, Tyrus, Willy, Johnny, Lew, Otis, Lance, and Pancho were sitting around a table in the kitchen eating sardines and crackers they had found in the cupboard. Lance said he was impressed by the gourmet food that the governor stored in his pantry.

A few minutes later, the front door opened, and Jim Brown appeared with the informant he had picked up at Palm Beach International Airport. Lew, Willy, and Otis all did double-takes, then dropped their half-eaten crackers on the floor. They all stood up and appeared to be shaking and speechless, staring at the two folks who had just entered Daughtry's house. The informant froze in her tracks, staring back at Lew with her mouth wide open while tears formed in her eyes. Then Lew made a mad dash to the informant, gave her a big kiss, and nearly squeezed the life out of her with an enormous hug.

"Janet, you're alive!" yelped Lew, barely able to breathe. "I was told you were on the Heartland Lakes flight that crashed this week. Oh my God, you're here, alive and well!"

Janet didn't let the embrace go. She whispered to Lew, "I love you, but I've done some bad things. Can we talk?"

“Bad things?” Lew looked puzzled. “Sure, let’s go somewhere private.”

But just then, Lew and Janet turned to find Willy and Jim Brown in a massive bear hug, two humongous men with tears flowing down their cheeks.

Willy took a step back and looked at his boyhood friend Bo Yardly from his head down to his toes. “Bo, you are dead, man. I went to your funeral!”

“The funeral you attended was for Gaspar Millage, a close friend in the same regiment. Got blown up walking on a landmine twenty feet from me. His mom abandoned him and his little brother when he was five-years-old, and his dad’s now serving life in prison for killing his little brother. He had no one left back in the States to give him a proper burial, so I let him be me. It was closed casket, no one knew.”

Willy was in shock, and so was Otis. But Tyrus just looked at his two brothers sympathetically. He knew why Bo had sacrificed everything, including his family and friends back home in Seminole Bend. Tyrus nodded at Bo, then started rubbing his hands nervously.

”Mind if we sit down?” asked Bo. “It’s time you all know the truth and what’s happening.”

Everyone slid backward, and two more folding chairs were set up around the table in the gaps. Bo and Janet sat down in those chairs, and the kitchen became quite crowded. Bo took a deep breath, trying to think where he was going to start with his story.

“I was assigned to a special task force named Espy. Three of us were asked personally by President Nixon to identify CIA counterspies and eradicate their plans for treason. Nixon caught wind of double agents planning to overthrow American democracy that would place our government in the controlling hands of an unknown foreign leader, but he didn’t have any specifics. Nixon produced letters embossed with the presidential seal that gave Espy permission to act on its own, basically open orders to examine any and every part of every

American intelligence agency. We acted covertly and uncovered a dangerous operation being carried out in Florida, in fact, right here where we sit. Following leads, I located Tyrus a few years back in Columbia and brought him into the loop to help us infiltrate the group. Together, we assassinated Roy Jackson's head of operations in Columbia to promote Tyrus to the top spot."

"Assassinate?" asked Willy. "That doesn't sound like you, Bo. How did you do it?"

"We drowned him in his own swimming pool and made it look like an accident. And you're right, Willy, it doesn't sound like me. I felt I had to do it to save our nation from destruction."

"You joined this Espy task force on your own? Or were you ordered?"

"I agreed to it. President Nixon had flown to Saigon and spoke only to the three of us aboard Air Force One. He had no aides or even Secret Service on board at the time. This was his furtive theorem, and he wanted complete privacy. Keep in mind, it was CIA miscreant agents we were looking for; thus, he trusted no one."

"Bo, you gave up an NFL career to join this task force? Man, you're my hero once again, dude!"

"What's an NFL career without a country? You would have done the same thing, Willy. I know you! But two other folks are sitting in this room who are just as much, or even more so, heroes than me." Bo grinned and pointed at Tyrus, who gave an appreciative nod in return, then smiled at Janet. Lew looked at his wife, then back to Bo. He was hoping for an explanation.

"Both of these courageous souls risked everything for the sake of their country. Tyrus hasn't seen his son or girlfriend since the night Tyrone was born. He had the chance to return after we killed the chief over in Columbia, but he insisted on seeing our plan through to save many, many more lives. And

Janet, she kept me posted on Roy's activities for several years after I located her in Pennsylvania."

Lew was perplexed. He turned to his wife and asked nicely, "Is this part of the 'bad things' you wanted to tell me about?" Janet affirmed with a nod.

"Lew, I haven't been faithful to you, and that was even before I knew anything about this operation." She paused for a moment as dead silence filled the room, and tears sprung from her eyes. "After we were first married and you were on the road selling insurance, I met a man named Roy Jackson, whose name you've heard by now, and we had an affair." Lew frowned and pulled out a hanky from his pocket to wipe his forehead. His eyes glistened with salty fluid.

"It's okay, you can tell me later," said Lew as his voice crackled. He was embarrassed, but doing his best to control his anger. Right now, just having his wife alive and well were the most important things.

"No, Lew, I can't." Janet paused but decided to tell him the rest. "Brett is not your son, Lew. He's Roy Jackson's son."

The room was completely mute. You could have heard a pin drop. Everyone was thinking about the implications of Janet's last statement, especially Lew.

"It was a one-night stand. I don't know why I did it, I just did. I was working at the Greyhound station when he came in on the bus and started sweet-talking me. You were in Harrisburg on business, and well, we had dinner, and he spent the night. I found out that he went to work at Marks, Taylor, and Smith law firm, and when I knew I was pregnant with Brett, I went to his office to tell him. I knew it had to be his because you were gone quite frequently back then when you first started selling insurance, and the one-night stand fit the time frame. Anyway, he wasn't in his office, so I left him a note telling him I was pregnant."

Janet paused for a moment to regain her composure and pulled out a Kleenex to wipe off the tears that had destroyed today's facial makeup. Black mascara was forming a river from the corners of her eyes down to her chin. Lew was angry and confused but didn't say anything. He just waited for his wife to continue.

"To make a long story short, Roy blackmailed me. Every now and then, he would call and threaten to tell you about the affair if I didn't cooperate in some plot he was cooking up. Later, he even said he would kill you if I didn't do what he said. His actual words were, 'dispose of your hubby.' When he thought that I might spill the truth and tell you about the affair, he threatened to kill me.

"As the years went on, Roy would demand that I meet him for coffee or lunch. He was going to use me in this wild get rich and powerful scheme of his. He had moved away from Pittsburgh but kept coming back just to harass me. I found out he had purchased an enormous ranch in southern Florida, but I could never figure out why. He didn't seem much like someone who wanted to work the land or milk cows for the rest of his life.

"Brett never knew it, but Roy paid for his college, and then Roy donated $100,000 to the Seminole Bend athletic department with one catch—they had to hire Brett as the head basketball coach. The corrupt athletic director never blinked an eye or even said a word to the school board. From what I heard, the school district never saw a penny of that donation.

"But Brett was still in love with his childhood sweetheart, Sheryl Babbitt, and she didn't want to move to Florida. She was very close to her family and agreed to marry Brett only if he would stay in Pennsylvania. When Roy found out that Brett might back out of the job that he had bought for him, he flew to Pittsburgh and followed the Babbitt family around one night. Mom and dad had picked Sheryl's brother up from practice and were going to pull into Burger King for dinner on the way home. Roy was right behind them, and while they were waiting for oncoming traffic to make a left turn, Roy smashed into their bumper, forcing the Babbitt's car to be hit head-on by a dump truck. They were killed instantly. Roy told police his brakes had failed and then had some buddies from Marks, Taylor, and Smith get the case against him dismissed out of court.

"Meanwhile, Sheryl was devastated at losing her entire family, and decided that she wanted to get out of Pennsylvania and start over in Florida. Roy told me what he had done over lunch the day after the accident. I was frightened and appalled, and I knew if I tried to go to the authorities, he would have Lew killed. Then he started to tell me more about his grandiose plans to take over America, and I was terrified. That's when I met Bo."

Bo continued with the story, seeing that Janet needed a break. "Our task force secured the names of every CIA agent living in the United States and abroad. President Nixon gave us the list personally, and it contained the names and addresses of both active and retired agents. Then Nixon told us not to make contact with him again. We were told to locate and eliminate any and all threats to the United States without alarming the general public. He also said he would vehemently impugn any orders he had given if we were caught, and he would claim that the permission letters signed and sealed by him were fakes. So we knew it was kill or be killed, no help was coming. And when Jimmy Carter was elected, we knew we were really on our own.

"President Nixon opened up and financed an offshore bank account in the Cayman Islands so our task force could fund operations until we succeeded. His last phone call to me was very brief. He asked how the mission was going and what we had found since he left office. Then Nixon said if we were successful with our quest, we could keep whatever was left in the account for our retirement. After Watergate, we never heard from him again.

"We investigated the CIA agent list as thoroughly as we could, but with only three people, it took a great deal of time. Then we found out that one of the supervisors of the agency,

Oliver Harfield, had built a considerable estate on a golf course in Seminole Bend. Because that was my hometown, I took a particular interest. On a wing and a prayer, I called the sheriff's department and said I was with the IRS, and we were investigating a tax situation with Harfield. I never said what kind of tax situation, but I asked if the department had ever received a complaint about him. I lied and said that Harfield may have some friends in the area who might be hiding some income from real estate investments. I was fishing for anything. I was hoping to find out if others in the area were associated with Harfield that we could follow up on. I left a phone number for a motel I was staying at in Moore Haven, then decided to get back on the big lake and break some bass necks. I had really missed those days.

"The next day, I got an anonymous phone call from someone at the sheriff's department in Seminole Bend telling me to check out a rancher named Roy Jackson. Then he hung up before I could ask any questions. So one night, I decided to drop in on Roy, but I couldn't get past the two guards he had posted at his driveway. Right then, I knew something suspicious was going on. No rancher needs two armed guards unless he's doing things he shouldn't be doing. The next day, I rented a crop duster from a farmer in Pahokee and flew several times over the Jackson ranch. I noticed he had guards all over the property. As I was turning back to Pahokee, a small plane was descending below me and heading for the swamp behind the ranch. I watched the pilot drop several containers from a cargo hold into the water, and then ascend back into the clouds and turn south. Four or five boats scrambled out to the containers from Jackson's ranch and picked them up. I figured Roy was dealing drugs.

"The next night, I rented an airboat from Bennett's Airboat Palace, hoping that Phil, the owner, wouldn't recognize me from my days playing ball in Seminole Bend. Fortunately, he didn't, and I headed back to the ranch by going up the Kissimmee River until I found a break in the mangroves that led to Jackson's swamp. I hid the boat and swam across the swamp amidst a family of gators who must have just eaten. They left me alone. I snuck up to the barn and noticed what appeared to be an office attached to it, so I broke in.

"There was a shortwave radio, which was odd, and a bunch of other stuff you would typically find in an office. I found nothing to implicate Roy in any drug dealing or different scheme with Oliver Harfield, so I decided to leave and call the FBI when I got back to the motel. They could investigate Roy, but I needed to get back to my mission. I would start with the next name on my list.

"But as I was about to leave, I noticed a name and phone number pinned to a cork bulletin board above the phone that was on Roy's desk. I took it off and saw Janet's name on the note with a Pennsylvania area code. I stuck it in my pocket and turned to leave when I accidentally knocked a framed picture off of Roy's desk. As I was putting it back on the desk, I glanced at the photo, then did a double-take. Roy was standing next to someone that looked very familiar as he was raising a ten-pound bass high in the air by the gills. Then I remembered seeing the other man in a file that our task force kept. It was Ray Jackson, who worked closely with Oliver Harfield. I assumed that Roy must be Ray's brother. I pulled the note back out of my pocket and looked at it again. I thought Janet Berry might be able to give me some information, so I planned to start with her."

Lance stood up and went over to the cupboard. On the top shelf were all sorts of bottles of liquor. He reached up and grabbed a fifth of Jack Daniels. "Anyone else need a drink. This story is getting complicated!" Everyone nodded. He didn't bother trying to find glasses. Where he lived down by the phone booth, his buddies just passed the bottle around. That seemed to work for everyone sitting at the kitchen table, including Agent Jones and Agent Tecka, who were busy taking notes while Bo spilled his guts.

Bo continued, "I phoned Janet, and she met me at a coffee shop in Pittsburgh." Then he paused and glanced over at Lew and Janet, not sure how he should approach this topic. Lew could read his mind. Janet gave him an affirmative nod.

"Go ahead, Bo," stated Lew confidently. "I can handle it."

"Well, Janet obviously didn't want Lew to know what was happening, but she was very clear it was to protect him." Bo locked eyes with Lew. Bo knew Janet was courageous in her actions, and he wanted that bravery to be evident to her husband. "I lied to Janet and told her I was with the FBI, and we were investigating Roy for fraud and other possible crimes. I couldn't reveal to her that I was part of a special task force, nor what our real mission was. Thankfully, she never asked for a badge."

Lew turned to Janet and interrupted, "How much did you know about Roy's activities?"

Janet responded, "After I met up with Bo, he asked if I could help him out. He assured me that he would protect me. So I convinced Roy that my life was miserable and I would like to become part of his operation. He bought it, and then filled me in on what was happening."

"He bought it?" asked Lew. "Did you have to cozy up again to make that work?" He was being sarcastic, but deep down, he wasn't sure.

"Lew, I wasn't involved sexually with Roy Jackson after that one-night stand. I'm sure later on he wanted me again, but I only led him on to get information. That's all. I swear it!"

"It's true, Lew," inserted Bo. "She may have saved our country from ruin."

"Go on, please!" said Agent Jones. "We need to get to the bottom of this soon. Time isn't on our side!"

Bo continued, "Roy told Janet that he offered Brett a new house, car, and a boatload of money to join him in his scheme. Brett never knew that Roy was his father. Then, at a teacher retreat last June, Brett met Norma Foss, who was a fifth-grade teacher at the elementary school. The kids call her Miss, but actually, she's married. After the retreat, he began an affair with her. She became pregnant almost right away, which was a shock to her family and friends because she had told them that her husband, Doug, couldn't have kids due to a low sperm count.

"Meanwhile, Sheryl Berry had become pregnant at about the same time. Brett confided to Roy what had happened, and Roy knew he needed to fix the problem. Roy decided that it was best to simply get rid of Sheryl Berry. But he didn't tell Brett his plan, and the night of the basketball game, Brett actually thought Sheryl drove the truck into the culvert. Roy hadn't planned on Brett being killed trying to save Sheryl. That was just an accident, and it devastated Roy personally. It also threw his mission into turmoil.

"Now, I have to admit what I'm about to tell you next was improper and covert, but you need to know the truth to validate what I'm going to say. It came from the FBI report that surfaced following your investigation." Bo looked right at Jones and Tecka. They both looked stunned.

"Surfaced? FBI reports aren't made of Styrofoam; they don't just float! How did you get an FBI report?" asked Jones angrily.

"Well, I'm sure you will soon guess, so I might as well tell you. Yes, you have a CIA mole in your office. Now don't get excited, we have moles in every major FBI office in the United States."

Jones and Tecka glanced at each other and looked livid and perplexed. Then Jones said in a subdued tone, "Well, go on. Tell them all what our theory is!"

Bo continued again, "Roy substituted a dead male body for Sheryl and placed him in the truck. That turned out to be a mistake because Coroner Cliff Sutton determined that the charred bones could only be from a man over six feet tall. Anyway, from the video room right here in Daughtry's house,

Brett's truck was driven from the high school to the culvert, then steered into it."

"How?" asked Johnny Murphree. "Are you talking about those joysticks in the video room? That's incredulous!"

"No, Johnny, it's not," replied Willy. "I found a metal box in Brett's truck over at the impound lot connected to the steering wheel. It had some sort of electronic gadget in it, like a radio receiver. And the box had an engraving on it that matched the engraving on that big dish outside of Sam Dulie's office window."

"I'll get to that, Willy," inserted Bo. "It's Arabic writing. I'll explain in a little bit. Anyway, going back to Roy, he decided to kidnap Sheryl and keep her around until the baby was born. This sounds crazy, but Sheryl and Norma Foss's babies are technically Roy's grandkids. That may be his one and only soft spot, I guess.

"But then Oliver made the decision to test the radar jamming equipment, which was being assembled in Columbia, to make sure he could count on the devices. We're not sure who installed the jammers on the planes or in the air traffic control center in Miami."

"NTSB," interrupted Willy. Everyone looked at him. "It was someone from the NTSB."

"Why do you say that?" inquired Bo.

"There is a video recording of a car pulling up to the NTSB office in Tampa after the crash this week. I have a gut feeling the person installing the jammers is NTSB. Makes sense, aren't they the only ones who would be allowed to fiddle around in the control towers without raising suspicion? They could say they were there to check out the system."

"You might be on to something," said Agent Jones. "But it would have to be an NTSB higher-up to make this scheme work. We'll get to the bottom of it when we get back to the office. Please go on with your story."

"So when Roy found out that Oliver was successful in causing a midair collision over Miami, he decided to eliminate Sheryl, cut off her hand, and plant it at the crash site. He hoped the FBI would find it, then identify the wedding ring and assume she died in the airplane accident."

"You stole the report about Sheryl's wedding ring, too?" asked Agent Tecka with a disgusted look on his face. "I hope you realize that when we find your mole, he'll waste away in a prison cell!"

"Bo, that's not exactly what happened to Sheryl," muttered Janet in a low voice, not sure she wanted to say anything at all. "I haven't told you something." Now all eyes were staring at Janet.

CHAPTER 81

Sunday, March 14, 1982
7:30 p.m.

"Sheryl's not dead," murmured Janet. "Roy cut off her hand to stage the accident, but he's keeping her alive until the baby's born. He pretended to have her board the Trans South jet in Miami."

"For God's sake, where is she?!" yelped Lew at his wife. "That plane crash was a month ago. We need to find her!"

"She's doing fine. Father O'Shea is keeping her in the basement of the Catholic church in Seminole Bend. Roy's thugs kidnapped Father's younger brother and sister and are holding them ransom. He threatened to kill them if Father turns him in. Sister Mary and Sister Roberta patched up her hand, I mean wrist, and are watching over her pregnancy."

Agent Jones was nervously clicking his pen cap with his thumb. "Get back on track, Bo, there's a huge gap in your story you haven't told us. You talked about finding Roy and Janet back in '74 or '75, but you obviously had a lot of leads to follow since that time that brought you here today. I'm not buying that Janet gave you all this information from her few chats with Roy Jackson. Yet, you seem to know this scheme of Harfield's pretty much inside and out. Come clean, Bo, what are you leaving out?" Jones had drawn a bubble map and flow chart on his notepad and was trying to organize this plot in his mind. "How did you find Tyrus? I can't see a connection between Janet and him."

Bo looked over at Willy, then to Johnny Murphree and back at Jones. Tyrus stretched out his fingers like a web and covered his face. Everyone wanted to know the answer to Jones' question.

"You should tell them," uttered Tyrus. "We've got more work to do and will need their help. They need to know everything."

Bo looked at each and every person in the room before responding. He clamped his arms behind his back and paced the room, staring down at the floor as he tried to gather his thoughts. Then he came back to the table and stood while everyone looked up with anticipation at the man who had been a high school, college, and NFL star running back. They wanted to hear what their one-time hero had to say.

"I mentioned we had a mole in every major FBI center in the United States," said Bo in a restrained voice. "Well, I've had an inside person in Oliver's little group of friends for several years. I was trying to avoid telling you to keep all this confidential and also to protect you. If Harfield finds out, everyone in this kitchen would be in grave danger."

Everyone in the room looked at each other, trying his or her best to picture the members of Oliver's gang of criminals.

"Our inside man is Sheriff Al Bonty," stated Bo. There were loud grunts, and then everyone in the room started talking at once. A conversation taking place in the Tower of Babel would be better understood than in Daughtry's kitchen at that moment. Bo motioned with his arms to quiet down, like so many quarterbacks that he played with did in tight games and loud stadiums.

"Can't be!" proclaimed Willy as he stood and faced his best friend. "The man's a total ass! He fired me as a deputy sheriff, Bo!"

"I asked him to fire you, Willy," replied Bo as he stepped forward and affectionately patted Willy on the shoulder. "You were getting too close to finding the truth. You would have been killed by one of Roy's goons. Bonty was the anonymous caller from the sheriff's department who tipped me off while I was in Seminole Bend, and he also pointed me in the direction of Tyrus. Al knew you were my best friend and thought that I could convince Tyrus to risk his life and join our side. And obviously, that was no problem. Tyrus wanted no money, the only thing he wanted in return was a promise that someday he would see Abby, Tyrone, and his brothers again."

"But Sheriff Bonty?" inserted Johnny Murphree. "He's been nothing but a jerk to everyone in the department."

"That was the plan, Johnny. To give us a chance and allow us to infiltrate their group, Bonty had to be a tough guy and prove to Roy and Oliver his value. But Sheriff Bonty also had another reason. A personal one." Bo turned away, not really wanting to say anymore.

"Tell us," ordered Agent Jones, the ballpoint of his pen pressed against the notepad. "What was Bonty's personal vendetta all about?"

Tyrus nodded at Bo to finish the story. "Al Bonty was a happily married Seminole Bend deputy sheriff back in 1964, who had a son in '65 and a daughter in '67. His wife was an attractive, loving soul that had many friends and no enemies. The marriage was blissful, but ended when Roy Jackson forced them into a staged divorce two months after Al's daughter was born."

"Bonty wasn't married, and he didn't have no kids," interrupted Johnny Murphree. "He never talked like he was ever married, and he had no pictures in his office. What are you talking about, Bo?"

"Let me explain. Roy needed an insider at the sheriff's department to make his plan work. Al was a vibrant and outgoing young man and well-liked by everyone in the county. He gave almost everybody a warning instead of a speeding ticket, and he smiled a lot back then. That was until he met Roy. Roy kidnapped Al's wife and sent her to Jasurbia, where his brother Ray had presented her as a gift to the royalty. Today, she's part of a harem, but even Ray isn't sure where exactly.

"Anyway, Roy took the babies and raised them at his ranch. Jimmy and Jenny Jackson are Sheriff Bonty's kids."

"What?!" gasped Willy, Otis, and Johnny almost in unison.

Bo continued. "Roy has never been married, nor has he ever had so much as a live-in gal around the house. He told Jimmy and Jenny that their mom was killed in a car accident. He told Al Bonty that he would allow him to watch the kids grow up, but he was never to speak to them. Then he shared the masterplan with Al and said that if he joined along with the grand scheme, when it was all over, he would release his wife back to him. The blackmail has loomed heavily over Al, but he's played his role well.

"A month after the kidnapping, the Seminole Bend sheriff, Al's boss, mysteriously moved to Oregon. No one knew why, including me, even though I have a good idea. He was a southern boy who liked to soak up the sun and fish the big lake. Starting a new life in Oregon made no sense.

"And Judge Boone was one of Roy's fishing buddies who also chaired the county commission. When the search began for a new sheriff, Boone immediately recommended Al Bonty, and the rest is history."

"What part did you play in all this, Tyrus?" asked Agent Jones.

"Bo and me, we teamed up in South America and gambled that I had gained enough of Oliver and Roy's trust through the years to be their number two guy. We drowned the chief of Oliver's Columbian operations, and then I was appointed to run the show down there. Had I not been put in charge, we had no backup plan. Once I was picked to head up their Columbian mission, I disabled the last few shipments of jammers, but several original boxes made it to Florida before I took over. Those are dangerous and in the wrong hands as we speak! I conned Oliver into believing that I had a good person working with me who could run the Georgia Nike base, his name being Jim Brown." Tyrus pointed at Bo.

"Thanks to Sheriff Bonty, we knew about the video controls implanted into airplanes and cars and the remotes used to maneuver them. Janet called me after her last meeting with Roy in Harrisburg, and she was terrified about something." Bo looked at Janet, and she nodded back at him. "I guessed Roy was becoming suspicious of her, but then Bonty told me about plans that had been made to test the new lethal combination of a radar jammer together with a video remote controller in an aircraft departing from Chicago. I remembered that Roy had asked Janet to fly down to Florida to meet up with Lew so he would stop snooping around. Least that's what Roy told her. When I found out that Roy booked her on a connecting flight through Chicago instead of a nonstop from Pittsburgh, I figured Roy planned to take down that Heartland Lakes jet with Janet on it. I intercepted her at the connecting gate just ten minutes before it was to depart. I had no badge, but I approached the CSRs at the desk and demanded the plane be grounded. I was restrained by airport security but broke free, grabbed Janet, and ran. Meanwhile, the flight took off. And–it didn't land."

Bo walked over to Lance and finished off the last of the Jack Daniels. But whiskey would not fade his memory of what could have been prevented had he only had more time.

"When Harfield took down those planes last week, I realized I needed to step up my game quickly. Ray Jackson devised the plan to send me to Baku so I could bribe a Soviet pilot, then steal a MiG-25 and rig up nuclear weapons to nuke South Florida. Ty found out about the plan from Bonty. Ray's mission was to destroy all the evidence in this house we're sitting in and force the president to fly down from Washington and declare a state of emergency. Then, Ty was supposed to launch a short-range Hercules missile from the Nike base to take out Air Force One. If that didn't work from down here, I was the backup stationed at the base in Georgia with a more extended range Zeus-B missile. But I had a different idea, one that I didn't share with Tyrus.

"Years ago, Oliver had requisitioned from the CIA a HoftanJet HJ-15 to have at his disposal when needed. It was waiting at the Gainesville airport to take me to Baku. But I knew I needed to get back to the US faster than that thing could get me here, so I went with my own Plan B. You see, back in the late sixties, our squad was trained to fly jet fighters as soon as we joined the special ops force. President Nixon secretly placed an F-4 Phantom fighter jet and an AH-1 Huey Cobra chopper at our disposal before he left office, and we've been flying them covertly ever since. There's a secluded desert airstrip in eastern Turkey near Kars that is near the Soviet border. We planted the chopper there a week earlier, hoping it wouldn't be seen. I convinced Oliver's pilot in Gainesville that plans had changed, and I wouldn't need his service and told him to go home and wait for orders. Our Phantom was hidden in a private hangar we had purchased at the Gainesville airport. I flew it to the airstrip in Turkey, then went to Baku with the Huey at night so I could fly below the Soviet radars. Ty thought I was going to replace the MiG's nukes with incendiary bombs. I didn't want to tell him the truth, or he would have insisted on coming with me. Chances were slim that I could pull this off, and I wasn't about to have my best friend's brother killed in action." Bo paused and grinned at Willy.

"So I broke into the Soviet jet and rigged up the camera and remote controllers, then left the nukes in place. Prince Adil had already taken care of paying off the Russian pilot, so I got out of there as fast as I could with the chopper. I knew I was cutting it close, but I got back to the Gainesville control center shortly before the MiG took off. Ray Jackson was napping on a cot and never did see me turn on the TV and operate the joystick. It was time to end the Jasurbian connection, and the MiG-25 brought a conclusion to that nightmare. Then I ended the nightmare that was Roy Jackson's big brother."

Everyone in the room glanced at each other and gave slight nods. They were starting to see a clear picture of how a third world war may have been prevented.

"Your actions kept the president from flying to Miami," pronounced Agent Jones with a slight nod to Bo. "This goes beyond the Medal of Honor, Mr. Yardly! Our nation will be forever in your debt."

"I appreciate your words, Agent Jones," replied Bo. "But my name can never be associated with these events. As far as America's concerned, I'm dead, and it needs to stay that way. All of this is top secret, and we need to protect Richard Nixon's enshrouded orders. His courageous actions and enormous risk-taking measures are to be commended! But we are not finished until we put an end to Oliver Harfield and his band of outlaws. And it's time for Tyrus and me to complete this mission."

"Bullshit, my friend," stated Willy matter-of-factly. "Two things. One, you are a hero, and every dog gets his day. I will make sure of that! Two, you and Ty are not going at this alone. You got a full ride to 'Bama cuz I blocked so damn well for you in high school! Teammates for life, bro! I'm with you from here on out, you got that?!"

Bo was shaking his head no and about to respond when Agent Jones spoke up. "The FBI is in. We will protect your identity and mission, forever if need be. Nothing in a report whatsoever, but we're in, and that's not a request."

"If my two big bros are in, me and Lance here ain't 'bout to be left out neither," proclaimed Otis proudly. "Besides, we are now wise detectives, ain't we, Lance? We got skills!"

Janet put her arm around Lew's neck and drew him close. "We all love this country," she said, looking around the table. "We all want to help." Everyone nodded in agreement.

Pancho stood and raised his glass of Jack Daniels, then turned to the group. "For mi amigo, Miguel. For what they did to my friend." He quaffed down the whiskey and slammed the glass on the table. Then Pancho walked up to Bo and saluted. “To my death, señor.”

CHAPTER 82

Monday, March 15, 1982

1:15 a.m.

Oliver's personal pilot was refueling the private aircraft from the jet fuel pump next to Roy's barn using only the light from the full moon. Onboard, its tired passengers were getting comfortable in their leather seats. The flight to Gainesville would be a short one, and no one had much sleep in the past twenty-four hours, so it was time for a quick doze. Roy, Oliver, Governor Daughtry, Sam, and Yussef had etched out their plans moving forward, and that meant using the secret Murphy O'Sullivan Center location as their only base. Ray should be waiting when they arrived; however, Roy hadn't been able to get ahold of his brother on the shortwave. Perhaps he was sleeping, but that would be strange considering everything that had happened on Sunday.

The group had come to the conclusion that Tyrus Banks and Jim Brown were most likely double agents who were working against them. Sheriff Bonty commented that it would "pleasure him to no end" to drive down to the Nike base in Homestead and "take care of that rat" Tyrus. Roy agreed to let him go and even thanked him for his efforts.

While the group was trying to catch a few winks in the Learjet before takeoff, the sheriff went into the Jackson house and found Jenny sleeping on the couch with Norma Foss's newborn son nestled comfortably on her chest. The baby was as conked out as his babysitter. Al quietly approached the daughter he barely knew and stroked her hair. He hadn't touched Jenny since she was an infant not much older than Norma's baby. Then Sheriff Bonty did something he hadn't done in years. He cried.

"What do you want with my sister, Sheriff?" came a voice from the doorway. Al turned toward the sound and saw his son. He had seen both Jenny and Jimmy many times during the years, but only from a distance.

"Your dad wants me to take all of you to my place in Seminole Bend," lied Al. "He's planning on doing some renovations around here in the morning and wants all of you out."

"So, who is this baby's mother and father, Sheriff? My sister was convinced he belonged to me. Now we would both like to know what's going on!"

Jenny was awakened by the conversation and almost forgot the infant was lying on her chest. She arose slowly, cradling the baby in her arms. "Sheriff Bonty? Why are you here?"

"Jenny, you and Jimmy need to pack a suitcase for a week. You'll be coming with me to my house to stay while your house is being renovated."

"Daddy never said anything about a renovation, and I don't want to go away for a week." Jenny's stubborn eyes met Al's. She could detect a bit of panic in the way the sheriff raised his eyebrow.

"Something's come up. I'll explain later. Please pack and hurry along." Right then, everyone in the house could hear Oliver's Learjet take off from the decrepit landing strip. No one even bothered to look outside. Small planes had been coming and going for years on the Jackson ranch.

* * * * *

While Jimmy and Jenny were packing and the baby asleep in a wicker basket overstuffed with blankets, Sheriff Bonty went out to Roy's office and unlocked the closet. He then unfastened the handcuffs and removed the gag.

Norma Foss rubbed her eyes and gasped for a breath of fresh air. As Bonty led her out into the office, she noticed that no one was around. She looked in all directions, then turned back to the sheriff. "Where is everyone? Where is my baby?!" She grabbed Bonty's shirt with both hands and shook him. He understood her frustrations and just waited for her to calm down. That could take some time, considering she was drenched in sweat and blood from head to toe.

"Norma, we're going into the house to get your baby boy. He's doing fine. But then we're taking Roy's teenage kids and all going to my house."

"Your house? Why your house? I did my part. Just let me take my baby and get away from here. You'll never see or hear from me again! I promise!"

"It's not that simple. Come on, get moving, and I'll explain when we get to my house."

Norma didn't need any prodding. Her baby was in the house, and she moved swiftly to the door with Al trotting behind. She opened the door and found her newborn son sleeping in a basket on the living room coffee table. Norma carefully lifted her son out of the basket and cradled him hard. She would never let go.

A few minutes later, Jimmy and Jenny came down the stairs, each clutching a large duffel bag. Sheriff Bonty greeted them at the base of the stairs with a stern look on his face. "I said suitcase, not duffel bags."

"We've decided we're only going for one night at the most," said Jenny as she returned a stubborn look right back at Al. "If Daddy doesn't want us back here, we got plenty of friends we can stay with."

Jimmy looked over Al's shoulder and noticed a lady hugging the baby in the living room. "Hey, isn't that Miss Foss, our fifth-grade teacher?"

Jenny sidestepped Al, and she and Jimmy both went into the living room. "Miss Foss, is that you?" asked Jenny as she saw what a mess her teacher from five years ago had become. "Are you alright?"

Norma turned to her past students, still embracing her new bundle of joy, and cried. "Never better, Jenny. Never better."

"Is he your baby?" asked Jimmy.

"Yes, Jimmy, he's my son. I'm going to name him Brett in memory of his father, who he will never know."

"The baby's father died?" inquired a puzzled Jenny. "But your husband's name is Jim Foss, not Brett. And ain't nobody I know in town said your husband's dead, ma'am."

When Norma didn't reply and turned to face the window, Jimmy took a step toward her. Gently, but to the point, he asked, "The baby's father is Coach Berry, isn't he? He's the only Brett I know who died."

"But coach Berry's wife was pregnant too," inserted Jenny, who was trying desperately to figure out this mystery. Her naiveté broke into pieces, then it dawned on her what had happened. She stared indignantly at her former fifth-grade teacher, who happened to be her all-time favorite. Jenny's face turned bright red with anger, and she stormed towards the hallway, but Al caught her and gave her a hug. Jenny retracted with a push, then looked up at the sheriff's face and thought she saw a tear.

Jimmy glanced at his sister and saw it, too, and he was baffled. "Sheriff Bonty, I do believe you're crying. Well, that's a first!" Jimmy walked over, grabbed Jenny by the arm, and pulled her away from Bonty. "Come on, Sis. We're out of here. I'll drive." The sheriff released his embrace and watched as Jimmy and Jenny picked up their duffel bags and headed toward the front door.

Norma looked at Bonty and said, "You need to tell them, Al. You need to tell them now before they leave."

As the front door opened, the sheriff took a step forward towards the siblings and with a loud, forceful tone, declared,

"Wait! Jimmy and Jenny, there's something you need to know." He paused, unsure of how to say it. "I'm your father!"

Jimmy and Jenny froze in their tracks, and both duffels dropped simultaneously at their feet. As if they were performing a synchronized swimming event, they both turned with their hands on their hips and muttered the world's shortest, but most frequently asked question: "What?"

CHAPTER 83

Monday, March 15, 1982

7:00 a.m.

Getting FBI agents out of bed on a Monday morning after they had picnicked with their families all day Sunday was not an easy task. The government operatives cherished the minimal hours they had with their wives and kids and did their best to stretch every pleasurable moment out as long as possible before donning the blue suits once again. Agent Tecka rounded up fifteen coworkers, and by dawn, they were swarming Daughtry's house in the Everglades. He remained with them to supervise the confiscation of all evidence, mainly the videos.

Meanwhile, Agent Jones had faced similar frustrations as Tecka had following a phone call to the Orlando FBI office. Only one agent was on duty as two others had called in sick. It took most of the night, but finally, thirty agents from Central Florida Headquarters were gathered, awaiting Jones' arrival and their subsequent orders. Jones also called the Gainesville police department, and they assured him that the SWAT bus would be ready for action when the FBI arrived. He opted to drive the Ford LTD up the Florida Turnpike instead of waiting for a government Learjet to be prepped.

Bo Yardly rode shotgun in the passenger seat, while Tyrus, Willy, and Johnny Murphree sat in the back. Willy glanced over Jones' shoulder and noticed the speedometer was buried to the right, just past the 140 mph mark. The car was moving so fast that it was doubtful anyone seeing the FBI vehicle approaching would even notice the blue flashing light on the dashboard. The southern Florida sky was its old gorgeous springtime self: light blue with a few puffs of clouds. They would be meeting the Orlando-based agents in the parking lot at Tinker Field. Jones and company needed to arrive and get out of there before the spring training crowd of Minnesota retirees started filling in to watch the Twins host the Tigers. It was nearing ten o'clock, and they had just flown past the Fort Pierce exit. At this speed, they would be in Orlando by eleven and Gainesville by noon, barring any left lane-hogging snowbirds out admiring the citrus blossoms along the highway. The accelerator was jammed to the floorboard.

Lew was following a not-so-safe distance of fifty yards behind Jones in the Trans Am. But he had no problem keeping close. It was, after all, the Bandit's getaway vehicle! Janet was next to him in the front, while Otis, Lance, and Pancho held on for dear life in the backseat. Jones had told Lew that they would need to wait at the Gainesville PD once they got up there, and Lew lied and said they would. But no one in the car, including Janet, had any plans to sit back and wait. After leaving Orlando, they would head directly to the O'Sullivan Center and wait for the FBI agents and SWAT team to arrive.

It wouldn't make much difference where they waited, however, because Harfield, Jackson, and the rest wouldn't be there when they arrived. Nor would the O'Sullivan Center.

*****

Roy hadn't slept much on the flight from his ranch to Gainesville. He was restless thinking about how the mission that his brother and Oliver Harfield had designed had changed over the years. Now with the latest complication, would the plan ever be successful? Roy reclined his chair and looked out into the night sky, seeing only the blinking blue light at the tip of the Learjet's wing. Memories of the last twenty years were a neuronal mishmash of impulses swirling around in his brain:

When the CIA had carried out President Kennedy's secret mission in December of 1962 and built an underground nuclear control facility in Gainesville, no one could have predicted that the University of Florida would grow so fast. And when university officials broke ground in October of 1977 on the Murphy O'Sullivan Center, architects were told that an old, dormant sewage facility lay ten feet below the ground. The design professionals wanted to extract the tank prior to excavation for the new basketball fieldhouse but were told that the storage container was owned by the federal government and must be left in place. No one questioned why the feds wanted to preserve a tank full of excrement and unidentified amoebas, so university officials simply built the center over it, end of story.

This had caused a big problem for Oliver and Ray. Previously, the entrance to their secret base of operations had been disguised as a manhole cover, and they came and went only during the darkness of night. But by New Year's Day in 1978, concrete had been poured on top of the manhole cover by university construction workers. The cover had been built of ferromagnetic materials with a transponder embedded in the iron. The transponder was powered by a small nuclear battery that had a lifespan of a hundred years. President Kennedy had feared that Soviet missiles could create significant earth movement, and if one landed in central Florida, he wanted the ability to locate his subterranean control center quickly. The manhole cover could be detected even if it was smothered under a large quantity of dirt.

Oliver and Ray had to wait for a year before they could return to their op center. The men's basketball locker room was built directly over the buried manhole cover, and during the Christmas Holiday in 1978, when construction workers had been given days off to be with their families, Oliver brought in twelve men to covertly create a new entrance into the underground control center. They chipped through the floor tiles and the concrete foundation, then dug down to the manhole cover. Then they framed up a four-foot by four-foot steel encasement in the tunnel leading from the locker room to the control room and finished by welding steps onto one wall. The trick was to design an undetectable entrance, which happened to be in the equipment room, using tiles glued onto a wooden trap door. After several adjustments had been made, there was no way to see it with the naked eye.

However, there was still one obstacle in the way of their master plan. Once the fieldhouse was in use, which would be the fall of 1980, the only people who would be allowed in or out of the men's locker room would be their coaches, managers, and players. And after hours, the entire Murphy O'Sullivan Center would be protected by security guards.

That's when Ray Jackson had an idea. His nephew Jimmy was a decent player on the Seminole Bend High School basketball team. Perhaps Roy could persuade Coach Brett Berry to do whatever it took to get Jimmy a scholarship to the University of Florida. The mission to hold America hostage would begin in early fall of 1982, and it would be imperative to have access day and night to the operations center. If Jimmy were playing for the Gators, he would have access to the locker room.

Brett never knew why Roy was so intense on Jimmy playing for Florida. He had no knowledge of Roy's clandestine activities and didn't know that Roy was his father. The only thing Brett was aware of was that Roy

Jackson was a ruthless son-of-a-bitch and a man to be feared. But with a chance to beat Martin Park and win the title, Brett opted to play his best players, which most likely ended Jimmy Jackson's chances of playing NCAA Division I basketball, not just at Florida, but anywhere. And after the game, when he didn't see his wife or Roy anywhere in the gym, Brett was terrified that he had made the biggest coaching mistake of his life.

Roy never cared much for Sheryl, and it didn't faze him to murder her family so she would move to Florida and marry Brett. But he had no intention of killing her until after his grandson was born, and he was devastated that Brett got himself killed trying to save the life of a man who was already dead and placed posthumously in Brett's own pickup truck. Roy wondered if Brett recognized Doc Stanley at the wheel of the truck before it collapsed on top of him. What a shame that the only doctor in town who still made house calls accidentally came to the wrong house—at the wrong time. Doc Stanley was very good at delivering babies but very bad with addresses. Roy was trying to figure out where he could find a body for the decoy maneuver he had planned when the doorbell rang. Doc had semi-retired a few years back and lived alone. He ran a small office where he saw a handful of patients once a week, but only if the fish weren't biting. Yes, he would be the perfect decoy.

Roy kept Doc's decomposing body rolled up in horse blankets out in the barn until the cadaver was needed. Over the phone, Roy plotted out the accident with Sam Dulie. The DNR chief remotely controlled Brett's truck from the video center in Homestead and caused the fiery crash into the culvert.

At the end of the basketball game against Martin Park, fans were celebrating like wild lunatics. Nobody noticed Roy Jackson pull out a small gun from his pants pocket and force Sheryl Berry out the door of the gymnasium. Still furious that the University of Florida coaches left without seeing Jimmy shine on the court, he returned to the ranch driving recklessly with one hand on the wheel while the other waved the gun at various points on Sheryl's face. After shoving Brett's wife through the front door of his ranch, he threatened to kill her unborn child. Roy then made plans to make sure Sheryl was never seen or heard from again.

But then that damn coroner, Cliff Sutton, found out that the skeletal remains in Brett's truck were from a big man, not a young lady. Time for Plan B or C or wherever they were now in the alphabet: cut off Sheryl's hand and place it at the scene of the midair crash in the Everglades. And that meant that is was also time to recruit Norma Foss into the scheme.

Norma's best friend was Judge Boone's daughter Maddie. She had confided to her about the affair with Brett Berry at the teacher retreat the previous summer. Maddie wasn't the best person to confide in because it was painful for her to keep a secret, and sure enough, she told her dad the story one night at the dinner table. The next day, while out trolling in the weeds off the north shore, Judge Boone revealed the affair to Roy. Most folks in Seminole Bend knew that Norma's husband was sterile (rumors spread quickly in a small town), so when Norma got pregnant, the good Christians of the community assumed it was a miracle. Roy, however, because he caught wind of Norma's affair, reckoned it was most likely Brett's baby.

Brett never knew, nor did Norma, that Roy was Brett's father. Norma would have had a massive coronary if she knew that the baby forming vocal cords in her tummy would one day use them to call the badass rancher Grandpappy!

Norma resembled Sheryl in many ways: face, size, age, and figure. She was married to Jim Foss, a very well-liked and respected member of the community. Roy figured that blackmailing her would be easy. Norma was angry, but she went along with Roy's plan so she could save her marriage now that Brett was gone. She could also save her teaching job at the elementary school, and yes, save her own life! Besides, since falling in love with Brett, she hadn't much liked Sheryl anyway. So she agreed to pretend that she was Sheryl.

Norma drove to a travel agency in Orlando and bought tickets for the Trans South Airlines flight from Miami to Atlanta, and then checked in at the Miami airport. But she never got on the airplane. Afterward, Roy was worried that Norma would run and tell authorities about the plot, so he forced her to stay with him. But he would only keep her around until his other grandson was born. He decided that once Sheryl and Norma had delivered their babies, they would be erased from this earth, and Roy could one day tell his grandsons that they were twins.

CHAPTER 84
Monday, March 15, 1982
7:30 a.m.

Oliver's Learjet touched down at the Gainesville Regional Airport just before dawn was awakening, and Florida could once again make a claim as the nation's true Sunshine State. During the flight from Seminole Bend, he had tried to radio Ray but without luck. A good CIA agent has a unique sense of intuition and can surmise when something has gone wrong, and Oliver's thoughts were troubling.

Even more troubling was what Oliver saw in an open hangar as the jet touched down. It was an F-4 Phantom fighter jet, just like the ones used by the Special Operations Unit back in the early '70s. As everyone was headed for the terminal, Oliver excused himself and walked briskly towards the hangar. He was met outside the large open door by two men in khaki pants, light blue shirts, and tennis shoes. One had a Brave's baseball cap pulled down tightly on his forehead, but other than that, they looked like they were wearing some sort of casual uniform.

"May I help you, sir?" asked the man in the cap.

"Yes, I would like to know why this Air Force jet is parked in this non-military hangar," replied Oliver in an authoritative tone.

"Whom may I inquire is asking?" replied the cap man in an equally directorial voice.

Oliver pulled out his badge. "CIA. Now could you please answer my question?"

The man without the cap took a close look at the badge, then replied, "Your badge is CIA alright, but it says *retired*. Now, may I ask what your business is here?"

"Retired or not, I hold a high rank in the United States government! You will explain to me what an F-4 Phantom jet is doing in this hangar! The F-4s were buried years ago, son. I will be on the phone to the White House if you don't answer my question immediately!"

"We have presidential orders to commandeer this hangar," said the man in the cap as he threateningly took a step towards Oliver. Yes, he did have presidential orders, but they were from Richard Nixon. Hopefully, the retired CIA man wouldn't ask to see them. "Our mission is top secret. Now step away and get along on your business."

Oliver knew he wouldn't get any further. He had noticed both men were carrying pistols strapped inside their belts, and he was confident they wouldn't hesitate using them. Yet, Oliver was curious. Why would the president have two plainclothes agents guard a military aircraft instead of uniformed soldiers with automatic weapons? And why was a retired Phantom jet now back in use? And what was that jet doing in Gainesville right now while he was about to execute a mission that he had planned for twenty years? Coincidence? Oliver didn't believe in coincidences. Without acknowledging the two men, he turned and walked to the terminal.

*****

Oliver didn't speak a word while driving the limousine carefully at the speed limit through the city. He wasn't about to be pulled over by some rookie cop playing around with some Doppler speed radar as rush hour was commencing. But everyone in the car could tell by Oliver's silence that something was bothering him. They hadn't noticed the

Phantom fighter upon deplaning at the airport, and Oliver hadn't mentioned a thing to them.

"Something bugging you, Oliver?" asked Roy.

"Nothing. Just thinking, that's all. We need to hurry and get to the O'Sullivan Center before the coaches and students start arriving."

"Won't need to worry about the students," replied Governor Daughtry. "The university is on Spring Break this week. I'm sure they're all partying in Daytona Beach as we speak."

"Well, someone will be around. And we heard that security was going to change the locks over the break. If my master key doesn't work, we'll have to eliminate another guard like before, then fiddle around trying to find the right key on his belt."

Ten minutes later, the limo parked sideways, blocking three handicapped slots in the O'Sullivan Center lot. Oliver hung a blue and white handicapped permit on his mirror, one he had stolen from a car whose unlucky driver had left the window open. All the men exited the vehicle and walked towards the back entrance that was reserved for coaches and administrators. Hopefully, if security were watching, they would think university president Robert Marston was showing off the new basketball facility to some other important people. Oliver slid the master key into the door with no problem. The locks had yet to be changed.

With no coaches or anyone else in sight, Oliver and company entered the men's locker room. The door locked automatically when it was closed. In the back near the showers was the equipment room, which needed to be locked manually after exiting. Today, it wasn't locked, and the secret trap door embedded into the floor tiles was wide open. Everyone paused for a moment and glanced at one another with cold sober looks on their faces. Something was wrong, something was very wrong.

Each of Oliver's accomplices pulled out a weapon. Roy descended the steps first. He feared the worse for his brother. The manhole cover had also been displaced and was leaning up against the wall, another major security breach for this team of gangsters. Oliver and the rest waited impatiently for Roy's prompt that would signal it was okay to enter. It came, but it wasn't the signal they were expecting to hear.

"No!" cried Roy as his voice echoed from the operations center to the equipment room above. "Ray, oh my God, Ray!"

Ray Jackson was lying face-up on a small cot with his eyes wide open and staring at the ceiling. Unfortunately, he had witnessed his own death. His neck had been slashed from ear lobe to ear lobe, and the small traces of blood still left in his body were trickling out of his carotid artery. He was white as a ghost, which of course, he was. The murder weapon lay on the floor next to the cot. It was a stainless steel Gillette safety razor blade.

Roy pounded his fists on his brother's deflated chest. "Who did this to you? I will kill him, Ray, I swear I will get revenge! No mercy!"

Oliver stood behind Roy and patted his back, a sympathetic gesture to the brother of his best friend. Then he kneeled down and whispered to Roy, "This is a tough time, but we need to work fast. Are you up for it?" Roy nodded, then stood and placed a nearby blanket over Ray, covering his body and the red, blood-soaked sheet he was lying on. Everyone else in the room remained motionless, wondering if it was time they gave up and got away while the getting was good.

"Our moles must be Jim Brown and Tyrus Banks," confirmed Oliver. "Jim Brown must be Air Force or Special Ops. There was an F-4 Phantom fighter jet in a hangar at the airport. That's where I was while you were waiting in the terminal."

"F-4?" questioned Governor Daughtry. "Those have been retired from the military for quite some time. Banks doesn't know how to fly, so Jim must be a pilot. How did he get ahold of a Phantom, and why is it parked at the Gainesville airport?"

"Those are questions for later. Come over here and take a look." Oliver signaled for the group to approach three televisions bolted onto the counter. The screens had been smashed, and the remote controllers were missing. There was an empty space where a fourth TV had been placed. "Jim took out our video system and stole the remotes and a television. Sam, what are our options here? By now, Banks and Brown will have secured the Homestead facility, so we can't go back there. Two of the nine-passenger jets we rigged with cameras and jammers are scheduled to depart later this afternoon, and Tassett has installed jammers in the control towers at their destinations. I know we weren't planning on doing this for a couple of months, but can we somehow get this mission initiated today?"

"We haven't fully tested the equipment, Oliver," answered Sam Dulie. "I don't know if we can pull this off that soon."

"The hell with more testing! We've taken down four passenger jets in two mid-air collisions in the last month! I think the equipment works just fine!"

"Can we deploy the USS Halibut right away?" asked Daughtry. "We'd have some excellent bargaining leverage if we controlled a sub carrying two nuclear missiles on board."

"Yes, I'll get on the phone with Admiral Inman up at Kitsap. He will be devastated when he hears that his good friend, Ray, was killed. He told me earlier that he could have the sub into the Pacific within an hour or two of my call. But he has no idea we need it ready this soon. He's a good man, he'll make it happen. I know we can count on him." Oliver walked to the shortwave and found it was working. "Thank God Jim didn't take out our communications. He must have wanted a quick exit."

Five minutes later, Admiral Inman confirmed that he would have the USS Halibut deployed and through the Puget

Sound and into Pacific waters by no later than two that afternoon, which was five o'clock on the east coast.

"We have a stock of remotes back on my ranch," informed Roy. "But I don't have video equipment, so the cameras embedded in the nose of the planes will be useless."

Sam looked at Yussef. "You have the radio frequencies for the target jets, don't you?"

"Yes, of course," replied Yussef. "Why?"

"We can plot coordinates by listening to the pilots communicating with the air traffic control towers. From there, we can maneuver the jets in the direction we want. I know it sounds haphazard, but I think it will work."

"What are the two planes we are targeting?" asked Daughtry. "Where are they coming from and going to, Oliver?"

Oliver glanced at a printout that was tucked neatly into a folder. It listed the flight schedules for the next three months of each jet that had video cameras and jammers installed in the cockpits. Oliver knew when each plane was flying and when they would be scheduled for maintenance downtime.

"Coastal East 561 from Tampa to Atlanta leaving at 5:55 and Bayou 444 from Orlando to Dallas leaving at 6:10. Jack Tassett has jammers installed and ready to go in all four of those airports.

"Well then, we're wasting time here," replied Daughtry. "Oliver, we need to roll!"

"Scoop up what we need. I'll rig the auto-destruct mechanism. There will be nothing left but a hole in the ground."

"What about Ray?" asked Roy. "We need to get him out and give him a proper burial."

"No time, Roy. And even if we got him out, where would we put him?" Roy looked at Oliver but said nothing. He knew Oliver was right, but leaving his brother's body to be blown to bits was simply wrong. Oliver detected his hesitation and embraced Roy. "Look, Roy, your brother was my best friend.

This is hard on me, too. But I know he will be happy laid to rest right here where his life's mission took him. Come on, let's go."

A W-54 nuclear warhead was rigged to a timing device when the underground operations center was built in the early '60s. In the event of an emergency evacuation due to the close proximity of an enemy, such as the Soviets approaching from the Atlantic or Cubans advancing northward from the Keys, President Kennedy wanted a self-destruct mechanism installed that would leave no trace of military intelligence. This handy device was encased in a small cylindrical container but could wipe out three or four city blocks in an instant. While the others gathered equipment that they could carry out in a hurry, Oliver set the timer. They would have two hours to get out of Dodge, or they would melt like a candle in the fission of the nuclear blast. It was 9:00 a.m.

CHAPTER 85

Monday, March 15, 1982

10:00 a.m.

Lew was fueling up the Trans Am at a turnpike service area a few miles from Leesburg, while the FBI team of sixteen identical Ford LTDs were getting on I-4 after their slight detour to Tinker Field when it happened. The blast sounded like ten sonic booms going off simultaneously, and a rapidly moving cloud of gray smoke could be seen rising above the horizon. Manatee sea cows surfaced in the Crystal River to sneak a peek at the phenomena in the sky sixty-five miles away, while tourists searching for eternal life at the Fountain of Youth in Saint Augustine now feared the end of the world.

Agent Jones radioed the Florida Highway Patrol and ordered them to get every vehicle off the turnpike. The Ford LTD parade of expertly trained FBI drivers was sizzling the asphalt with Goodyear rubber, moving so fast that Daytona 500 winner Bobby Allison wouldn't even catch them in his Gatorade Buick Regal. Lew didn't bother hanging up the gas hose before firing up the Trans Am and storming back on the turnpike. Two miles up the road, he passed a state trooper who was trying to signal him to pull over and clear the highway. But Smokey never could catch the Bandit, and Lew was doing his best Burt Reynolds escape artistry imitation. Pancho leaned over Otis and puked out the open window.

The SWAT team in Gainesville didn't wait for the FBI after the explosion rocked the city. They joined every policeman, fireman, and paramedic, both on duty and off duty, in their slapdash race to the University of Florida campus. Or what used to be the University of Florida campus, that is.

Seats from Ben Hill Stadium, the Gator's football arena that set adjacent to the O'Sullivan Center just across Gale Lemerand Drive, could be seen splashing down in Lake Alice a couple of blocks away. The giant red bricks from the College of Engineering were scattered among the grass and trees of Reitz Union North Lawn, and the concrete dust, which was all that was left of Trusler Hall, completely consumed Hume Pond. The pond sat across a salmagundi of tar, gravel, and crushed rock from a street that two minutes ago was known as Museum Road. Most of the college's buildings that hadn't skyrocketed simply collapsed into a giant sinkhole.

Within minutes, the huge mushroom cloud darkened the skies, and traffic moving about the entire city came to a standstill. Pedestrians dove to the ground covering their heads with their hands. From miles in every direction, kids could be heard screaming and dogs barking. Cars and trucks speeding down nearby Interstate 75 lost control and flipped into ditches, and small planes rolled and were whisked away like paper blowing in the wind. The Gainesville emergency rescue teams gathered at the VA Medical Center on Archer Road, which miraculously was untouched by the explosion or flying debris. But they remained paralyzed in the parking lot, shocked and stunned at what they saw. Thoroughly trained in handling automobile crashes and even gunshot wounds, the EMTs, police, and firemen had no idea where to begin searching for bodies.

But God works in mysterious ways, and this day was no exception. Professor emeritus Gregory Coakley, perhaps the most well-liked member of the University of Florida faculty, a renowned research expert in the area of physics and a weekly columnist for *Scientific American* magazine, had retired three weeks earlier. He was affectionately nicknamed "Unlucky Coakley" by his colleagues who would take annual junkets to Vegas, and Professor Coakley would be stymied continually at the blackjack tables. Last year, he doubled down on three consecutive elevens and couldn't be dealt a face card to save his life. He lost $3,000 at the Stardust on the first day and had to spend the evening listening to Wayne Newton woo the ladies with *Danke Shoen*. For all the money the friendly professor had put into the Stardust's coffers, Wayne should be thanking him. Professor Coakley's final unlucky hand was dealt three weeks ago, the day he purchased a ticket to Germany as a vacation to celebrate retirement with his wife, Clare. On the way home, the couple changed planes in Chicago and boarded the doomed Heartland Lakes flight to Tampa, which was the last leg of their journey. Today, the entire faculty, support staff, and administration attended Coakley's memorial service in his hometown of Spring Hill, and the only personnel left on campus when the bomb exploded were security guards. The handful of students who remained in their dorms for Spring Break were injured, but every one of them survived.

CHAPTER 86

Monday, March 15, 1982

1:45 p.m.

President Donald Layman was intently watching the disaster unfolding in Gainesville via CNN from a portable television that had been placed on his desk in the Oval Office. Chief of Staff, Gordon Brubaker, had called Tallahassee an hour ago wanting to speak to Governor Daughtry, but the governor's office said he was at his vacation home in Homestead. Brubaker ordered Daughtry's office staff to place top priority on reaching the governor and have him call the president immediately.

Layman was waiting impatiently when the private phone on his desk rang. Brubaker reached over the president, grabbed the receiver, and answered with one simple word, "Yes?"

"CIA four six one, H as in Henry, five. Agent Oliver Harfield speaking. I need to speak to the president. This is a matter of national security."

Gordon Brubaker had met Oliver Harfield at Langley, and he also knew Harfield had been retired for some time now. Why would he be calling for the president using his retired security number?

"Oliver, this is Gordon Brubaker. We are waiting on a call from Governor Daughtry in Florida and can't tie up this line. What's up?"

"Gordon, I have Governor Daughtry with me. You need to hand the phone over to the president."

Brubaker pushed the hold button and gave the receiver to President Layman. He had the most inquisitive look in his eyes. "It's one of our retired CIA agents, Oliver Harfield. Says he has Governor Daughtry with him."

Layman quickly grabbed the receiver and pushed the hold button again. "Harfield. Let me speak to Daughtry."

Oliver had taken his last presidential order several years ago. He was now the man in authority and would be making directives from here on out. "Mr. President, I now have America under siege, and your time is running out for doing something about it. Many, many civilian deaths will occur before the end of the day without your immediate actions. Do I have your attention?"

"What are you talking about?" asked Layman. "Are you insane, Harfield?"

"Perhaps, sir, but I also plan on becoming very rich. Do you have a pen and paper handy?"

"Yes, of course. Get to the point, Harfield. And by the way, you are in big trouble."

"My problems are coming to a close. Yours are just beginning, Mr. President. Now write this down. Routing number is 6877934810. Account number 45-00328654. You will transfer one billion dollars into that account before midnight tonight, or two jetliners will be sent spinning out of control from 35,000 feet to whatever lies below them. Also, two nuclear weapons are aimed and locked on Los Angeles and Washington. If you attempt to put a tracer on those accounts, I will know, and the Washington Monument will collapse into your bedroom. Do you have any questions, Mr. President?"

"No one holds America hostage, Harfield. You of all men should know that. I will not be threatened by your nonsense!"

"You would risk the lives of millions of Americans, sir?" responded Harfield boldly. "And you called me insane? Get a clue, Mr. President. The midair crashes in Miami and Tampa were my doing. The bombing in Gainesville was my doing.

That was to show you that I'm not playing games here. It's two o'clock. You have exactly ten hours. You better get hustling, sir!"

Oliver didn't wait for a reply. He hung up the phone on his Learjet as it touched down on the cracked asphalt runway at the Jackson ranch.

CHAPTER 87

Monday, March 15, 1982

2:15 p.m.

Norma Foss sat on a couch feeding her infant son while Sheriff Al Bonty sat at his kitchen table having a Coke with Jimmy and Jenny Jackson. He had just finished explaining how it came to be that their mother was in a Jasurbian harem and why Roy Jackson had raised them as his own. This was the first time he had spoken to his kids since they were infants.

"A harem? In Jasurbia? Sheriff, you're in the business of proof. My sis and me need some evidence of this story if you don't mind." Jimmy was having a difficult time swallowing the story and was using sarcasm as his defense mechanism. Jenny was just sitting at the table, motionless and speechless. She was beginning to think the story could be true, but like Jimmy, wanted to hear more.

From the couch in the next room, Norma, the kid's beloved fifth-grade teacher, decided it was time to say something. "Kids, the sheriff is your father. Everything he has told you is the truth. We don't have much time, so please trust me—and him."

"Listen to me," inserted Sheriff Bonty. "I promise you that it is my life's mission to find your mother and bring her home. But I need to move quickly, and I need to make sure you two are safe. Please lock the doors when I leave and stay away from the windows."

"No, sir," said Jimmy and Jenny at the same time, both shaking their heads.

"What do you mean, no, sir?" asked Al.

"If you're our dad, we're going with you!" pronounced Jimmy as he rose and pounded his hand on the table. He looked at his sister, and she jumped up and nodded back. "There's got to be some way we can help. From now on, we're in this together."

Al stood up and stared at his children, thinking about the years he missed watching them grow up. He was frozen in time, and tears were flowing down his cheeks. Jimmy looked at Jenny, and their hearts began to melt. Their father's sincerity was real, as was their own compassion toward him.

The siblings walked over and embraced their dad. Norma wiped off her own cheeks and squeezed her newborn. They were all thankful to be out from under the clutches of Roy Jackson.

*****

Now that it was inevitable that Jimmy and Jenny were going to tag along, the sheriff changed his plans and asked Norma to come with, as well.

"Why?" inquired Norma, still clutching her newborn. She wasn't about to let anything happen that could separate herself from her baby. "Where are we going?"

"There's some laundry that needs airing before we go any further, plus I know a very safe place for you and your child."

Norma gave Al a puzzled look, then repeated his words in the form of a question. "Some laundry that needs airing, you say? What are you talking about?"

Al asked Jenny to call Tyrone Banks and have him meet them at the Catholic church at 3:00 p.m. Sheriff Bonty wanted to see if Tyrone had any idea where to find Willy. Al was ready to tell Willy everything and to enlist his help in stopping Roy.

Seeing it was Spring Break at Seminole Bend High School, Tyrone was just hanging around the house, bench pressing

400 pounds in his front yard where all the neighbors could watch. Sure, he would love to hang out with his girlfriend, but an afternoon date at the Catholic church didn't sound like a great time seeing they both were Baptist.

"The Catholic church?" asked a skeptical Norma. "Why? What's at the church?"

"You'll see. And after we're done with some business, Father O'Shea and the nuns will take good care of you and the baby."

No one said a word in the fifteen-minute drive to the church. Everyone had many questions, but no one was sure where to start. Tyrone pulled into the parking lot in his rusty Volkswagen at the same time the others arrived. He was wearing a muscle t-shirt and work out shorts. The sweat had already dried to his skin.

When all the pleasantries were done (Jenny hugging Tyrone and Jimmy giving him a high five), they all turned in a semi-circle toward Sheriff Bonty, waiting for guidance and instructions.

"There's someone here you need to see. Follow me." The three high schoolers glanced bewilderedly at each other, and Norma gave a perplexed look at Al. Then, they all moved toward the church entrance.

Inside, Father O'Shea was replacing the altar candles. He turned towards the door as it opened. He wasn't exactly excited to see his guests, but it was his job to make everyone welcome in the Lord's house.

"Hello, Sheriff Bonty. I doubt you're here for confession, so I'm assuming you are on official business. I see you brought Roy's kids with you. Jimmy, Jenny, good to see you. And Miss Foss, it appears you've had your baby. How nice. Now, how may I assist you today?" Father O'Shea was appalled at the sight of every one of them. Thus the reason his words had been cold and blunt.

"Actually, Father, I am here to confess. Would you be so kind as to hear me out?"

"I doubt all of us would fit into a confessional booth, so would you like to take a seat at the table in the corner?" Father motioned to a folding table that had stacks of brochures entitled *Convert to Catholicism Today* and collection envelopes so numerous that there would never be enough Sundays or generous parishioners to fill them all up.

Once they all were seated, Sheriff Bonty detailed the grand master plan put together by Roy and Ray Jackson, Oliver Harfield, and Governor Daughtry. He purposely didn't mention that Tyrus Banks was involved, seeing Tyrone had no idea his father was even alive. He would wait for a better time to mention that detail. Bonty guaranteed Father O'Shea that he will do everything in his power to find and release the priest's brother and sister from the place Roy is holding them captive.

Father O'Shea was in deep shock and disbelief. He had spent every evening praying for the well-being of his siblings and also praying for the forgiveness of Roy and company for the sins they had committed. He personally had a tough time forgiving those bastards, but his faith and duties to the Lord required it. Now, like a lightning bolt sent from heaven, Father finds out that Sheriff Al is a good guy after all!

An air vent ran from the floor directly underneath the table to the basement of the church, and Sisters Mary and Roberta could overhear the conversation taking place directly above them. Sheryl Berry came over and listened too. She was astonished to discover that Sheriff Al was actually a mole who was playing along with the scheme just to save his wife and kids.

The elephant in the room was getting bigger by the minute. Sheryl now understood why the sheriff came to the church. She started up the stairs with the nuns following right behind.

As she approached the table, Sheryl was looking at only one person. Norma Foss saw her coming and the two locked eyes. A mix of fear and anger spread across each of their faces. Then everyone else at the table turned and noticed the pregnant gal heading their way.

"Oh my God!" Jenny, Jimmy, and Tyrone sounded like a choir in perfect harmony. They all stood up and covered their mouths, then Jenny ran to the coach's wife and wrapped her arms as far as they could reach around her gravid waist. "You're alive!" As Sheryl returned the embrace, they all could see the stump where her left hand used to be.

During his confession, Al had described the role Norma played when she disguised as Sheryl. He emphasized that Norma was forced into the plan to save her own life. Bonty had looked at everyone sitting around the table and asked them all to forgive Norma. She lowered her head in embarrassment, gripped her baby, and spilled tears over the newborn's soft little head. The sheriff had purposely failed to mention that Sheryl was alive and well in the basement of the church.

"Sheryl," muttered Norma, half aloud and half under her breath. "I'm so sorry. I'm so very sorry. Please forgive me!"

"Forgive you?" replied Sheryl, trying unsuccessfully to hold back her rage. "Not even in a Catholic church will I ever forgive you! First, trying to steal my husband, and second, trying to end my life." She then raised her stump above her head. "Nor for this, either. So, go to hell, my dear!" Father O'Shea's eyelids opened to their fullest extent. Sheriff Al stood up to separate the ladies.

As Norma turned away to protect the baby, Sheryl wagged a forefinger at her. "That child of yours. Well, there's something you should know. Brett—" Sheryl stopped suddenly while everyone waited on pins and needles to hear what she was going to say.

Not telling Norma the truth would be Sheryl's revenge.

CHAPTER 88

Monday, March 15, 1982
4:00 p.m.

CIA Director Bill Knutson vacillated for some time but made the decision at 4:00 p.m. to reveal Classified File Number 6441 to President Layman and his lead administrative team. The executives and the Joint Chiefs of Staff were in a frantic and frenzied emergency meeting in the War Room at the White House. In 1972, President Richard Nixon had boldly handwritten the words *Top Secret (CIA Director's Eyes Only!)* on the file and affixed the gold presidential seal. It was to be distributed to high ranking personnel only in the event of a "dire threat to national security." Knutson had already shared the file with Secretary of Defense Carlyle Liston to ensure the file's perpetuity in the event of Knutson's death.

"Bill," said the president in a serious tone as he opened the meeting with no greetings or salutations. "You have something to say before we begin?"

"Yes, Mr. President. I am holding a top-secret document that has been locked in the CIA director's desk since Richard Nixon gave it to Director Richard Combs back in 1972. None of the subsequent directors have revealed its contents until I shared it with Carlyle a few months ago."

"Well, get on with it, Bill, we have little time to waste," inserted Layman.

"Do you all remember NFL football player Bo Yardly?" Every one of the Joint Chiefs and top aides were big fans of the pigskin, as was the president. They all nodded eagerly, reminiscing in their minds the touted running back out of Alabama.

"Sure we do," responded Secretary of State Walter Cletes. "He was killed in Nam. Pretty sad loss for sports fans."

"He's alive, Walt. And working for us." The words landed with a thud on the ears of all those listening. Everyone was in a state of shock and disbelief. "His death was faked in order to transfer him into a special operations force that would seek out and destroy corruption in our own department. Three men in that clandestine task force spent the last ten years probing and scrutinizing malfeasance within the CIA. To their families and friends, they are dead. It's a long story that I will tell you all about later, but for now, I need to get to the nuts and bolts of this file. I believe it could affect what we all decide in the next few minutes."

"Get on with it, Bill," urged the president.

"Bo and his team were provided an F-4 Phantom fighter jet and a Huey chopper to have at their disposal. They carried presidential orders allowing them to refuel and stock up on ammunition at naval air bases throughout the world, and the billing would go straight to the CIA director himself. Embedded into their radar tracking system was a clearance code giving them carte blanche access to worldwide airspace, both in the United States and that of our allies around the globe. The fighter jet and chopper have a tracking beacon, so we know where they are at all times. Both are currently sitting at the Gainesville Municipal Airport in Florida."

Director Knutson paused for a moment so others could begin to understand where he was going with this. "Coincidence, perhaps, that Bo's task force would be in Gainesville at the same time the University of Florida campus gets destroyed? I seriously doubt that. Carlyle and I both believe Bo had been tracking Harfield and was close to disposing of him and revealing his mission when Harfield accelerated his plan."

"So you think Bo's team could help us?" asked Cletes.

"I know you've stated that we won't negotiate, Mr. President, so I think Bo could be a viable option. I suggest before we make any further decisions today that we locate him and find out what he knows."

Just then, the door to the War Room opened, and General Ross Clifton entered with a folded piece of paper between his fingers. He apologized for interrupting, walked over to Director Knutson, and handed him the note. "Sorry, sir," whispered Clifton to Knutson, then walked back out. All eyes were on the CIA director while he opened the paper and read it.

"We won't need to locate Bo Yardly," stated Knutson. "Seems he has located us. He's on hold on the phone over at my office."

"Patch him through to the War Room," ordered President Layman. "Make it quick!"

* * * * *

For one hour, Bo briefed the president's cabinet with critical details of Oliver's masterplan and his involvement for the past decade. When grilled by Walter Cletes on why he hadn't come forth to authorities earlier, Bo explained his orders from President Nixon had specified that his special ops team of three was to take all measures necessary to liberate America from any dangers posed by CIA corruption, and then to terminate all persons involved in such perilous activities. Nixon was very blunt when he told Bo off the record, "Spare American taxpayers the cost of lengthy courtroom trials for any bastards you catch red-handed." The ops team was ready to take out Harfield when the bomb went off in Gainesville.

Before Defense Secretary Liston could call Kitsap Naval Base, word came from his office that the USS Halibut had been commandeered by unauthorized personnel led by Admiral Inman and had entered the Puget Sound. There was confirmation that two long-range nuclear missiles were on board. Liston ordered all available ships to follow the sub, but not to take any measures to stop or detain it. He didn't want a nuclear explosion ripping across the Pacific Northwest. But Admiral Inman had given all his unsuspecting sailors stationed at Kitsap a three-day shore leave, leaving the base staffed with only military police and the officer who was second in charge. When Inman sliced the throat of that officer, the entire unit of MPs was in a state of chaos. Trying to get a fleet deployed to chase the sub would be impossible.

Bo knew the USS Halibut would be in the Pacific Ocean within an hour and then cruise undetected in deep waters. Timing was now at a critical stage, and Bo wished he had completed the mission on his own and not involved the president. It was now five in the afternoon in our nation's capital.

"Do we evacuate Los Angeles and Washington, Mr. President?" asked Chief of Staff Brubaker.

"First, we need to ground all air traffic," inserted Vice President Matthews. "That's a no-brainer."

Layman paused for a few moments and looked closely at the stupefied faces of each man in the room. The air was thick, and all showed deep concern as reality set in. His next decision would determine his presidential legacy.

The choice to alarm or not alarm American citizens weighed deeply on each of their minds. Panicking a nation of 232 million people by grounding air traffic was one thing, but the inevitable trauma caused by the evacuation of two major cities would be even worse. It could lead to unnecessary casualties as people trampled over one another to get out of Los Angeles and Washington. The other option was to pay the ransom, but trying to keep that secret from the American public would be impossible.

Although Bo could not see what was happening in the War Room, he could hear and feel the tension through the telephone lines. So many times in his football career at a critical point in a game, Bo would enter the huddle and ask for the ball on the next play. Now it was his time to take the ball and run with it for his country.

"Gentlemen, I have a solution for you," announced Bo over the speakerphone. "I'm standing next to a fully loaded F-4 Phantom fighter jet. My orders from President Nixon are still in effect, and I need no permission, but I would like your blessings. Mr. President, members of the cabinet, I am going to take out the Halibut myself."

* * * * *

"Bo, the ammunition aboard the F-4 cannot penetrate ocean water at a velocity needed to do any damage to the sub," said Barney Watkins. He and Ben Smith were both Air Force majors who were selected to the special operations team of three along with Bo.

"I think he knows that," stated Ben, then looked at Bo. "What's our plan, Buddy?"

"I need you and Barney to fly these folks back to Seminole Bend in the chopper," said Bo as he motioned to Willy, Tyrus, and the others who were listening intently inside the hangar. "Then take out Jackson's ranch. They must be heading back there because they know we've got the Homestead base swarming with Fibbies. Roy's office is next to the barn. Light it up good, but be careful. Two teenagers are living in the house. They're innocent."

"You need someone in the second seat of the F-4 running radar navigational guidance," stated Barney bluntly. "Ben can handle the Huey by himself. I'm going with you."

"No, Barn, I've got a different idea. I'm in charge, and you're to go with Ben. That's an order, friend." Ben and Barney looked at each other with a deep level of concern that was easily detected by all the rest.

"I'll go with you then, Bo," stated Tyrus. "You need some company up there."

"You need to go back to Seminole Bend and be with Abby and your son, Ty. It's been way too long. You and Willy need to do some fishing too. Now, I don't want no arguments, you hear me?" Bo's voice was cracking, and moisture was clouding up his eyes.

Willy knew his best friend well enough to know there was nothing he could say that would change Bo's mind either. He stepped at him and embraced him with all his might. Bo responded in kind. The tendons and tissues from those four biceps could lift an elephant! Finally, Bo broke first and pushed his friend gently backward. "It's time to go." He then saluted and walked up the portable steps to the cockpit.

The F-4 Phantom was airborne and out of sight within minutes. Flying twice the speed of sound, Bo would reach the Strait of Juan de Fuca as the sun was setting over the Pacific Ocean. However, the sonic boom blast emitted by the fighter jet was muted by the sounds of fire engines and ambulances circling the city of Gainesville.

Meanwhile, President Layman decided he would wait to see if Bo was successful in his mission before making a pronouncement that would put America in a state of hysteria and fear. The fate of the nation now rested in the hands of Seminole Bend's gridiron hero.

CHAPTER 89

Monday, March 15, 1982
5:15 p.m.

Following a plane crash, the flying public is hesitant to board an aircraft, especially in a city where the last major aviation disaster just occurred the previous week. It's human nature, no matter how brave the appearance of the seasoned traveler seems to be. Pending the outcome of the initial investigation into the Heartland Lakes and Sky Tropic Airways midair collision, Tampa International Airport had shut down operations. Today, the NTSB lead investigator, Jake Tassett, had given the thumbs up for flights to start again. The first flight would be Coastal East 561, departing at 5:55 p.m. That flight, along with every other one leaving tonight from Tampa, had a big list of cancellations. Seems this evening, most people would rather drive seven hours to Atlanta where they would have complete control of their Ford or Chevy cockpit.

Jake Tassett met the customers that decided to brave the airways, mainly businessmen who needed a good night's rest before their early morning meeting, at Gate 14A. He said he would personally check out the cockpit and controls to ensure everything was in proper working order. Then he boarded the aircraft to make sure Connor Herman had the video, remote receiver, and jammer installed correctly. Connor and his twin brother, Casey, had maintained and repaired satellite equipment for NASA's Space Shuttle missions until one night at a Titusville bar they got drunk and beat up two astronauts in training. A short time later, they needed a job, and Jack Tassett needed them. Jack opened a duffle bag with $200,000 inside in various denominations and explained what their job description would be if they accepted his offer. He would fly them to multiple airports to rig up the videos, remote receivers, and jammers, and then pay them very handsomely for doing so. Connor and Casey never knew it, but had they turned down this incredible opportunity, they would have found eternal rest and peace in the dented dumpster out back.

WTSP was the highest-rated local news channel in Florida, with in-depth coverage stretching from Tallahassee to Naples. The station's newest reporter was Dustin Royce, a recent graduate of Florida State University's School of Communications. His first assignment was to cover the reopening of Tampa International Airport following the midair collision last week.

"The National Transportation Safety Board's lead investigator, Jake Tassett, has assured restless travelers that it's safe to take to the skies again following the disaster over Lake Okeechobee last Wednesday. As you just heard, Mr. Tassett will personally perform a preflight check on Coastal East 561 here at Gate 14A. Flight 561 is the first flight out of Tampa since the shutdown, and Tassett wants to demonstrate the serious nature that the NTSB takes when it comes to ensuring safety for all passenger planes within America's airspace. The Coastal East flight is scheduled to depart in a few minutes. Let's ask a passenger here at the gate his feelings about flying tonight.

"Excuse me, sir, are you feeling any apprehension about boarding tonight's flight in the wake of two midair collisions in the past month?"

"Not at all, son," replied Ed Knowles, a senior executive for Florida Sugar Company. "I fly in and out of Atlanta every week to visit our biggest client, Coca-Cola, and I can tell you after driving down the I-75 speedway that flying is still the safest form of travel."

"Well, there you have it," concluded Dustin as he turned to face the camera. "Reporting live for WTSP from Tampa International Airport, I'm Dustin Royce."

Meanwhile, back at police headquarters in Gainesville, Agent Tecka had just arrived on an FBI helicopter from Homestead, where his colleagues were still gathering evidence from Governor Daughtry's vacation home. In the conference room, the FBI and police were laying out a strategic plan of action to investigate the campus bombing. WTSP was being broadcast on a thirty-two-inch television in the corner of the meeting room. Police in many cities monitored news events to pick up leads in unsolved cases. Agent Tecka noticed the live feed coming from the Tampa airport, and he rose from his seat as if he had just sat on a tack.

"Jack, look!" said Tecka as he pointed to the screen.

Agent Jones glanced over to the television, then quickly got out of his chair and walked over to the corner. "Well, I'll be damned. There's Jake Tassett. We've got an APB out on him all over the country, and instead, he miraculously appears right before us!"

"Jack, that flight. Coastal East 561. He said he's 'personally' going to prepare the preflight check. I don't like this."

"That's it, Tom! He's rigged the flight deck. We can't let that plane leave the ground! Get on the phone to FBI headquarters in Tampa. Now!"

Everyone in the room sat in stunned silence. The police had not been briefed on Oliver Harfield's master plan, but they could infer from Jones' and Tecka's conversation that another jet was in imminent danger and that the NTSB's chief investigator was involved.

While Tecka was calling the Tampa FBI headquarters, Agent Jones was calling the head of operations at Tampa Saint Pete airport. He was waiting very impatiently on hold, pounding his fist on the desk. "Come on, damn it! Pick up!"

At six o'clock, Operations Supervisor John Duerty answered. "John Duerty. How may I help you?"

"Mr. Duerty, this is Agent Jack Jones of the FBI. I need you to ground Coastal East 561 immediately. The flight is in grave danger!"

"What? Grave danger? What do you mean? The flight rolled back five minutes ago. It should be airborne any minute now."

"Call the tower! Stop it from taking off!" Just then, an enormous cheer could be heard in the background. All airport employees were whooping and hollering, celebrating things finally getting back to normal in their workplace. Coastal East 561 had just lifted off.

"Sorry, Jones, but the flight is airborne. And I don't have the authority to bring it back. Once in flight, only the FAA can do that."

Frantically, Jones pulled out a piece of scrap paper from the wastebasket under the desk. "Please check who performed or signed off on any maintenance to Coastal East 561 the past few days."

"That will take a few minutes. I need to pull the file in the next room."

"I can wait. Please hurry!" While on hold, Jones yelled across the room to Agent Tecka, who had just hung up his call to the Tampa FBI. "Tom, call the FAA. Fill them in so they can notify the pilot. Fast, please!"

Five minutes later, Duerty came back on the line. "Well, this is strange, Mr. Jones, very strange."

"What is it, Duerty?!"

"Normally, Coastal East has a maintenance supervisor that signs off on all their jets. But this time, an NTSB employee gave the okay. His name is Connor Herman." Agent Jones scribbled the name on the scrap of paper, thanked Duerty, and hung up.

A Gainesville police sergeant typed the name *Connor Herman* into the computer database, and within seconds his picture appeared on the screen. Below the image was a brief bio and a statement that caused Agent Jones to pound his fist through the thin sheetrock wall in front of him:

Connor Herman was arrested and booked on two charges of assault and one disorderly conduct. Charges dropped at the request of National Transportation Safety Board Chief, Jake Tassett.

CHAPTER 90
Monday, March 15, 1982
6:00 p.m.

"Your attention, please. This is the final call for Bayou Airlines 444 to Dallas. All passengers should be on board." The intercom was cracking and difficult to hear, and the majority of passengers didn't want to go home to Texas. The Youth Christian Club of Fort Worth, an organization dedicated to bringing happiness to needy children from the inner city, had sent seventy-eight over-the-top-with-excitement kids to Orlando on Friday for two full days at the Magic Kingdom. The boys and girls, ranging in age from nine to thirteen, had spent today killing time at Gatorland while waiting for their night flight back to the Lone Star state. They cheered like crazy every time the giant alligators would leap up from the swamp and swallow a whole chicken that was dangling from a human feeder's skinny and shaky hand. By the time the kids stopped for Happy Meals at McDonald's on the way to the airport, the ten moms who were chaperoning were totally wasted. But the plane was on schedule, and they smiled at each other, knowing that they would be home in their cozy beds in plenty of time for Johnny Carson to put them to sleep.

There were only a handful of other passengers who were not associated with the youth group on board Bayou 444. They longed for peace and quiet amidst this group of rowdy kids so they could catch a few winks on the westward flight. Chances were slim of that happening. Sitting in a middle seat in the last row next to the bathrooms was Harley Hutter, a

Bayou pilot who was deadheading to Dallas to catch his early morning flight to Mexico City. Harley was returning from an extended leave of absence following the death of his brother, Harry, who had piloted the fateful Trans South flight that crashed in the Everglades last month. Harley's mother had tried in vain to talk him into a new career, perhaps cleaning jets instead of flying them, after Harry's memorial service. Harley assured her that lightning never strikes a family twice, and she should have no reason to worry. Besides, Harley flew his jets carefully and by the book, unlike his wild and crazy brother who longed for a little shaky-shake from the turbulence dance in the skies.

Harley's mom didn't buy his assurance because, quite frankly, her sons were like two peas in a pod. Whatever Harry could do, Harley thought he could do better.

*****

Federal Aviation Administrator Hubert Combs had been appointed to the top position by President Layman a year earlier. He was a well-decorated Marine Corps veteran, a Navy test pilot, and a really nice guy—who didn't put up with crap. Three months after heading up the FAA, Combs fired three air traffic supervisors in Washington for coming back two minutes late from their coffee break. One was Combs' nephew, who was living with him in a Virginia suburb.

The call came from FBI Director Morris Clements, who informed Combs that NTSB Chief Investigator Jack Tassett had broken bad and was a top suspect in a criminal investigation into the two Florida midair disasters this past month. He had been briefed on the case from Jack Jones, one of his most trusted field agents who had pleaded with Clements to take immediate action. After a five-minute discussion with the FBI Director, who had mentioned that Tassett was just seen on a live TV news program from Tampa International Airport, Combs grounded all planes. Every flight currently in US airspace was ordered to land at the first available airport. He assumed President Layman would be furious that he placed the directive without his permission. He was right. Within ten minutes, the president was on the phone.

"Who the hell do you think you are, Bert, grounding all planes without even speaking to me first?" President Layman was beside himself. "Can you even comprehend the panic you've just created in the minds of all Americans?"

"I had to make a quick decision, Mr. President. Many American lives are at risk. I'm more concerned with protecting human blood than I am with image." Combs then proceeded to inform Layman about the conversation he just had with FBI Director Clements. The president softened up, then apologized to Combs.

"What's your plan, Bert, I mean, where's your focus at this point?" inquired the president.

"The two midair collisions occurred in Florida. Tassett was last seen at Gate 14A in Tampa advising the public that he himself would be providing the safety check for Coastal East 561, the first flight out of there since the crash over Lake Okeechobee. I believe that flight, which lifted off before six, is in grave danger. We are unable to contact the cockpit; however, the pilot has been transmitting coordinates with somebody on the ground. Middle Eastern accent, but we have no idea where it's coming from. The pilot believes the person to be legit. I have no doubt it's fraud. Also, sir, Clements informed me about a plot to control airplanes with some sort of remote control device and that Tassett had loaded air traffic control centers and certain aircraft with radar jamming equipment. There's a chance the Coastal East flight is being controlled by whoever is on the ground, and the pilot doesn't know it. His radar panel could be displaying false data."

"Do you think any other flights are being controlled by this person?" asked the president.

"I'm sorry to say, but the chances of that are very good, sir. We found out that Tassett was at Orlando's airport a few days ago making what he recorded as 'safety adjustments' to the air traffic control center there. He was also seen tinkering around with an airplane that was down for a few days of scheduled maintenance in a hangar. I hate to say this, but that plane just took off for Dallas with a large group of kids from the Youth Christian Center in Fort Worth. And yes, we are unable to hail the pilot, but once again, he is making voice transmissions to someone on the ground. Same Middle Eastern accent."

"Oh my God! This is nuts. Will someone please arrest Tassett. I don't want him to see the light of day ever again! Bert, you have my full support on whatever you need to get those planes home safely. Keep me posted. I will keep a line open here in the War Room."

"Yes, sir. Thank you, Mr. President."

CHAPTER 91

Monday, March 15, 1982

6:35 p.m.

Jack Tassett quietly walked away unnoticed from the news cameras following his inspection of Coastal East 561 and headed for the National Transportation Safety Board office located near the charter terminal. When he arrived at 6:45, the last employee was getting into his car. Jack waited in the shadows until the man drove away, then unlocked the door and walked to his office in the back. As he entered, the phone on his desk rang, and he debated answering it. He knew the feds would figure things out soon, and it was time for him to finish the job and drive down to Roy Jackson's ranch. Jack decided to let the phone go to the answering machine.

"Tassett! Are you there? Damn it, pick up now, this is Harfield."

Jack lifted the receiver. "Go ahead, Oliver. I'm here."

"The FAA just grounded all flights. We barely got both in the air before the order went out. We have no video access, but Dulie and Yussef have the joysticks. Dulie's controlling the Coastal East jet while Yussef is handling Bayou, which just took off from Orlando. Yussef was able to scramble communications with both jets and intercept cockpit transmissions through our satellite. The pilots think Sam and Yussef are their air traffic controllers, and they are relaying flight data to him. Dulie and Yussef are controlling the flight by providing headings and bearings, but it won't be long before the pilots realize the plane's not going in the right direction to get to their destination. Where do you have jammers in place right now, Jack?"

"Every major airport in Florida, plus Chicago, Dallas, both Washington airports, Denver, Houston, St. Louis, and Minneapolis. I can turn on the jammers from my office at any time with a computer link."

"Hit the switch, Jack. It's time to play hardball with the president."

"One problem. The jammers are all on the same code and frequency, including the Coastal East and Bayou flights. If I shut down the towers, your flights will be jammed, too. That means your pilots won't be able to transmit their locations to Sam and Yussef."

"Hold on," shouted Sam, who was listening to the conversation. "If you can give us ten minutes, we can have both planes close enough to Seminole Bend so we can see them. As soon as that happens, we can guide them around from right here. Make them do parade laps around Lake Okeechobee until the president gives in."

"Okay, did you hear that, Jack?" asked Oliver, holding the receiver out a small distance from his ear.

"Affirmative. At seven sharp, I will jam all our equipment, and then I can meet up with you by nine o'clock at the ranch."

Jack Tassett could hear sirens coming from all directions and several helicopters overhead. He knew the FBI was on his tail and converging fast. Holding off until 7:00 might prove to be a complicated mess.

CHAPTER 92

Monday, March 15, 1982
6:50 p.m.

Above Roy's office was a makeshift rectangular-shaped control tower for his own little airstrip with glass on all four sides plus the ceiling. It looked like a greenhouse in the sky. The satellite receiver and communication's antennas were bolted to all four corners of the roof. There was a computer and a radio in the tower that was connected to the equipment downstairs. Sam and Yussef dashed up the metal staircase into the glass enclosure and continued their transmissions from there.

"Coastal East 561, this is Sam in Tampa Tower," announced Dulie into the microphone. "Continue on course heading one-seven-zero and level off at four thousand feet. Hold tight at 250 knots."

"Tampa Tower, this is Coastal East 561," replied the Coastal East pilot. "Roger that, Sam. But we're heading to Atlanta. Why bear south-south-east with minimum altitude?"

"Report of high turbulence over the Gulf of Mexico. We're looping you around Lake Okeechobee, and then you will climb to ten thousand near Melbourne with a course heading of three-four-zero up to Atlanta."

"Roger. My radar is showing no weather activity over the Gulf, though."

"We received reports from earlier flights out of Miami and Orlando, so just advising a safer path for all your high paying clients."

"Roger that. Coastal East 561 out."

Meanwhile, Yussef was plotting a southeasterly course for Bayou 444, also at a low altitude, much to the confusion of the pilot. Yussef claimed the same turbulence theory, then ordered the pilot to go around it from the south. Harley Hutter leaned over and peered out the tiny window from his uncomfortable middle seat, much to the annoyance of the window seat passenger trying to catch a few winks. Why was a plane that should have a straight course over the Gulf of Mexico now turning left in a southerly direction? And why the hell was it flying so damn low?

At precisely 7:00 p.m., Jack Tassett flipped several switches, and all radar equipment in the targeted cities and onboard the Coastal East and Bayou flights went blank. Sam and Yussef could see both aircraft in the distance, but just barely. They pulled out their joysticks. This should be fun!

*****

"Coastal East 561 to tower. Sam, I've lost all radar functions. Also, rudder pedals and control wheel are moving on their own. I've disengaged autopilot with no luck. Ailerons are flopping, and I can't control my pitch or roll. Need to declare an emergency!" Coastal East pilot Aaron Douglas had never trained for anything like this in a simulator. Copilot Keith Carver had been a Navy electrician during the Vietnam War and guessed the problem was electrical, but couldn't seem to pinpoint where to start looking.

"Coastal East 561, this is Sam. Sit back and relax boys, I'll take care of you from here."

"What's that supposed to mean?"

"Well, let me show you," replied Sam as he pushed the joystick up with one hand, and then an accelerator switch forward to increase speed. The HJ-15 jet began to climb at a forty-five-degree angle. Then Sam slid the joystick to the left, and the plane banked into a 30-degree turn. The Coastal East passengers and crew would now be doing a counterclockwise lap around Roy's ranch every two minutes. In the background, Sam could hear screams echoing from the cabin into the cockpit. He smiled.

Bayou 444 pilot Rich Auferdahl had radioed Yussef with the same radar and flight control malfunctions that Coastal East 561 was experiencing. Yussef's response was the same as Sam's, and he was now banking the Bayou jet clockwise just 125 feet above the Coastal East jet. Passengers in window seats on both aircraft could see the other plane circling just above or below them. To keep from panicking, the kids from the Youth Christian Center joked to one another that they were back riding Disney's Space Mountain roller coaster. But soon they went silent, and fear was embedded into their eye sockets. The barf bags were getting quite a workout.

Harley Hutter unbuckled his seatbelt and made his way to the cockpit, falling twice on aisle passengers as he tried unsuccessfully to compensate for the crooked fuselage and turbulence. Under orders from the captain, the flight attendants were strapped into their jump seats. They, too, feared the worse. Harley pounded on the cockpit door, and Co-Captain George Alvin reached back and opened it.

"I'm Captain Harley Hutter, deadheading to Dallas. Do you need some help up here?"

"Yes, please, we'll take any help we can!" answered Captain Auferdahl frantically. "We've lost all cockpit functions, including radar, flight control, and communications. Our ATC's name is Yussef, but he has now hijacked the plane!"

"How the hell can an air traffic controller hijack a jet?"

"I have no idea, but he is now flying this plane from somewhere on the ground, and either he or someone else is most likely in control of the Coastal East jet below us." Harry leaned forward to get a better look at the other aircraft flying dangerously close and at a ridiculously low altitude. He had read the NTSB report in detail following the midair crash that had killed his brother and remembered that the air traffic control center in Miami was malfunctioning at the time of the accident.

"We need to get into the control deck and find the device that is steering this plane remotely."

Captain Auferdahl and Co-Captain Alvin both stared blankly at Harley. "Obviously, it's happening, Captain Hutter, but how?" inquired Auferdahl.

"Quite frankly, I'm not sure. But we need to find out. Grab your toolkit. And just call me Harley, okay?"

CHAPTER 93

Monday, May 15, 1982

7:10 p.m.

Lew drove the Trans Am back to Seminole Bend while Janet sat silently daydreaming, staring blankly out the passenger side window. In the back seat, Otis, Lance, and Pancho were snoring in harmony. At 7:10, they were nearing the Yeehaw Junction exit off the turnpike when Lew tapped his wife on the arm and pointed up to the sky.

"Look up there. Those two planes must be in some kind of air show. They're circling around awfully close to–. Hold on, I think they are passenger jets!" Janet leaned forward to get a good look, then she covered her mouth with both hands.

Meanwhile, Major Barney Watkins brought the Huey Chopper down softly on the Seminole Bend High School football field. Before leaving Gainesville, Willy had phoned the sheriff's office and told them to find Sheriff Bonty and send him over to the stadium immediately. Bonty left Norma Foss and Sheryl Berry with Father O'Shea at the Catholic church, but Jimmy, Jenny, and Tyrone demanded to go with him to the high school.

Major Ben Smith dropped the ramp and was the first one out of the chopper. Bonty and the kids were standing by the visitor's bench on the fifty-yard line watching as the others disembarked. Willy glanced up and noticed Bonty had brought Jimmy and Jenny Jackson and his nephew Tyrone with him. He walked over to Sheriff Bonty and shook hands. "I heard, Al, what you did, and I'm very grateful. I apologize for being an ass."

"You're a good man, Deputy Banks," replied the sheriff. "And I'm glad to have you back on the force." He winked at Willy.

Willy nodded at Jimmy and Jenny, then put his arm around his nephew and led him back to the Huey. "Tyrone, there's someone here I would like you to meet."

Tyrus was the last one off the chopper, and he froze in his tracks when he noticed Willy approaching with a teenage boy. His mouth dropped wide open, and tears ran down his cheek. He knew it was his son - there was no doubt in his mind.

"Tyrone, let me introduce you to your dad," said Willy as he stepped back. Tyrus embraced his son with a bear hug while Tyrone stood completely still. Then, Tyrone reached up and pushed his father's chest, releasing Tyrus' clutch and causing him to stumble backward.

"You're not my dad," retorted Tyrone. "You abandoned me!"

Willy grabbed Tyrone from behind and turned the boy to face him.

"Your father is a hero, Ty. He left you only to save your life and that of your mother. I will explain everything to you later."

Tyrone dropped his head and wiped the tears from his cheeks. Willy and Tyrus embraced him and each other. America was in a state of siege, but family still came first.

CHAPTER 94

Monday, March 15, 1982
7:30 p.m.

Barney Watkins noticed it first. "Ben, look up."

Ben Smith glanced westward where Barney was pointing. "Awesome sunset, Barn, but we need to refuel the Huey. Let's get this party over and get moving."

"That's not what I mean. Look again. Those two jets are circling as if they were in a holding pattern, but they're flying dangerously low and way too close. And they're flying in opposite directions!"

Sheriff Bonty saw the two special ops pilots pointing to the darkening sky, and he looked up, then began a sprint to the chopper. While running, he shouted over his shoulder, "Willy, Johnny, and Tyrus, over here!"

The family embrace suddenly became unlocked. The two brothers joined Deputy Murphree, and all three jogged back to the Huey, where Al was now watching the aerial show with Ben and Barney.

"What's going on, Al?" asked Johnny.

Barney had grabbed a pair of binoculars from the chopper and aimed them towards the distant sky. As the sun set below the horizon, he could barely read the writing on each of the plane's fuselages. "Those are civilian passenger jets. The lower one is Coastal East, and the upper one is Bayou."

"Jackson and Harfield!" exclaimed Sheriff Bonty. "They've got control of those planes, and they're flying them over the ranch! We've got to get over there and put an end to this. Now!"

"Hold on, Al," said Tyrus. "If we just rush in, they'll crash those planes. I'm assuming the remotes, jammers, and video cameras were installed. They're most likely using joysticks, and I bet they've jammed the radar."

"The radio!" shouted Willy as a thought just occurred. "Ty, you know where they attached the remote receptors in the cockpit. Can you locate the pilots' frequencies and talk them through disabling the equipment?"

Barney Watkins had thought of that before Willy mentioned it, and he was hailing on all frequencies from Huey's cockpit.

"No luck. I've got the Tampa control tower holding, and they too can't reach either plane. And damn it, their radar is jammed, as is Orlando's."

"Oliver has somehow taken control of the communications," inserted Tyrus. "That was never part of the master plan. It must be Dulie or Yussef. They've intercepted the transmissions and are probably impersonating air traffic controllers!"

"Roy's got a mini control tower on the roof of his office next to the barn," stated Bonty. "I've seen a satellite dish attached to one corner."

"So somehow they've scrambled communications," said Tyrus. "If we could disable the satellite, then we should be able to reestablish a connection with the pilots."

"If they see us, they will definitely crash the planes!" replied Bonty with a nervous tone.

"Not necessarily. If they take down the jets, Oliver will have nothing but the USS Halibut left to use as collateral. The two planes appear to be securely under his control, but the Halibut is not yet a given at this time. Would he take that chance?"

"The Halibut has two nukes aimed at Los Angeles and Washington," replied Ben Smith. "The death toll would be extraordinary!"

"We can't have another air disaster in Seminole Bend," said Bonty firmly. "This is my county to protect, and I will make the decision. Somehow, someway, we must covertly take out the damn satellite dish and do it before Oliver or Roy even realize it! Then Tyrus can contact the pilots and disconnect the remotes.

With a trace of skepticism, each one nodded in affirmation. Jimmy, Jenny, and Tyrone were huddled behind the adults and listening intently. Before Sheriff Bonty could lay out his furtive plan, Jenny took a step forward.

"Me," she said. "I will do it." Everyone turned and stared at Jenny.

"What are you talking about?" asked Bonty.

"Roy doesn't know that I now know you are my real father. He's always been very protective of me. I can go into his office and disconnect the wiring from the satellite dish."

"Absolutely not! You, Jimmy, and Tyrone are going to take the squad car and go back to my house, where you will be safe. The rest of us can get close to the Jackson ranch with the Huey, and then hike to the barn."

"And then what, Dad? You won't be able to get to the dish without them knowing it. But I think I can."

"No, it's too dangerous!"

"He's right," said Tyrone. "I don't want you hurt."

"I can do this!" pleaded Jenny, then went up and gave her newly found father a hug. "You have no other good option."

"I have an idea," said Barney. "We can sneak into the barn and hold tight with weapons drawn. Then, see if Jenny can get the job done. If not, and she's in danger, we strike fast and kill the whole lot of them. Besides Oliver and Roy, the only ones in the office will be Sam, Yussef, and Governor Daughtry. Only Oliver is trained to use deadly force. We'll have Ben, Tyrus, and me, plus three of the sheriff's finest. I like our odds!"

"What if Jenny is caught in the crossfire?" asked Jimmy. "I don't like that risk! Let me go instead!"

"No, Jimmy. I stand a better chance of making this work without raising suspicions. I will take cover if the shooting starts."

Reluctantly, Sheriff Bonty nodded his approval. "Jimmy, Jenny, and Tyrone take the squad car and park it off the main road in the ditch near the entrance to the Jackson ranch. From there, it will be a fifteen-minute walk up to the house, but wait until I call you on the car radio. I will have a walkie-talkie, and when we are all in place in the barn, I'll give you the signal to get moving. Jimmy and Tyrone, wait in the car for further instructions, okay?"

Barney and Ben buckled into the Huey's cockpit and fired up the rotors, while Tyrus, Willy, Johnny, and Sheriff Bonty strapped themselves into their seats. The chopper lifted off the football field and headed in a northwesterly direction. They would circle the ranch out of Sam's and Yussef's line of vision, and land in an area next to the swamp. If all went as planned, they would avoid interference from a hungry alligator or a lost Brahman bull grazing on a nighttime snack in the pasture.

Jimmy drove the sheriff's car with Jenny riding in the passenger seat. Tyrone was behind the cage in the backseat. Jenny's foot accidentally tapped on a hard metal object attached to the bottom of the front seat with Velcro. While Jimmy was adjusting the mirrors and trying to figure out how to work the radio, Jenny unbuttoned her blue jeans to loosen up the fit, slipped the object into her pants, and then re-buttoned. Jimmy was too busy to notice.

Jimmy slid the automatic transmission into gear and drove off. Jenny bit her lip, trying to hold back a smile of relief. She now felt much safer. She was packing a Beretta M418 pocket pistol in her pants.

CHAPTER 95
Monday, March 15, 1982
8:00 p.m.

"Oliver Harfield on line two for the president," said the White House operator to Gordon Brubaker. The Chief of Staff slid the phone in front of Donald Layman. Line two was blinking.

"It's Harfield," said Brubaker. The president picked up the receiver and pushed the blinking button.

"This is the president. Go ahead, Harfield."

"You grounded the planes, Mr. President. Big mistake. There are a Coastal East jet and a Bayou jet full of taxpaying citizens doing parade laps at 4,000 feet above my head. They have no radar, no flight controls, and, most importantly, no way to call anyone except me. And to top that off, I just got off the phone with Admiral Inman. Seems the USS Halibut has just left the Puget Sound and is in Pacific waters with one nuclear warhead aimed at Los Angeles and one aimed right about where you are sitting in your comfortable chair. So let's talk expediency for a moment if you don't mind."

"You're a stupid fool, Harfield!" shouted President Layman into the phone. The War Room became very silent.

"Excuse me, sir, but I didn't ask for your opinion. Now just shut your trap and listen to me. Due to your lack of love for the people of your country, many who cast votes to put you in the White House, you have now placed them in monumental peril. However, I'm giving you one last chance to do the right thing and save what little grace you have going for you. I've given you the routing and account numbers. I said you had until midnight, but now that you've taken evasive action, you will make the call right now to transfer one billion dollars from the US Treasury. It's eight o'clock. That transfer must be complete by eight-thirty, or it will be raining human beings once again from the moonlit Florida skies."

"Oliver, stop this nonsense right now, and I will give you and your cronies a full pardon. If you don't, you realize I will put a full military priority on hunting you down and killing you. No trials to waste time and money. Just a bullet or two that will shatter your face into tiny bits!"

"You're down to twenty-nine minutes, Mr. President. Goodbye."

The president hung up and looked at his Secretary of Defense. "Carlyle, what's the word from Bo Yardly? Where is he?"

"He's approaching the Puget Sound as we speak, but if the Halibut made it to sea, he wouldn't be able to stop him. Bo's flying a fighter jet, and his ammunition won't be able to penetrate ocean water enough to do any damage beyond twenty feet. We've deployed every ship we have from San Diego, Hawaii, and Alaska to find the Halibut, but they are too far away. Admiral Inman put all our sailors who were stationed in Kitsap on shore leave for three days, so trying to find a chaser fleet up there has become next to impossible, sir."

"What about our west coast missile bases?"

"They are ready and on standby with orders to seek and destroy the nuclear missiles if they are launched. But Admiral Inman has somehow found a way to scramble data and cloak the submarine."

"Speak English, Carlyle. What does that mean?"

"We can't track the Halibut's exact location. If he was able to scramble the sub's global positioning coordinates, he might have found a way to do that with the nukes, too. We just don't know. The only way to verify the sub's exact location would be with sonar."

"We can't evacuate LA and Washington in twenty-five minutes," the president stated as he glanced at every person in the room. After a few seconds of deep thought, he slammed his palm on the table and briskly stood up. "Gordon, transfer the ransom money now! Do it quickly. I'm going back to the Oval Office."

At 8:25 p.m., the money had been routed to an unknown, untraceable offshore account. Oliver received confirmation of the transfer when the phone in Roy's office rang, and the voice on the other end said one word: "Done."

Oliver hung up the phone and got on the radio to Admiral Inman. "Launch now, Admiral. The money's in the bank."

Roy walked over to the staircase leading up to his makeshift control tower and yelled his orders to Sam and Yussef. "Fly those metal birds over Lake Okeechobee and crash them. I don't want dead bodies littering up my beautiful ranch, got that?"

CHAPTER 96

Monday, March 15, 1982
8:45 p.m.

"Daddy, are you in here?" asked Jenny as she opened the door to Roy's office. Everyone inside froze, including Sam and Yussef, who were about to engage in a fun little game of Bloody Red Baron with the Coastal East and Bayou jets.

Roy hustled over to the door to try and keep Jenny from going any further, but she had entered and was nodding and smiling at the entire group. Oliver was fit to be tied.

"Jenny, I've told you that my office is off-limits, so now go on back to the house," ordered Roy.

"But Dad, I've got some really good news to tell you," said Jenny, but then paused and took a step toward the man sitting in the corner of the room. "Hey, you're Governor Daughtry, aren't you? It's a pleasure to meet you, sir!" The governor stood up, and Jenny extended her arm and shook hands with him.

"Jenny, we're really busy here," interrupted Roy. "Your good news will just have to wait for an hour or so until we're finished. Now scoot on back to the house."

"Sure, Dad. Will do." Roy turned his back and walked to the door to let Jenny out, but Jenny didn't follow. Instead, she headed for the staircase, and just before taking the first step, she looked up to the second floor and said, "Hey, what's up here? Wow, this is like a cool observation deck. Can I take a peek?" Jenny hastened up the steps before Roy could stop her, then stopped at the landing and stared at Sam and

Yussef. They had halted their fun and games and were now sitting straight up, trying to block Jenny's view of the control panel.

"Oh, I'm sorry," said Jenny. "Who are you?"

"Jenny, get down here!" howled Roy. "Now, young lady!"

Jenny noticed the cable coming through the glass wall that was attached to the satellite dish. It ran from the roof to the floor and into a splitter, then branched off into two cables, one running downstairs and the other to the computer where Sam and Yussef were sitting. Jenny had taken a pair of spring-loaded wire cutters from Sheriff Bonty's squad car before leaving, and they were in her left pocket. She slowly slipped her hand into the pocket, carefully removed the tool, and opened the vise grip with her thumb. The gun was out of sight and held in place by her waistband, but there was a noticeable bulge pressing on her blouse, and she was worried someone would see it. Jenny glanced down the stairs where Roy was standing with both hands firmly perched on his waist, his red face about to burst into flames.

"Okay, coming, Dad." Jenny turned to descend the steps backward so her left hand was on the left side rail. She was pretty sure Roy couldn't see her arms as she twisted her body in an awkward angle that prevented a clear view. The cable was a foot away, easily within reach, but the only way her idea would work would be if Sam and Yussef weren't watching her. Just before taking the first step, Jenny pointed to the dark sky and asked, "Hey, look at those planes up there. Wonder what they're doing so close together." Both Sam and Yussef looked through the ceiling glass, and then realized they needed to grab the joysticks or the jets would collide right on top of them. Both turned back to the computer screen.

As Jenny took the first step down, she reached out with her left hand, placed the open vise grip blades over the cable, and squeezed with every bit of strength she could muster. With the massive adrenaline pumping through her bloodstream, she could have cut through a steel pipe, if need be!

Immediately, the computer screens went blank, and Sam blurted out, “Hey, what the hell?!” Yussef turned and shot an evil glance at Jenny as she was trying to hide the wire cutters in her palm. But the tool slipped out of her hand and fell down the stairs landing at Roy’s feet. Oliver heard the commotion and pulled out his handgun. He pushed the stunned Roy out of the way and aimed the weapon at the back of Jenny’s head.

“You have exactly five seconds to come down these steps and place your hands in the air, or I will shatter your skull bones into tiny fragments!” Jenny took two steps and jumped down, then raised her arms in the air. If looks could kill, Oliver and Roy would need no weapons.

From the observation deck, Sam shouted down to Roy and Oliver, “We’ve lost our remote control functions and our communication lock. The pilots will be able to hail a control tower now if they realize it.”

Oliver shouted back up to Sam and Yussef, “What about their cockpit radars? Are they still jammed?”

“Yes, and there’s no way for the pilots or the air traffic control centers to unjam them. Also, they won’t have any way to steer their aircraft unless they remove the remote controller. They are now locked into the holding pattern we gave them. When they run out of fuel, they’ll crash right on top of us.”

“Then we need to get out now. The money’s been transferred, and the Halibut will take care of LA and Washington. America will be cleaning up that mess for quite some time. It’s time we start living our life of luxury on our own private island. We can be there in about two hours.” Oliver put the barrel of his gun on Jenny’s forehead and said to Roy, “You want me to do it, or would you like the honors?”

Jenny’s frightened expression gave way to tears, and she looked pleadingly at the man who had pretended to be her father. Roy wiped the sweat from his forehead with the back of his hand, then said to Oliver, “Don’t. Let’s just cuff her to the stairs and leave. When the planes come crashing down, she most likely won’t survive anyway. And even if she does, she has no idea where we’re going. Just don’t shoot her in front of me, Oliver.”

Just then, the door slammed inward, and two boys were aiming Smith and Wesson .38 Special revolvers at Oliver. Jimmy and Tyrone had never given one thought to staying put in the sheriff’s car and had followed Jenny without her knowing.

“Drop the gun, Mr. Harfield,” ordered Jimmy. Oliver quickly assessed the situation and could tell by the way both boys were holding their weapons that they had no idea how to use them. Roy didn’t have to assess, he knew the boys were basketball stars, not gunslingers. Oliver lowered the gun to his side, but held it firmly in his hand, finger ready on the trigger. Jenny reached in her pants and pulled out the Beretta M418, then jammed the barrel into the back of Oliver’s skull. Governor Daughtry backed deep into the corner, searching for something on the counter to protect himself. Sam and Yussef peered down from the second level.

Everyone waiting in the barn had seen the boys approach the office and knew something terrible was about to happen. Johnny Murphree told the others to hold tight while he would try to stop the boys from going any further. He dashed to the office entryway but was too late. When the boys pulled out their weapons, Johnny ducked down and crawled forward so he wouldn’t be seen through the window.

Oliver’s skilled training and experience was no match for the three kids. Reaching back with his left arm, he grabbed Jenny’s waist and spun her around in front of him so fast that the Beretta flew out of her hand. The boys just moved their pistols hopelessly in all directions. Oliver then aimed his revolver and fired two shots. Jimmy fell to his knees, then his chest heaved forward, and his face slammed into the floor.

Tyrone staggered backward a few feet, then his legs gave way beneath him, and his head smashed into the ground outside the doorway. Jenny screamed while Roy ran to Jimmy and cradled him in his arms. When Johnny saw Tyrone hit the ground, he sprang to cover him. Oliver fired one more shot that entered Johnny's skull in the temple, and he collapsed on top of Tyrone.

"No!" screamed Tyrus as he witnessed Tyrone's head hit the ground, and Johnny's mad dash effort to save him. Sheriff Bonty had heard his daughter's scream, and he, Tyrus, and Willy sprinted to the scene, weapons drawn, but stopped suddenly when they saw Oliver in the doorway clutching Jenny from behind with a gun to her head.

"Stop right there, or she dies!" shouted Oliver. Sam and Yussef had scampered down the steps and were standing directly behind Oliver. Governor Daughtry had lifted Roy up from Jimmy's bloody body, and he was consoling him in the back of the pack. Roy was just starting to come to his senses.

"Bonty, you're our traitor! Well, I should have known!" Oliver chuckled as he clutched Jenny even harder. "Now, you boys will drop your weapons and clasp your hands behind your heads." The sheriff, Willy, and Tyrus carefully placed their guns on the ground, then stood up and did as they were ordered. Meanwhile, Barney and Ben were still hiding in the barn, watching closely, ready for their chance.

"Now, we're going to walk to my Learjet and get on board. Any slight movement, and you'll need to dig one more grave for this pretty girl. Do you understand?"

"Let her go, Oliver!" demanded Sheriff Bonty. "You have our word we won't try anything."

"Your word? Well, that's a joke, Al. You tried to con us, and now you want us to trust you? You know what. I'm going to let you live, Al, because living will be worse than dying, knowing your son's dead and your wife soon will be. Yes, that's right, Mr. Sheriff. As soon as we reach our destination, I will be calling our friends in the Middle East and order my one final hit. Now, if you behave yourself for a few minutes, I'll let your daughter live so she can grieve alongside you."

With Oliver leading the way, walking backward so he could face Bonty, Willy, and Tyrus and using Jenny as a shield, his men climbed aboard the Learjet. Oliver waited until they had entered, then slowly ascended the ramp with his back to the fuselage. After boarding the jet, he released Jenny but ordered her to stand perfectly still on the top step. She did as she was told, and Oliver left the hatch open and walked to the cockpit. Sam and Yussef appeared in the doorway with rifles as soon as Oliver disappeared from sight. Sam's weapon was aimed at Jenny, while Yussef made sure Bonty, Willy, and Tyrus stayed put. Two minutes later, the aircraft rolled down to the end of the runway. The hatch was closed, and the Learjet readied for takeoff. Jenny slowly walked down the ramp steps, then fainted.

Willy ran into Roy's office and called for an ambulance, while Tyrus tore off his shirt and was applying pressure to Tyrone's bullet wound. Bonty was doing the same for Jimmy while yelling at Willy to hurry. Neither boy was conscious. Blood was everywhere. Johnny Murphree was dead.

CHAPTER 97
Monday, March 15, 1982
9:00 p.m.

Otis was breathing heavy but was the first one to arrive. He practically dove on his brother Tyrus to see if Tyrone was alive or dead. Pancho came next, followed by Lance and Lew. Janet ran to Jenny to give her some comfort.

When Lew noticed the planes circling the Jackson ranch, he gunned the Trans Am from Yeehaw Junction all the way to Seminole Bend, then slowed down slightly through town, running two red lights on his way out to Angler's Delight Marina. Several rescue airboats had been docked at the marina ever since the midair crash last week. No one was around the boats, and Lance had a knack for hotwiring anything that had an engine attached. They all loaded up, and Pancho directed them to the small creek that was the hidden entrance to Roy's property, the same place he had saved Willy's life.

Lew parked the airboat at the edge of the swamp. In the distance, they could see Oliver's Learjet sitting near the runway with the hatch open and the ramp pushed up against it. They noticed lights on in Roy's office and guessed the Learjet was empty. No one had any idea that Willy and his entourage were waiting in the barn, or that Jenny would soon be making her fateful entrance.

It had been Lance's idea, actually. They all knew the Learjet was probably Roy's method of escape, so they devised a simple plan to stop him. Next to the jet was a water pump with a 100-foot rubber hose attached that was most likely used to wash off boats and farm equipment. Otis pushed the portable ramp underneath the starboard side secondary fuel tank that was located on the wingtip, then unscrewed the cap. The jet fuel drained quickly, then Otis stuck the water hose into the inlet valve and refilled the wingtip tank with H2O. When that was finished, Otis unscrewed the main fuel tank in the wing itself and drained most of the fuel. Lew had told him to leave a small amount of fuel so that the Learjet could taxi and take off before the water in the wingtip tank transferred through the valve into the main tank. That would happen automatically as soon as the main tank became empty. When Otis finished on the starboard side, he moved the ramp to the port side and did the same thing. Then, they all ran as fast as possible back to the airboat to watch.

Moments later, they heard gunshots, then witnessed Jenny's kidnapping and the Learjet takeoff with a planeload full of thugs. When Otis saw Tyrus running towards a body that had collapsed near the office door, he sensed it was his nephew Tyrone.

* * * * *

Ben ran up to Tyrus, who was applying intense pressure to Tyrone's wound, and touched him on the shoulder. Willy had just made the call for an ambulance and was now standing hand-in-hand with Otis directly behind Tyrus watching helplessly. Everyone wanted to pitch in, but no one was trained on how to stop the flow of blood from a .45 caliber bullet that had penetrated the upper chest area and exited out the back. Prayer seemed like the only logical treatment.

"Barney ran to get the chopper and will put down here," said Ben. "Tyrone and Jimmy don't have enough time to wait for the ambulance. We'll fly them over to Gregorson."

"What about Roy and Harfield?" asked Willy. "We can't let them get away!"

Lew was panting, puffing, and resting his hands on his knees, gasping for breath. Then he looked up at Willy. “You don’t need to worry about Roy Jackson again, Willy. He’s not going far.”

Willy and Sheriff Bonty knelt down next to Johnny Murphree’s bullet-shattered and bloody face and motioned with their hands the sign of the cross over their fallen hero. Bonty unzipped his jacket and covered Johnny’s upper torso the best he could.

The Huey landed a few feet away, and the men wrapped Tyrone and Jimmy in blankets and carefully laid them on the floor of the chopper along with Johnny Murphree’s lifeless body. Tyrus, Willy, Otis, Sheriff Bonty, Janet, and Jenny all buckled up for the five-minute ride to the hospital. Lew, Lance, and Pancho headed back to the airboat. They were planning to hang around near the swamp and see how far the Learjet got before the sputtering began. Jenny was in shock as Janet embraced her. In her mind, Jenny believed she was responsible for the deaths of her brother and boyfriend.

The chopper was just lifting off the ground when the call came over the radio.

“Huey 618, this is Bo. Are you on board the chopper, Barney, and Ben?”

“Ten-four, Bo. Problems at the Jackson ranch, and we’re headed for the hospital.”

“What kind of problems?” asked Bo with a concerned tone.

“Long story,” replied Barney. “Tell you later. What’s your location and TOA to the Halibut?”

“USS Halibut made it to the Pacific, but I now have a visual. It appears they are at a depth of thirty to forty feet, but not moving. Wait a minute, that’s curious.” Bo clicked off the microphone. Ben glanced at Barney and shrugged his shoulders.

“Bo, we lost you. You were saying something’s curious. Please repeat.” They waited almost a minute before Bo responded.

"Oh my God!"

"Bo, what is it?"

"They've opened the missile silos and are ready to deploy!"

"We need to alert Washington!" shouted Barney into the mic. "I'll take care of it from here!"

"Too late," replied Bo. "They won't have time to evacuate the city. I'll take care of this myself."

"What do you mean, Bo? Your ammo can't penetrate saltwater to that depth enough to do any damage."

"No, Barn, you're right. But my F-4 Phantom traveling at Mach-2 can stop them."

"Absolutely not, Bo! Damn it, don't do it! We need you alive! This country needs you alive!" Barney was now screaming into the mic, pleading with Bo.

Willy unbuckled his belt, then leaned forward and snatched the mic from Barney. "Bo, this is Willy! Hey man, we're all in the chopper listening. Don't do it, my friend, please! Turn around and come back home!"

The F-4 Phantom shot straight up to an altitude of 50,000 feet before Bo leveled off. From that height, he lost visual contact with the sub but believed he could regain an optical lock around 10,000 feet, even though he would be traveling at 1,400 mph. The trick would be to thread the needle and drive the jet directly into the Halibut. A near miss would do no good. He had one chance and one chance only.

Then Bo remembered that Coach Bear Bryant had said the exact same thing to him during a final timeout against arch-rival Auburn in the 1967 Iron Bowl. Down three to nothing, ball on the two-yard line with fifteen seconds remaining and no timeouts, Bryant opted to go for the win instead of a tie. After all, he had Bo Yardly, the best college running back in the nation. During the timeout, he motioned for Bo to come to the sideline.

Bear grabbed Bo's face mask and shook it, then said, "You're getting the ball. Your blockers can only give you a split second to hit the hole and go in for the touchdown. A near miss will do us no good, Bo. You have one chance and one chance only. Now go be a hero!" Bo crashed through that hole and rammed the middle linebacker with a helmet to helmet crunch that echoed throughout the stadium. Alabama won and would play in the Cotton Bowl on New Year's Day.

Bo got back on the mic. From the altitude he was now traveling, his voice crackled with static on the Huey's receiver. But his words were understood loud and clear.

"Barn and Ben, it's been a pleasure, boys. But now I must carry the ball for the final time and win one for our great nation. Until we meet again in a much better place, God bless you both. And Willy ..." Bo paused for a moment and tried to clear his throat. "And Willy, my lifetime best friend for all of eternity—I love you, man!"

The F-4 Phantom turned nose down and sped to earth with extraordinary velocity. At 8,000 feet above the Pacific Ocean, the jet's extraordinary pilot locked his eyes onto the USS Halibut. The fate of America would be decided in the next few seconds.

CHAPTER 98

Monday, March 15, 1982
9:15 p.m. (EST)& 6:15 p.m. (PST)

A clear day in Seattle is somewhat of an anomaly. But as the sun was nearing the horizon on the west coast, a cloud of saltwater could be seen by diners enjoying the view from the Space Needle. The radioactive geyser rose and then spread wide, splashing down in a radius of fifty miles from where the F-4 Phantom hit dead on target with the USS Halibut. The nuclear explosion caved in the seafloor and rocked the coastline of Washington. The cliffs surrounding Neah Bay and the Makah Indian Reservation broke off from the Olympic Mountain range and were now resting on the floor of the Juan de Fuca straight. Two rescue boats were sent from Port Renfrew on Vancouver Island across the straight to try and assist any Native Americans that didn't have time to get to higher ground, but one vessel capsized in the rough seas.

Earth vibrations caused the Juan de Fuca tectonic plate to shift, separating the Cascadia fault and generating a small earthquake in the city of Victoria. The esteemed Empress Hotel collapsed into the harbor, spreading fiberglass splinters from the marina's small boats and big yachts onto Government Street.

The 130-foot Tsunami that was created traveled westward across the Pacific Ocean and would hit landfall at Sendai, Japan, in nine to ten hours. Over three million lives would be at risk if the Japanese weren't warned to evacuate. Hugh Boyd was the lone scientist on duty at the National Oceanic and Atmospheric Administration Center in Toke Point when Bo blew the USS Halibut into oblivion. As the ground below him shook violently, Hugh believed an earthquake would be the cause of death written in his obituary. He dove from his workstation to the floor and covered the back of his head with his hands as if that would do any good. After lying there muttering a continual stream of "Hail Marys," he finally realized he was safe, thanked the Lord, and returned to his desk. It was then he noticed the blip on his computer screen. A tsunami was moving at 500 mph in a westerly direction across the Pacific Ocean.

Hugh tried to call his boss in Seattle, but the phone lines were dead. So he reached for the ship to shore radio and pushed the emergency button. A Coast Guard cutter was just offshore in Willapa Bay. Captain Keith Adams answered and scribbled Hugh's data on his clipboard, then shoved the throttle to full and raced southward down the Pacific coast. The 120-foot cruiser docked in Astoria, Oregon, an hour later, and Captain Adams immediately called the Japanese consulate in Portland. The shocked Consulate General quickly relayed the oceanic data to Prime Minister Suzuki's office in Tokyo. Within minutes, a mid-afternoon evacuation was ordered for the entire east coast of Honshu Island.

*****

Barney touched the Huey down lightly onto the Gregorson parking lot next to the emergency entrance. Those automatic doors had seen a lot of action in the past week. The ambulance that Willy had called for was already halfway to Jackson's ranch. In the haste to get everyone in the chopper, he had forgotten to call off the paramedics.

The emergency room staff ran to meet the Huey, and within minutes, Jimmy, Tyrone, and Jenny were all being rushed into the hospital on stretchers. Barney and Ben remained in the chopper and tried to hail the Coastal East and Bayou jets. They hoped that their communications were re-established when Jenny cut the cable to the satellite dish.

Ben dialed in emergency voice frequency 121.5 on the Huey's radio. "Coastal East 561, this is Charlie Alpha six-two-zero. Do you read?" No response. "Bayou 444, do you read me?" No answer. Ben repeated the hailing for several tense moments.

Ben looked at Barney, and with a stressed voice, asked, "Why won't they pick up?"

Barney just shook his head. "You got me!"

CHAPTER 99

Monday, March 15, 1982

9:30 p.m.

After unfastening the last bolt on the center panel, Harley Hutter, with the help of Captain Auferdahl and Co-Captain Alvin, carefully pulled back the entire cockpit dashboard of the HoftanJet HJ-15. Harley shined a flashlight into the mess of tangled electrical wires and then noticed a strange metal box with every color wire imaginable running into and out of it. A tiny green bulb was blinking faintly.

"This isn't right," stated Harley. "Hand me the manual."

George Alvin handed him the thick HJ-15 operations manual, and Harley quickly opened to the page he was looking for. "Just what I thought. This box is not supposed to be here." Harley shined the flashlight towards the box that was fastened to a bracket as Auferdahl and Alvin peered inside the dash.

"What is it?" asked Auferdahl.

"I'm not sure, but wires are leading to the switch panel that appears to be overriding the autopilot, hydraulics, rudders, spoilers, flaps, and yaw damper system. I'm assuming the metal box acts like a receiver that has a switch, which allows for both pilot control and some sort of remote control."

"Are you kidding me?" responded Captain Auferdahl.

"Wish I was. But if I can disengage the remote, we should be able to regain control."

"We tried to shut down the autopilot, but we weren't able to."

"Well, the autopilot is still engaged, which means whoever is controlling us from the ground has locked us on this holding pattern and has also done the same with the Coastal East jet."

Co-Captain Alvin pointed at a different wire inside the dash. "Look at this purple wire. It's running from the metal box to the radio." All three pilots were on their knees studying the complicated wiring system.

"It appears to be connected directly to the radio's fuse box," said Harley. "That must be how they shut down our radio communications. They blew a fuse. But take a look, the orange wire that runs from the box to the radar controls is not connected to the fuses. Which means it must be sending incorrect or scrambled data directly into the radar's mainframe."

"If we can shut down the metal box functions, will we then have control of our radar and hydraulics again?" asked Auferdahl.

"In theory, we should. But I'm only guessing. If they installed a tamper switch to the box, we'll be in big trouble."

"What's a tamper switch?"

"The military uses them all the time. If an enemy captures one of our fighter jets or naval ships and tries to operate it without a proper code, the jet or ship will blow up."

"So, you think whoever did this to our plane may have installed an explosive inside the cockpit, or worse yet, anywhere in the fuselage that would go off if we try to override their controls?"

"Yes, Captain, that's exactly what I'm trying to say." Auferdahl and Alvin glanced at each other, and both wiped the sweat that was rapidly beading up on their foreheads. Neither knew how to respond. That's when Harley made the decision for them. "We have no choice. Even if we can regain radar functions, we have no communication ability with the ground. It will take some time to put the cockpit back together and fly blindly to a landing location, and we only have a couple hours of fuel left. We have to get this bird back on the ground, so we must take that risk. Go out to the cabin and prepare the passengers. And see if we have any clergy on board with all those kids. A prayer or two couldn't hurt."

The tropical depression that had moved into the Bahamas yesterday turned into a tropical storm with sustained winds of sixty-two miles per hour. It had changed directions and was now picking up speed and velocity, bearing due west towards the Gold Coast of Florida. With everything else happening in the Sunshine State, no one gave it much thought. Besides, a March hurricane was too rare to even seriously consider. Tell that to the overnight boaters now rocking between twenty-foot swells in the Bermuda Triangle.

CHAPTER 100
Monday, March 15, 1982
9:40 p.m.

The Learjet climbed to five thousand feet, and Oliver waved his wings at the Coastal East and Bayou jets that were locked into a dreadful date with destiny. They would soon run out of fuel, and Florida would be picking up the pieces of its third civilian airline disaster in a month. Oliver thought about circling a few thousand feet above them and watching the planes hit the ground and burst into flames, something he found more entertaining than a science fiction movie, but then decided to fly onward after noticing dark clouds forming to the east where his entourage was headed. He shoved down on the throttle, and the Learjet was at ten thousand feet within seconds.

As the aircraft rose above the clouds and the full moon was lighting up the night sky, the Learjet's General Electric CJ-610 turbojet engines began to misfire. The passengers in the cabin looked out the window and saw lightning flashes in the darkness ahead of them to the east. Within seconds, the brilliance of the orange moon was quickly disappearing behind the storm clouds, and the small jet began to shake. Governor Daughtry grabbed the armrests tightly, and Roy glanced over and smiled, saying, "Relax, Hank, have you never flown in turbulence?"

But up front in the cockpit, Oliver knew something was seriously wrong with the jet. First, the engine failure warning light for the starboard turbojet came on, and within seconds, the port engine failed, and that red light began blinking. The

Learjet started to drop and was soon back under the cumulonimbus clouds. Roy unbuckled his seat and walked up to the cockpit.

"Everything okay up here?" asked Roy as he sat down in the unoccupied copilot seat. Oliver had several copilots on the payroll, but they weren't invited to his retirement party, so he was flying the bird by himself.

"As a matter of fact, no!" answered Oliver without looking at Roy. "We've got double engine failure, and I can't seem to locate the problem."

"Holy crap!" yelped Roy. "What are you going to do?"

"We've got to bring this down. Take a look out there." Oliver pointed out the narrow windshield to the storm brewing in the east. From up front, the lightning strikes appeared much more vicious than from the cabin. A few seconds later, the jet's nose rose several degrees, then suddenly dropped. The aircraft rolled to starboard before Oliver could regain control. Learjet's glide ratio was the best in the business, but the weather was getting rough, and Oliver was losing speed and altitude. "It looks like Palm Beach and Fort Lauderdale are socked in with that storm. I'm going to declare an emergency and request priority runway clearance at Miami International." Roy buckled up in the copilot's seat.

"Hey, what's happening up there?!" shouted Daughtry as he leaned into the aisle and looked toward the cockpit. He tugged the seat belt tightly, nearly cutting off the blood supply to his legs.

"Miami tower, this is echo victor three niner declaring an emergency. We have dual engine failure and request runway clearance. Over." Oliver, trying not to sound panicked, was beginning to have heart palpitations. "Miami tower, do you read?"

"EV39, we are experiencing a complete radar malfunction, and visibility is less than ten percent due to the storm. All southern Florida air traffic centers are out of commission.

Suggest trying for Orlando as visibility is better; however, be aware that their radar is out, as well." Roy's and Oliver's eyelids suddenly opened wide, and they gave each other a petrified look. It dawned on them that they had disengaged their own lifeline.

"We need to try and get back to your landing strip," said Oliver frantically to Roy. "But if the engines shut down completely, we'll never make it." Roy was shaking and speechless.

Oliver turned the Learjet around and was traveling in a northwesterly direction. Belle Glade, at the southern tip of Lake Okeechobee, was directly below. He was at 3,000 feet, losing altitude and airspeed fast, and needed to fly another sixty miles back to Roy's airstrip.

Oliver yelled through the cockpit doorway, "Sam, get up here! Now!"

Sam Dulie unbuckled his seat and dashed up to the cockpit. "What is it?"

"You tell me! The fuel tanks are reading half full, but the engines are misfiring. I turned around because we screwed ourselves when we knocked out the air traffic center's radars, damn it! And that blasted weather is blanketing the east coast with massive thunderstorms, so we can't see to land. We've got to get back to the ranch!"

"What's our gross weight?"

"Just slightly over 15,000 pounds. We've got cargo in the back that is full of all sorts of pleasurable weapons to hunt with in our retirement. What the hell does the weight have to do with the engines malfunctioning?"

"Nothing, but I was wondering about our ability to make it back to Roy's airstrip. We're too heavy unless we can pick up airspeed and altitude, then glide in." Sam leaned in and looked at the instrument panel. "Oliver, we're flying at ninety-three knots! The stall speed on this thing is ninety-one knots! Roy's airstrip is about fifty miles away. We're never going to make it!"

Oliver unstrapped his harness, grabbed the Glock pistol that was attached to the underside of his seat, and forcibly pushed Sam into the pilot's seat. "Take over! I'll be right back." He tucked the revolver into his pocket and walked to the back of the plane. Governor Daughtry and Yussef watched him precariously but asked no questions.

"Hank and Yussef, come back here!" Oliver waited while his two remaining passengers hustled to the rear of the aircraft. "The Learjet is overweight. I need your help. These weapon cases each weigh a hundred pounds. We're going to dump them into Lake Okeechobee. Quickly!"

The weapon cases had rollers attached and could be moved easily. Hank and Yussef each pushed one towards the cabin door, then looked back and saw that Oliver was behind them, but empty-handed.

"Hit the door switch, Hank. We're flying too low for any cabin depressurization problems, so you'll be just fine." Daughtry and Yussef held on tight to grips that were bolted into the fuselage on either side of the door, but Hank paused, his hand only a few inches from the red button. Something was bothering him, but he couldn't quite pinpoint it. Then Oliver barked at him, "Right away if you don't mind, Mr. Governor. We need to dump the weight if we're going to make it back in one piece!"

Hank hit the emergency hatch release switch, and the rollup door slowly opened and began to lift upward. The drag caused the plane to turn sharply to port, but Sam corrected the steering. As soon as the aircraft steadied, Oliver pointed at the cargo and motioned for them to push. Hank and Yussef let go of the grips, and both dropped to their knees behind the cases. They got down on all fours so that the momentum wouldn't carry them out the hatch with the cargo while they were pushing. Each gave a heave, and 200 pounds of confiscated CIA weapons were now at the disposal of any criminal catfish that might be bottom-feeding in the big lake.

Using the grips to steady themselves, Hank and Yussef stood up and turned to get some more cargo, but were met by Oliver who was pointing a Glock in their faces.

"Sorry, boys. This should take care of our weight problem." In less than a second, one nine-millimeter bullet ripped through Hank's forehead and another through Yussef's heart, and both men fell simultaneously backward through the open hatch into their water cemetery. Oliver then pushed the emergency release twice in a row, and the cabin door jettisoned from the fuselage.

Sam and Roy both heard the gunshots from the cockpit. Sam was flying the plane, but having a difficult time controlling the shaking in his hands. You didn't have to look at him to see his fear; you could feel it in the air. Roy glanced at the cabin behind him to verify that what he thought had happened was what actually did happen. It was, and Roy looked back at Sam and laughed. When Oliver reentered the cockpit, Sam's whole body was convulsing.

Oliver pointed the gun at Sam and said, "We just dropped about 600 pounds. Now can we make it?"

Sam's voice quivered as he responded, "It might be too late. Airspeed is ninety-one knots, which means we will be going into a stall any second now. I don't think we have the altitude to make it. We've dropped to 1,750 feet. Angler's delight is ahead on our left."

Oliver suddenly regained the composure and self-confidence that had advanced him up the CIA's corporate ladder in just a few short years. He laid the gun down and calmly asked Roy to get up so he could take over in the copilot's seat. Roy obliged and walked back to the open hatch in the cabin and grabbed onto the grip.

As the Learjet passed over Angler's Delight at 1,100 feet, the turbojet engines both stalled at the same time. The edge of Roy's airstrip was not visible in the night sky, but Sam was gliding the aircraft by reversing the navigation path they had used for takeoff. Glancing up through the windshield, Oliver could see the Coastal East and Bayou passenger jets circling perilously, and he smiled, thinking about the horror and hysteria that must be going on inside those cabins. He knew he was only ten miles from the airstrip. They should have no problem reaching it safely.

But just then, Sam made a fatal error in judgment. Instead of waiting until the last moment, he panicked and lowered the landing gear, and the drag caused the Learjet to drop from its glide path. Roy peered out the open doorway and could see the plane was now over his own property, but just a few hundred feet in the air. Believing the aircraft didn't have the velocity to reach his airstrip, Roy jumped to the swamp below and hit the water feet first.

The Learjet continued to fall, and Oliver screamed into Sam's ear, "You dropped the landing gear too early, you idiot! Pull up, pull up!"

The nose of the jet dipped down and struck the swamp twenty feet short of the runway. The aircraft flipped end over end eight times, veered right, and then slid upside down fifty feet before crashing into Roy's office. The makeshift observation tower collapsed onto the belly of the plane, and the jet burst into flames. When emergency teams arrived, they saw that the plane's fuselage had melted to ash, but the cockpit was basically intact. The EMTs found the charred remains of Sam and Oliver harnessed in their seats upside down. The blackened bones of Oliver's hands were firmly clenched around Sam's neck.

Roy broke both legs when the appendages jammed into the swamp's sandy floor, but he was able to move his arms and propel himself to the surface. An airboat could be seen in the distance making its way rapidly towards him. Roy began waving his arms frantically, trying to get the attention of the driver. Then he started yelling.

Unfortunately, the yelling woke up the family of alligators who were snoozing on the shore under the mangroves. Papa Gator was none too happy about this loss of much-needed sleep, and either was Mama. Papa was a sixteen-foot bull, and Mama was a fourteen-foot cow, and they spent most of their free time guarding their fifty-five hatchlings that were nesting on dry land. When the gators heard the man screaming and struggling only thirty feet away, it was Papa's idea to round up a human liver to make a nourishing breakfast for the kids. But Mama was hungry now, and she decided there was nothing better than a midnight snack. Papa agreed, and the two gigantic reptiles slid into the dark water and swam slowly towards Roy.

When the airboat was only a hundred yards away, Roy saw the two snouts and four fluorescent eyes moving insidiously in his direction. Roy stopped yelling and waving, then a tremor of terror bolted through his entire body. Even if he had good legs, he knew he couldn't outswim the rulers of the swamp!

The noisy airboat's engines momentarily stopped the gators in their tracks ten feet away from where Roy was treading water. The boat's driver shut off the engines and coasted toward him, now only nine feet away, but on the opposite side of the gators.

"Thank God!" shouted Roy to the silhouette figures on the airboat. "Come quick! My legs are broken, and there are two alligators on the other side of me!"

A figure on the boat reached over with an oar and paddled up to Roy, but as Roy began to reach up and grab the side panel so he could climb aboard, the figure slammed the oar onto Roy's wrist. Bones could be heard cracking, and Roy dropped back into the water. The gators once again began moving toward him.

"What the hell are you doing?" yelped Roy, his right wrist dangling on top of the water.

The silhouette who had been piloting the airboat stooped down and leaned forward. Roy's eyes widened in fear when he recognized him.

"Well, well, are you out for a midnight swim?" asked Lew Berry.

"Please, let me onboard!" pleaded Roy. "I assure you I can make you a very wealthy man if you do!"

"That sounds like the same nonsense you used to lure my wife away many years ago. Sorry, Roy, but tonight you are nothing but gator meat."

Lance paddled the boat a few feet backward, then laid the oar on the floorboard. He, Pancho, and Lew plopped foam air cushions under themselves and sat comfortably poised to enjoy the show. Seconds later, Papa Gator's jaw clamped around Roy's broken legs while Mama's clutched his neck. Papa rolled in one direction, and Mama rolled the opposite way, screwing Roy's torso around so that he looked like a donut twist. With a violent jerk, Papa ripped Roy's thigh away at the hip and began chomping on it. Mama let loose her grip to see what Papa was dining on. Roy was in immense pain and barely alive, but he watched in agony as the alligator blissfully chewed the muscles and bones of his lower extremity. Mama decided she was in the mood for that delicious gray matter after all. She opened her jaws as wide as they would go and slid her mouth directly over Roy's skull, resting his head on her tongue. Mama Gator's salt glands began to excrete just the right amount of flavor while her sensory pits bolted into action. She snapped down with full force, her molars easily shattering Roy's neck and spine. Roy's torso and innards would be dragged back to shore for the starving hatchlings to enjoy tomorrow.

CHAPTER 101
Tuesday, March 16, 1982
12:10 a.m.

Shortly after midnight, Harley had removed the alien wiring and reconnected the airplane's control system. The dashboard had been loosely reassembled, but it should hold up until the plane landed. Harley couldn't locate a fuse to replace the burned-out one in the radio, which meant there would be no communications with air traffic towers. But that really didn't matter seeing the navigation equipment on the ground was still inoperable, as were the devices in the cockpit. The tropical storm was now pelting the fuselage with hail and rain, while the clouds had covered the aircraft, and visibility was near zero. Sobs and screams filled the cabin as all passengers remained in a crash position.

Harley motioned to Captain Auferdahl to take his seat, but the pilot shook his head. "Captain Hutter, please, sir, do me the honor and fly this baby home." Harley nodded and smiled, then strapped himself into the pilot's chair. Co-Captain Alvin moved to the jump seat in the back of the cockpit so Auferdahl could take his spot in the second chair.

Harley pushed down on the throttle and pulled back on the wheel. Immediately the aircraft lifted. All three pilots let out a sigh of relief. Harley knew the Coastal East jet was still in a holding pattern somewhere below, but he couldn't see the plane. Harley was praying that the Coastal East pilot had figured out that his control panel had been tampered with and would soon have it fixed too. Bayou's fuel gauge was nearing empty, and Harley assumed Coastal East's HJ-15 would be in the same predicament.

As soon as Harley reached 5,000 feet, wind shear from the tropical storm lifted the jet another 1,000 feet. Then the bottom gave out, suddenly dropping Bayou 444 back down to 4,000 feet and shifting the nose to starboard before Harley could regain control. He pushed the rudder pedal to compensate for the adverse yaw, but the turbulent conditions were wreaking havoc. The warm air from the ground was rapidly rising, while the cool air from above was sinking, catching the HJ-15 in a microburst that banked the left wing to almost vertical. Items in the overhead compartments were dislodged and flying around the cabin. Harley decided to execute an aileron roll to regain control. He throttled back to 200 knots and stabilized the elevators in a neutral position. The nose angle lowered, and the jet began flying upside down. Co-Captain George Alvin was strapped in the jump seat, puking on the ceiling.

Harley completed the roll, and the jet was back on course heading due east when the fuel gauge warning light began to flash. The roll had forced the plane down to 3,000 feet, and there was no visibility. Complete silence eerily replaced the piercing screams that had dominated the cabin. Harley wondered if he was losing passengers to heart attacks.

* * * * *

As the massive cumulonimbus cloud encompassed Coastal East 561's remote-controlled nonstop circle of death, an immense lightning bolt lit up the night sky and illuminated the aluminum fuselage. Everyone on the flight shrieked in terror as the lights flickered in the cabin, and then went out. The antenna that Jack Tassett had installed into the nose of the plane to receive satellite signals had acted as a lightning rod, and soon smoke was circumventing the cockpit. Captain Aaron Douglas grabbed the fire extinguisher and sprayed wildly in the direction of the flight controls. Little did he know that at that moment of hysteria, an act of God had occurred.

Within seconds, the fuse from the alien switch box burned out, and the actuator was now back to functioning through the jet's own electrical system. As the plane lurched off its circuitous course, Douglas dropped the extinguisher and grabbed the wheel. He quickly shoved down hard on the throttle and applied the up elevator to try and get over the thunderstorm, but the turbulent air pockets caused the plane to porpoise. The barf bags in the cabin were now being reused.

Then came the fuel warning light. Captain Douglas couldn't see anything outside through the rain and clouds, and the radar wasn't functioning. And because his communications were out, he had no way to issue a "Mayday." He lowered the elevators and throttled back to save fuel. Good thing. The Bayou jet dropped down in front of his eyes, its tail just missing the Coastal East jet's nose by less than fifty feet.

"Holy crap, watch out!" yelled Co-Captain Carver. Douglas veered left but stayed close, and Carver thought he felt a bowel movement coming on. "What are you doing, Aaron?! Take evasive action!"

"That Bayou jet may have a working navigation system, Keith. We don't! Our only hope is to follow its path and try to land behind it."

The Coastal East jet was now yawing and porpoising violently while both pilots secured the wheel and planted their feet firmly on the rudders.

"Wake turbulence! We can't fight this, Captain!"

"Positive thinking, Keith. We can and will!"

"But if we do manage to follow Bayou in, if he brakes faster than us, everyone on both jets is doomed!"

"I understand. But it's a risk we have to take."

*****

Harley peered down at the altimeter. Bayou 444 was holding firmly at three thousand feet when the engines sputtered and died. The fuel lamp was now lit bright and steady, and warning beeps were echoing off the cockpit's walls. A sinister computer-recorded voice was yelling, "Pull up! Pull up!"

Captain Auferdahl couldn't hide his anxiety. He glanced at Harley, and his voice squeaked, "Now what, Captain?"

"The HJ-15s have a seventeen to one glide ratio," replied Harley immediately. "At three thousand feet, we can glide for about nine and a half miles. But we need to put down now."

"Nine and a half miles won't get us to Palm Beach International, Harley."

"I know. I think our only option is the Beeline Highway. It's a straight shot from Seminole Bend to Riviera Beach. According to my calculations, which are all just flashes of instinct lighting up my brainwaves, we should be near Indiantown right now. I have one of those fancy watches with a built-in compass that I use when hiking. Unfortunately, it's our only navigation that is working, so I will use it to try and find the Beeline."

"Your hiking watch? My God, Harley, we have 150 passengers on board! We're going to put their lives in the hands of your watch?!" Captain Auferdahl was concerned, but he trusted Harley. "What if there are cars on the road?"

"I thought of that, Rich. It's past midnight, and the Beeline is a low-traveled road at night. With this stormy weather, hopefully, no one will be driving."

"Our visibility is so bad that we won't be able to see any car headlights until we're down to about a hundred feet, and we obviously will have no lift that close to the ground."

Harley was about to respond when he saw a small break in the ground fog, and a rain-soaked road appeared out of nowhere about 500 feet below. Curiously, he noticed four sets of high-powered aircraft guidance lights reflecting off the shimmering wet asphalt. Harley knew two sets of lights were reflections coming from his own wings, but where were the other two sets coming from? He guessed right away, and he guessed right.

"Rick, look down there. Four sets of flood lamps and I do believe that's the Beeline!" Harley pressed the compass button on his watch, and the position and direction appeared. He confirmed with the map that was tucked into a leather pouch next to him. But at that second, Rick wasn't thinking about the road. Why were there four sets of lights instead of two?

"Four sets of lights, Harley? How could that be?"

"Well, if these dang airplanes had a rearview mirror, I could probably tell you quite certainly. But my best-educated guess is that Coastal East 561 is following us."

"Based on the distance and angle of the lights," inserted George Alvin, "that plane is only a hundred or two hundred feet behind us!"

"Good point," replied Harley. "That means once we touch down, we need to slow brake to give them time to stop so we're not rear-ended."

"And that means we'll need to hope God gives us two or three miles of no car traffic," stated Captain Auferdahl solemnly.

*****

The porpoising on Coastal East 561 became minimal as Douglas and Carver were suddenly able to regain control of their HJ-15.

"No wake turbulence anymore, Captain," said copilot Keith Carver. He quickly wiped off the sweat accumulating on his forehead with the back of his right hand.

Without hesitation or even a second thought, Aaron Douglas responded, "They're out of fuel, Keith. They're gliding down to that road."

Carver raised his head and leaned forward so he could see the road below. It appeared to be a long and narrow stretch of asphalt.

“I think that’s the Beeline Highway down there,” declared Carver. “State Road 710. Road my motorcycle on it last year to eat lunch at a catfish place in—”

Captain Douglas interrupted as he screamed out an order, “Shut down the engines! Now!”

Carver was startled and confused. “Shut down, why?” He didn’t wait for the answer because it was an order. He hit the kill switch, then stared at Douglas.

“If they’re gliding, they must be planning on putting down on the Beeline,” answered the captain. “That means their airspeed is gradually declining. We’d ram them in the tail before they even touched down with our engines running! We need to glide, too.” Carver nodded his head. That made sense. He agreed, but now two fully loaded HJ-15 civilian planes were going to attempt a landing in the middle of a tropical storm on a public road with no power to lift their wings. He glanced out the cockpit window, looked upward towards heaven, and mumbled a short prayer.

Meanwhile, the momentum of the Coastal East jet was propelling the aircraft treacherously close to the tail of the Bayou jet.

When Captain Douglas saw that Carver appeared to be offering up a prayer, he grasped the pilot’s wheel with a sturdy grip and whispered to his co-captain, “Put in a good word for me, too. I’m going to need it.”

CHAPTER 102
Tuesday, March 16, 1982
12:30 a.m.

"This is your captain," shouted Harley Hutter into the cabin intercom system. There was no need to hide the anxiety in his voice. Trying to be calm would fool no one. "I need all passengers seated behind row fourteen to immediately move to the front of the plane and lie on the floor. Lie on top of each other if you have to, but do it quickly!"

"What the hell, Harley?" asked Captain Auferdahl. "What are you doing?"

"Rich, get back there and help those passengers in the back of the plane move up. Throw them over the seats, if you have to, but just do it! When they are all lying down, go open the tail door and lower the stairs!"

"Open the tail stairs in flight? Harley, no, what are you doing?! Those stairs will snap off on touchdown!"

"Just do it, Rich! As soon as the stairs are down, run up as far as you can and hit the floor, too!"

Captain Auferdahl was clueless, but jumped out of his seat and raced to the back of the plane. That section was filled with kids from the Youth Christian Club. They were mobile and quick, but they also had excellent lungs as the terrified wailing echoed around the fuselage walls. The stewardesses were moving them rapidly forward, except for Bonnie Woodman, who was right out of Bayou's training school and on her first flight. She had wet her pants and locked herself in the restroom.

Harley hadn't had time to explain. He had a sixth sense about some things, much like his brother Harry. Harley sensed the Coastal East aircraft was flying too close and fast and wouldn't be able to stop. He guessed right.

Captain Auferdahl blasted the emergency crossbar with his hand and cranked it upward. The crossbar prevented the tail door from opening during flight. Then he flipped the switch, and the tail door began to lower. As it did, the stairway unfolded. Rich got on his knees and peered out, then stared in disbelief as he saw the Coastal East jet only 100 feet behind him with its nose up and landing gear down. Rich lowered his view. The stairs were now fully dislodged and only ten feet above the Beeline Highway. He hastily stood up and rammed into Bonnie Woodman as she was coming out of the restroom. He grabbed and carried her to Row 14, and then slammed her face-first on top of Reverend Alice, who was a chaperone for the youth group. The clanging of the stairway lasted only a split second before it snapped and bounced off the nose of the rapidly approaching Coastal East jet.

Both jets were gliding without engine power; thus, the reverse thrusters would not be operable upon landing. Harley lowered the Bayou's flaps and raised the spoilers. Miraculously, the jet touched down softly in the pouring rain and whipping wind. Harley didn't use the airbrakes. His gut feeling told him to wait for the Coastal East jet to land.

Seconds after Bayou 444 touched down, Coastal East 561 landed, but as Harley predicted, it was moving much faster than his jet. The nose of the Coastal East plane hammered into the open tail section of the Bayou aircraft, thrusting the rear engine and wing compartment of the Trijet upward. As Coastal East's cockpit was jamming its way through the tail of the Bayou jet, Captain Douglas switched on the airbrakes. Co-Captain Carver's mouth was wide open, about the same size as his eyes, as the nose of the Coastal East jet came to rest in Row 15 of the Bayou cabin.

Harley felt the jolt and waited a few seconds before deploying Bayou's airbrakes, hoping that the Coastal East jet was doing the same. Both airplanes were gradually slowing and had used up a mile of State Road 710 when Harley saw headlights approaching through the fog. If he hit head-on with the car, chances were excellent that the car's gas tank would explode, sending all the good folks on board both jets to eternity.

Just a short distance to the southeast, Harley saw what appeared to be the entrance to some sort of factory. He yanked the plane's steering wheel to the right as the station wagon heading northwest on the Beeline slammed on its brakes.

The Bayou jet rolled on to a concrete driveway and crashed through a security gate as the Coastal East jet fishtailed behind, stretching Bayou's fuselage to its limits. The factory's security guard, who was sitting in his chair finishing off a bag of microwave popcorn, never saw the dual jetliners approaching, nor what hit him. The elevated security tower was ripped apart just below where the guard was perched, and it and the aghast guard came to rest on Bayou's tail section. The guard held on tight to a piece of metal protruding from the fuselage and watched in horror as the jet crossed the railroad tracks and crashed into a large aircraft hangar door on the grounds of Pratt Whitney. Ironically, all six JT8D turbofan engines on the Bayou and Coastal East jets were assembled only yards away from where the planes came to a stop, one tucked neatly into the hind end of the other. There were multiple bumps, bruises, and broken limbs, but everyone aboard both planes survived.

The stunned security guard resigned the next day and went to work in his brother's comic book store.

CHAPTER 103

Tuesday, March 16, 1982
12:45 a.m.

Barney and Ben watched in awe from the Huey's cockpit as the Coastal East jet rear-ended the Bayou jet on the Beeline Highway. They weren't able to keep up the airspeed, but using specialized telescopic night goggles, they witnessed the most incredible emergency landing in the history of avionics. The Huey landed in the Pratt Whitney parking lot two minutes after the HJ-15s had come to a stop in the hangar. Barney radioed the Jupiter Medical Center, and ambulances, fire trucks, and police all began arriving within twenty minutes. Meanwhile, Ben rushed to help passengers who were using the inflatable slides next to the exit doors on the wings to evacuate.

At 3:00 a.m., Barney called the president and briefed him on the situation. President Layman said he was sending Air Force One to Palm Beach International immediately and asked Barney to fly the Coastal East and Bayou pilots to the same airport. Layman wanted them to board the world-famous presidential jumbo jet and fly back to Washington as soon as they were medically cleared. They would be transported from Andrews Air Force Base to the White House by the Secret Service. Finally, the president ordered Barney to ensure that the pilots didn't speak to anyone from the media.

Harley Hutter refused to go with Ben and Barney. He wanted no credit for his heroic actions, instead he claimed he was just helping out, something any pilot deadheading on a doomed flight would do naturally. "Two wonderful pilots, Rich Auferdahl and George Alvin!" said Harley to Barney. "They're the reason everyone is alive tonight." Then Harley checked on all the passengers who were wrapped in blankets waiting for medical vans that would transport them to the hospital. Afterward, he began a brisk twelve-mile walk along the ditch that paralleled State Road 710 to Indiantown. From there, he would hitchhike to Seminole Bend and hope to catch a bus up to Tampa. When dawn arrived a few hours later, he stuck out his thumb and a nice fellow driving an Oldsmobile Cutlass convertible pulled over and offered him a ride.

"Where ya headed?" asked the driver as Harley closed the passenger side door. He glanced in the back seat and noticed it was loaded to the gills with bags of pita bread.

"Texas," replied Harley.

"That's a long ways, son. I can get ya up to Seminole Bend, though. Still a long way from Texas, but it's a start. I'm going to see my cousin Lance up there in Seminole Bend. By the way, my name's Lenny Billips. What's yours?"

Harley reached over and shook Lenny's hand. Then he noticed that the keychain hanging from the ignition had a picture of a young blond gal embedded into a medallion. "That your daughter?"

Lenny's face turned bright red when he realized that the car he had stolen could be easily identified by the keychain.

"Yep, yep. That's my daughter, Peggy Lou. Bought her this here automobile for her sixteenth birthday. Mine broke down, so she's letting me borrow it today."

Harley did a double-take at the picture and could tell the girl was at least thirty years old. The car was brand new. He chuckled under his breath. After last night, he had no plans to get involved in someone else's problems by turning in a car thief. Harley was just happy for the free lift.

"So, ya hear 'bout that plane crash last night over at Pratt Whitney?" asked Lenny, mainly to change the subject. "Been blasting all over every AM station this morning. Seems like it's becoming a weekly occurrence, it damn sure is! Too bad we can't train our pilots how to fly them metal birds the right way! Well, I'll tell you what. You ain't never getting me up in one of them things. How 'bout you? Bet you don't want to fly neither, now do ya?"

"Nope, can't say that I do." Harley laid his head on the headrest and dozed off.

*****

Willy Banks waited until he had a definite prognosis for Tyrone from the doctor before he called Abby. By 8:00 a.m., Tyrone was groggy but awake and in pain. In the recovery room next door, Sheriff Bonty sat firmly by Jimmy with his hands folded in prayer. Both boys spent four hours in surgery, and it appeared that their athletically healthy bodies would overcome bullet holes to their torsos. Jenny had fully recuperated from her fainting spell and spent the early morning hours traveling back and forth from her brother's room to her boyfriend's room.

Tyrus, Willy, and Otis sat stupefied in chairs near Tyrone's bed watching the live CNN reports coming from Pratt Whitney. The pictures of the Coastal East jet's nose cone lodged inside the tail of the Bayou jet's fuselage and everyone alive to tell about it was beyond comprehension! Passengers were telling reporters how Captain Auferdahl had ordered everyone behind Row 14 to hustle and lie down on the floor ahead of the wing exits, then bravely opened up the tail staircase, which kept the Trijet engines from simply being shoved forward through the cabin. They believed it was a miracle that the Coastal East nose cone stopped exactly at Row 15, and no one was killed. The passengers mentioned that a person seated in the back row had gone up to the cockpit to help out, but they weren't quite sure if he had done anything significant.

Perhaps the most interesting interview came from the security guard as he described his adventure sliding across the fuselage and becoming moored to the vertical Trijet engine compartment. The future comic book salesman embellished the story a little more each time he told it to a different reporter.

At 8:30 a.m., Abby Charles sprinted down the hallway at Gregorson Hospital to Tyrone's room. When Willy called, she was still in bed. Abby slipped on a pair of blue jeans and a white t-shirt from the laundry basket and ran barefoot to her car. There was no time for makeup today. Without looking at anyone in the recovery room, she hastened to her son and gently stroked the top of his head, almost ripping off the IV in the process. Her eyes were a mess, flooded with tears.

That's when two strong arms reached around Abby from behind, pulled her back from the bed, and turned her about. She looked up at the man she had last seen kissing her in the maternity ward the night her son was born. Tyrus clutched her waist with his left arm and wrapped his right arm around her neck, pushing the back of her head to his chest. Soon, everyone in the recovery room was wiping tears away. Tyrone stared at his mom and dad and smiled. The pain in his shoulder could no longer be felt.

EPILOGUE
Billy Joe Gormon

FBI Director Morris Clements came on *Sixty Minutes* and told Harry Reasoner that all the terrible events that took place in February and March of 1982 were just a coincidence. He said the airplane accidents were a result of a major malfunction in our nation's air traffic control radars due to a computer glitch. President Layman reprimanded the Federal Aviation Administration and replaced the computer company that was under contract. He assured the citizens of the United States and our friends throughout the world that the radar systems were all fixed, and the skies were safe for travel.

Mr. Clements then claimed that the University of Florida blew up because of some underground gas leak. My brother Kenny wasn't too happy about that neither because the Gator's basketball team had to play their home games for a year at Moses Junior High down in Ocala. He tore up the letter of intent he had signed, but Mama taped it back together again. She then sat Kenny down on the couch and gave her lecture on "commitment" while Daddy just rolled his eyes.

Finally, Mr. Clements told Mr. Reasoner that the submarine, you know, the USS Halibut, exploded when it accidentally struck a jagged underwater ledge while doing training maneuvers in the Strait of Juan de Fuca. The other TV guy, Mike Wallace, got really mad at Mr. Clements, and it sure sounded like he didn't believe him. Mr. Wallace wanted to know why there were nuclear weapons on a training vessel.

Mr. Clements just shrugged his shoulders and said, "No comment."

Then Mr. Reasoner asked why news reporters weren't allowed to speak to anyone up at Kitsap Navy Base.

Mr. Clements said that all military operations, training or otherwise, are top secret. Mr. Reasoner shook his head and said it sounded like a cover-up.

Well, I'll tell you what. Mr. Clements turned all red in the face like he was really getting mad. Then, on behalf of the president, he apologized to the Makah Indians, because I guess about fifteen of them were never found when their reservation collapsed into the ocean. He said that the president is mailing a load of taxpayer money to them so they can rebuild, but ain't it kind of hard to rebuild when the land you own is now on the bottom of the sea?

Anyway, the *Seminole Bend Gazette* had to hire two more reporters because of all the crazy news going on. Then, for some unknown reason, the editor got arrested by the CIA, or something like that, and ain't nobody ever seen him again. Mama and Daddy were telling me about that peculiar vanishing act at the kitchen table yesterday. They was saying the editor got arrested because his reporters were digging up a bunch of strange and unbelievable new evidence around town. Didn't know that was illegal, but must be.

So, do you remember them pilots that landed those passenger jets down on the Beeline? Well, they all were flown up to Washington to meet with the president, and just like the editor, no one has seen them since. Daddy says ten or so fellas in dark blue suits went to their homes and packed up their families and sent them somewhere nice to live. No one knew where, but my guess is that it was New York. What could be better than being a fan of both the Yankees and the Mets?

Down here in Seminole Bend, Sheriff Bonty turned into quite a nice guy. Surprising, because no one ever cared much for him before. He held a press conference at the high school football stadium a few months after things settled down that totally confused everyone who came to listen.

First, he introduced his wife and said that she had been living for quite some time over in the Middle East somewhere. Who knew? And then he called Jimmy and Jenny Jackson up on the stage to join him. In front of a thousand or so puzzled onlookers, the sheriff gave them a big hug, and dang if it didn't look like they actually enjoyed it! Mr. Bonty then told everyone that he and his wife were going to adopt the Jackson kids now that their daddy Roy was dead. People started clapping, they sure did! Brought tears to my eyes!

I forgot to tell you about Roy Jackson, didn't I? Well, I guess that SOB, sorry about my language, but that's what Daddy still calls him, was fishing out in his swamp and fell out of the boat and got eaten by an alligator. Daddy and Uncle Johnny chuckled when they found out, so Mama got very upset and left the room.

By the way, you won't believe the scandal that swept the town. Daddy said it was just rumored, but Mama claimed it was the truth. Mama said she was disgusted hearing about Coach Berry's affair with none other than my favorite teacher of all time. Yep, Miss Norma Foss. And to top it off, Miss Foss gets herself knocked up!

But before Coach Berry hooked up with Miss Foss, his wife, Miss Sheryl, wanted to have a baby. However, Coach Berry didn't want children. So then Coach gets a vasectomy so he can't have no kids. Ouch! Just saying that word is painful to me! Sorry, I got sidetracked again. Anyway, Mama said that when Coach got himself "fixed," it made Miss Sheryl real mad, and she was determined to get even with her husband. So she secretly went and got herself artificially inseminated, and a short time later, she was pregnant. Coach Berry assumed the vasectomy was a failure and having a child was just meant to be.

Now, this is where it gets really complicated. Miss Foss figured Coach Berry had to be the father of her child after that fling at the teacher's conference. There was no way her husband could be the daddy because a few years earlier, Jim Foss went to the doc and found out he was sterile and wasn't able to make babies.

Miss Foss didn't know about Coach Berry's vasectomy. Well, it turned out that a couple of months after the baby was born, the doctors gave the infant a blood test, and it was the same type as Norma's husband. Seems the sterility test he took years earlier was mixed up with some other guy's test by a stressed-out clinic laboratory nurse. The nurse later realized she had made a mistake, but didn't tell anyone. The doctor gave the news to Norma and her hubby that they would never have any babies. The nurse kept her secret for fear of permanent unemployment. But after the blood test, she came clean. And then she was fired.

Speaking of fired, Miss Foss ain't gonna be a teacher no more. Sheriff Bonty locked her up in the jail. The sheriff said that my former best-teacher-of-all-time tried to kill Miss Sheryl so she could have Coach Berry all to herself. Needless to say that it was like a scene from the *Twilight Zone* when Miss Sheryl turned up alive down at the Catholic church missing a hand!

Despite the tragic news that came out of Florida, the snowbirds continue to make their annual trek to the Sunshine State for a great climate, good fishing, and fresh-squeezed orange juice. Deputy Willy Banks still runs traffic radar out in the ditch by my house. Willy's a good guy, you know. He invited me to join him and his brothers when they go fishing next week down at Nubbin Slough. Can't miss that. I hear the speckled perch are biting like crazy!

Oh yeah, one last thing that my friend Jesse Dagos told me on the phone. He ran into Judge Boone in BoldMart a week or so ago. The judge was buying a bunch of suitcases and beach clothes. Judge Boone used to speak to Seminole Bend

Elementary School classes about how good, lawful citizens made America great, and how students should start right there and then obeying all the laws of the land. Anyway, Jesse tells me something the judge said to him that makes my hair stand up because Jesse doesn't know what I know. I think maybe I should tell someone, but with all the terrible events that took place in my hometown, maybe it's best to let sleeping dogs lie.

Jesse, trying to be nice and make small talk because, well, that's the kind of fella he is, asked Honorable Judge Boone if he was going to give his *America Great* speech to school kids anymore, and the judge shook his head no. When Jesse asked why not, he said him and his buddy were moving to some remote island down in the Caribbean to retire. Said they found a treasure chest full of money and we're going to live the high life.

I asked Jesse who the Judge's friend was, and Jesse says, "I think he said his buddy's name was Jack Tassett or something like that."

AUTHOR'S NOTE

My inspiration for writing Seminole Bend came as a result of teaching, coaching, and living in the small, wonderful community of Okeechobee, Florida, shortly after graduation from college. Because my story included some wild and crazy events fictitiously taking place there, I changed the book's title out of respect for the town and its amiable, caring citizens. Okeechobee is a prime example of Southern hospitality at its finest!

The culture of the Seminole Nation that surrounds the area is vibrant in its art, Sweetgrass basketry, beadwork, and food. A visit to the Sunshine State should include a day or two of discovering the history and traditions of this fascinating tribe.

With that said, any resemblances regarding people, places, or events that were not of a historical or factual nature are purely coincidental. I also want to thank my good friend Oliver Harwas for allowing me to simulate his name as the highest-ranking villain in my story. In reality, Oliver is one of the nicest men you will ever meet! I wish he would learn how to properly place a minnow on a hook, though.

ACKNOWLEDGMENTS

Thanks to all the good folks who supplied edits, feedback, suggestions, and encouragement. And kudos to my patient wife, Meg, for questioning, clarifying, editing, and advising while carefully reading through the manuscript. Also, thank you to Luke Hansen Media for your creative direction and design of the cover!

ABOUT THE AUTHOR

Tom Hansen is a native of New Richmond, Wisconsin. He holds a BS from the University of Wisconsin-River Falls and an MS from Nova Southeastern University. Tom has lived in or traveled to seventy-two countries and all fifty states. He is currently a resident of Arizona. Tom has dedicated most of his life to the field of education as a teacher (Dhahran, Saudi Arabia, Okeechobee, Florida, and Orlando, Florida), principal (Hazel Green, Wisconsin and Mesa, Arizona), educational consultant (State of Arizona), college professor and administrative director (Scottsdale, Arizona). This is his first novel.

CHARACTER REFERENCE CHART

(cast of characters alphabetized by last name)

LAST	FIRST	ROLE
Adams	Marvin	Personnel Manager at POWVAC in Pittsburgh
Alvin	George	Copilot of Bayou 444 (Orlando to Dallas)
Auferdahl	Rich	Pilot of Bayou 444 (Orlando to Dallas)
Banks	Mama	Willy's mother (died of heart attack during high school graduation)
Banks	Otis	Willy's younger brother (struggled to get good grades in school)
Banks	Tyrone	Willy's nephew (center on Seminole Bend HS basketball team)
Banks	Tyrus	Willy's older brother (father of Tyrone Banks & fiance to Abby Charles)
Banks	Willy	Seminole Bend Deputy (fired by Sheriff Bonty for investigating Roy J.)
Bennett	Phil	Owner of Bennett's Airboat Palace (became a close friend to Lew Berry)
Berger	Johnny	Copilot for Trans South Airlines (flew with Harry Hutter)
Berry	Brett	Head Boy's Basketball Coach
Berry	Janet	Mother of Coach Brett Berry (lives in Pennsylvania with husband Lew)
Berry	Lew	Father of Coach Brett Berry
Berry	Sheryl	Wife of Coach Brett Berry (disappeared from Seminole Bend HS gym)
Billips	Lance	Homeless man (friend of Otis Banks who lives in a phone booth)
Billips	Lenny	Lance's cousin (sells pita bread & delivers MD20 wine to Lance)
Blanchard	Susan	Mysterious woman who was in seat 14C on Trans South Airlines crash
Bonty	Al	Sheriff of Seminole Bend
Boone	Judge	Judge in Seminole Bend (close friend of Roy Jackson)
Boone	Maddie	Judge Boone's daughter (best friend of teacher Norma Foss)
Boyd	Hugh	Scientist (on duty at the NOAAC when Tsunami began)
Brewer	Toby	FBI Agent (investigated the South Florida DNR's office)
Brown	Jim	Double Agent (decoy name - member of special ops team)
Brubaker	Gordon	White House Chief of Staff (member of President Layman's cabinet)
Bryant	Paul	Alabama Head Football Coach (recruited Bo Yardly)
Carnes	Amos	Non-starter for Seminole Bend HS basketball team
Carter	Tim	Non-starter for Seminole Bend HS basketball team
Carver	Keith	Copilot of Coastal East 561 (Tampa to Atlanta)
Charles	Abby	Tyrone Banks' mother (worked in photo shop at BoldMart)
Cleaver	Marcelus	Starting forward for Seminole Bend HS basketball team's
Clements	Morris	FBI Director in the 1980's (under President Layman)
Cletes	Walter	Secretary of State in the 1980's (under President Layman)
Coakley	Gregory	Physics Professor at U of Florida (died in Heartland Lakes crash)
Combs	Hubert	FAA Director in the 1980's (under President Layman)
Combs	Richard	CIA Director in the 1970's (under President Nixon)
Cummings	Bob	Head of NTSB for Miami Region (in charge of the Trans South crash)
Dagos	Jesse	Billy's classmate (witnessed Willy Banks save a dog from an alligator)
Dasani	Mustaf	Head of Miami Air Traffic Control (friend of Pilot Harry Hutter)
Daughtry	Hank	Lawyer in Pittsburgh who later becomes Governor of Florida
Doth	Doris	Marks, Taylor & Smith (Pittsburgh) law office front desk receptionist
Douglas	Aaron	Pilot of Coastal East 561 (Tampa to Atlanta)
Douglas	Donny	Worker at McDonald's (gave leftover food to his friend Lance Billips)
Duerty	John	Tampa Airport Operations Supervisor
Duff	Albert	Owner of Duff's Motor Lodge (murdered a man he caught with his wife)
Duff	Gertrude	Wife of Albert Duff (ran Duff's M.L. after husband was sent to prison)
Dulie	Sam	South Florida DNR Supervisor (aka Abdul Samad, friend of Yussef Jasur)
Dulles	Alex	CIA Director (promoted Oliver Harfield & Ray Jackson as CIA supes)
Evans	Carla	Staff assistant for Governor Daughtry (Deputy Murphree's fiancé)
Foss	Jim	Husband of Norma Foss
Foss	Norma	5th Grade Teacher at Seminole Bend Elementary School
Gibson	Buck	Owner of Gibby's Glass Warehouse
Gormon	Billy	Narrator (age 11 in 1982, son of Marvin & Maxine, brother of Kenny)
Gormon	Johnny	Billy's uncle & Marvin's brother (known for "telling it like it is"!)

Gormon	Kenny	Billy's older brother (best shooter on HS basketball team)
Gormon	Marvin	Father of Billy & Kenny (dairy rancher near Seminole Bend)
Gormon	Maxine	Mother of Billy & Kenny (wife of dairy rancher, Marvin Gormon)
Granger	Jimmy	Dartmouth College student (friend of Abdul Samad, aka Sam Dulie)
Harfield	Oliver	CIA Supervisor (rogue agent who teams up with Ray Jackson)
	Miguel	Oliver Harfield's groundskeeper (lives in a hidden equipment shack)
Herman	Casey	NASA Maintenance Worker (resigned after bar fight with an astronaut)
Herman	Connor	NASA Maintenance Worker (resigned after bar fight with an astronaut)
Hoyt	Jessica	News anchor for the World Broadcasting Network
Hudster	Elmer	Owner of Elmer's Hardware Store (found Max Miller lying in blood)
Hutter	Harley	Pilot for Bayou Airlines (brother of Harry Hutter)
Hutter	Harry	Pilot for Trans South Airlines (crashed plane in Everglades)
Hyle	Ernie	Taylor Creek locks operator (noticed Pancho Sanchez go through locks)
Inman	Admiral	Navy Admiral in charge of Kitsap Naval Base on Puget Sound
Jackson	Jenny	Daughter of Roy Jackson (cheerleader for Seminole Bend HS)
Jackson	Jimmy	Son of Roy Jackson (expects to earn a basketball scholarship to Florida)
Jackson	Ray	Roy's older brother (cheated his way into becoming a CIA agent)
Jackson	Roy	Ray's younger brother (dairy rancher who began life of crime)
James	Greg	Assistant Boy's Basketball Coach
Jasur	Adil Al	Prince of Jasurbia (son of Mustafa, brother of Hakim, father of Yussef)
Jasur	Hakim	Defense Minister of Jasurbia (oldest son of King Mustafa)
Jasur	Mustafa	King of Jasurbia (father of Hakim & Adil)
Jasur	Yussef	Prince Adil's Son (develops radar jamming & video equipment)
Jones	Jack	FBI Agent (Lead investigator of Trans South Airlines crash)
Jones	Johnny	Starting forward on Seminole Bend HS basketball team)
Kennedy	John	US President (ordered covert nuclear weapons control facility built)
Kline	Ralph	Neighbor of Lew and Sheryl Berry in Pennsylvania
Knutson	Bill	CIA Director in the 1980's (under President Layman)
Layman	Donald	US President during the 1980's
Liston	Carlyle	Secretary of Defense in the 1980's (under President Layman)
Loughten	Mister	Principal at Cocoa Beach Causeway HS & former US Congressman
Mann	Willis	Starting point guard on Seminole Bend HS basketball team)
Martin	Danny	Roy Jackson's body guard (Max Miller's partner)
Mathune	Clevus	Starting guard for Martin Park HS (high school All-American)
McCone	John	CIA Director (succeeded Alex Dulles as director of the CIA)
McCormic	Sam	Seminole Bend Deputy (Willy Banks' partner)
Merrick	John	Reporter for the World Broadcasting Network
Millage	Gaspar	Army soldier in same regiment as Bo Yardly
Miller	Max	Roy Jackson's driver (followed Calvin Potts to the sheriff's office)
Morris	Karen	Saleslady for Everglades Estates (found Willy Banks' dirty clothes)
Mucker	Matt	Owner of Mucker's Produce (hired Otis Banks as a janitor)
Murphree	Johnny	Seminole Bend Deputy (friend of Willy Banks who works front desk)
Nixon	Richard	US President (started covert operation to identify rogue CIA agents)
Officer	Mel	Tamiami Police Officer (arrested Willy Banks)
Officer	Todd	Tamiami Police Officer (arrested Willy Banks)
O'Shea	Father	Priest at Seminole Bend's Catholic church
Patton	Mickey	Billy Gormon's classmate who Billy put a King snake in pants
Peters	Gloria	Head nurse at Gregorson Hospital
Plank	Bobby Joe	Billy Gormon's best friend (witnessed Roy Jackson threaten Willy Banks)
Potts	Agnes	Wife of Calvin Potts (killed by Danny Martin, Roy Jackson's body guard)
Potts	Calvin	Retired appliance salesman (boat was stolen by Pancho Sanchez)
Pritchard	Ev	Lance Billips' married Friday night fling
Rambert	Mister	Principal at Seminole Bend Elementary School
Rambus	Tony	Non-starter for Seminole Bend HS basketball team
Reasoner	Harry	CBS Sixty Minutes Reporter (interviewed Morris Clements, FBI Director)
Royce	Dustin	WTSP News Reporter Covered the reopening of the Tampa airport
Samad	Abdul	MIT Graduate in Electromagnetism (Yussef's friend, aka Sam Dulie)
Sanchez	Pancho	Citrus Picker for Gold Coast Fruit (saved Willy Banks' life)

Scott	Buck	Private in Vietnam War (saved by Willy Banks' during Viet Cong attack)
Sister	Mary	Nun at Seminole Bend's Catholic church (provided care for Sheryl Berry)
Sister	Roberta	Nun at Seminole Bend's Catholic church (provided care for Sheryl Berry)
Shubert	Jerry	Tamiami Police Officer at front desk (checked Willy Banks' credentials)
Slivko	Yakov	Russian Air Force Pilot (piloted the Mig-25 Foxbat)
Smith	Bard	Sports columnist for Miami Sentinel
Smith	Ben	Special Operations Team Member
Stanley	Doc	Family doctor who delivered Tyrone Banks at Gregorson Hospital
Sutton	Cliff	Seminole Bend County Coroner
Swenson	Cal	Second-In-Charge of Miami Air Traffic Control
Tassett	Jake	NTSB Lead investigator into the Trans South Airlines crash
Tecka	Tom	FBI Agent (partner of Agent Jack Jones)
Timkins	Gordon	Seminole Bend HS basketball fan (sits behind the coach)
Turloney	Bill	NTSB Go Team Member who Investigated Trans South Airlines crash
Wallace	Mike	CBS Sixty Minutes Reporter (Interviewed Morris Clements, FBI Director)
Watkins	Barney	Special Operations Team Member
Woodman	Bonnie	Stewardess for Bayou Airlines (trapped in restroom on Bayou 444)
Woods	Martin	Head Basketball Coach of Florida Gators (recruited Kenny Gormon)
Yardly	Bo	Willy Bank's best friend (college football star, drafted into the US Army)

www.ingramcontent.com/pod-product-compliance
Lightning Source LLC
Chambersburg PA
CBHW020616310726
48979CB00008B/1506/J

* 9 7 8 1 7 3 2 8 1 8 2 3 1 *